SLAVES OF VALHALLA

Book 2 of The Prometheus Wars

by

Luke Romyn

This book is a work of fiction. Any resemblance to any person, living or dead, any place, events or occurrences, is purely coincidental. The characters and storylines are created from the author's imagination or are used fictitiously.

Editor: Chuck David

If you are interested in more writing by Luke Romyn, be sure to visit
http://www.lukeromyn.com

Dedicated to my good friend and fellow

scribbler, Claude Bouchard.

May we both survive this hellish ride.

Acknowledgements

Many thanks to all those involved in bringing this novel together.

My proofreaders, Karen Hansen, Sarah Dougherty, Claude Bouchard, and Joanne Chase, are fantastic. Thanks for finding all the pieces that don't fit.

Chuck David's editing helps me sleep better at nights.

And a special thanks to every single person who has ever encouraged me with this dream. Writers are some of the most self-conscious individuals alive, and we survive on the support of those who read our words. Never underestimate the effect your encouragement has.

PROLOGUE

The cold tore at his skin, ripping away the thin veil of comfort which had cloaked him in its illusory embrace. Trying to rouse himself, the stranger struggled free of the congealing remnants of his unnatural slumber, battling to gather thoughts and memories.

Such a task was like grasping an oiled eel, however, and the more furiously he tried to call to mind what had occurred, the more his recollections seemed to slip through his fingers. Images drew tentatively close, but then fled, leaving him empty and alone once more.

Okay, he needed to keep it simple. Basic things first, that was the secret to these things. What was his name…?

Panic flooded through him. He couldn't remember who he was!

The stranger paused, breathing deeply and evenly, controlling the forest fire of panic erupting within his belly. Such lack of control would not help his situation in any way, shape or form, and as such was useless to him at this time. He emptied his mind, not a difficult task under such circumstances, and pictured an empty field. Allowing his thoughts to roam across the field wherever they may, he journeyed with them when they tugged him in various directions, this way and that, following as they ultimately began to hurtle across the field toward a target he could not perceive.

Slowly, like a tiny trickle of oil from the delicate fingers of a Thai masseuse, images began to unfold in his mind. He recalled an enormous three-headed dog snapping and snarling right before he'd sliced through one of its necks, wielding a glowing sword which glittered and hissed with energy unlike any he had ever known.

Another vision exploded within his mind of an intensely tall man, a towering individual clad in black armor, whose sword had seemed to suck the light from the world around it. This giant had battled a man of myth, whose bulging muscles swelled and strained against his bronze breastplate as he swung a blade glittering with dazzling radiance – similar, but different to the one he'd held in his own battle.

These recollections dribbled into the stranger's memory, their agonizing slowness crowded by a myriad of other smaller images. A man who fought against his own fear in order to prevent a calamity across time.... An enormous orange rock perched in a red desert, plunging into the ground after the timid man played a strange kind of tune.... An incredible city under the ocean, a towering statue of a legend standing guard at its gates....

Yet his own name remained elusive.

The stranger gazed around him and winced as a bolt of pain shot through his head. Raising a hand to his scalp, he felt something sticky. Rubbing his fingers against his palm he saw the smear of crimson which could only be blood. Stumbling over to a cracked mirror on the wall, he stared at his reflection. Dark, mocking eyes peered back at him as he parted the matted and bloodied brown hair to gaze at his wound. Shallow wound, but it would need stitches or some medi-foam –

What the hell is medi-foam?

He pushed the thought aside. "Well, at least you're a good looking bastard," he muttered, "even if you *are* forgettable." He winked and moved away from the mirror.

He cast his gaze across a scene of carnage, bodies and mutilated limbs flung around haphazardly like items hurled from an angry woman's purse. Whatever had happened here had been terrible, yet oddly the stranger felt no discomfort as he stared at the horror and destruction. Upon closer inspection, he saw many of the corpses appeared to have been wrenched apart by physical force, though how he knew this fact remained a mystery.

Had he been in some sort of plane crash?

Looking at himself, the stranger regarded his faded combat fatigues, their desert camouflage pattern of mottled sandy colors smeared with drying blood he guessed was not his own. He bore no weapons, but attached at his left hip was an empty scabbard. Confusion suffused him. The image of hacking a glowing sword through the three-headed dog's neck returned again. What sort of beast had that thing been? What sort of man was *he* to be fighting it?

The stranger checked himself for further injuries. Apart from the gash to his head, he seemed pretty much intact, unlike the building around him. It was virtually demolished, and as he stepped through its smoldering husk, he observed dozens more bodies torn to pieces around the ruins.

This entire place appeared to have once been an armed forces installation. Its Spartan militaristic layout and near-obsessive categorization survived even beyond its demolition. It was a style the stranger felt strangely used to, a home-like sensation, and he glared at the destruction, wondering what could have possibly caused it.

Was there a war?

Glancing down, the man saw something strangely familiar and stooped to pick it up. The name of the item came back to him in an instant. It was an M4A5 carbine assault rifle and fitted his hand like a glove. Expertly checking to see that the clip was full, he chambered a round and raised the weapon to his shoulder in a move so fluid it bespoke years of practice.

Yet he still couldn't remember his name.

Shrugging aside the problem, the stranger moved through the structure. Climbing a set of stairs, the next floor revealed a wall of windows exposing the outside landscape, and he realized he had actually ascended from below the ground.

Looking through the windows in the cement-block walls of the military building he noted perimeter fencing topped with razor wire, beyond which stretched a desert so red it almost defied belief, the same desert from his memories, where the rock – *Ayers Rock!* – had dropped into the ground.

His mind trickled on, putting the pieces together with agonizing slowness.

He was in Australia!

The stranger moved outside the devastated building – his assault rifle up and aimed wherever he looked – only to be confronted with even more destruction. Gazing through the scope of his carbine, the man shuddered at the damage wreaked upon this place. The building he had awoken in was one of seven, and the only one not razed completely. Bodies were everywhere, male and female alike, some with weapons and military uniforms, others wearing lab coats or engineering work gear.

Under the waning daylight, the stranger realized several of the victims had been bitten, as if by huge jaws, but he didn't linger in his examination. He had a strong sense that whatever had attacked this place was long gone, but couldn't be sure. Whatever it was might return at any moment to finish the job, to finish him.

Traveling cautiously between the buildings, the stranger came upon what looked like the ruins of an aircraft hangar. Secure doors, three-feet-thick and crafted from solid steel, lay bent and discarded amidst the rubble. Several fighter jets, along with a number of helicopters, lay crushed beneath crumpled blocks of concrete. Their technical names lay tantalizingly close to the surface of the stranger's memory, but were brushed aside hastily as he spied a singular means of transportation which appeared untouched by the devastation surrounding him. It seemed a bland option in the midst of so many vehicles engineered for destruction, but the stranger's heart hammered in his chest at the mere sight of it.

It had three axles, sported ten rubber tires, and chrome letters spelled out *MACK* across its front grill. The large tank upon its back confirmed its purpose.

Yep. It was a septic tanker.

And his name was Wes.

CHAPTER 1

Zoe crawled from under the sheets and rose from the bed, tripping on a shoe before cursing and kicking it away to slap against the wall. Grumbling incoherently to nobody, she stumbled across to the bathroom and gazed at her reflection, shaking her head softly before washing her face with cold water, trying to fully rouse herself from the last remnants of slumber still clinging to her brain.

It didn't help.

Glancing again up into the mirror, Zoe saw her bright blue eyes glaring accusingly back at her, but as usual she ignored the memories they brought with them, of another set of eyes she could never escape. She pushed her hair behind her ears to cascade over her shoulders.

Men had always been drawn to her, like hormonal prairie dogs, all of them panting and wanting to mount her, but she had much more important priorities in her life than being a Barbie doll-esque bimbo who relied on her looks to survive. She admitted to liking her long, black hair, but the whole beauty regime so many women adored did not appeal to her in the slightest. She detested the concept of a woman having to primp and preen herself while men simply rolled out of bed, scratched the thing between their legs, belched and strolled out the door. Disgust at the thought crossed her features, and her nose crinkled slightly.

Her mother had always been the beautiful one, which possibly why Zoe abhorred it so much. It wasn't like Zoe hadn't gotten along with her mother – far from it, she'd loved her deeply – but the memory of her brought with it pain and an aching sense of loss. For years every time she glanced in a mirror, she only saw how much she resembled her and nothing else. No matter how much she changed the way she looked, her eyes were always her mother's.

Zoe didn't have an aversion to being beautiful, it was just that it didn't matter much to her. Perhaps if she'd been born with a big toe where her nose was supposed to be things would have been different, she might have craved beauty. But she hadn't been born that way, and she often took her looks for granted.

Like this morning.

Moving away from the mirror, Zoe returned to the bedroom and swiftly changed, emerging into the lounge a moment later clad in jeans along with her sports bra under a loose gray t-shirt. She wore a pair of comfortable running shoes and, checking that the sink wasn't overflowing and the stove was turned off, she walked briskly to her front door.

Swinging the door open, Zoe was confronted by a man dressed in full combat fatigues, his hand raised as if about to knock on her door. The stranger carried an assault rifle slung over his right shoulder.

"Who the hell are you?" asked the man, his voice thick with an odd accent. It rang similar to someone from the British Isles, but subtly different.

"I'm the person who lives here. Who the hell are you?"

The man ignored her demand and pushed his way past her and into the apartment. "Hey, Talbot!" he shouted into the empty apartment. "Doctor Harrison, where are you? We have a situation!"

"Why are you calling out for my father?" demanded Zoe.

The stranger spun back around to stare at her as though he'd been stung. He grabbed her firmly by the shoulders, pinning her in a vice-like grip and gazing intently into her eyes. "You're Talbot's daughter?"

"I'm Zoe Harrison," she replied, her curiosity rising as she began to suspect who this man might actually be. "Talbot Harrison was my father." The disbelief was evident in his eyes, and Zoe swallowed heavily. She got the distinct impression that this man could prove a very dangerous enemy; she'd have to tread very carefully if he were to believe her.

"*Was* your father? What do you mean?"

"Let me go, you freak," snarled Zoe, hoping bravado would help get her out of the situation. It worked; the stranger glanced down as though noticing for the first time he was clutching her. Slowly he relaxed his grip.

"Sorry," he mumbled, raising his intense gaze once more. "What did you mean, though? Where is Talbot? And how can he have a daughter as old as you? He's not much older than me."

"Who the hell *are* you?"

"My name is Wes. Talbot and I –"

"You're Wes?" gasped Zoe. "*The* Wes? As in the Aussie commando who saved my dad's ass? But you're too… young."

"So is your dad…I mean Talbot…. Whatever! This is his place, I know that. Now where is he?"

Zoe stared hard at the man claiming to be Wes, a figure from her father's stories, one she had come to believe was almost as mythical as the monsters involved. Looking into his eyes, however, she saw something in the intensity of the Australian which slotted perfectly into the mold she had always imagined Wes fitting – brash, rough, and uncouth.

Zoe's father had recounted a seemingly constant stream of tales about the crazy commando who fought against the creatures contained within the world of Tartarus. They were the only stories he'd ever told her.

Her father's tales were becoming very real in the space of a few heartbeats – the man standing before her was direct evidence of them.

"If you really are Wes, what happened to Heracles in Hades?" she asked.

The stranger's eyes narrowed in concentration, as though having to focus heavily in order to remember. "Gigantor promised to get us to Hades, but then Kharon the Ferryman wouldn't let us cross unless we paid him. Heracles sacrificed himself in order to get us across the river Styx; Kharon sucked him dry, and not in a good way either. He absorbed him and took over his body or something. Next thing we knew, the guy was wearing Heracles's skin like it was a Halloween costume. Luckily, Heracles was later able to convince Kharon to release him, coming to our aid in the nick of time."

Zoe felt shaken. Not just from the accuracy of the stranger's recounting of her father's tale, but from the rough way he did it. His speech was exactly the way she had envisioned it from her dad's stories, although from her father's telling she would have expected him to swear a lot more. Maybe this wasn't Wes.

"So, are you going to tell me what the fuck is going on or what?" he snapped.

Okay. It was definitely Wes.

"I don't know how to tell you this," began Zoe, "but Talbot is dead."

Wes frowned. "How and when?" he asked, his tone subtly changing to one of decisive action.

"About six months ago. He was involved in something for the military along with his brother Thomas. He wouldn't tell me what it was, but they were both killed in some sort of rockslide."

"*Rockslide?*" hissed Wes. "Is that what they told you?"

Zoe nodded.

"Damn them. Those bastards can't even be bothered to come up with new cover stories." He looked away.

"What do you mean?" asked Zoe.

Wes's gaze returned to her once more. "That's what they told Talbot – your father – when his brother got killed… the first time."

"Are you saying those stories my dad told were true?"

Wes nodded. "If you mean the ones involving big-ass monsters from Greek mythology popping up and trying to chew our heads off every five minutes, then yes."

"So my father was right," gasped Zoe. She sat back on the arm of her couch.

"Exactly," muttered Wes. "Now, fill me in on how the hell you came to be. I copped a knock on my head recently, and everything inside it got jumbled. Is your mother named Suzanna?"

Zoe's eyes flared. "Why?"

"Talbot mentioned her one time, that's all. From the way you're talking, she's not around anymore either."

"My mother died when I was young," Zoe hedged. "Talbot had to raise me on my own. He did a pretty good job. He used to take me around with him on archaeological digs and stuff. I mean, how many other kids get to go to Egypt and be there when they crack open the newest tomb in the Valley of the Kings?" She sensed the commando was beginning to believe her.

"Not many, I'm guessing," replied Wes. "When did he go back to working for the Government?"

"About a year ago. Some guys just turned up on the doorstep and that was it. I got calls from him occasionally, but the conversations were always blunt, like he was holding something back. I always had the feeling someone else was monitoring what he was saying."

"Yeah, probably. Those guys are the leaders of the arsehole brigade, that's for sure. Did he manage to tell you anything we can use? Anything at all?"

Zoe shook her head. "I can't think of anything offha –"

SMMMAAAASSSHHHH!!!

The small apartment was suddenly enveloped in chaos. Wes instinctively grabbed Zoe and shielded her with his own body as the roof of the apartment caved in. Dust billowed and bricks rained down, but luckily none hit the duo. Slowly the haze receded, and Wes spun around, his M4A5 up and aimed directly at something which should not exist. Zoe saw it, towering within the dust, but still could not credit what her eyes told her. It wasn't feasible; there was no way it could possibly be here.

The enormous creature shuffled around on four legs, each as large as a medium-sized tree trunk, folding its huge wings in close to its body as it did so. The midday sunlight shone brightly through the demolished roof and glinted from the plate-like scales which covered its hide. The alligator snout snorted at the still drifting dust, and the beady, heavily-lidded eyes studied them with something akin to amusement as its forked tongue flitted from within a lipless mouth. It reared up on its hind legs and roared, causing more plaster and bricks to rain down.

It was a… a *dragon*.

The beast suddenly shimmered and shrunk, swiftly diminishing in size until it stood around double the height of a tall person. As it did so, its features twisted and remolded into those of a man – albeit a man standing almost fourteen-feet-tall.

"Prometheus," growled Wes.

"Hello, Wes," said the tall man, who Zoe now saw had lidless eyes filled with thick, smoky, black orbs.

A single shot from Wes's assault rifle cracked the air, and the tall man's head snapped back. Instantaneously a hole appeared in his right cheek, and gore spewed from the rear of his skull as he crumpled to the ground.

"What –?" Zoe began, but Wes waved her to silence, keeping his gun aimed at the corpse.

Zoe looked back at the body on the floor just as it gave a huge shudder and twitched rapidly. The head turned and the body raised itself once more to its feet, the skull swiftly reforming, the wound in its cheek sealing in an instant. Within seconds the figure was standing before them whole and uninjured once more.

"I thought you would have learned by now, Wesley."

"Don't call me that, fuck-hole," snarled Wes. "What are you doing here? How'd you come back this time?"

"That is hardly of consequence at this point," said Prometheus, "but let's just say your Government had a lot to do with it, or don't you remember?"

Zoe stared at Prometheus with dread in her heart. She knew exactly what this man, the Titan Wes had fought through so many dimensions, was capable of.

"Pr – Prometheus?" asked Zoe, her nerves making her stutter slightly.

The tall figure raised an eyebrow. "And who are you? You must be someone of importance to understand what I'm saying in Olympian. Your meat-sack friend here –" he pointed at Wes "– had the talent unlocked by my old nemesis Zeus during our last encounter, but you weren't around back then. So how is it you can comprehend what is going on? Unless…." Prometheus assumed an almost predatory expression. "Unless you are either Olympian or from Tartarus, which I doubt. Perhaps you are somehow related to a person versed in the Elder-tongue and against all odds that talent has passed to you."

Prometheus took a step toward them, and Wes squeezed the

trigger once more, hitting the Titan in the chest and knocking him backward, but not dropping him to the ground this time.

"Will you stop doing that? You have no idea how annoying it is!" snarled Prometheus, his eyes never leaving Zoe.

"Well, you just hold your ground and answer some questions," responded Wes.

"Oh, all right, you stupid ape. What do you want to know?"

"What the hell is going on here? How come it seems like years have gone by, and yet I haven't aged? Why can't I remember anything? And what's with the whole dragon thing? I don't remember anything about dragons last time we met."

Prometheus chuckled darkly. "I have been traveling. I went back to a time where your race was easier to manipulate and impress. Have you perchance heard of the Age of the Aesir?"

"What's that?" asked Wes, his gun unwavering. He obviously couldn't kill Prometheus, but it seemed to deter him enough to allow Wes to maintain some sort of control over the situation.

"There was once a wonderful race of people who were so superstitious – even more so than your ancient Greeks – that it was easy to manipulate them to my own ends. I mean, the last time we met, I manipulated you and that pathetic monkey Talbot like stringed ants. It was only through luck that you prevailed and quashed my plans. But that is all beside the point.

"I went back in time to the Age of the Aesir, when your people slaughtered each other in the hope it would gain them access to the halls of Valhalla."

"You're talking about Norse mythology," interjected Zoe.

Prometheus turned his smoky eyes toward her, studying her face, and Zoe felt her heart race. "Yes, the people of the Norse, I believe they were also called Vikings. I traveled to their time with the hope that I could meet up with my people's sister race, the Aesir, a peaceful people who wouldn't think of harming –"

"Cut the crap, Prometheus," snapped Wes. Rage flashed across Prometheus's brow, but Wes merely grinned maliciously. "Get on with the fucking story."

"I wanted to create a new army with which to attack Olympia and finally destroy those pesky Olympians once and for all. You are right, human, the Aesir are indeed warlike and powerful, much like my own race was... *before* they were destroyed by the Keres during our last encounter." His words dripped with malice, and Zoe was amazed Wes could stand so casually.

She remembered from her father's stories that the Keres, an incredibly powerful race of creatures, had joined forces with the Olympians and saved them during the final battle against the Titans. However, it wasn't until they realized they'd been fooled by Prometheus, and discovered their lord Hades had been slain and replaced by the shape-shifting Titan, that they had acted. From what Zoe's father had said, the revenge of the Keres had been both awesome and horrific to witness.

"I stayed with the Aesir for a long time, but was unable to sway their confidence enough to get them to follow me. During my time with them, I adopted the guise of one known as Fafnir, a shape-shifter and dragon of incredible power – hence my most recent appearance."

"Are these Aesir living in a different dimension like the Olympians were?" asked Wes.

"No. They fled their land when another race invaded it. They came to your realm and established themselves within the domain of the Norse people; swiftly becoming their rulers because of their natural human weakness, utilizing their superstitions to great benefit. The Aesir dabbled in things unheard of in this realm, but their main ambitions were violent and warlike, hence the creation of myths which led the Vikings to believe they had to die in battle in order to receive glory in the halls of Valhalla."

"What's Valhalla?" asked Wes, his eyes never leaving the towering form in front of him, the gun never wavering.

Prometheus peered down at him. "Your memory must be bad indeed if you, a soldier, don't recall the legend of Valhalla. It was the realm where all Norse warriors traveled if they died gloriously in battle; a place where their cups would be filled with mead by the most beautiful maidens in existence. Only the souls of the greatest warriors were chosen to enter Valhalla, and there they were to wait for the time of Ragnarok, when the final battle would commence. To my knowledge this never happened."

"What is this place called, the land the Aesir fled from?" asked Wes.

Prometheus's features instantly became slightly more rigid, though he tried hard to mask his discomfort. "It was a world called Vanaheim," he replied stiffly, offering no more information.

"I have heard of Vanaheim," interjected Zoe, "along with many of the old Norse myths, especially a place called Asgard. It is said the only way to reach Asgard was by crossing Bifrost the Rainbow Bridge. Could this have been a reference to a rift like the ones used to travel to Olympia and Tartarus?"

Prometheus looked uncomfortable at the question, though Zoe wasn't certain. What she did know, however, was that Prometheus could not be trusted for a moment, and thus any expression might simply just be a ruse to lull them into a comfort zone.

It was obvious Prometheus wanted something from them, for even though he appeared compliant, Zoe knew Wes's gun was not really deterring him. This outpouring of information was much more than simple conversation. Glancing at Wes, she guessed he knew it too. Her father had always alluded that the Australian was far more intelligent than he ever let on, and quite possibly a much more dangerous man as a result. Dangerous and unpredictable.

"Well, answer the woman!" snapped Wes, waving his M4A5 at the Titan.

"It is likely that the Rainbow Bridge is a reference to one of the rifts, though I cannot be certain. It was before my time."

"What was before your time?" asked Wes.

Prometheus seemed to bite back a curse, a look of loathing crossing his features. "I was not alive when the Aesir were driven from their home."

"Was it your people, the Titans, who invaded them?" asked Wes, his gaze piercing. "Is that why you're so upset about these questions?"

"My people colonized many worlds."

"Let's just cut through all the crap. What do you want, Prometheus?" snapped Wes.

"I want to atone for my past actions. I want to assist you both by giving you information."

"What a crock of shit. I've had to deal with your information before," said Wes bitterly, "and it almost destroyed the universe. What bullshit do you want to share with us now?"

"It's really quite simple," replied Prometheus, turning and grinning maliciously, directly at Zoe. "I just want to tell you that Talbot Harrison is still alive, and trapped among the Aesir."

Wes's jaw dropped, but Zoe never saw it. She took a step away from Prometheus, his glaring orbs seeming to strip away all her defenses, and she tripped. Wes, with cat-like reflexes, spun and caught her, but when they turned back, Prometheus was gone!

CHAPTER 2

Wes cursed himself. In the split second his attention had been distracted by Zoe falling, Prometheus had transformed back into the dragon's form, lifting into the air and disappearing in the blink of an eye – a staggering feat for something so huge.

Wes hauled Zoe to her feet. "Gotta go. I've had a great time, thanks for everything." He moved toward the front door, currently hanging from only one hinge – a reminder of Prometheus's entrance.

"Wait!" called Zoe, leaping to her feet. Wes turned, his hand resting on the doorknob. "You are *not* going to leave me here after what just happened."

Wes shrugged nonchalantly. "Well, I was thinking about it. Why should I let you come?"

"He's my father!" yelled Zoe.

"That may be true, but I'm not a babysitter. I was for Talbot, but this time, I know what we're going up against. There's no way I'd ever put someone in the way of the crap we went through before without a damn good reason."

Zoe paused. "He said I must be able to speak the Elder-tongue," she eventually replied.

Wes wracked his brain for a way to refuse her request, but knew she was right. He'd need the power she possessed, and the only thing that kept popping into his head was a single word:

Checkmate.

"Damn," Wes muttered. The last thing he needed was luggage, even super sexy luggage like Zoe. Just looking at her made him think of –

She's Talbot's daughter!

Yeah, alright. It was wrong to be thinking stuff like that.

"Okay, let's go," he muttered gruffly.

"I'll just be a minute," said Zoe, running back through the devastation.

"Shit," mumbled Wes to himself. "Now she has to go and pack her hair dryer. Good work, numbskull."

But Zoe emerged moments later wearing thick, black cargo pants and hiking boots along with a heavy, nylon, dark-colored top. Her hair was tied in a neat braid, and she had a light pack on her back.

"What's in the bag?" asked Wes. "Tampons?"

"Why? Do you need some?" snapped Zoe. "I thought some MREs might come in handy."

Wes's raised an eyebrow; this was an unexpected twist of events. A staple in any soldier's diet during warfare, MREs were exactly what the name said: meals, ready to eat! Wes had eaten so many over the years he preferred them to normal food… almost.

"Fair enough," he said. "Let's get going then."

Moving to the door, Wes kicked it, snapping the remaining hinge and knocking it flying across the hallway. The duo carefully navigated their way through the destroyed apartment building and out to the street beyond.

"Where's your car?" asked Zoe.

"Over there," said Wes, indicating across the road, beyond the hundreds of onlookers who had gathered to stare at the partly-demolished structure. Whether they had witnessed Prometheus in the guise of the dragon crashing through the building would remain a mystery Wes didn't care to investigate. He hid his M4A5 as best he could, hoping the people in the crowd were too preoccupied with the teetering structure to notice.

They pushed through the crowd and suddenly Zoe stopped. "You can't be serious."

"What?" asked Wes, looking around.

"Is *that* what I think it is?" She pointed at the septic tanker parked on the side of the road.

"Depends on what you think it is."

"I think it's the same truck my father told me about in his

stories."

Wes paused. "Then you'd be right," he replied finally, resuming his stride. Zoe skipped slightly to keep up.

"So you mean *all* my father's stories were true?" she asked.

"That depends."

"Depends on what?"

"It depends on what his stories were," replied Wes casually, striding up to the tanker and placing his hand on the door handle. The septic tanker instantly transformed, the outline shimmering as though they were peering through a heat haze as it remolded into a sleek, futuristic-looking silver jet.

Zoe's jaw dropped as she stared up at the awesome craft, such a contrast to the septic tanker parked there only moments before. Then her mouth snapped closed, and she regarded the people moving along the street.

"Say hello to Bessie," said Wes.

"Why aren't they reacting?" she asked Wes.

Wes glanced around, looking at the gawkers passing within meters of them. "People see what they want to see," he said. "Plus the camouflage system extends out a few feet from the hull of the ship. All these sheep see is a septic truck, and when we take off they'll see nothing at all. The ship has the ability to refract light around it, effectively becoming invisible."

"How does it do that?"

"Who cares?" replied Wes with a shrug of his shoulders. He pressed a panel, and the outer hull of the ship swirled, creating a hatch in the side of the craft. Wes climbed inside.

Zoe stood motionless for a moment, unsure of how to proceed until Wes poked his head out from the darkness. "Well, are you coming or not?"

She clambered aboard.

***

The interior of Wes's ship appeared exactly as Zoe had imagined it: an empty shell with two metallic pillars toward the front of the vacant space. The ceiling height allowed her to easily walk upright within the craft, and she moved with unconcealed curiosity to the two pillars. Zoe had heard endless hours from her father about this craft which Wes and Talbot had used to travel back in time. It had been one of the main tools in thwarting Prometheus the last time, and as such had become a near-obsession of her father's.

The pillars – Physical Control Monitors or PCMs for short – worked as a kind of safety harness in addition to functioning as a control console. From what her father had told her, this craft had supposedly been built in the future and stolen by Wes when he went AWOL from the Australian army. The former SAS commando had traveled back in time before crashing into the ocean and sinking an aircraft carrier in the process.

"Look," said Zoe, "I'm not sure I'm ready for this."

"Don't let the door hit your arse on the way out," replied Wes.

Zoe glanced back at the entrance and faltered; she had to stay with the commando if she were to achieve her objective. Talbot was trapped in the past with a race of people they knew almost nothing about, and the only way he could escape was with the help of Wes… but Wes would need her aid if he were to succeed. Zoe knew this without a doubt.

She had envisioned a quest like this for as long as she could recall, but now that she stood on the threshold of it, she found herself hesitating. This was not make-believe anymore, and Zoe realized she could very well die if she continued. The excitement of finding out Wes was real had blinded her to reality. Both Wes and Talbot had been very, *very* lucky to survive their last encounter with Prometheus. Perhaps this time would be different.

Prometheus's claim to be there to help them didn't fool her. He was an incredible manipulator of events, and she had no doubt he had a hand in Talbot's current situation. In fact, Talbot might not even be alive at all; Prometheus might have lied about this as well.

Even as she thought about it, Zoe realized she really had no real choice in the matter. The simple fact that Talbot *might* be alive was enough, and now that Wes was here, she had the aid and the transport she needed to rescue him; it was almost like serendipity… or manipulation on a brilliant scale. The kind of manipulation Prometheus was renowned for.

It didn't matter.

"Let's go," said Zoe resolutely. "How does this PCM thingy work?"

Wes chuckled. "Like this." The commando pointed his arms toward the metallic pillar in front of him, and it instantly began to liquefy. The entire PCM smeared itself like butter across Wes's hands and arms, progressing to his shoulders and around behind his neck while spreading over his chest, back and down over his legs. In the blink of an eye, Wes was covered from neck to toe by the metallic substance. Beneath the surface of the liquid metal Zoe could see his hands moving, manipulating something.

He looked back at her. "Just point your hands toward the PCM, and it'll do the rest."

Zoe did as he bid, and the metal instantly flowed up and over her fingers and hands, swiftly covering her body in the same manner as it had Wes. It even encased the pack looped over her shoulders. The consistency of the PCM was not of metal, more like… like….

"Yeah, you're in a booger bath," said Wes, grinning.

"What do you mean?"

"It feels like snot, right?"

Revulsion flashed through Zoe. "That's not what I was thinking at all. I thought it was more like exfoliating body-scrub."

Wes stared at her blankly for a moment. "This is going to be a long trip," he muttered, shaking his head before turning away and once more manipulating something beneath the surface of the PCM.

Zoe felt around inside her own PCM, but could find nothing which felt like controls. A screen dropped down in front of the commando's face, and for several moments he studied it intensely while operating the controls within the PCM.

The entire wall in front of Zoe suddenly shimmered and misted, becoming first opaque, and then snapping into focus. It took her a moment to realize it was an outside view of the ship, whether by camera or another means. The only thing she could tell for sure was that it wasn't glass; it was more like the entire front panel had become a crystal-clear plasma-screen. As she watched, the whole scene abruptly dropped away, and Zoe realized they were taking off, shooting directly up into the sky. The buildings around them rapidly disappeared as the craft shot up and forward at an astonishing rate.

Within seconds they were racing across the ocean, and Zoe gaped in awe at the unbelievable velocity with which the jet shot through the air. If her father's stories were true, this craft could travel between countries at much the same rate as a person traveled between rooms in a large house.

She was enjoying the amazing view so much, in fact, that she almost missed seeing something miles off in the distance burst out of the ocean and shoot toward them. Zoe squinted, trying to make it out. What the hell was –?

"Oh shit!" barked Wes from the PCM beside her. "Brace yourself!"

She glanced back at the screen just in time to see the *thing* – it looked like some sort of three-pronged missile, sparking with electricity – smash directly into the front of Wes's ship! The screen began to flicker on and off, and Zoe felt the jet pitch forward.

"Fuck it!" snarled Wes. "We're going down. We need to eject."

"Eject? But I thought this thing was impervious or something."

"Obviously not," replied Wes caustically. "Prepare yourself; this might be kind of… unsettling."

Zoe saw Wes manipulating his controls as the ocean rushed toward them, and the craft tipped further forward, smoke beginning to obscure the already flickering view.

Without warning, her PCM surged forth, rising up and over Zoe's entire face and head. Panicking, she fought to break free, but the PCM held and controlled her, swaddling her form without completely solidifying. In her terror, Zoe opened her eyes and saw something resembling an LCD floating unsuspended just in front of her eyes, giving her a perfect picture of everything she would normally have seen. She also realized that despite the PCM now encasing her, she had no problem breathing, and could even turn her head slightly.

And then she shot directly up through the roof of the ship.

Zoe let fly a muffled shriek as she blasted high into the air, reaching the zenith of her ascent at the same time she realized her eyes were closed tightly. She opened them just in time to momentarily see Wes, similarly encased in the shiny metallic skin of the PCM, shoot up beside her.

And then she dropped.

Her eyes squeezed shut yet again as the shrieking took over once more.

It took a moment, but Zoe eventually realized her descent toward the ocean was somehow controlled. She hadn't felt the jolting which usually signaled the release of a parachute, but opening her eyes a crack, she looked down and saw several small jets had deployed through the 'skin' of the PCM and were now pushing high-pressured air directly downward, slowing her plunge, balancing her perfectly, and keeping the PCM vertical. It wasn't enough to halt the descent, but it proved sufficient to reduce her speed and make the fall safe.

The surface of the water rushed up toward her.

Zoe's main concern now was sinking like a stone. The PCM had shown it could provide oxygen, but it would do no good if she sank to the bottom of whatever ocean this was and couldn't get free from the cocoon-like creation designed to keep her alive.

She could see the cresting waves and cringed behind the cover of the PCM. The water came closer....

And closer....

The PCM jets blasted away at the surface, but didn't stop her.

The water seemed to reach up for her, eager to swallow her within its depths. Her breath rasped inside the coffin-like enclosure and she clawed hysterically and futilely at the elastic skin, trying to free herself.

The base of her silvery casing touched the surface of the water, cutting through it like a knife. It immediately sank down, the water rising past the level of her legs and rapidly reaching the height of her hips....

And in a blink everything changed.

The PCM unraveled with such velocity it seemed merely a blur to Zoe's eyes. One moment it was swaddled around her, and the next it was flat and spread across the surface of the ocean, floating like a cork. It thickened upon the water, stabilizing and raising its edges at the same time, shifting its form to become a life raft.

Zoe lay back, staring at the cloudless sky, stunned. She floated on the water supported by something which had successfully worked as a seatbelt, ejection seat, parachute and now a *lifeboat*. She had little time to ponder this marvel as Wes hit the water beside her and she sat bolt upright.

From her new perspective, Zoe realized she hadn't really been going as fast as she'd thought. Wes's thrusters were extremely effective at slowing him, and the moment his feet dipped into the ocean things began to happen. The thrusters disappeared beneath the metallic surface of the PCM, and before he dropped waist-deep in the water, the PCM exploded outward, flattening to become identical to the raft Zoe now sat upon.

"WOOHOO!' shouted Wes. "I'm glad that shit worked!"

"What do you mean?" called Zoe across the short distance of ocean between them.

"I mean the ejection system has never been fully tested before."

Zoe's stomach dropped. "Are you saying you had no idea if we'd live through it?"

"None at all," replied Wes. "But it seemed better than the alternative."

"Which was?"

"Burning horribly as the ship crashed into the ocean, and then choking on toxic fumes as we sank beneath the surface of the water, praying the hull would breach so that we could taste the sweet oblivion of death through drowning instead of being cooked alive."

"Oh…. When you put it like that, I see your point," said Zoe.

Wes began to reply, but stopped and twisted around, his gaze suddenly serious, searching the surface of the ocean. "Do you feel that?" he asked.

"What?" Zoe couldn't feel anything.

"Something big is moving beneath us."

Zoe held her breath, willing her senses to probe the ocean depths, but couldn't tell if there was anything beyond the ordinary splashing of waves against the side of her raft.

"Move!" shouted Wes. "Move now!" he immediately picked up a small paddle – one of which also clung to the side of Zoe's raft – and began to furiously push his way through the water toward her. Zoe fumbled for her own paddle with hands which seemed to have doubled in size. Finally freeing it from the clasp, she plunged it into the water –

The ocean erupted with such force Zoe's raft bounced on the surface. Something dark green surged from beneath the water, flopping heavily onto its belly. The resulting wave flipped Zoe's raft, and she went flying into the ocean, plunging beneath the surface before clawing her way back up, coughing and spluttering. She spied the upturned raft drifting several yards away and swam over to it, her heavy, water-logged clothes and boots weighing her down in the water. Grasping the side of the raft, Zoe glanced around and realized Wes had disappeared. He'd been directly under the huge thing when it had splashed down.

And now he was gone.

Zoe had no time to mourn the lost commando, however, as she gazed up at the enormous creature which now lay floating calmly upon the surface of the ocean. The waves from its unannounced arrival had begun to fade now, and she had a moment to realize how big the thing actually was.

Shaped roughly like a whale, it was bigger than any marine creature she'd ever heard of – even a blue whale, the largest living animal on the planet. It was green, but that may have simply been from the vast amounts of algae accumulated upon its exterior and over the enormous, pectoral-fin-like protrusions from its sides, slicing into the water and helping to stabilize the thing as it sat upon the ocean's surface.

Zoe peered further along the creature and saw something resembling an enormous vertical tail splashing from side to side just beneath the surface, the upswept portion rising high above the water. Seeing this, Zoe realized the thing was different in shape from a whale in that whales had a tail fin which spread out horizontally, and thrust up and down through the water. This tail was more like a fish's… or a shark's. Glancing at the head, Zoe saw it was indeed slightly pointed, but more resembling the roundness of a killer whale than the sharp predatory nose of a shark.

Without warning, a man appeared on top of the creature, standing calmly atop its back.

At first, Zoe thought it was Wes, judging from his broad shoulders tapering down to narrow waist, but this man was slightly taller. The stranger was also dressed differently; he wore long flowing robes the color of the ocean, which seemed to shimmer and change shade as he moved across the top of the beast.

She had heard enough from her father's stories to know that everything was not always as it appeared when dealing with these situations. Zoe saw the man, his hands calmly clasped behind his back, talking to another who had also seemingly appeared out of nowhere. This second man nodded and moved out of sight once more. Moments later, Zoe heard a thunderous *crunch*, and the side of the water beast cracked, sliding open like a door. Light erupted from within and a ramp splashed into the water, several figures moving down it toward her.

Not knowing whether these were friends or enemies, Zoe splashed away from the ship – for that must be what it was – one hand holding onto the capsized raft. She tried to kick out to move more swiftly through the water, but her heavy hiking boots made this task almost impossible.

Bubbles erupted and at first Zoe thought they were from her thrashing, but in moments the surface of the ocean surrounding her was breached as trident-like spears emerged from beneath the water. The skulls of the creatures which followed were scaled, with leathery skin similar to that of an alligator, their faces bearing warthog-like snouts, from which the bubbles Zoe had noticed emitted. At least a dozen of the figures were now floating in the water all about her, their tridents coursing with electrical sparks. A small corner of her mind wondered how they didn't electrocute themselves beneath the ocean. The greater part of her mind focused on not losing a grip on her rising panic.

Zoe gasped, "What do you want?"

One of the creatures nodded at her and silently pointed its spear toward the ramp hanging from the side of the ship. She looked from the creature's snout to the trident and decided against arguing. Splashing out in the direction of the ramp, Zoe suddenly felt hands clamp her upper arms, and glanced around to see two of the creatures had grabbed her and were now propelling her through the water, seemingly without any effort on their behalf.

Upon arriving at the ramp, Zoe was roughly assisted from the water by the men there as half of the water creatures clambered out of the ocean on either side of her. The other half silently submerged once more. She was marched up the ramp by both humans and water creatures, none of whom would answer any of her questions.

They halted at the top of the ramp in front of the man who had stood atop the ship. Up close, the enigmatic figure appeared even more imposing. His dark hair was closely-cropped and cut squarely, his thin moustache and sharp, pointed beard stabbing downward, all indicating the man who possessed them was unlikely to be jovial or benevolent. His eyes burned a startling blue in contrast to his tanned features.

This was definitely not a sedate figure, not a leisurely man who reveled in the luxuries of life. Everything about him screamed hardship and adversity, and yet he stood seemingly unscathed by the ravages of age – he could have been thirty or fifty. To Zoe he radiated mystery.

"Who are you?" demanded the stranger, his voice as cold as the ocean she'd just been plucked from.

Zoe thought about ignoring him, but one look into his eyes told her he would tolerate no insubordination. "I'm Zoe Harrison. Talbot Harrison's daughter."

The man's lip curled at the mention of Talbot's name. "I never met the man, but his actions almost killed my race. Him and the idiotic braggadocio from the land called Australia. They brought about one of the most dangerous threats my people have ever had to battle. Unfortunately I was not there, but I can promise you things would have ended differently if I had been. Rather than your father and the strange-talking fool named Wes being lauded as heroes, I would have had them clapped in restraints and watched them rot away in the deepest cell imaginable for the rest of their lives."

"So," began Zoe carefully, "I take it you're an Olympian."

The man stared at her, his expression disappointed. "As Talbot's daughter I have to assume he passed on the skill of the Elder-tongue to you. If I didn't require such an ability I would throw you back to act as food for my pets."

"Who? These pig guys?" snapped Zoe, indicating the odd-looking creatures around her.

The man chuckled humorlessly and indicated to one of the creatures who reached behind its head and abruptly peeled away – a mask!

"These are the underwater breathing devices my crewmembers use when they need to work outside my ship… or in the odd case where we need to capture a rogue female who may hold the fate of our people in her hands. No, my pets are much nastier than my crew. Pray you never meet them."

"Who are you?" asked Zoe.

The Olympian grimaced. "I am Zeus's brother, my name is Poseidon."

Zoe's jaw hung open, and she simply stood there, gaping at the man, speechless. She had heard stories from her father of the leader of the Olympians named Zeus and his son Heracles along with others, but now that she actually stood before one of the Olympian 'gods' she felt her courage flee.

"At least your brother had some fucking manners."

Poseidon spun around. Zoe's heart jumped in her chest, and she turned and saw Wes, M4A5 aimed directly at Poseidon, materialize from the shadows of the ship.

"So," said Poseidon calmly, "the idiot emerges. I was wondering when you would show your face. You can lower your weapon, it is useless onboard my vessel." The crewmembers holding tridents raised them, preparing to defend their leader.

Wes aimed the assault rifle at one of the divers to the left of

Poseidon and squeezed the trigger. Nothing happened.

"Oh well," said Wes amiably, dropping the barrel of the gun to point it at the floor. "Any of you guys got a towel?"

The crew looked to Poseidon for direction, and he nodded slightly. Three of the divers with electrified tridents moved toward Wes, their weapons pointing directly at him.

"Now, don't do anything silly, boys" said Wes, dropping the assault rifle to the floor and sliding his right foot back.

All three rushed at once, striking toward Wes with their electrified tridents. A second later, all three were laying senseless on the floor, and Wes was leaning casually upon one of their tridents.

Zoe was stunned.

The clash ended so quickly her mind hadn't been able to take it all in. She replayed the memory, slowing it down, and recalled seeing Wes leap over the first strike, grasping the handle of one of the tridents. The commando had then pulled the Olympian holding the trident forward, forcing his opponent into the other two weapons. The attacker had been knocked flying into the wall, rendering him unconscious. Wes had landed and swung the trident he now held in a sweeping motion, taking out the remaining two assailants with a single blow.

The entire action had held an incredible, almost graceful, economy of movement, and no one watching failed to realize the talent involved. The fact Wes had made it seem so effortless only bespoke of how skilled he actually was. The rest of the crew looked to Poseidon for direction once more, and Zoe saw several expressions of relief when the Olympian leader shook his head.

"Can I have that towel now?" asked Wes. "If I get much colder my old fella is likely to fall right off."

"Your what?" asked Poseidon.

Wes glanced at Zoe, and then shrugged. "My dick, mate. I didn't check with Zeus, but I assume you guys have one too."

Poseidon frowned, his displeasure at Wes's informality evident upon his features.

"Get them towels," he instructed one of the crew who saluted by hitting his fist on his chest, and then raising the same fist to his forehead. The man moved off.

"Nice salute. What do they call you; *mein fuhrer* perhaps?"

"You are as arrogant as Zeus told me," replied Poseidon, "but do not think I will put up with it as he did. It is through my sufferance you aren't now in the hold, as your experience and skills may actually be of assistance. Do not make me regret my decision."

"You won't regret it, buddy, I'll keep you warm at night. Speaking of which, where the hell are those towels?"

Zoe gawped at Wes's audacity. She'd heard of it from her father, but until now had never realized how close to the mark his stories about Wes had actually been. She'd always assumed his tales of the arrogant Australian were slightly far-fetched, but she now saw that, if anything, the accounts had been understated. The SAS commando was by far the most confident – or arrogant – man she'd met in her life.

As if on cue, the crewmember returned bearing towels. He approached Zoe first who took hers with a smile and a thank you, and then he moved to Wes who grinned and slapped the man on the back.

"Good work, mate. You're a legend."

The crewmember looked around at Poseidon, confused and unsure of how to react. Poseidon ignored him, and he hurried away.

***

"Ah, that's better," said Wes after toweling himself down. He'd shown no embarrassment stripping naked in front of everyone, whereas Zoe had merely patted her drenched clothes down as best she could. It did little to actually dry her off, but she felt slightly better by the end of it.

"So, Poseidon," said Wes, wrapping the towel around his waist and standing bare-chested, "what the hell is going on this time?"

"You don't know?"

"I woke up in an Australian military base with no memories after the last time Talbot and I wrangled with the Titans. Since then, Prometheus – a guy I've seen killed twice – has turned up looking like a fucking dragon, and this chick here –" he indicated Zoe, "– is claiming twenty years have gone by, and she's Talbot's daughter. Oh, and I haven't aged a day. Now you've shot my ship out of the fucking sky with a giant spear thing, and your pretty little guards have tried to attack me. So what the hell is going on?"

Poseidon appeared thoughtful, his arms folded across his chest. "I couldn't permit you to proceed as Prometheus's puppets. He would have manipulated you much as he did the last time, resulting in catastrophe once more. I will not allow you to endanger my people again."

"He spoke about Zoe's father, Talbot, being stuck in the past with a group called the arseholes or something," said Wes.

"The Aesir," corrected Zoe.

"Whatever. Prometheus said Talbot was trapped by those guys. He told us he'd been trying to use the Aesir to invade Olympia once again."

Poseidon looked aghast. "You cannot be serious!" he said.

"That's what he told us. Why? Who are these people?"

"They are a race known to us through legends, much as Greek gods are known to you. The Aesir were forced from their home world by the Titans, defeated despite their own destructive nature. The Titans opened a primitive rift and forced the Aesir to flee through it into a place known as Asgard."

"The land of the Norse gods," murmured Zoe, awestruck.

"That is one of the guises the Aesir went under when they successfully opened a rift into your world. Their rift was nothing like the ones my people developed; it cut back and forth with its resonance and proved unreliable to say the least, many Aesir dying or becoming lost in the mists between dimensions as a result. They were trying to find a way back to their home world, but had instead stumbled upon your plane of existence. They kept the rift open for several of your generations, but eventually the alignment of the planets altered too much for the resonance to remain constant and the rift failed.

"It may be that the planets have now realigned enough for this rift to have once again unlocked, opening your world to the Aesir once more. With the guidance and manipulation of Prometheus they will invade your world, destroying Earth, and then using Talbot, he will open the Syrpeas Gate, leading them into Tartarus. From there they can get to Olympia, the world Prometheus has always yearned to rule."

"Not good, huh?" asked Wes.

Poseidon shook his head.

"Well that's all you had to say. I didn't need the doom and gloom speech, but thanks for creeping out young Zoe here. Great work, Possy."

"What did you call me?" asked Poseidon, astounded.

"We've got more important things to worry about right now." Wes unashamedly dropped the towel and proceeded to dress in his fatigues once more. "You just shot down the one thing that could get us to where we need to go. How the hell are we supposed to travel around the planet now?"

"This is all a manipulation by Prometheus," replied Poseidon, ignoring Wes's question. "I cannot allow you to be controlled by him."

"Ah, but that's the problem with Prometheus's plans," said Wes. "If we just sit back and do nothing he'll get his way anyway. I'm sure he needs us to be involved in this somehow, but even if we're not, he'll probably get those other arseholes to help him out. Before you know it they'll sodomize Earth before sliding on through the rift gate and prison-raping Olympia."

Poseidon appeared to ponder Wes's words. To Zoe they seemed to make sense, and she could tell Poseidon was now weighing his choices. He could either admit he'd been wrong in destroying Wes's ship, forcing him to aid them, or he could kill them both.

"I will take you to the site of the Aesir rift and from there we will decide how to proceed," said Poseidon finally.

"Nice," replied Wes. "So why the hell did you have to shoot down my jet? I would have been there by now, and I'd probably be wiping my arse with Prometheus again."

"You hardly wiped anything with him the first time," countered Poseidon. "If you had, he wouldn't be here bothering us now, would he? As for your flying craft, that was regrettable, but I had to know what your intentions were."

"Good point," replied Wes. "Remarkably stupid reasoning, but good point nonetheless. So, how are we supposed to get back in time now?"

"What do you mean?" asked Poseidon.

"That's where they're holding Talbot, in the past in that place called Asgard."

"Prometheus told you this?

"Yeah, why? What's the big deal?"

"I had thought they'd somehow reopened the rift in this time, and it would be a relatively simple task to go there and close the rift. If he somehow traveled into the past, that means whatever damage he managed has already been done."

"You're forgetting something," interjected Zoe.

"What's that?" asked Poseidon.

"These Aesir have Talbot, and Talbot has the power of the Elder-tongue. If they somehow coerce him into using it, they'll be able to open a rift gate during a time before the Olympian wars. Your people will have to face the double threat of attack from the Titans as well as the Aesir."

Poseidon paled as he realized what she meant. "But that's not possible. The past has already happened and cannot be changed."

"Sorry to shatter your dreams, buddy, but it most definitely can happen," said Wes. "Trust me, that's how we stopped Prometheus the last time; we traveled back through time and prevented him from the very start."

Poseidon's brow furrowed. "If what you say is true, we must find a way to get you into the past."

"You don't say? We were actually on our way to do exactly that when you shot my ship out of the sky. Well done, by the way."

"I was acting on the information that you were being influenced by Prometheus," replied Poseidon defensively. "For all I knew you were already set on a course which would have seen the end of my people forever."

"So you shot me out of the sky. You're not American by any chance, are you? You know, shoot first and ask questions later?"

If looks could have killed at that moment, Zoe thought Wes might have dropped dead in an instant. As it was he simply grinned roguishly.

"Well, first things first," continued Wes. "We need to find a way to get to the time when Prometheus fucked around with stuff. He got back there somehow, and we just have to figure out how he did it. Can you take us to Washington, or as close as you can get in this rub and tugboat?"

Zoe picked up on Wes's innuendo instantly, choking back her laughter with difficulty, and Poseidon studied them both for a moment before nodding somberly.

"I understand now why my brother aided you as he did. You are a fool, but I seem to have little choice in the matter if I want my people to remain safe."

"Yeah, that sucks," said Wes. "So how fast can this heap of green shit go?"

"The journey you speak of will take less than a week."

Wes nodded approvingly. "Not bad, Possy." The Olympian shook his head and moved away, indicating the rest of the crew should follow him.

"Why are we going to Washington?" asked Zoe once they were alone. The giant ramp lifted laboriously from the water, clanging loudly as it sealed with the rest of the hull.

"I thought that would have been obvious," replied Wes. "We're going to go and meet the President of the United States."

Zoe's heart fluttered. "Of course we are," she replied.

***

If Zoe had been impressed by Wes's futuristic jet, it was nothing compared to Poseidon's submarine. The scale of the ship, combined with its aesthetic and almost living beauty, made it more like traveling within a breathing creature rather than a vehicle. Zoe had to constantly remind herself that the submarine – which she discovered was called the *Ketos Aithiopios,* or Ketos for short – was a machine created by the Olympians, and not an actual animal.

However, this did nothing to lessen the impression that the Ketos emulated a living, breathing creature in almost everything it did. Her father had told Zoe about the incredible creatures the Olympian named Hephaestus had constructed; beasts created from metal which moved and acted like living beings.

Remembering her father brought a deeply-embedded anguish she feared would never leave her, and she roughly suppressed the memories battling to break free. Stories of Wes and Talbot had been iterated so many times she knew them as if they were her own, and at this moment, surrounded by the incredible beast that was the Ketos, she understood why. Zoe had never really credited how amazing such a thing was until this moment, when she traveled inside a fabled sea beast.

For that was what the Ketos was – a sea monster straight out of myth.

The ship had been referenced in Greek mythology as a monster Poseidon conjured to attack the lands of Ethiopia as punishment for having the audacity to proclaim Princess Andromeda more striking than the Nereides: water nymphs of the sea. The truth, as Zoe discovered from one of the more loose-lipped crew, was that the Ethiopians had nothing to do with the attack. Rather, the Titans had set up a fortress just off the coast of Africa which the Ketos had destroyed spectacularly with its trident-like Olympian missiles. This tale had somehow become warped over the centuries into a story of a horrific creature attacking Ethiopia after Queen Kassiopeia's boasting.

Such was the way with legends, Zoe supposed. They eventually took on a life of their own, until the original tale was so distorted as to be unrecognizable.

"How did you all end up here?" Zoe asked Pheres one day. He was the crewmember who had divulged the information. She had a sneaky suspicion the Olympian was smitten with her, and she played on it to find out as much as she could.

"Lord Poseidon has brought us here to investigate something," boasted Pheres one day. "He told us there was an issue with the rifts. The Ketos remained in your world when we left the first time – only years for us, but apparently centuries for your people."

"How could the ship have remained hidden for all that time?" asked Zoe.

Pheres grinned. "Lord Poseidon disguised it as an outcrop of stone off the coast of a city called Joppa. I am unsure what this place is called now."

"It's in Lebanon. I read about it in the Bible or something."

"What is a *bible*?" asked Pheres innocently.

Zoe shook her head. "It'd take too long to explain. Please continue."

"The Ketos remained undetected until the time we returned."

"From what my father told me, your people were decimated after the battle against the Titans."

"Yes, those living atop Mount Olympus were almost completely annihilated, but we live on the coast of Olympia. Our city was largely untouched by the wars, and our population has always been larger than that of Mount Olympus."

"How many cities are there in Olympia?"

"There are seven," replied Pheres. "My home is in Artemisium. We are a people who spend as much time upon the oceans as we do on the land – often more so."

"Were you involved in the first war?" she asked.

"No. It was years ago by our time, and I was only three then – too young to go to war. I reached my age of majority last year," said Pheres, "and could have fought in the clash your father was involved in, but the battle against the Titans took place atop Mount Olympus, many days distant. My people didn't even hear of the conflict until the Titans had been chased back to their own realm by the Keres."

Zoe knew the tale well. The Keres were a race of beings composed of nearly pure energy and almost invulnerable. The ferryman, Kharon, was one of them, and they had been led by Heracles, arriving just in time to vanquish the Titans. Their hatred of Prometheus was so intense they had viciously attacked the Titans, slaying thousands and hounding the rest through the rift, back into Tartarus, following and sealing the gate behind them.

"And Zeus opened the gate for you all to come through?" asked Zoe.

At this Pheres appeared uncomfortable. He glanced around nervously, but at a small smile from Zoe he seemed to give in. "No. It was our lord, Poseidon, who opened the gate. He believes – as do we all – that Prometheus poses the greatest threat to all of Olympia. There is something within the Titan that despises our race, and he will not rest until we are utterly vanquished."

"So Zeus doesn't know you're here?"

Pheres swallowed heavily. "I do not think so."

This was interesting. In the couple of days they'd been aboard the Ketos, there had been little to no mention of Zeus, and Zoe had begun to wonder if there was some sort of split between him and Poseidon. The crewmembers aboard the Ketos were extremely loyal toward Poseidon, and Zoe found herself amazed Pheres had divulged this tiny tidbit of information.

"This fucking thing is awesome!" called Wes as he entered the area where Zoe and Pheres stood. "No matter how much I wander around, I never get bored with all the weird shit whirring and goo squirting out of places and the slime and stuff."

Zoe glanced at Pheres and noticed a narrowing in his gaze when he looked at the Australian. It took her a few moments before she realized the young Olympian was jealous of Wes.

"I have to go," muttered Pheres.

"See ya later, Pheromone," said Wes. Pheres scowled at him and looked to Zoe. She smiled and his face brightened somewhat before he turned and stalked away.

"You didn't have to be so mean to him," admonished Zoe.

"Was I mean?" asked Wes, adopting a surprised expression.

"You know you were. The poor kid looked like he was about to cry."

Wes chuckled. "It's not my fault he's got his balls in a twist over you. That's assuming these Olympian guys actually have balls. They might have tentacles or something."

"We need their assistance if we're going to make it through this," she countered.

"Just remember what your father told you in his stories," said Wes.

"What do you mean?" asked Zoe, somewhat defensively.

"Any one of these fuckers could be Prometheus. This entire thing might be one big trap set up in order to make us do something he needs us to do. You're no longer Zoe Harrison, hot chick and daughter of a guy who went missing. Now you're the one person on this planet with the ability to discern the script of the Elder-tongue. That makes you an extremely valuable commodity to whoever has their hands on you."

Zoe felt her palms begin to sweat as the weight of Wes's words sank in. She couldn't trust anyone except Wes, but even he could be suspect at any time. Prometheus could take on the guise of anyone he wanted, and he had already set them upon a path of his own design by telling them Talbot was still alive and trapped in the past. Everything they had done since then had been in reaction to this news. But they had no choice. Talbot held the answers they needed, and they had to get him back at any cost.

Zoe straightened her back and raised her steady gaze to meet Wes's. The Australian grinned lopsidedly. "That's the spirit," he said, clapping her on the shoulder.

She stumbled forward slightly before righting herself, and frowned at Wes. "What's our plan of action?"

"At the moment we have none. Even though this thing goes faster than I would have imagined possible for something of its size, we're still a couple of days away from the coast of the United States. For the time being we just have to wait and not stick our necks out too much. I know Prometheus made out like he needs us for now, but it doesn't mean he has to like it. I'd bet my left nut he's onboard, and I'd bet my right one he wouldn't mind taking a cheap shot at either one of us."

"Why me?" asked Zoe, her gaze narrowed.

"Because your dad is the one who thwarted his plans the last time."

"Oh," said Zoe. "Right."

"And I can assure you," continued Wes, "your perky boobs and tight butt aren't going to coerce Prometheus as easily as…. What's that guy's name?"

"Pheres."

"Right, Porous. Anyway, Porous might be easily distracted by your looks, but Prometheus is more likely to take a bite out of you than drool over you. Don't ever forget that."

Zoe knew the truth in what Wes said, possibly more so than anyone else aboard. Not only was Prometheus a genius and incredible manipulator of events, he was also virtually invincible, having the ability to assume the appearance of anyone he chose. For all Zoe knew, it was Prometheus she now spoke to instead of Wes. She stared at the commando, gazing deep into his eyes, searching for some indication it might not be him.

Wes looked intently back at her, holding her gaze for what seemed like an eternity, and then he let loose an enormous belch.

Well, that was one problem solved.

"What happens when we finally get to Washington?" she asked.

Wes scratched at the stubble on his chin. "We start by meeting with the President and finding out what the hell is going on."

"Just like that. We just walk up to the front gate of the White House, and they're going to let us in."

Wes chuckled. "Not exactly," he said. "But I'm sure I'll think of something."

"What do we do after that?"

"I've got no idea," replied Wes with a shrug.

Zoe was aghast. "What do you mean? I thought you had a plan."

"I do have a plan. It's to get to Washington DC and find out why I haven't aged in twenty years and why I can't remember anything."

Zoe looked away. "Perhaps you somehow traveled forward in time after the incident with the Titans."

"No, it's impossible to travel forward into a time which hasn't been created yet," said Wes. "Time is like traveling along a suspension bridge which splits into a myriad of possible directions with every decision we make, but only one direction is solid. The thing only becomes solid once you pass over it. If you try to jump ahead, nothing exists yet and you will disappear into oblivion."

Wes's simplistic speech and mannerisms altered slightly during his explanation, and Zoe recalled what her father had told her about the many different layers of the man named Wes. It seemed hard to believe this was the same tactless buffoon who had been belching and bastardizing names a moment ago.

Zoe wondered if it was all an act, or if Wes's genius had fractured his personality in such a way as to work as a form of protection. She remembered hearing her how the commando had been immune to the toxin Prometheus had released into the air around the city of Hades, but which had rendered Talbot susceptible to suggestion. Perhaps it was because of his strange multiple personas. She pushed the issue aside for the time being.

"But wouldn't it exist if you'd already traveled back from the future?" she asked.

Wes laughed, snapping back to his roguish demeanor. "Back from the future, just like the movie, eh? As far as I know, nobody before me had even traveled backward through time, and the first time I did it was only a fluke. There's no way I could have traveled forward in time, and even if I did, it doesn't explain my amnesia."

Zoe decided to let the issue go. She sensed she had touched a raw spot when she'd brought up the subject of traveling through time.

Traveling through time!

Talbot was trapped in the past. They were going to try to save him and stop the Aesir from being duped by whatever scheme Prometheus had devised, but in order to do so they had to get back into the past. And the only machine capable of traveling back in time now rested at the bottom of the ocean.

Zoe looked at Wes once more, finally understanding the nerve she had touched when talking about time travel. They had to somehow travel back in time to avert the coming disaster, but Wes's craft, the only thing on the planet which had proven it could do something like that, had been destroyed.

CHAPTER 3

The Ketos cruised within the depths of the ocean like a predatory juggernaut, surging ahead, silently searching for its prey. The shark-like tail cut through the water more effectively than any propeller, and the sleek prow of the submersible vessel drove the ocean aside like mist.

Zoe and Wes hurried through the stairwells and halls of the enormous submarine. They had been summoned to the bridge of the Ketos by Poseidon, and it would be their first meeting with the Olympian leader since their unusual introduction. Several days had passed, and Zoe knew they must be close to reaching their destination.

Climbing the last set of stairs, they followed their escort through the doors to the ship's bridge. Beyond the sliding double-doors was an extraordinary control room, and glancing at Wes, Zoe could tell the normally stoic commando was also impressed.

The most prominent feature of the bridge was a huge glass bubble-like wall through which the various crewmembers could peer into the murky depths in front of the Ketos. On closer inspection, however, Zoe realized the wall was not actually curved at all; rather it was some sort of viewing screen which displayed like a huge bubble. The screen seemed similar to the one upon Wes's jet, but on a much larger scale and convex like a fish-eye in order to make the most of the view outside the Ketos.

The entire effect was amazing, but Zoe realized she shouldn't have been so surprised. After all, she *was* traveling through the ocean in a giant machine designed and built thousands of years ago that resembled an amalgamation of shark and whale.

The crew, both male and female Olympians, were either standing or sitting in front of foreign instruments and controls, none of which appeared even remotely similar to anything Zoe had ever seen before. Poseidon sat in a large, unadorned chair in the center of the room, the heart of a controlled maelstrom, calmly surveying the activity taking place all around him, occasionally relaying orders to the crew.

As though sensing their arrival, Poseidon spun his chair to face Wes and Zoe, pinning them both with a piercing stare.

"We are traveling north along the coast you described to us, currently navigating through the western part of your North Atlantic Ocean."

"The *western* part?" asked Wes dramatically. "As in the part to the west of the center? As in the area of the North Atlantic Ocean between Miami, Puerto Rico and a little island called Bermuda?"

Poseidon stared at Wes quizzically. "What are you babbling about?"

"Those three points mark out an area of the North Atlantic Ocean known to most people on Earth as the Bermuda Triangle."

"But surely that's just superstition," cut in Zoe.

"Not necessarily," said Wes cryptically.

"Forgive me for seeming ignorant," spat Poseidon, "but what in the Deep Green are you talking about?"

Wes turned his gaze toward Poseidon. "The Bermuda Triangle is a place which has always had weird crap going on in it. A lot of what is said about the place is bullshit, but there're some facts mixed in there as well. Flight 19 definitely disappeared in 1945 under some strange-arse circumstances, and the way the USS Cyclops vanished way back in 1918 during the First World War has never been properly explained."

"How do you even know that stuff?" asked Zoe.

"I get around. Anyway, my point is the Triangle has always had weird shit going on, in or around it."

"Tell me," said Poseidon, "did their directional instruments begin to act oddly before these incidents took place?"

"Yeah, I think so, at least for Flight 19. Why?"

"It may be this Triangle you speak of is actually a junction point for inharmonious resonance waves," said Poseidon.

"Inhar… what?" asked Wes.

Poseidon frowned at him slightly. "They are like the negative version of the energy we harnessed to create rift gates. For it to influence machinery on your planet without being tuned in for such a thing must mean it is incredibly powerful. I shall alter course for now, but this is something which is both very disturbing as well as potentially positive."

"What do you mean by that?" asked Wes, but Poseidon ignored him. Instead, the Olympian barked orders for a change to their course, and crew members quickly scrambled to obey.

The external view of the ocean displayed through the convex viewing screen tilted as the monstrous craft banked smoothly to the port side, and then righted itself, powering forward through the dark emerald water.

"This diversion from course in order to avoid the Triangle you speak of will add several hours to our journey," said Poseidon. "I hope your information is true, otherwise we are simply wasting time. Be ready when we arrive."

"All right," snapped Wes. "I'll just be up on the deck sunbathing, okay? Let me know when you want to talk to me a bit less like I'm your dog."

He moved to leave, but two male crewmembers stepped in front of the doors, barring his exit. "Now boys, you don't really want to do this, do you?" asked Wes with a grin. Zoe saw from their expressions that the two Olympians were nervous, but they seemed more scared of failing Poseidon.

"One moment," called Poseidon, and Zoe thought she could see the two crewmembers exhale in relief as Wes turned back to the Olympian leader.

"What can I do to you – I mean for you?" Zoe saw a malicious gleam in Wes's eye and, without realizing it, she placed a hand upon his arm. He glanced at her and beamed a dazzling grin before snapping his gaze back to the Olympian.

"I need you both to realize how dangerous this entire enterprise is, not only for myself and my crew, but our entire world," said

Poseidon.

"What do you mean?" asked Wes cagily.

"I mean Prometheus obviously needs you for his plans to succeed. By assisting you we might be playing right into his hands. As such, I am somewhat limited in the information I am able to relay to you. Do you understand?"

Wes stood silently for a moment, looking thoughtful. "The opposite is also true, though," he said finally. "Perhaps Prometheus planned for all of this. I mean, crashing into a building in New York City dressed as a fucking dragon is hardly the most subtle way to give us a message, is it?"

"But why would he do that?" asked Poseidon.

"At the very least it would achieve what is happening right now; a total lack of trust on both sides. At the very best it would result in either you killing us or us killing you. I mean, your first move was to shoot my jet out of the sky, and now we have no immediate way to travel back in time in order to get in on the action. However it works out, Prometheus wins. Everything turns to shit as we argue and bitch amongst ourselves, and in the meantime he can wander around and do whatever the hell he wants."

Poseidon stared at Wes, his stony gaze drilling into him in a way which would have made a strong man cringe, or at the very least look away. A weak man might have burned crimson with a shame similar to what a child feels when caught doing something they shouldn't.

Wes scratched his crotch and yawned.

"You certainly are an odd individual," said Poseidon. "But you make a very valid point. We can argue about Prometheus's intentions all we want, and they still won't become any clearer; the Titan is nothing short of a genius at such things, as you have already been witness to. Very well, we will proceed as you have suggested, but with one small alteration. This leader of yours; this... *President*. When you go to meet with him I will be with you."

Zoe's eyes bugged out of her head, and she spun around to look at Wes. How would they explain Poseidon – in fact, how would they explain any of it – to the President of the United States?

"Yeah, alright," replied Wes with a grin. "That should be good for a laugh. You might want to have a wash first, though. That fishy smell might go down well with all your little mermaids – or mermen, if that's your thing – but the Prez kinda has higher standards." Poseidon huffed slightly, and Wes grinned triumphantly. "I'll lend you some deodorant to cover up the stink, okay?" The Olympian sat back in his command chair and waved them away dismissively.

Wes chuckled and strode off the bridge, pinching one of the crewmen who had prevented his earlier exit on the butt as he passed. Zoe stood shocked for a moment before shaking her head in wonder and following the Australian. Her father had told her stories about Wes, but nothing could have prepared her for the reality.

***

Wes stared at the pencil. It rested on the small table beside his single bunk, but now rolled all the way across the top, the most movement he'd noticed in the craft's level since they'd finished diving. The gauge was surprisingly effective, but hardly rocket science.

They were surfacing.

He rose from the bunk, slipping out the narrow door and into the hallway, walking along it briefly and knocking on the next door. A couple of moments passed before a bleary-eyed Zoe, her hair looking somewhat like a bird's nest, opened the door and blinked groggily up at him.

"What is it?" she mumbled.

"We're surfacing."

"Oh. Hang on." She closed the door in his face, and Wes leaned against the wall of the hallway. At least Zoe wasn't like other women who needed forever and a day to get ready, a fact he was constantly impressed with.

Moments later, Zoe opened the door once more. This time she had her hair pulled back into a neat ponytail and wore her cargo pants and black t-shirt.

"What are you waiting for?" she asked him, her face expressionless. "Let's go." She strode off down the corridor. Wes grinned and shook his head, following her.

"How are we going to get from the coast to the White House?" asked Zoe once he'd caught up.

Wes shrugged. "Poseidon reckons he's got a way to fly us there. I hope it's not flying horses again, though. They were seriously cool, but the last time I rode one of them my balls hurt for a week."

Zoe snickered. "My father told me about that; although his version was slightly different."

"You try riding a flying horse while chopping up a half-lion, half-eagle thing the size of an elephant without getting some vice-like activity going on in your nether regions."

"Thanks for the image."

"All jokes aside, I have no idea what Poseidon has in store for us. Washington's not exactly accessible in this giant condom, so we'll need some sort of transport to get us to the White House. Preferably I'd like something the Air Force isn't going to blow out of the sky the moment they notice it, but we'll just have to wait and see."

"That's reassuring," muttered Zoe over her shoulder.

"If you want reassurance, talk to a priest," snapped Wes. "Don't whine when I tell you the truth."

"What's up your ass?" replied Zoe, rounding on him and halting their walk at the base of a set of stairs.

Wes avoided her accusing stare. "Nothing. I just had a bad sexual experience in the bathroom this morning, that's all. My hand rejected me."

"You're not going to joke your way out of this one, Wes."

He looked Zoe directly in the eye, seeing the compassion there, as well as the capacity to accept whatever he had to tell her. Or so she thought….

"I –" began Wes, but got no further.

CLANG!!! An enormous crash sounded through the Ketos, resonating through the hull like an enormous bell.

Zoe flew across the corridor, and only Wes's lightning-quick reflexes stopped her from cracking her head on the handrail. He grabbed her arm and hauled her back to her feet in one smooth motion.

"What was that?" gasped Zoe, regaining her composure.

"No idea," replied Wes. "But I have a feeling it wasn't anything natural. I think we're under attack."

"How can you tell?"

"Because the collision came from on top of us, so unless the East coast of the USA is now frozen with ice it's likely something's assaulting us from above. Judging by the sound and feel of the impact, I don't think it was a missile, so that leaves me with the impression it's more likely a physical attack."

"What do you mean by 'physical attack'?" asked Zoe.

Wes turned to gaze at her, excitement burning deep within him at the prospect of finally seeing some action after such a long voyage trapped within this stifling vessel. "It means I think we're under attack by something big enough to knock a submarine from Olympia around like it's a Tonka truck."

"Uh oh," muttered Zoe.

Wes laughed. "Let's get to the bridge before we miss out on the fun," he said, striding up the stairs like a kid racing to the arcade, eager to play his favorite video game.

But this was not a game.

***

Zoe followed as quickly as she could, but Wes was practically running, the anticipation of discovering what was happening propelling him forward. By the time she caught up with him, he was striding through the doors to the bridge. Zoe followed, seeing Olympian crewmembers scurrying back and forth, several relaying orders through odd communication devices; some boxes mounted on walls, others hand-held with cords linking back to control consoles.

"What's happening?" asked Wes.

"We are under attack," answered Poseidon rigidly.

"No shit. Thanks for the update, Captain Obvious. What's attacking us?"

Poseidon glared at Wes, but refused to be baited. "I have no idea. I have never heard of or encountered anything like it before. Perhaps you have. We managed to get a look at it before our view was obscured completely."

The Olympian captain barked an order to one of the crew who immediately began keying controls on his panel. An image, frozen in place and slightly blurred, flashed onto the viewing screen. The natural distortion of the screen added to the haziness of the picture, but Zoe could definitely make out enormous fish scales, each around the diameter of a tree-trunk, and an extremely thick, serpentine neck. There was also a single eye, its predatory pupil staring at them from the center of the image.

"Could it be a dragon? Could it be Prometheus?" suggested Zoe.

Wes shook his head. "I don't think so. That dragon thing he turned up as at your place was big, but nowhere near the size of this thing." A huge shudder of the Ketos made Wes lurch, but he caught his balance almost immediately. "For this tub to get shaken like a piñata would take something around the size of Paris Hilton's ego. I doubt even Prometheus's ability to shape-shift could make him that large. If he could, why wouldn't he merely attack Olympia on his own?"

"Good point," said Zoe. "But it doesn't answer the question about what's attacking us right now."

"Well, if it's not from Tartarus or Olympia like Captain Stubing reckons –" Wes waved a hand toward Poseidon, "– and it's not from Earth, where else could it be from?"

Zoe wracked her brain. "Asgard? But how could it get here?"

"That's not the problem at the moment. Living through this shit is the real issue. Hey Possy! What weapons do you have on board?"

Poseidon glowered at him so hard Zoe had the distinct impression he would have preferred to use those weapons on Wes rather than whatever was outside.

"We have seventeen electrified tridents such as the one which struck down your flying craft." Zoe thought she saw a tiny smirk cross Poseidon's face, but it vanished before she could be sure. "And we also have nets harnessing the same power. Various weapons on the exterior of the hull are designed to target smaller objects. The issue with the tridents is the close proximity of the beast. It appears to be wrapped around the outside of the Ketos, attempting to constrict it. The ship was designed to stand up to almost any of the beasts we knew about, but this was not among them. Whatever we are facing is at least four times the length of the Ketos."

"That'd make it about a mile long!" gasped Wes. He let out a whistle. "That's one big motherfucker of a fish... or whatever it is."

"We are unable to utilize our external viewing screen while the beast covers the optical source with its body. As such, we cannot properly triangulate coordinates to fire our tridents lest we miss and hit the ship."

"What are your smaller weapons?" asked Wes swiftly, getting the gleam in his eyes Zoe was beginning to associate with the commando formulating a plan.

"We have several turrets capable of loosing Olympian arrows charged with the power Hephaestus refined during our first war against the Titans. We also have charged blades which we extend from the sides of the hull to carve our way though ice when necessary."

"Right, here's what I'll need you to do," said Wes. He swiftly outlined a plan which seemed both implausible and tremendously risky. Looking at Poseidon, she saw her own doubts mirrored there. "But wait a few minutes until I give the word," said Wes at the end. "And give me someone to guide me to one of your turrets."

"Anything else?" asked Poseidon, crossing his arms, unimpressed once more with the commando's lack of respect.

"Yeah, there is, but I won't say it out of politeness to you, your godliness. I'd hate to get you more pissed off than you already are." Wes chuckled and moved toward the door, calling to one of the Olympian crewmen, a young man barely more than a boy, to guide him. The crewmember glanced at Poseidon, but he looked ready to erupt at any moment. The leader of the Olympians nodded stiffly at the crewman before turning back and snarling orders at the other crewmembers.

Zoe raced after Wes once more, the crewman trotting along behind her. They caught up with the commando almost immediately and slowed slightly to his extended pace.

"What's your plan, Wes?" asked Zoe.

"I'm gonna kill whatever's out there," replied Wes calmly, as though it would be the simplest task in the world. "Hey you, smiley or kid or whatever you want to be called," Wes said to the crewmember, who swallowed heavily. "How do your turrets work? Is it a simple matter of pointing and squeezing a trigger, or do I have to do a rain dance while holding my left nut before it'll fire?"

The crewman's eyes narrowed quizzically. Most of what Wes had uttered must have gone straight over his head, but enough made sense for him to be confused as to whether the commando was joking or serious.

"The power for the arrow turrets is activated when the operator sits in the control seat," he said nervously. "There are two handsets which control the movement of the pod while a finger control mechanism fires the arrows depending upon required velocity and pitch. The arrows are self-loading, but occasionally jam, requiring blunt-force adjustment."

"Meaning I have to kick it, right?" said Wes, grinning.

The young Olympian returned the smile uncertainly. 'Err... yes."

"Good shit. What's your name, kid?"

The young Olympian blinked. "It's... um...."

"Come on, boy," said Wes, marching along just behind the Olympian. "Spit it out!"

"My name is Ganymedes," uttered the nervous young man finally.

"See, that wasn't so hard now, was it?"

"No sir," said Ganymedes.

"Alright then, Genitalis. Now, how far away is this damned turret? I'd prefer to get there before the ship gets squashed like a soup can."

"Not far, sir. But my name is Ganymedes."

"Of course it is," replied Wes, patting him on the shoulder.

"Don't worry, I won't forget it."

They made several twists and turns through more unfamiliar corridors until finally Ganymedes moved to a circular hatchway and gripped a lever to the side of it, pushing it down. The entire door rolled sideways into the wall of the ship, exposing a small compartment perched outside of the hull.

"I just need a moment to prepare the turret," said Ganymedes.

Another echoing reverberation shook the Ketos and all three had to grasp the rough walls to avoid sprawling across the floor.

"Well, you'd better hurry up, sweetheart," said Wes, "because I don't think whatever's outside is going to wait for much longer."

Ganymedes jumped into the cramped compartment and pressed several panels. The controls appeared to be made of stone, but the way the Olympian nimbly manipulated the buttons and dials made Zoe think they were created from something synthetic. The board began to glow slightly after several adjustments, and the entire front of the turret abruptly split, peeling apart down the middle like an eyelid opening. Beyond the dome-like, toughened crystal, Zoe could see the ocean. They must have surfaced enough for daylight to filter through the depths, because streaks of light shone within the emerald water.

And then she saw it.

The serpent – at least that's what it looked like – was enormous, bigger even than she had imagined from the blurry image on the bridge's control screen. They had guessed the beast would be around a mile long, but looking at it now, Zoe could tell this estimate was way off. It was much, much larger.

The body of the beast was several yards wider than a jumbo jet, but it was the length of the creature which defied belief. Zoe found herself unable to make any sort of accurate guess of its total size from what she could see, and the fact it was wrapped around the hull of the Ketos didn't help either, but she saw enough to suggest what it must look like.

The Ketos shuddered again, and this time a long shrieking sound, like steel screaming, echoed through the vessel.

"I think I know what this thing is," said Zoe.

Wes climbed into the seat of the turret and slid his hands into the control pads as Ganymedes instructed. "Let me guess, it's a snuffleupagus."

"A what?"

"You know, that thing off Sesame Street with the big nose that used to hang around with the talking yellow bird."

"That was like an elephant or mammoth," said Zoe. "And how is it you remember that, but can't remember what happened right before we met?"

"I guess it left an impression. But seriously, what is this thing?"

"I remember reading about something like this in Norse mythology, so it's possible it comes from our friends the Aesir."

Wes shifted in the turret, and the long barrel-like tube swung through the water, aiming directly at the beast. "Well, don't leave me hanging; what is it?"

"I think it's Jörmungandr," replied Zoe.

"Well thanks for clearing that up," muttered Wes. He turned and called out to Ganymedes, "Hey, Grannytitties, can you let the bridge know we're good to go? Thanks buddy." The young Olympian moved to one of the wall panels that functioned as an intercom and proceeded to speak into it.

Zoe squatted down beside Wes in the turret, finding a position where she could get a clear view of what was going on without being in his way. "I'm serious, Wes. That thing isn't like those pesky creatures you had to deal with from Tartarus. Jörmungandr is described as The World Serpent for a reason. It was thrown into Earth's oceans by Odin, King of the Norse gods and ruler of Asgard. It eventually grew so large it came to surround the world. They believed it would eventually destroy the entire planet. This is not something you can take lightly!"

Wes turned, calmly fixing her with an icy stare. For just a moment Zoe saw beyond all the wisecracks and name calling: here sat an intelligent and dangerous man used to violence, one who knew exactly what he was facing.

In an instant, however, the expression was gone, like a mask sliding into place once more. In its place was Wes, grinning at her from the seat of an ancient turret on the side of an incredible alien submarine, about to take on a sea monster like it was nothing out of the ordinary.

Which for him, was probably true.

Zoe had to remind herself that Wes, more than anyone else, had been instrumental in combating the worst threats the world had *ever* faced. Sure, there were other things which had come close over the Earth's history, but Prometheus's plans of conquest had proven a climactic event. Wes and Talbot were the only ones from this realm directly involved, and they had won, mainly due to Wes and his incredible skills. Prometheus, of course, remained the only living evidence of his limits.

Wes spun the turret to point directly along the hull toward the closest coil of the beast. The turret and external barrel appeared minuscule in comparison to the behemoth Wes hoped to tackle.

"Now, Ganymedes!" roared Wes, amazingly getting the boy's name correct.

Ganymedes hollered into the intercom, and the blades designed to slice through icebergs snapped into place. The coils of the serpent bore heavy scales for protection on its back, but its underside, pressed tightly against the hull of the Ketos, was softer, less protected: the belly of the beast.

The blades slashed outward. Staggered some twenty feet apart, they ran in lines down the entire length of the Ketos. Olympian energy sparked and popped within the ocean.

The constricting coils were slashed to ribbons, and the huge beast immediately struggled to free itself of the Ketos. The enormous head, similar to a horribly mutated salamander, arced toward the turret. Wes instantly jammed his right hand forward.

A single electrified projectile – more like a spear than an arrow, but still looking pitifully small – blasted out of the turret's barrel and raced through the flickering water toward the serpent's head.

The thickest and most armored part of the entire creature. Zoe wondered why Wes would have....

The beast twisted slightly and Zoe saw it, almost gasping as she did.

The eye.

Wes's Olympian arrow sliced through the water and plunged directly into the orb of the serpent, piercing deeply. A hideous shriek reverberated through the ocean, vibrating the crystal dome. To Zoe it sounded like a cross between distorted whale-song and the muted cry of a small child, as the serpent finally detached itself fully and began to glide away swiftly, its incredible length stretching after it, swirls of blood darkening the water in its wake.

"Wait for it," murmured Wes so softly it was almost a whisper. Zoe wondered what he was talking about. Something flashed out of the corner of her eye, and she turned back, staring hard through the lens of the toughened-crystal dome.

A huge, missile-like trident, fired from the side of the Ketos and pursued the immense creature through the water. "Damn. Too soon," muttered Wes. At the last moment Jörmungandr arced down, diving deep, and the trident passed harmlessly above it.

The serpent continued down, disappearing into the murky depths within seconds.

"Well, that was fun," said Wes chirpily. "Well done, Ganderpants."

The young Olympian merely stared at Wes, something akin to worship now glinting in his eyes. Zoe guessed Wes could now call Ganymedes whatever he wanted without upsetting him. Not that Zoe could blame the young Olympian. She had heard the tales of Wes's prowess in battle from her father, and had seen the ease with which he had incapacitated Poseidon's men. Still, to witness the calm with which he faced down a beast alleged to have the power to bring about the end of the world was something else entirely.

CHAPTER 4

The sun shone down warmly, and Zoe closed her eyes, tilting her head back and smiling slightly. It had only been a few days, but their time on the Ketos seemed so much longer. She was thankful to be standing in the sunlight within the hold where they'd first met Poseidon, the huge ramp open and leading down to the ocean.

"I wonder what joyous mode of transportation Poseidon has in mind for us," murmured Wes beside her, making her jump slightly. She hadn't even heard him approach. Zoe glared at him as he adjusted the strap of his M4A5 slightly to sit more comfortably on his shoulder.

"How should I know?" she snapped, harsher than she'd intended, but annoyed by his interruption.

Instead of returning her anger, Wes began to laugh, which only made Zoe grumpier. She would have stormed off in a huff, but she really had nowhere to go. Poseidon had ordered them to wait here in order for them to disembark on their way to Washington, so she couldn't exactly leave. Looking around, there really wasn't anywhere she could go out of view of Wes, so she satisfied herself with glowering at the Australian commando, wishing he would just burst into flames.

He didn't.

Poseidon entered the area, striding regally through the double doors and approaching where they stood. He held a large trident, bigger than the weapons his crew had carried days before when taking them prisoner.

"You really get off on the whole trident thing, don't you, Posies? Is that a tiny wiener issue? Maybe a little bit of shrinkage below decks?" commented Wes.

"This staff allows me to affect the atomic structure of solid materials in such a way as to –"

"Uh huh," cut in Wes. "Sounds fascinating. So where's our transport?"

Poseidon's brow thundered, but he refused to be baited, merely murmuring something to one of the crew. The man nodded and ran to the back of the area, pressing his palm against a hand-sized panel.

The entire back wall of the hold slid open silently. Over five times the height of Wes and at least two bus-lengths wide, the heavy-looking wall inexplicably slipped aside like a silk curtain. Beyond the partition was their transport, the thing which was going to take them to Washington DC to meet the President of the United States....

It was a gryphon.

The elephantine beast had the body of a lion, but wings and a head like that of an enormous eagle; a snake's reptilian tail flicked about its rear as it stretched its wings. In a split second Wes swung his assault rifle to his shoulder, aiming directly at the creature.

"Do not shoot!" commanded Poseidon and, strangely enough, Wes obeyed. But he didn't lower his weapon.

"What the hell is going on here, Poseidon?" demanded Wes, for once using the Olympian's true name. Perhaps that was the only time Wes adhered to formality; when action was close.

"This is the only gryphon we were able to successfully capture from the Titans. We have since gained its trust sufficiently to partially tame it, enough so that we will be able to ride it to your city; barring the possibility that your military attacks us."

"Of course they're going to attack us!" snapped Wes, his rifle still trained on the huge beast. "The last time anyone saw one of these fuckers it was cooking marines with its shitty breath!"

"Well, we shall have to hope they don't," replied Poseidon, "because while the gryphon is largely immune to your human weaponry, we are not."

"No shit. Surely there's another way."

"We have no other option, I'm afraid. I have several chariots drawn by horses designed and created by Hephaestus on board, but they will not be fast enough, and I'm afraid will gather even more attention than the gryphon."

Wes stared hard at the enormous creature, which in turn seemed to glare balefully back at him, its dark eyes unflinching.

"Fuck it, let's go," Wes said finally, looping the strap of the M4A5 over his shoulder once more.

"Whatever happened to the sword you had which my father used to tell me about?" asked Zoe. "What did he call it? The Sword of Chiron?"

The commando appeared discomfited. "I don't know. When I woke up in the base it was gone, but I was still wearing a scabbard, so I have to think I had it on me when whatever happened... happened. You know?"

"You think whatever attacked that base also took your sword?"

"Chiron's sword," corrected Wes. "But yeah, that's the only thing that makes sense."

"Bummer," said Zoe.

"You're telling me. It'd be nice to have it right about now in case we have any problems with fluffy here." He indicated the gryphon.

"We need to leave," said Poseidon.

"Just waiting on you, Pollyanna."

The Olympian paused mid-stride, shook his head slightly and resumed walking toward the giant gryphon without looking back. Wes chuckled softly and turned toward Zoe. "I think I'm growing on him, what do you reckon?"

Zoe smiled, but said nothing, preferring instead to follow Poseidon. The gryphon was terrifyingly large – at least the equivalent of an Indian bull elephant – and she wondered at something so big being able to fly. She recalled her father saying these beasts were also remarkably agile when airborne, but was dubious about such an assertion.

The gryphon flared its eagle-like wings out wide – as broad as a bus was long – and Zoe's doubts lessened somewhat. Its wickedly hooked beak looked sharp enough to effortlessly shred her apart, and she remembered her father also saying these creatures were able to spray a liquid which somehow combined with the air and ignited like napalm.

And they were going to ride it.

Yippee.

Poseidon strode directly up to the beast, which seemed to glare at him slightly, but otherwise appeared docile. Wes followed the Olympian's lead, and both turned to look back at Zoe. Swallowing her trepidation, she ran over to the gryphon, which seemed to grow larger the closer she got.

"So how do we mount this fucker?" asked Wes.

Poseidon barked a command, and the gryphon smoothly squatted down on its haunches, looking much like a domestic cat in its movements. The coarse fur of the beast's huge body – the result of Titan gene-splicing – was tawny brown, tapering away to darker brown feathers which covered its shoulders, neck and head as well as the gigantic wings. The gryphon's trashcan-sized hind paws boasted claws, each easily longer than a butcher's cleaver.

Wes fearlessly approached the beast, patting its flank. "Good kitty."

Grabbing a handful of the thick fur just below the feathers, he stepped off the beast's foreleg and smoothly hauled himself up. In a moment he was seated just behind the huge wings, looking like he had been born to ride the gryphon. "What are you guys waiting for?"

"Well, I was waiting for my men to bring the saddle, but I guess we can forego that now. As long as the lady doesn't mind, that is," said Poseidon, looking at Zoe.

She smiled at his condescending tone and shook her head. "I'm sure I'll survive."

"Just hang on to me, baby," shouted Wes jovially.

"You wish," Zoe called back. "Now can somebody at least get me a box so I don't look like a complete idiot trying to climb onto this thing?"

***

Wes had soared through the skies above Mount Olympus upon a pegasus, but the sensation was somewhat different sitting atop the enormous gryphon. The creature soared through the clouds; the ride nowhere near as jerky as Wes would have anticipated, considering the size of the beast. As long as it had no problem with them riding astride its back, everything seemed like it would be okay.

And then four fighter jets shot into view.

Shit.

"Poseidon, you'd better let me take the reins for this one," Wes said, pointing toward the fighter planes – F-22 Raptors from the look of them.

Wes knew the F-22 was one of the best fighter jets ever designed by the Air Force, and certainly one of the most dangerous. It had been created to take over from the old F-15 fighters used since the late 1960s, and the most advanced technology and weaponry of modern times had been incorporated in its design.

This wouldn't be fun.

Wes kind of leap-frogged over Poseidon and gathered the thick, heavy reins. Poseidon protested loudly, but Wes ignored him. They had bigger issues at hand than the sensitivities of a Greek god.

Banking the gryphon to the right, Wes headed directly toward the oncoming jets. He had seen firsthand how tough gryphons were, but knew that while a single missile hit from the F-22s wouldn't injure the winged beast, it would probably leave the beast's three passengers crispier than French fries. Even if this weren't the case, he could hardly battle it out against the United States Air Force when he was coming here to ask the President for his help. He only had one hope – and even this chance was slimmer than a Hollywood starlet.

Wes eyed the four jets as they shot toward the gryphon. They were still several miles away, but it was lucky they hadn't fired on them already. The F-22s' AMRAAM missiles were designed to fire from beyond visual range, meaning they could shoot a target out of the sky or on land before it even knew they were there. The fact they hadn't fired yet meant they were instructed to investigate only, with no 'kill' orders issued… so far.

Damn it, he really didn't want to do this, but saw no other way out. He had to do it *now*.

Wes stood up on the back of the gryphon and began to wave his arms in the air, madly trying to get the attention of the F-22s' pilots. Each fractional second passing brought more hope that they might see him, but even this didn't guarantee they wouldn't fire. It all came down to what orders were relayed when they passed on the information of a crazy man jumping around atop the back of a giant flying monster. These pilots would in all likelihood have no knowledge of the existence of gryphons in the universe – the last instance being classified beyond top secret – thus their tension would be ratcheted even higher than if it were an invading force from another country or a terrorist attack. That was stuff they'd been trained for. This was not.

The jets flew closer.

Wes began to wave more frantically, shouting despite knowing there was zero chance they would hear him. Zoe and Poseidon were yelling something at him, but he ignored them. He saw the nodding helmets of the pilots, and willed them not to blow him out of the sky. He could imagine their frenetic calls back to base requesting orders.

The jets continued to race through the air toward them.

It was like an insane game of chicken. The difference being Wes was riding a mythological splicing of lion, snake and eagle, and the pilots commanded millions of dollars of high-tech war equipment.

Okay, maybe not so much like chicken.

The pivotal moment came. The jets were too close for missiles and would have now switched to guns – an M61A2 Vulcan 20mm cannon; more commonly known as a Gatling gun. The six barrels rotated to avoid overheating as they fired more bullets than a hiccupping redneck holding an Uzi.

The jets thundered closer.

Wes waved more frenetically.

They shot past, two peeling away on each side of the gryphon, and Wes whooped with excitement, turning to comment to Zoe and Poseidon –

The backwash from the jets hit him like a low hanging bridge and Wes was launched from the gryphon, Zoe's scream following him as he plunged helplessly through the sky....

***

Wes plummeted through the air, tumbling like an out of control acrobat as he fought down panic and tried to clear his mind. He'd been in this position before, but at that time he'd had Talbot there to fly in and rescue him.

Talbot wasn't here this time.

Flattening himself so that his body was parallel to the ground, Wes finally stabilized his fall. The wind stung his face, and he felt tears streaming from his eyes, but struggled to look around just in case....

Just in case *what*?

He had no idea, but it couldn't end like this. There *had* to be something he could do. The hero in the movies always thought of something, so why couldn't he? Wes considered flapping his arms, but... er... no.

He was going to die.

The thought was startling. While he'd never deluded himself about his mortality, Wes had always believed he was somehow luckier than other men. He'd thought he could walk through any fire life might throw at him and stroll out the other end with scorched pubes and a wicked grin. Wes knew it was arrogant, but he'd always been right before.

Gravity was about to prove him very, very wrong.

The earth shot toward him, and Wes closed his eyes, hoping he'd at least make a decent impression on the ground when he impacted. God knew he was hurtling faster than a falling meteor. Where the hell was Bruce Willis when he needed him? He opened his eyes once more, determined not to be afraid.

He was plunging so fast now everything became a blur. There were buildings in the distance, but the only clear thing Wes could see was the wide expanse of grass beneath him. Maybe it was a cemetery.

That would be somehow ironic, and a pretty cool way for him to end things; by burying himself.

Wes heard a sound and it took a fraction of a second to realize it was his own voice yelling. There was very little fear inside him, more an exhilaration bordering on rapture. This was the culmination of all his years, of everything he'd ever done. It all came down to this.

Fertilizer.

Unable to stop himself, Wes squeezed his eyes shut just before the point of impact. He hit the ground like a bullet....

And the earth sagged down, compressing like an enormous mattress, or a huge, building-deep airbag, cushioning his fall, stopping Wes from being crushed and broken like a psychotic kid's action figure. He sank at least thirty feet before the area around him compressed once more, and he was gently raised up to the surface. Rolling to his back, Wes first checked his testicles, and then his spine for any sort of injury, but found nothing.

Okay. That was unexpected.

The sound of wings garnered Wes's attention, and he spotted Poseidon and Zoe landing the gryphon approximately thirty feet away. The Olympian held his trident aloft, aiming it toward Wes. As soon as the beast touched down, Zoe leaped from its back and ran over to Wes, hauling him to his feet and embracing him, her sobs muffled as she buried her face in his shoulder.

Wes hugged her back, shock over what had just happened making his brain foggy. What the hell *had* happened? He saw Poseidon dismount and walk leisurely over to where he stood, Zoe still weeping quietly in his arms. The shock slowly began to dissipate, and Wes's heart rate returned to normal. He stared hard at the Olympian.

"What the fuck was that?" he asked.

Poseidon grinned, the action stiff and out of place upon his normally stoic face. "This," he indicated his trident, "is more than a mere weapon. As I attempted to explain to you before we departed, it is designed to transmit sound vibrations on a certain level and pitch. With it, I am able to manipulate various forms of matter."

"Like the ground. You turned the ground into a giant vat of jelly... but with no hot chicks wearing bikinis wrestling in it. Do you reckon you can manipulate up a couple of those next time? If it's too hard, they don't really need the bikinis."

Poseidon stared hard at Wes, his expression a mixture of confusion and annoyance as he attempted to decipher what the Australian meant. Eventually, he seemed to just give up, shaking his head slightly before continuing.

"I merely vibrated the atomic structure of the earth below you and altered it slightly, giving it much more elasticity than it would normally have. I have done similar things before, but usually the result ends with the land cracking and breaking, rather than what happened here. I'm rather happy and surprised it worked, to be honest."

"Not as happy and surprised as me, mate," replied Wes, prying himself out from Zoe's grip and grasping Poseidon's hand, shaking it firmly. "You're a fucking legend."

"So I have been told," replied Poseidon. "But it's always nice to hear."

Wes looked around, realizing for the first time where they were. People were running across the perfectly manicured lawn toward them from all directions, several of them shouting. He looked beyond them toward the building, the iconic white structure that the free world looked to for guidance –

The White House.

The men wearing suits – Secret Service agents – had their guns drawn as they ran toward them, shouting demands. Wes chuckled and strode up the grass toward them. 'G'day fellas," he said, waving.

"Get down on the ground now!" yelled one of the agents.

"Not right now, buddy," replied Wes. "I'm not sure if this is still valid, but I need to implement Code Epsilon-Four-Eight-Delta."

The Secret Service agent stopped as though he'd been hit in the face with a hammer. "You're –?"

"Yes, I am," replied Wes, cutting him off. "And we need to see the big man straight away."

"Yes, sir," replied the agent. "I'm Special Agent Delafore." He glanced beyond the group, paling slightly as he saw the gryphon.

"That's really special, Special Agent Delaforeskin. I'd leave fluffy alone for now, if I were you," said Wes, nodding toward the gryphon. "We'll figure out what to do with him a bit later."

The Secret Service agents glanced nervously at the gryphon, which screeched loudly and beat its wings several times before folding them alongside its body. Several agents spoke into their wrist-mounted microphones, but Wes just chuckled.

"Lead the way, Agent Delaware," he said.

"It's Delafore, sir," corrected the agent.

"That's what I said," replied Wes smoothly. The agent appeared confused, but seemingly let it go and began to lead them up the lawn toward the White House.

"So what's this latest president like; is he as much of an arsehole as the one I used to know?" asked Wes. "I mean, twenty years ago when things used to get kinda rough, the President was a bit of a soft-cock."

Wes grinned, imagining Special Agent Delafore's eyes bugging right out of his head behind his reflective sunglasses. Wes had always disliked the Secret Service for some reason. Their pretentious demeanor rubbed him the wrong way. He couldn't help himself; the need to somehow put these guys in their place always overpowered the impulse to shut his mouth.

"The President is well," replied Agent Delafore stiffly. "And I'm sure I don't understand what you mean about a different president."

"The President in power when I was here before used to fancy a bit of donkey porn now and then, did you know that?"

Special Agent Delafore's expression remained hidden behind his glasses. "I was not aware of that, sir."

"Yeah, nothing he liked better than relaxing in the tub with a bit of donkey porn playing on the TV. I guess it was the only way he could wind down… or maybe it was the only way he could gear up for his 'special time' with the first lady. What do you reckon?"

"I think that's enough talk like that, sir. I've heard of your reputation, but disrespecting the man who leads our country is not something I am prone to take lightly."

"Well said," grunted Wes. "I like a man with a bit of backbone, Agent Delores."

"Delafore, sir."

"Whatever," replied Wes. "So, are you guys up to speed with the current situation?"

"What situation?" asked Special Agent Delafore.

"I'll take that as a resounding *no*. Hopefully el Presidente is up to date with current events, or this is going to be a very long meeting."

The rest of the journey up the hill was shrouded in silence, but just as they reached the rear door of the White House, Poseidon suddenly asked, "Where is your companion?"

Wes glanced around, noticing for the first time that Zoe was missing. He'd been so distracted, first by the Secret Service, and then by what he'd have to say to the President, he hadn't noticed her disappear.

"Where the hell is she?" he mumbled. He'd remembered her getting off the gryphon and hugging him, but at the time Wes had still been rattled by the near-miss of having almost been spattered like a watermelon dropped from the roof of the Ed Sullivan Theatre by David Letterman.

"Sir, the President is waiting," said Special Agent Delafore.

"Huh? Oh, okay," murmured Wes absently, still looking around for some sign of where Zoe had disappeared to. He followed the agent and Poseidon through the door.

"The President is waiting for you in the Oval Office. The Secretary of Defense and head of the CIA will also be there."

"I hate those guys," muttered Wes.

"Is there anyone here you *do* like?" asked Poseidon.

"I'm beginning to like Delaforeplay, here. But that might just be his cologne."

They moved through the halls of the White House and eventually came to what Wes recognized as the main corridor leading to the West Wing. More Secret Service agents were placed at specific locations, but Special Agent Delafore strode past them all with Wes and Poseidon in tow. Arriving at the door to the Oval Office, Delafore gave a brisk double knock before opening the door and holding it for Wes and Poseidon to enter. He then stepped back out of the room and closed the door behind him.

Wes sauntered toward the center of the room, but stopped so

abruptly Poseidon almost slammed into him from behind. This couldn't be right. There was no way the man standing behind the desk was the President of the United States of America. Not after twenty years had passed.

It was the same president as during Wes's last visit!

In a nanosecond, the pieces flew together in Wes's mind, and he silently cursed. The jets that had flown to intercept them were not advanced enough, the base in Australia had not altered dramatically since the last time he'd seen it. Talbot's apartment was almost exactly the same.

Nothing had changed.

Which made only one thing certain; there was no way twenty years had passed since the last incident with the Titans. Wes hadn't been suffering amnesia, losing over two decades worth of memory, and he hadn't traveled forward in time. It had all been a lie. Everything had been one huge lie, which led back to the person who had conveniently disappeared.

Zoe.

"Are you alright?" asked the President, peering at Wes oddly. The Secretary of Defense stood in front of the huge timber desk. Wes stared beyond them to the beautiful bay window, the view from which overlooked the South Lawn of the White House.

"Fuck me," he muttered.

"Excuse me?" The President's brow narrowed.

His eyes snapped into focus. "Sorry, Mister President, I just realized something which will probably come back to bite me on the arse. Hopefully it's nothing too serious."

The President gazed at him for a moment longer before nodding. "I'm sure if it is something serious you won't bother bringing it to my attention as usual."

"Hey, at least I'm predictable," said Wes, trying to cover his concern. "Oh, and let me introduce you to Poseidon."

Both men stared at the imposing figure of Poseidon, complete with his trident. The Secretary of Defense looked as though he'd choked on a fly. The President admirably kept his composure.

"As in Poseidon from Olympia?" he asked.

"Is there another one?"

"Good point," agreed the President. "Welcome to America, sir," he said, moving around the desk and extending his hand. Poseidon stared at it as though it were anathema, until the President awkwardly let it drop back to his side.

"Yeah, that's awesome," said Wes. "Now, Mister President, sir, we have a whole roll of shit to drop in your lap. I hope you're ready for it."

"What's going on? From the presence of Mister Poseidon here I'm guessing there has been a resurgence of activity with the Olympians – or more precisely the Titans."

"Worse than you know... and worse than I know too, come to mention it. Can you guys tell me what's going on with Talbot Harrison?"

"Why do you ask?" asked the President.

Wes took a deep breath and looked the leader of the free world directly in the eye. Without embellishment, he relayed the entire episode up until the point where they had noticed Zoe was missing. He told the President about waking up in Australia without a memory, meeting the supposed daughter of Talbot and being told twenty years had passed, the appearance of Prometheus and attack on the Ketos – all of it. Somewhere during the retelling Wes came to realize what an idiot he'd been, and wondered how much it had to do with Zoe's appearance.

"So who is this Zoe woman?" asked the President when he'd finished.

"I'm not sure," replied Wes. "I have to assume she's working for the Titans. Between her and the arrival of Prometheus, they're the main reasons I started this crappy journey. She probably expected us to fly straight back in time to save Talbot – which is exactly what would have happened if Poseidon here hadn't shot us down. Well done by the way, Poseidon."

"Now you decide to use my proper name?"

"I have no idea what you're talking about," said Wes with a grin.

The Olympian merely stared at him coldly before turning back to face the President. "My people have no record of this woman, and I personally have no idea who she is. Throughout our many dealings with the Titans, I cannot recall anyone similar. If not for the fact that this human," he indicated Wes, "had seen Prometheus and her in the same room, I would be inclined to believe she was Prometheus in another guise."

"Could the Titans have developed another shape-shifter, or whatever Prometheus is?" asked the President, seemingly understanding Poseidon's Olympian speech without issue. Perhaps the brother of Zeus also possessed his talent of mental manipulation. Wes considered it momentarily and then disregarded it; other issues were far more important at the moment.

"It is doubtful," replied Poseidon. He made no direct inflection, but Wes had the feeling the Olympian was talking patronizingly to the President. "From what we managed to learn of Prometheus, he is something of an anomaly. Nothing even remotely similar has ever come out of Tartarus."

"So what *do* you know?" asked the President, his tone hard. Wes guessed he'd also picked up on the Olympian's attitude.

"Very little," interjected Wes, trying to divert the conversation from dissolving into a pissing contest. "That's why we're here. Where's Talbot?"

The Secretary of Defense spoke up. "Doctor Harrison has been missing for several months after assisting us in some of our trials. His brother is with him."

"Can't you dumb motherfuckers avoid losing these guys just *once?* And how the hell did you manage to convince Talbot to help you after what happened the last time?"

The Secretary of Defense glanced at the President. "I'm afraid that's on a need-to-know basis."

"Well, I need to know," said Wes. "And if you've got a problem with that I'll just bust your dumb redneck skull open like a walnut. So where the *fuck* is Talbot?"

"You can't talk to me like that!" fumed the secretary.

"Just answer him, Bill," said the President, rubbing his temple. "It saves time."

"I don't know why you put up with his attitude –"

"That's because *you* don't *need to know*," snapped the President, slamming his open palm onto the desk. Wes always liked him when he got like this.

The Secretary of Defense swallowed heavily. "Talbot Harrison and his brother Thomas were assisting the Government to research an unknown dimension which opened up through an anomaly known as a rift. Due to their previous security clearance and experience it was decided they were the prime candidates to assist us in our studies. We lost all contact with their team as soon as they entered the rift, and soon after that time the rift itself closed, cutting us off completely."

Wes glanced at Poseidon. "Just so you know, not all humans are as dumb as this motherfucker." He turned back to the secretary. "What the hell does any of that mean? Did you just literally regurgitate one of your media conference statements to me? That was bullshit. Where did the rift lead?"

The secretary looked to the President once more, who nodded slightly. "We were researching the field of time travel, and somehow linked with a rift many centuries in the past. This provided a direct link into Earth's past without the need to utilize the technology, such as your craft, while also linking with a separate dimension."

"You're telling me you found a way to journey into another world as well as travel back in time? So what Prometheus was saying was true?"

"It would appear so," said the President, his expression thoughtful. "We should never have delved into researching time travel, but the opportunity was just too great to jump ahead of ourselves in regards to knowledge. I mean, imagine if we could go back and actually witness all the great works throughout history."

"I've told you it doesn't work that way," said Wes.

"I know, I know. We just got greedy." He shot an accusing glance at the Secretary of Defense.

"All of this is extremely fascinating," cut in Poseidon, "but it ultimately avails us no information relevant to our immediate concern. We need to concentrate on facts and how to proceed in order to defeat Prometheus."

Wes nodded. "Poseidon's got a point. So now we know

Prometheus was telling us the truth, at least partially, and Talbot is indeed in the past. Zoe's a rogue element we know nothing about, which we need to put aside at the moment and try not to worry about. The question is what do we do now?"

"We need to stop Prometheus at all costs," said Poseidon. "He threatens my entire world as well as your own."

"That's a pretty obvious starting point," agreed Wes. "The issue comes back to what he's up to. At this time we really don't have enough information to work off, except for the fact he somehow wants us to go back in time to save Talbot and Thomas, which is probably the last thing we should do."

"And yet that is what you're intending on doing, isn't it?" said the President.

"Pretty much," replied Wes brightly. "I reckon –"

Without warning, the bay window shattered outward, something tearing half of the wall away in an instant. Instinctively, Wes leaped over the desk and drew his M4A5.

An enormous gray wolf hunched beyond the ruined window, standing almost the same height as a gryphon. The beast's hackles were raised and its lips curled back as it snarled at the four men within the partially demolished Oval Office. Finally its gaze fixed on Wes, the expression in its eyes malevolent.

"I know you," it growled, surprising Wes.

"Well, you do look like one of my ex-girlfriends."

The doors into the Oval Office banged open. Wes surmised it was merely the Secret Service agents finally responding. He didn't turn around to check, his eyes never wavering from the snarling threat in front of him.

Several guns cocked. "Hold your fire!" Wes ordered. To the wolf he called, "Who are you, curly?"

The wolf sneered at him, the expression terrifyingly human. "I have merely come to see who opposes me. I am not impressed. My people will not suffer at your hands again as they did before, regardless of who stands beside you. This journey has cost me a great deal and sapped much of my energy, but now I know you are allied with the Aesir and we will prepare for your trickery once more. Know this: come against me again and your death will echo through the annals of eternity."

"I think I just peed a bit," jibed Wes, but his expression was deadly and his gun never wavered.

The tawny eyes fixed upon him with such focused malice that Wes almost dropped his gaze, but with an effort he stood firm. "You are stronger than I remember," snarled the wolf. "Come visit me if you dare; I promise you won't get away as easily as the last time."

"Prometheus? Is that you behind all that fur?" asked Wes.

The beast let forth a tremendous howl, vibrating the walls of the Oval Office. Bits of plaster crumbled from the already damaged ceiling. "Do not speak that name to me! You know what he has done, just as you know who I am. Do not play the fool with me."

"My memory's kinda foggy at the moment," said Wes. "What was your name again?"

"I am Fenrir," roared the giant wolf. "Our destinies are so intertwined we will forever know one another, so don't feign ignorance. My time here is finite, but I needed to be sure it was you, my old nemesis, who was planning this foolish quest. I will see you soon, and then I will destroy you."

Piercing through the tension, a high-pitched shriek sounded, and Wes's gaze snapped up just in time to see the enormous gryphon hurtling out of the sky, crashing heavily into the form of Fenrir. The giant wolf seemed momentarily shocked, and the gryphon took full advantage, tearing into it wildly with both its hooked beak and its razor-sharp claws. The element of surprise lasted only a second, however, before Fenrir recovered.

Rolling the tremendous weight of the gryphon away with devastating ease, Fenrir snatched the great beast by the neck. The giant wolf jerked the gryphon violently, shaking the huge body like a rag doll in the jaws of a house pet. The strength of Fenrir's jaws was such that combined with the savagery of the attack it tore through the hapless gryphon's throat – flesh which Wes knew was capable of withstanding a direct missile hit. Snarling contentedly, Fenrir hurled the bleeding carcass aside like a piece of trash.

Not a cut, not a mark, scarred the wolf. It brought its fearsome stare around and pierced Wes one last time, a dark promise of some pre-ordained battle glinting in its shadowy orbs. Its gaze flicked skyward momentarily, eyes narrowing, before turning and bolting across the grass, slowly blurring until it finally disappeared altogether.

Wes turned, seeing the group of Secret Service agents surrounding the President with their weapons drawn. "Well done, boys. You can go back to your coffee and donuts now," he said, shouldering his M4A5.

The Secret Service agents slowly moved away from the President.

"What was that beast?" asked Poseidon.

"I'm not certain, but I'm sure it'll become vividly apparent in time."

"What do you mean?" queried the President, trying hard to regain his composure.

"It's all about time. But we need to get you to a more secure location first," replied Wes, gazing out through the demolished wall beyond the dead and savaged gryphon at the spot where Fenrir had disappeared.

***

The bunker beneath the White House's East Wing – known as the Presidential Emergency Operations Center – was possibly the safest area of the White House. The Operations Center had been constructed during Franklin D. Roosevelt's term at some stage in the Second World War, the height of wartime paranoia. They had originally planned on moving the meeting to the White House Situation Room in the basement of the West Wing, but Wes decided the Operations Center – being on the opposite side of the building to where the attack had just occurred as well as being much more secure than the Situation Room – was the smarter choice under the circumstances.

"So will somebody tell me exactly what just happened? Why did it seem that giant wolf was talking to you?" asked the President.

Wes had to think for a moment, but what the President had said swiftly made sense. "When Talbot and I were in Olympia, Poseidon's brother, Zeus, entered my head. He had some sort of telepathic talent, allowing him to unlock my ability to understand the Olympians. I guess it helped with the wolf too." He looked at Poseidon.

"I didn't understand anything the beast said to you, just as much of what you said sounded like nonsense. But then again, Zeus altered my language ability in order for me to come to this place and deal with your kind."

"So *I* wasn't making any sense either?" asked Wes.

Poseidon shook his head. The President and the Secretary of Defense nodded in agreement. "It sounded like a series of growls and snarls," said the President.

"Hmm. Cool. I guess Zeus unlocked more than he told me," said Wes. "Good old Zeus, I always liked him."

"Can we get back to the issue at hand?" asked the President. "What just happened?"

"That big-arse wolf calls himself Fenrir, and he reckons he knows me. Now, my memory's pretty fucked up at the moment, but I'm almost one hundred percent sure I'd remember meeting a talking wolf the size of Kim Kardashian's arse. Anyway, he said our destinies were intertwined, or something like that, and he just wanted to come here and be certain it was me."

"Do you know what he meant by that?" asked Poseidon.

"I reckon something will happen in our future which will determine that I somehow end up meeting that fucker and clashing heads with him. Whatever I've done in his past seems to have really pissed him off – especially for him to come here just to threaten me. I don't understand it fully… at least not yet."

"But if Fenrir is from the past," said the President, "how could he come here, to the future? I mean, all research into time travel has indicated that traveling forward through time is impossible."

"Unless the rift you guys linked in with from the past has somehow allowed him to travel forward through a tunnel-like system.

In that way time might actually count as another realm, not merely an instance." Wes sighed, throwing an accusing look toward the Secretary of Defense. "This is what happens when you fuck around with shit you don't understand."

"We weren't to know…." The secretary's words trailed away.

"I'm sure that's what Oppenheimer said," muttered Wes. "What has just become incredibly apparent is the need to find a way back in time. I need to know what all this shit means."

"I may know of a way," said Poseidon.

"How so?" asked Wes.

"That triangle you described when we were traveling through your ocean, what was it called?"

"The Bermuda Triangle."

"Yes. I believe it may be a focal point for inharmonious resonance waves, working in such a way as to act like a kind of wormhole between the dimensions – in this case through time itself."

Wes instantly grasped what the Olympian was saying. "So you reckon we could travel through this wormhole onboard the Ketos?"

"Oh no! The Ketos would be crushed instantly under the strain. We need a craft which can travel faster than the speed of sound and can also withstand the same amount of pressure you would find at the bottom of your deepest ocean."

"I can only think of one vehicle which could do all that," said Wes. "Unfortunately it got shot out of the sky by a big fucking trident."

"Well, we need another one," said Poseidon, not looking the least bit embarrassed by Wes's implied condemnation.

"Any ideas?" Wes asked the President, who thought about it momentarily, shaking his head before turning to the Secretary of Defense.

The secretary appeared uneasy or unwilling to answer, but under the scrutiny of all three men he caved in. "There is a prototype jet fighter we were working on based on the technology of the futuristic plane you had. It can do everything you specified, as well as being dual-seated – so both of you will be able to travel."

"Where is it, sweetheart? Don't be shy, now," demanded Wes.

"It's at an undercover facility right here in Washington."

'Where exactly?" said the President.

"At Dulles International Airport, inside an underground research facility."

The President bent over his desk intercom and hit the button, requesting immediate transport for three to Dulles International Airport along with a full escort of United States Marines. He then strode over to Wes and Poseidon and shook their hands.

"Gentlemen, the very fate of the world – both our worlds, in fact – now seems to rest in your hands once again."

"To be totally honest," corrected Wes, "Poseidon wasn't involved in the last time. He had laundry or some other shit he had to take care of."

"However, I *was* involved the first time," retorted Poseidon. "I believe that was around three thousand years ago in your time, yes? Where were you then?"

"Okay, point taken," said Wes. "Let's go. Come, Mister Secretary, you don't want to be left behind."

"B-but –" began the Secretary of Defense, until a glance from the President silenced his protest. Wes grinned. The President was his sort of politician.

The guy really knew how to torment arseholes.

**

The flight in Marine One – the VH-60N military helicopter used by the President to travel short distances – was largely uneventful.

Wes sprawled haphazardly on the plush leather seat, snoring softly. Poseidon, in his dark, loose-fitting clothing of casual alien styling, sat bolt upright, his eyes calm, but alert. The Secretary of Defense, a miserable politician whose actions had, in part at least, contributed to the situation they were now trying to defuse, fidgeted nervously.

A motley crew to say the least.

Marine One flew low into Dulles International Airport, landing outside an immense hangar away from the main terminals. A CH-53E Super Stallion helicopter landed beside them, and a contingent of marines swiftly disembarked, surrounding Marine One, their M-16A4 and M4 Carbine rifles aimed outward, alert and tense.

Wes awoke with a snort and climbed to his feet. "Are we there?" he asked the Secretary of Defense.

The politician nodded miserably, climbing to his feet and moving to the door of Marine One, swiftly opened by the co-pilot as the attached staircase was folded down. The three men descended the stairs and moved toward the vast hangar.

"Is this it?" asked Wes, indicating the hangar.

"Of course not!" snapped the secretary. "I told you it was underground. What point would there be having it in one of these hangars where anybody could get a look at it."

"No need to get testy, Shirley," said Wes with a dark chuckle.

The Secretary of Defense mumbled something incoherent, but Wes just grinned and ignored him. They strode swiftly to a door marked as a utilities closet, their guards moving with them. The secretary produced a key from his pants pocket, slipping it in the lock and turning it.

"Wow," said Wes. "That's some high security you've got here."

"What's that supposed to mean?"

"It means you're all worried about it being too obvious if it were at ground level, and yet we're walking into a utilities room after having gotten off the President's helicopter surrounded by dudes with guns. Very subtle."

The Secretary of Defense looked as though he were about to argue the point, but decided against it and silently moved inside. Wes and Poseidon followed him, the marine contingent remaining in position outside the door. Once inside, Poseidon released the door, allowing it to swing closed behind them, and Wes saw they were actually in a long corridor. They followed the Secretary of Defense as he led the way down the hallway, at the end of which was a palm-print scanner next to a heavy steel door. The secretary pressed his palm against the scanner which emitted a low beep and the reinforced door slid silently sideways, unveiling an elevator beyond. All three entered the elevator, its door closing soundlessly before it smoothly began its descent.

After an eternity, the elevator came to a halt and the doors opened. Wes heard Poseidon's sharp intake of breath and found himself silently agreeing; what awaited them was nothing short of astounding.

Stretching out beyond the limit of his vision, the stunning underground base looked like something straight out of a Hollywood movie. To one side was some sort of testing area for what looked like a type of rail gun – a weapon which fired projectiles using magnetic fields and electricity. The resulting velocity exceeded more than seven times the speed of sound!

Wes didn't even look at it twice.

To the right was something that appeared similar to the technology used in both the thermo-shot and thermo-tube systems he and Talbot had used during their previous escapades. These transport systems used thermal energy beneath the Earth's crust along with reverse magnetic polarity in order to move vehicles along at astronomical speeds beneath the surface of the planet.

Wes ignored this as well.

He moved beyond these marvels, along with many others, his eyes fixed on only one thing. It was cooler than cool, so badass it would make Ice-T seem like a tree-hugging hippie.

"Gentlemen," said the Secretary of Defense with a note of arrogance in his voice which grated against Wes's nerves. "This is the MX-19 stealth fighter."

But it was not just any stealth fighter jet – Wes recognized that straight away. This was a thing of beauty.

He could see the distinct connection between this craft and his previous jet. There was no mistaking where the engineers had drawn their inspiration from in regards to design, but in other areas it looked completely different. This fighter was black, with a dark-tinted canopy and red air intakes. The wings were sleek, swept back, denoting how much it was designed for speed. But added to this was something Wes had to look at twice to make sure he'd seen it right.

There were no joins.

The entire fuselage of the MX-19 appeared to be without a single weld or rivet, as though it had been completely molded in a single piece. He stepped closer to make sure it wasn't constructed out of fiberglass or carbon-fiber.

Through some sort of process they had managed to closely imitate Wes's own jet – a design beyond anything this world was likely to come up with for a long time. This was probably the most aerodynamic jet on the face of the planet.

It couldn't possibly go as fast as Wes's jet had gone, he was sure of that. This time was nowhere near technologically advanced enough to recreate the system his plane had used to skim between space and time, but it was definitely the sleekest plane he had ever seen from this period. There was only one problem.

"Are you sure it'll be strong enough?" he asked the Secretary of Defense.

The secretary glanced over to a man standing nearby, some sort of technician or scientist from the look of him.

"The outer shell is constructed of titanium bi-weave alloy and can deflect most direct impacts from missile attack; both air to air as well as ground to air," the man informed Wes. "It is also able to journey in the upper-mesosphere, enabling it to travel much faster through the reduced atmosphere."

"So you're saying it's tough enough, is that right?"

The man looked perplexed. "Without knowing what you –"

Wes cut him off. "That's okay, buddy. You've been great. Now go and get yourself a massage with a happy ending to celebrate." The man stood still, looking confused. He glanced at the Secretary of Defense, and then back at Wes.

"Go away," snapped Wes. "Shoo!" He stood staring at the wondrous jet for a moment, thinking about –

"Shit!" Wes yelled, calling after the retreating technician. "Hey buddy, come back. How the hell do I fly this thing?"

***

Wes sat strapped into the pilot's seat of the MX-19, Poseidon seated securely behind him. According to the technician, the controls were loosely based upon those of his own jet, but without the technology of a PCM it remained a hybrid of a conventional fighter plane. The major difference was the addition of a second control stick, both seeming to float freely, rather than simply pushing forward and back or side to side. These sticks moved through a full seven hundred and twenty degrees – in other words, they were capable of full spherical direction.

The main reason for this was the wing-mounted funnels. The primary jet engines funneled power through exhaust points along the wings depending on the directions given using the control sticks. This was a vastly superior way of controlling the aircraft, enabling maneuverability previously unheard of – except from Wes's futuristic craft.

Each stick controlled the left or right jets of the MX-19, so that Wes could spin it on its axis either vertically or horizontally, bank at previously unheard of speeds and take off and land vertically like a Harrier jump-jet.

To put it mildly, this plane was the coolest thing to yet come out of the twenty-first century.

Wes lifted the controls slightly and felt the MX-19 rise from the ground. Looking directly up through the opening ceiling as the canopy peeled back for take-off, he could see a long vertical tunnel and a square of blue sky beyond.

"Hold on to your gills, Poseidon. This is gonna be one helluva ride," Wes called through the helmet microphone.

Before the Olympian could respond, Wes jammed the control sticks both straight up. The MX-19 responded instantly, shooting vertically so fast Wes thought his eyeballs might end up inside his scrotum. The jet was fully stealth-designed, so he wasn't worried about it being picked up on radar as he hovered momentarily, but he saw several members of the airport ground crew staring incredulously at the MX-19 from the tarmac. Wes just chuckled… and then threw the controls forward.

Over the radio, Wes heard Poseidon gasp at the rapid acceleration of the jet as it shot away from the airport. Wes whooped as the MX-19 cleared Mach Ten in a matter of seconds, and only their futuristic-looking suits – courtesy of technology from research on the encapsulating ability of the PCMs in Wes's former jet – stopped Wes and Poseidon from being crushed as the jet blasted beyond Mach Eleven.

Even though Wes had traveled faster – much, much faster – in his own plane, the MX-19 made the experience seem much more real. Wes's ship had always left him feeling as though it was just a procedure, rather than an adventure. The MX-19 thrilled him as the world whipped by, and the jet reached speeds in excess of Mach Twelve.

Yeah, this thing was the shit.

Controlling his emotions, Wes glanced at their heading on the digital Heads-Up-Display. They were right on course for the center of the Bermuda Triangle. At the mere thought of it, Wes sobered even more. He wasn't a superstitious man, and nobody could claim he was without bravery, but the mere thought of traveling into the Triangle set his nerves on edge.

He couldn't shake the feeling the Triangle was potentially more dangerous than any of them realized, and by traveling into it they might be setting the Earth up for something even more devastating than an invasion by the Titans or even these Aesir, whatever they were.

The enormous wolf, Fenrir, had claimed to recognize him, proclaiming they were enemies. The only way this was possible was if they'd crossed paths somewhere in Fenrir's past, a time that still remained in Wes's future. He shook his head at the complexity of it all.

The wolf had torn through Poseidon's gryphon, one of the most horrifying and powerful beasts Wes had encountered on their past encounter with the Titans, like it was a chicken. The incredible ferocity of Fenrir seemed almost elemental, and the fact that the wolf had just disappeared terrified him. Wes had laughed it all off in front of the others, but the truth was the beast scared him in a way he couldn't explain. There was something foreboding about it, the real possibility that it might ultimately destroy him.

Wes pushed the issue away. It would resolve itself one way or another in due time. For the moment he had larger issues to worry about. For instance, he had to focus on how to survive what Poseidon called the negative energy within the Bermuda Triangle to travel back in time to a land where Vikings traveled the coastline and believed in crap like giants, dragons and colossal wolves.

They would soon reach the edge of the Triangle, and if what Poseidon had predicted came true they would be sucked into some sort of tornado, a whirlpool through time....

His heart began to hammer at the mere thought of it.

This was ridiculous, he was better than this shit. Where the hell was his bravado now? It couldn't have departed, could it? Wes dipped the nose of the jet slightly, giggling loudly at the noise of Poseidon's choking breath coming over the headphones.

Then he saw it.

According to Poseidon, if they traveled toward the center of the conflux of negative energies at a speed greater than Mach Ten they would see the vortex begin to emerge in the atmosphere. The Olympian had speculated that the other documented occurrences had only happened during freak weather anomalies – like a one in a million chance.

And now, traveling at close to Mach Twelve, Wes could see it emerging. As the MX-19 sped toward the geographical center of the Bermuda Triangle, Wes saw the air split, almost like a giant set of hands had gripped it from either side and pulled. It was a most unsettling vision, and his instincts screamed at him to pull away before it was too late, but he kept the course steady, kept the nose of the jet aimed directly at the center of the hole through time.

As they maintained course, the air became turbulent, the jet shaking slightly. Wes forced his gaze straight ahead, watching the swirling and eddying air around the edges of the rip – a tear through the fabric of space and time. Within seconds the shaking increased to such a point it felt as though the giant hands which had torn the air apart were now intent on dashing the MX-19 into pieces for daring to approach.

Wes clung grimly to the controls, every ounce of strength and skill he possessed now battling to keep them on course. He had no idea what would happen if they hit the edge of the tear, and he didn't want to find out. The idea of half the jet getting sucked back in time while the rest remained behind did not appeal to him at all.

Glancing down at the airspeed indicator, Wes saw the entire console was going crazy; nothing made any sense at all. Fighting against the jolting sticks in his hands, Wes remembered the tales of the planes which had disappeared in the Triangle before and how they had lost all sense of where they were when their instruments failed. It was only moments after this that their radios had died and silence filled the airwaves.

Shaking aside the apprehension this image conjured, Wes glanced outside and estimated they were now hurtling through the air at close to Mach Thirteen. It had only been mere seconds since he'd glimpsed the tear, but seemed much, much longer.

Fuck it, thought Wes.

He jammed the controls fully forward and felt the MX-19 instantly surge. The engines screamed, forcing every possible ounce of speed out of the jet. The hole in space and time yawned open; a huge mouth waiting to consume them like a fat kid eating a Twinkie. Wes heard himself yelling as the MX-19 shot into the gullet of the tear....

And then the universe disappeared.

CHAPTER 5

Struggling back toward consciousness, Wes's head felt like it was full of ice shards as he tried in vain to open his eyes. Tearing off his right glove, he physically pried his lids apart, squinting against the harsh sunlight as flaking bits of blood fell away from his lashes. For the second time in his recent history, Wes had a gaping hole in his memory, unable to recall anything after they had shot into the rift, or conflux, or whatever the hell it was.

Glancing around, Wes saw his flight helmet first. It was split completely down the middle and ruined. Well, that explained the blood on his face. Looking further, he saw wreckage surrounding him, along with several small burning shrubs and charred trees close by. Following the trail of destruction, Wes saw what looked like a meteor impact, a huge gouge carved into the ground for around half a mile where something had hit the Earth at phenomenal speed.

Wes stood up to investigate, a parachute billowing out behind him, the light breeze filling it and pulling him backward. Catching his foot on a rock, Wes sprawled onto the ground, cursing softly.

Moments later, Wes had cut the parachute loose and was crouched on the ground, scanning the area for enemies. In his foggy condition, he hadn't gathered his senses as quickly as normal, and now his heart pounded heavily in his chest. Years of training had been forgotten in an instant, and he'd acted like a British tourist upon seeing the pyramids. A blind anteater could have done him in.

Without dropping his eyes, Wes felt inside his pressure suit, silently and swiftly removing the Heckler and Koch USP .45 handgun from its holster at his hip. It had been a long, long time since he'd been in the Australian SAS, but Wes had always been a stickler for tradition, and the USP had never let him down yet. His assault rifle had disappeared along with Poseidon and the....

The MX-19.

Wes stared once more at the fiery trail and suddenly everything fell into place. His mind remained hazy, but he still could have kicked himself for not realizing sooner that the burning surroundings and signs of impact were the result of him crashing. Searching through his jarred memory, Wes began to recall fragments – a kaleidoscope of colors, followed by the plane spinning totally out of control. They'd burst through the other side, and the jet had been spinning like a Frisbee; the computer had been screaming something... something....

EJECT!

So, the MX-19 had an automatic ejection system the technician hadn't told him about, and it had thrown them clear before the jet had crashed. Looking at the devastation, the deep gash slashed into the hard ground, Wes figured it was a pretty good call on the jet's part, and glanced again at the shattered helmet.

He'd gotten off lightly.

Satisfied nothing was of immediate danger, Wes swiftly removed the pressure suit and laced up his combat boots over the outside of his camouflage fatigues. Casting his gaze in search of Poseidon, the land seemed unfamiliar – flat and barren – and Wes figured that was probably a good thing. If he'd crashed into the middle of Las Vegas he would have known the whole traveling through the hole in the sky thing had been a waste of time – even though he could really go for some showgirls.

He was close to the coast, the blue of the ocean shimmering in the distance. From the position of the sun, Wes guessed it to be around ten in the morning... but he'd never really been good at that kind of stuff. It might just as easily have been two in the afternoon.

First thing he had to do was find Poseidon. He quickly scanned the surrounding area again. At first he saw nothing, and then an irregularity in the distance caught his eye. Wes jogged toward the shape, his pistol held ready.

He quickly discerned the shape was in fact a person – a

motionless one. After another check of the area to make sure it was clear to proceed safely, Wes moved swiftly closer to the figure, reaching it in moments. He couldn't tell if it was Poseidon, even as he drew closer, but he prayed it wasn't.

Because this body had been cooked.

Wes had no way of knowing if the toasting had occurred when the plane crashed, or whether the body had been burned in the resulting blaze. It was possible Poseidon's parachute had landed him within the flames, and if he'd been knocked unconscious like Wes, he probably wouldn't have noticed himself getting barbecued.

A whisper of movement came from behind him and Wes spun, dropping to one knee and bringing his .45 up, aiming directly at –

Poseidon.

"Will you please tell me how to remove this ridiculous helmet?" yelled Poseidon, his voice muffled by the still-closed visor. "And what is this ludicrous cape?" The Olympian indicated the parachute trailing behind him.

Wes chuckled and holstered his pistol. He moved over and twisted Poseidon's helmet slightly before lifting it clear. He then unharnessed the parachute, and the Olympian stepped out of it.

"That is a relief," breathed the Olympian. "Were we successful?"

"I have no idea. Up until a second ago I thought you were Senor Extra Crispy over there."

Poseidon moved to look at the corpse, shaking his head in amazement before glancing off to the right. "What is that?" he asked, pointing at something almost completely obscured in the dirt.

Wes jogged to where he'd pointed and saw what looked like the hilt of a sword jutting out from the ground. He tugged at it, having to yank several times before it finally came loose.

"Phew! Just like my sex life; three jerks and it's over." Grinning, Wes glanced over at Poseidon, who merely stood, frowning back at him. "Guess that must be an Earth thing." He returned his attention to the sword in his hands.

The blade itself looked to be around a meter long, with a wide guard. Wes noted the fuller running along the middle of the steel. The fuller was the area toward the center of the sword, usually the full length of the blade, significantly thinner than the outer steel. This was done to reduce the weight of the weapon, without significantly reducing the strength for the blade. The pommel on the base of the handle of this weapon was a full disc, designed to prevent the wielder's hand from slipping off the end as the blade was swung.

Wes grinned. He'd always maintained a fascination with things designed to kill people.

"I reckon we're in the right period," he said. "This sword our friend here was wielding is definitely from the Viking Era – so unless he was carrying an antique, we've landed in the right time and the right place. Well done, Poseidon."

"Now what?"

"Fucked if I know," replied Wes, looking around. "I guess we head up the coast."

"Why not down it?"

"Why not sideways? Why not bury your head in the ground and use your arse as a bike rack? Because I said so."

They began walking along the coast, Wes furiously trying to figure out how the hell he was going to find Talbot. There had to be a way....

"What is a bike rack?" queried Poseidon.

Wes's laughter rang out, and suddenly things didn't seem so bad. For now.

***

Talbot paused, wiping the sweat from his brow. The closest guard instantly shouted at him, and he swiftly dropped his head, digging laboriously once more.

Despite being an archaeologist back in his own time, he had no idea what they were trying to excavate, and really no time to contemplate the issue. Since they'd arrived – three months ago? Or was it four? – the entire US advance team sent through the rift had been split up. Talbot hadn't seen his twin brother, Thomas, since that day, and grimly pondered his fate.

Once durable military fatigues, Talbot's clothes were now little more than rags. In between shovel-loads of rock and dirt, he managed a swift look around, taking in the thousands of slaves also toiling in the dust. Surrounding them towered high rock walls, indications of how far down they had actually dug into the earth. The guards looked like Norsemen, their long hair and beards capped beneath helms of simple iron and toughened leather. They roamed between the ranks of slaves, their long whips held ready to punish any who were slow or who appeared to be disobedient.

But they didn't really need an excuse.

Since he had been brought here, Talbot had witnessed several executions, the last occurring just days ago when the guards had randomly selected one of the slaves – a slim man Talbot had never spoken to – and used him as an example. They had dragged the man from the line without warning and decapitated him using a *seax* – a large knife most of the guards carried in a sheath on their right hips, opposite the swords on their left. The result had been brutally terrifying, three guards holding the slave while a fourth sawed away at his neck. The man had not died quickly. The message had gotten through loud and clear: nobody was safe.

Talbot had managed to have whispered conversations with a couple of the other slaves, trying to find out as much about what was going on as possible. Most were reluctant to talk at any time, even during the three hours of non-labor allocated each twenty-four hour day, and he couldn't blame them for that. The gurgling sounds the decapitated slave had made still haunted Talbot's dreams, and he prayed when his time came that death would be swift.

Like Anderson.

Lieutenant Colonel Claude Anderson was the first man Talbot had seen executed by the guards after their capture, and the brutality of the incident had shocked the entire team of battle hardened soldiers. Talbot's brother, Thomas, had thrown up watching what they had done to the marine. But at least he had died quickly, not trying to scream, choking upon his own blood.

The dirt was solid, and at times it seemed more gravel and stone than actual soil, but nobody complained. Who would they complain to; the Union? Talbot almost chuckled at the thought, but swiftly caught himself, remembering Anderson's head dropping to the ground, and the sickly thud it had made striking that rock....

Talbot's primitive shovel struck a large rock and split down the middle, the poorly refined iron shattering, jarring Talbot's arms and shoulders.

Damn.

Talbot raised a shaking hand to gather a guard's attention, and immediately one moved toward him, fury burning in his gaze. So far, Talbot had managed to avoid being punished by the guards, but he knew the time would come when they would unleash their wrath upon him. He had not unveiled his ability to understand them through his skill with the Elder-tongue. Talbot kept his mouth shut at all times, attempting to gather as much information as possible, while drawing as little attention at the same time. Yet he knew it was only a matter of time until they tired of his being overlooked and decided to punish him regardless.

That time might be now.

He held up the broken shovel to the guard while keeping his eyes downcast. The guard glared at the broken tool and spat directly into Talbot's face. Talbot refused to react, nor did he raise his hand to wipe the spittle away as it began to dribble down his cheeks.

"If you were not so utterly pathetic," snarled the huge red-headed guard, "I would slice open your belly and feed you to the crows."

Talbot offered no reaction, showing none of the fear the words made him feel inside. If he responded it would tell the Norsemen he could understand them, and they might kill him simply for having deceived them.

The guard snatched the broken shovel out of Talbot's calloused hands, returning moments later with a primitive rock pick-like tool which he shoved at the archaeologist, who stood still with his head down, eyes downcast. Talbot reached out to take the tool, and the guard snatched it back. Confused, Talbot silently withdrew his hand and waited. The guard once more extended the pick toward him, but when Talbot went to take it again it was once more withdrawn.

Finally Talbot raised his glance from the ground and gasped.

"Happy to see me, fuck-face?" whispered Wes, his features obscured by the helmet and long red hair, which looked to have been cut straight from the guard's head. Looking him over, Talbot saw Wes was dressed completely in the garb of the Viking guards who patrolled the dig-site. He even wore the sword and seax knife of the Norseman.

"Oh boy, it's good to see you," replied Talbot in an excited whisper.

"Well, control your boner until we get out of here." Wes threw his arms around in the air while talking so as to give the impression he was admonishing Talbot for something. Talbot found it a very unconvincing piece of acting, but since nobody had stabbed them yet he figured he couldn't argue.

Motioning Talbot to move in front of him, Wes drew his sword, and they made their way through the lines of slaves. Talbot stepped as quickly as he dared while trying to keep his features downcast. His heart was thudding within his chest so hard he thought the guards might hear it, catching onto the fact that something wasn't quite right between the slave and the guard with very uneven braids.

Amazingly, nobody yelled. No alarm was raised, and no guards came running, waving their swords in the air as they sought to chop Talbot's buttocks off and wear them as ear muffs. Soon Wes and Talbot marched into the woods, swiftly disappearing within the trees.

Once he was sure they were fully out of sight, Talbot turned to Wes and swiftly embraced the man. "Thank you. You just saved my life... again."

"Yeah, whatever, cuddles," muttered Wes, prying himself loose. "Do you know how long we've been looking for you?"

"Well thank God you found me. I don't know how much longer I would have survived if you hadn't come along."

"I need to ask you about that, but not here. We have to get someplace safe before you can get too mushy. Watch out for that leg."

Talbot stumbled on something and looked down. Hidden beneath bracken and leaves was the naked body of the Norse guard who had spat in his face. Talbot bit back a cry of shock.

"I told you to watch out," reprimanded Wes. "Now move that branch back into position and let's go."

"Sorry," mumbled Talbot, covering the corpse once more and swiftly following Wes. No matter how much he saw of it, Talbot had never gotten used to death.

Wes, on the other hand....

The way he had spoken about the body was the same way someone else might chat about a tablecloth. The man always seemed completely untouched by the lives he took, and part of Talbot was immensely saddened as a result. Pushing away the feeling, Talbot remembered that if Wes wasn't like this, he would still be in the slave pit digging through the dirt, thinking each moment would be his last.

"Hang on a second," said Talbot. "Back there you said 'we' when you referred to looking for me. Who's with you?"

"You'll see," replied Wes mysteriously with a grin.

He led Talbot up a short hill and walked over to the rock face before turning sideways and disappearing. Talbot was momentarily stunned until he moved further to the right and saw a sharp crack carved in the face of the cliff through which Wes had vanished. It was marvelously concealed, and virtually invisible from the front. Talbot turned and slid between the two faces of rock, feeling somewhat claustrophobic as the air itself seemed to close in around him. Every conceivable fear about getting stuck flooded through his mind, and it was all he could do to avoid panicking.

Shimmying sideways for what seemed an eternity, the crack finally opened out into a cave. Talbot sucked in a relieved gasp as he stepped clear. Glancing around, he saw Wes stroll to the rear of the cavern, removing his Viking garb, while a tall, powerful-looking man stood studying Talbot. A small fire flickered at the back of the cave, its smoke drifting up and disappearing through a tiny crack in the ceiling which acted as a natural chimney.

"Talbot, this is Poseidon," said Wes casually, tugging at the thick Viking pants, trying to get them off from over his combat fatigues.

If Talbot hadn't gone through his previous quest and met with Zeus and Heracles, along with the rest of the Olympians, the realization of meeting Poseidon, the ancient Greek god of the oceans, would have possibly been too much for him. As it was, he was tired, and weak from hunger and cold.

"Hey, Poseidon, great to meet you." He gripped the Olympian's hand and moved to sit by the fire, holding out his hands to the flames and seeing how filthy they really were. The skin of his palms was cracked and broken from the many weeks working at the dig site.

Fatigue settled on Talbot like a heavy coat. For the first time in months he wasn't numb with terror and his exhaustion finally caught up with him. He needed to eat something... something....

***

"Wake up, but be silent," Talbot heard a strange voice whisper. He opened his eyes and saw the figure of Poseidon crouched over him, his face turned toward the exit of the cave.

"What's going on?" croaked Talbot, his throat dry.

"Your friend, Wes, believes your captors are close by."

"Do you have any water?" asked Talbot, realizing the irony of asking Poseidon such a question.

Poseidon stared at him and nodded before moving to the other side of the cave, grabbing a Norse water skin and handing it to him. The water skin was simple enough, utilizing a sheep's bladder in order to hold liquid, commonly sheathed in an animal skin, but as yet Talbot hadn't had to face the unpleasant task of drinking from one. He pulled the stopper clear and lifted the bag, allowing the water to pour down his throat. It tasted slightly stale, but still a hundred times better than the dirty water they'd been given in the slave camp; probably the best thing he was ever likely to drink from a bladder.

Remembering the slave camp, Talbot looked at his garb and realized he was no longer clothed in the tattered remains of his combat fatigues; he was now dressed in the garb of the Viking Wes had killed. The clothes were slightly baggy, and he smelled like some sort of farm animal, but at least they weren't rags. Wes had changed him in his sleep.

Creepy, but hardly the weirdest thing Wes had ever done. They had bigger issues at the moment, anyway. If what Poseidon had said was true, then the guards were close. Wes was never wrong about these things.

"Where is Wes?" he asked Poseidon.

"He left just before I woke you. Should we go after him?"

Talbot shook his head. "No, Wes works better alone."

"Good." Poseidon looked him directly in the eye. "There is much we need to discuss, and it will proceed better if we are undisturbed"

"Really? Like what?"

"Like the last time we met."

Poseidon suddenly stretched and grew, his form rapidly expanding into that of Prometheus. His eyes flickered, swiftly misting from brilliant blue to black cloudy orbs in an instant, swirling malevolently. Within a second he was fourteen-feet-tall, towering over Talbot, his frame garbed in the armor of the Titans, black as ebony with a metallic chest plate and shoulder guards. Full chainmail covered the rest of Prometheus's body, and an open-faced helm crowned his head. Talbot had never known whether the armor was truly metal or simply designed to look like it. He guessed it didn't really need to be steel, since as yet they hadn't found a way to kill Prometheus – at least not permanently.

"What do you want?" asked Talbot, retreating slowly.

"Now, is that any way to greet an old friend?"

"We were never friends, Prometheus. You tried to trick me into opening the gateway to Olympia so your people could invade."

"A task which you did anyway," observed Prometheus softly.

"I had no choice! I had to warn Zeus of your plans, and it was the only way back!"

Prometheus grinned. "There is always a choice. You just didn't want to die." His form shimmered once more and instantly he was clothed in a simple cotton shirt and loose drawstring pants. His features flickered as he shrank, morphing into Zeus, the handsome face of the leader of the Olympians smiling warmly.

"Zeus doesn't care about you, Talbot. Why risk yourself for him?"

"You're not Zeus," said Talbot, fighting to keep emotion from his voice. Where the hell was Wes?

Prometheus changed his features again. In an instant his muscles swelled, and he grew once more, but not as tall as his usual form. Talbot recognized the appearance of Heracles immediately; the short-cropped hair of the warrior framing his cleanly-shaven face and stern visage.

"I could have killed you by now; you know that, don't you?"

Talbot stared back into the now hazel eyes. "Then why haven't you?"

"I'm waiting to see if you try to employ that stupid chanting you so desperately used the last time we met. I wanted to see the look on your face when you saw it fail."

"It worked the last time," argued Talbot.

"Maybe that's simply what I wanted you to think. Perhaps I merely wanted you on this current course."

The thought troubled Talbot. He knew better than to underestimate Prometheus; the Titan was a genius when it came to manipulating events and people.

"If we were doing what you wanted, there's no reason you would be here right now. You'd leave us alone to continue until you had to prod us in a different direction."

The image of Heracles shifted and blurred, but not before Talbot glimpsed a look not unlike annoyance in his eyes. Seconds later Prometheus was back in his original form, although this time he was wearing a black Tudor suit, and he stood a mere six-feet-tall instead of his usual fourteen. His swirling eyes were now bright blue and stable. He looked like a regular New York businessman.

"I am not your enemy, Talbot," he said persuasively. "My people were slaughtered, and I am the last of my kind. You have no idea how terrifying that is, to be alone in the universe. I have a chance to be reunited with them through this period in history. By traveling backward through time we have reached a point where we can enter Tartarus and find my people whole again. I don't want to start another war, that's all behind me now. I just want to go home, Talbot."

The words were pleading, his manner desperate, and Talbot almost fell for it. Then he remembered the way Prometheus had tricked them before, and the results of the Titan's deception.

"You're fucking joking, aren't you?" Wes's voice echoed from the entrance of the cave. Prometheus spun toward the sound, and Talbot looked over to see Wes with his sidearm drawn and aimed directly at the Titan's brow.

"I was really beginning to like Poseidon," said Wes. "You didn't kill him, did you?"

"I needed a ride," stated Prometheus simply, shrugging his shoulders. "And to be honest, you never actually met the real Poseidon. It was me the whole time, but I'm a very likeable individual."

"You're about as likeable as gonorrhea. I wondered how he'd managed to get through that crack in the rock, but figured I'd ask later. Should have known it was your slippery arse sliding through there. How the hell are you still alive, Prometheus? I know we discussed it before, but I was sure you were done for when Talbot did his voodoo shit on you the last time."

"I must admit it was a difficult issue to overcome, but your government was very accommodating in allowing for my rehabilitation."

"What does that mean?" asked Talbot.

"I posed as one of your President's advisors for a time whilst recovering my strength – a time I also spent learning to protect myself from that little inconvenience. Besides having the ear of the President, I was also able to infiltrate their program to study time travel and rift manipulation. A few comments here and there allowed me to guide the entire operation in exactly the direction I desired. And none of it would have been possible without you." He pointed at Wes, unperturbed by the handgun still aimed at his head.

"What the hell are you talking about?" snarled Wes.

"You don't remember, do you?"

"I remember that you're an arsehole. What else is there?"

Prometheus grinned cruelly. "It is because of your ship that all of this has come to fruition. With it I was able to travel through time at will and manipulate events as I saw fit. That is how things began the last time; I journeyed back to the ancient Greece of your world and told my previous self of the things to come, so that he could be prepared. It's all very convoluted, and your primitive little brains would have no possible hope of keeping up, so I'll forego the rest of the explanation, but let me assure you that none of it could have worked if not for your assistance."

"So why are you telling us this now?" asked Talbot.

"I am merely gloating, you stupid meat-puppet. My plans are now so advanced nothing you do can prevent them."

"If that were the truth we'd already be dead."

"You think yourself quite intelligent, don't you? Perhaps I am merely leaving you for those bloodthirsty savages you call Vikings. Or maybe I still have other tasks which you will unknowingly accomplish for me. You'll never know."

Talbot began to say something, but suddenly Prometheus disappeared. At first he thought the Titan had discovered a way to vanish into thin air, but then he saw a large, black rat scurrying out through a tiny hole in the back wall of the cave. He started to call out to Wes, but the commando waved him to silence before holstering his gun and moving to stand beside him.

"Keep quiet," whispered Wes. "Let him think he has the upper hand for now. He's really screwed up by showing his hand so soon."

"How so?" asked Talbot softly.

"We're still alive. I don't know why, maybe what he said is true, and he needs us for something else, but while we're alive there's a chance we can stop whatever he has planned. We did it before; I don't care what he says. He can tell us it was all part of his plan, but that's bullshit. You don't go through all of that crap just to jump through hoops to get back to where you began, do you?"

"I have no idea what you just said."

"Exactly! It's all too confusing. Our Titan friend there didn't kill us today, and he's going to regret it. He didn't do it because he either still needs us, or he's not strong enough to do it. There might be a lot going on we don't understand, but for now we just have to keep going and see where all this shit takes us."

"I guess so. By the way, what the hell are you doing here?" asked Talbot. "Not that I'm complaining, mind you."

"Sit down, and I'll tell you all about it."

"Shouldn't we be worried about those warriors, the Norsemen, finding us?"

Wes shook his head. "Nah, that idiot –" he nodded toward the hole Prometheus had scurried through, "– just told me they were out there to get some alone time with you."

Wes then proceeded to tell Talbot of the events leading up to his rescue, brimming with expletives and elaborate gestures. In the end it was more like a one-man theatre show than a mere retelling of events.

"So who do you think that Zoe chick was?" asked Wes as he finished the story.

"I have no idea," replied Talbot. "Could she be another Titan like Prometheus? Or maybe she was Prometheus from a different time; the two of them teaming up like you did with your previous self when we went back in time to stop him in Atlantis?"

"I don't think so. She didn't seem anything like him, but then again I've been wrong before. Not often, though."

"How did she convince you twenty years had passed?"

"Dunno. I was still out of it, I guess, and just took her at her word. Guess I fucked up." Wes shrugged casually, seemingly unconcerned, but Talbot sensed an underlying agitation at the question.

"One more thing. Do you think Prometheus was telling the truth when he said he'd been Poseidon the whole time, or could it actually have been the true Poseidon with you at some stage?" asked Talbot.

"I'm not sure. If it *was* Prometheus the whole time, he had that crew wrapped around his little finger. Nobody suspected a thing. And there's no way they weren't all Olympians; plus the technology of the ship was definitely like that other crap Hephaestus built. Now what's your story? How'd you end up in Santa's little happy factory back there?"

"Not much to tell really that you don't already know or suspect. The Government convinced my brother and I to help them with a different kind of rift they'd found. We came through it and got caught straight away by those Norsemen, who killed most of the marines with us, taking the rest of us as slaves."

"How did those idiots catch you? Did they shake their little swords and scare the men with machine guns?"

"There were thousands of them, and they just appeared out of nowhere after setting a trap. Half the men were cut down before they'd recovered from the rift. I've been digging in that pit ever since, with no idea where any of the others are. They might be dead for all I know."

"Yeah, maybe," agreed Wes. "But that doesn't matter for now; we don't have time to launch a rescue attempt."

"But my brother's with them!"

"And dying isn't going to help him, is it? For now we have to find out what the hell is going on here, stop whatever plans Prometheus has, and find a way home. Simple huh?" Wes threw something to Talbot which he instinctively caught.

"Yeah, right," muttered Talbot, looking at the MRE in his hands with dread.

Wes suddenly laughed. "It's good to have you back, you little ray of sunshine. Bon appétit!"

Talbot grinned despite himself, and studied the instructions for cooking his Meal, Ready to Eat.

CHAPTER 6

A gaping hole appeared in Háleygr as the weapon of fire wielded by the stranger unleashed once more. Something exited from the warrior's back, taking out his spine at the same time. Háleygr barely had time to glance down at the blood spurting from his chest, a bemused expression crossing his features, before he toppled to the ground. His clansmen paused, shocked by the seeming magic of the oddly-speaking foreigner with the strange clothes and short hair.

"Come on then, you arseholes. I'll skull-fuck each and every one of you!" yelled the demon in human form.

Biaver, son of Gunnhvati, stepped forward, his shield lowered, but still in his hand lest the demon let loose his weapon of fire once more. The other nineteen warriors of his clan stood tensely, but seemingly uncertain. It was up to him as clan leader to resolve the situation.

"What are you, demon?" His voice held strong despite the nerves he felt fluttering in his chest.

"I'm the guy who's going to blow your head off if you attack us again, that's who."

"Do you serve the Aesir?"

"I don't serve anyone," snarled the demon, his weapon still aimed at Biaver's chest. Another figure stood slightly behind the demon, dressed as one of the followers of the Aesir, anxiously gripping a Viking sword, similar to Biaver's own Norse blade.

"Your companion wears the clothing of our enemies. If you also serve the Aesir we must battle unto death, for my clan defy the gods and their slavery in all its forms."

"Excellent!" replied the demon cheerfully, suddenly sheathing its weapon of fire and smiling broadly. "Luckily for you we're here to kill the Aesir. My friend is just wearing their gear in order to blend in better."

Biaver stood still, unsure whether to believe the demon's words or its actions. It was true that his warriors had been the first to attack the duo, and Háleygr had instantly paid for their rashness with his life. Biaver looked down at his cousin's body and grimaced. At least he had died with his sword in his hand.

Biaver shook his head slightly. The old superstitions remained difficult to relinquish. His clan was the only one to refuse to send people to work in the Aesir's slave camps, and they had paid for it dearly. Half their population had been wiped out in a single night, and the rest had scattered, hiding in the wilderness, only recently reforming, striking against the servants of the Aesir whenever they could.

But by far the hardest loss had been that of their religion.

Norsemen were taught from birth that to die in battle was the only way to ensure they would be accepted into the halls of Valhalla. By fighting against their gods, the Aesir, Biaver's clan had guaranteed they would forever be excluded from Valhalla.

But they would not send their people to work as slaves. If it ensured their children would be free of slavery it was a price worth paying.

The demon grinned at him. "My name's Wes. The guy crapping his pants over there is called Talbot. Don't ask me how I understand what you're saying, because I don't know. Zeus unlocked something in my head when I first met him, and now it seems I can translate what Olympians are saying – but you're obviously not Olympian, so I have no idea what's going on. Maybe he fucked up. Then again, I understood what Fenrir was saying too. I might be like you now, Talbot, what do ya reckon? Just with a bigger dick."

"You spoke to Fenrir the Wolf?" gasped Biaver, forgetting it was a demon he spoke to.

"Uh, yeah. He's not a friend of yours, is he?"

Biaver stared at the demon. Was this a test, or a trick? "Fenrir has vowed to destroy Odin."

"I'm guessing that would be a good thing, right?"

"If Fenrir destroyed Odin, half of our war would be over immediately. Odin rules the Aesir, and it is they who command my people to dig for them. Most clans agreed without contest, but my father, Gunnhvati, who was also my clan's leader, opposed them, refusing to send a third of our clan to their vile pits to dig through the earth like pigs. They killed my father, and I inherited his legacy. As the new clan leader it became my duty to continue the war against the Aesir."

"Right," agreed the stranger. "I didn't ask for all that, but thanks for the update. So Fenrir is good, is that what you're saying?"

"Not generally, no," replied Biaver cautiously, still unsure of these strangers. "But in regards to our quest he may prove invaluable. His hatred of the Aesir is equal to our own."

"That's awesome. Isn't it, Talbot?" The smaller man holding the Norse sword nodded slightly. He looked more like a scholar or poet than a warrior, thought Biaver. "So where do we go from here, champ?" asked the demonic stranger named Wes. Such a strange name, but somehow appropriate considering the oddity of his appearance.

"How do you mean?"

"Well, are we all good, or do we start killing each other again?"

Biaver was unsure, but couldn't show weakness in front of his warriors, who stood watching the exchange tensely. The stranger – or demon – had shown he had a weapon of incredible power which they could use against the Aesir. Perhaps they could combat the Aesir's weapons of magic with a magic of their own….

"We shall be allies," said Biaver. "But if you or the one with you decide to double-cross me or my people, we will carve the flesh from your fiendish bones."

"That's awesome," replied Wes cheerfully. "Do you guys have anything to eat? We ran out of MREs yesterday."

Wes and his silent companion moved past the group of twenty warriors, and Biaver could not help but think he had somehow made a mistake.

"Come on Beaver, what are you waiting for?"

He was almost certain of it.

***

"Well that's my luck used up for the next two weeks," said Wes.

Talbot nodded. "I thought they were going to gut us for sure, either that or take us back to one of the slave camps."

"It's just fortunate Heckler and Koch scared them."

"Heckler and Koch? Oh, your gun." Talbot eyed the semi-automatic pistol in its holster at Wes's hip.

"Stop looking at my dick."

"I-I wasn't –" stammered Talbot.

Wes's laughter sounded. "Maybe you prefer Heckler and cock!" he grabbed his crotch suggestively.

"Damn you, Wes," said Talbot, but he wasn't truly shocked. He'd seen Wes do much worse to relieve the tension, and Talbot grinned despite his embarrassment.

"If these boys weren't following us, I'd seriously man-hug you. You know that, right?"

"Stop it!" Talbot couldn't help but chuckle. He decided to change the topic of conversation. "You mentioned something about talking to Fenrir the wolf. You weren't serious, were you?"

"Yep. He tore half of the White House apart just to have a chat. Told me I was his enemy, yada-yada-yada, and then ripped apart a gryphon like it was a parakeet. Didn't I mention that before?"

"No," said Talbot, frowning.

"Oh well. At the time I figured it was something to do with my future and his past colliding, but now I'm not so sure. I mean, if he's fighting the same guys we are, why would he be pissed off at me?"

Talbot opened his mouth, and then quickly shut it again. He knew a rhetorical question when he heard it, and Wes didn't need to hear one of a million possible theories as to why a giant talking wolf from Norse mythology would be upset with him. Despite his outward displays of idiocy, Wes was far beyond genius, but like many people with an elevated IQ, he got bored easily, and mischief usually ensued.

"Exactly!" said Wes when Talbot failed to respond. "So Prometheus must have done something to piss him off back then… I mean *now*."

Talbot raised an eyebrow. "It's possible," he agreed.

Wes shook his head. "Nah, that can't be right. Fenrir just about freaked out when I mentioned Prometheus to him, so he's obviously met him or dealt with him before. I'm sure if he came close to the Titan he'd sniff him out for sure."

"Maybe." It was better not to get too involved in the conversation. Talbot was merely a secondary player in this discussion; his input wasn't really required. Wes was simply working things out in his own head, but preferred to do it vocally.

"Ah, fuck it. It doesn't really matter right now anyway. It's probably best not to mention it to these guys, though, just in case." Wes gave him a wink. Talbot grinned slightly and shook his head.

"What's our next move?" he asked Wes.

"Buggered if I know. I guess we need to find out what's going on here. Hey! Beavis!" Wes yelled at Biaver. "What are those guys digging for? The slaves, what do the Aesir have them looking for?"

Biaver swiftly caught up with them and spoke in a hushed tone. "It is unclear what they are truly searching for, and my men fear it may be sacrilegious to suggest it, but some speculate they search for the entrance to Valhalla."

"The entrance to Valhalla? What does it look like?"

"One of our people escaped from the dig site, grievously wounded, and he managed to give us a description of what they had been told to look out for during their digging. It was said to be a circle of standing stones, possibly still vertical or now fallen, which would open a door to Bifrost, the Rainbow Bridge, and from there to the Hall of the Heroes known as Valhalla."

"So these people the Aesir hold prisoner, these slaves," said Wes. "They're trying to find a gate to open a rift?"

Talbot glanced at Wes in shock, suddenly understanding what he was getting at. If the Aesir were looking for a gate – like the Syrpeas Gate – then Prometheus had to be behind it. And now Talbot and his twin brother, Thomas, the only people with the ability to read the language of the Elder-tongue and thus manipulate the machinery, were here also.

Ducks in a row....

***

Talbot roused himself with difficulty. He rose slowly to his feet, grabbing his pounding head as he did. Clutching the wooden wall of the dwelling, he tried to focus his eyes and remember where he was. The thick clothes of the Norseman felt rough upon his sticky and sweaty skin. He was tempted to remove them, but something within his bleary mind said to do so would be foolish. He figured he could handle the discomfort.

This headache, on the other hand, was proving utter torture.

He remembered arriving at the village – home to around sixty Norse men and women. Biaver had declared they would be given a welcoming feast. The last thing Talbot could recall was the crackling of meat on a spit over the fire – the same fire which smoldered within a pit in the middle of the huge hall he now stood in – and a goblet of drink being thrust into his hand. Talbot had drunk from the goblet, tasting something sweet, probably a type of honey mead. Beyond that first goblet, memories became decidedly blurry....

He looked around at the huge hall, recognizing it as a longhouse – a kind of main hall for the village. All around him, warriors were passed out, sleeping on benches around the walls, the air warm from the covered fire. Talbot moved to the large doors at the rear of the longhouse and pulled them open, stumbling outside.

The air outside was frigid, especially compared to the almost balmy longhouse, and Talbot was suddenly grateful for the thick garments he wore. Without warning, his stomach flipped, and Talbot ran to a nearby bush, retching loudly.

"I told you not to drink that shit," called Wes's voice.

Talbot wiped his mouth, amazed one of his kidneys hadn't

emerged along with the contents of his stomach.

"It would have been considered rude," he muttered, his voice hoarse.

"As opposed to spewing your guts all over their fruit plants?"

Talbot glanced down, noticing for the first time that the shrub he had vomited upon was a small strawberry bush. It stood only a couple of-feet-tall, struggling for life within the gravel-like soil.

"Oh no," muttered Talbot.

"You'd better find something to wash your puke away before those Vikings wake up and see what you've done. Maybe you should piss on it; that might fix the problem."

Talbot ignored Wes's laughter and raced over to the well on the other side of the longhouse, swiftly drawing up a bucket. Ice crystals were floating on top of the water, but Talbot didn't care. He raced over to the ill-treated bush and hastily dumped the water over it.

"You missed a bit. Looks like carrot," said Wes. He looked thoughtful. "How come whenever someone spews there's carrot? I haven't eaten carrot since I was a kid, but at the first sign of puke out pops a bit of carrot. Weird huh?"

Talbot graced him with a withering glance before stumbling to the well once more and drawing another bucket of water which he hurriedly carried back to the bush. Washing the rest of the evidence away, he stood back and surveyed the scene for any other sign of his mishap.

Not a speck remained.

A split second later, the large doors of the longhouse banged open and three Norse warriors stumbled out. Realizing he still held the wooden bucket in his hand, Talbot looked around for somewhere to hide it. There was nowhere.

"I was just... um... watering your lovely bush," he said, indicating the small shrub.

The first warrior lurched over and, without even looking at Talbot, heaved his stomach contents onto the pitiful plant. The second did the same while the third warrior stood still, appearing contemplative, as though unsure whether he needed to retch as well. After a moment, he stumbled away while the first warrior turned, wiped his mouth with his hand, and then patted Talbot on the shoulder, wiping his palm on Talbot's clothing. Tears ran down Wes's cheeks as he shook with silent laughter.

"Well, at least they didn't think you were rude," he said finally, gasping for air. "And look, carrots!"

Talbot shook his head and carried the bucket back to the well, hurling it into the inky depths and hearing its splash echo from the bottom. Tying the end of its drawing rope to the small hitch on the side of the well, he wandered off between the structures, heading toward the edge of the river or lake he could see beyond the buildings.

The village was beautiful in its simplicity. The dwellings were built from a combination of felled logs and primitive brickwork, the longhouse at the top of the hill, and the smaller dwellings built on the slope leading down toward the water. Two longships rested upon the stony beach, the dragon's-head carvings upon their prows staring sightlessly at Talbot like voiceless sentinels.

"They must have been hammered by the Aesir, or whoever attacked them when they refused to send their people to be slaves." Talbot jumped, spinning around to see Wes standing calmly beside him. No matter how many times he was surprised by it, the man's stealth never ceased to unnerve Talbot. "It was probably the other clans, or tribes, or whatever you call them. I imagine the Aesir wouldn't be so sloppy as to leave anyone alive."

"What makes you think they were decimated?" asked Talbot, his heart still hammering.

"Two boats for twenty warriors? I don't think so. Each one of those boats could carry between sixty to eighty warriors, judging by the thirty rowing benches. So we're looking at a combined carrying force of around one-hundred to one-hundred-and-sixty warriors. I'm assuming they don't use women as warriors, right?"

Talbot nodded. "The women stayed at home while the men traveled and warred – I mean they *stay* at home. I can't get used to this time thing yet. By the way, that kind of longship is called a *skei*, meaning: 'that which cuts through water'."

"What is this, a history lesson? It's a boat. Call it a boat. It's not like there's a whole fleet of battleships here. There are two boats, both called skei. What's your point?"

Talbot mumbled something, but knew Wes didn't mean his words the way they had come out. Sometimes the commando just liked to keep things simple. The truth was Talbot had begun to feel a bit useless. The last time he'd teamed up with Wes he had –

"Hey! Are you listening?" snapped Wes.

"Uh, sorry. What?"

"I said we might have trouble. Look."

Wes indicated across the water. Four dark longships were slicing their way through the water, heading unerringly toward the village.

"Time to go. Go wake up Belvedere."

"Who?" asked Talbot.

"The chief guy, whatever his name is."

"You mean Biaver."

"In the time you've been figuring that out you could have gotten him," snapped Wes.

"No need," replied Talbot. "He's already here."

Wes turned. "We need to leave, Benetton. Gather your warriors, and let's go."

"We won't escape. Those are the warriors of the Aesir. With only twenty warriors to row the longships, we will be too slow. We are doomed."

Talbot peered out across the glassy water at the four black longships powering toward the village. Something didn't seem right about the way they were moving, and it took him a few moments to figure out what it was. They had no sails out, their single masts were bare, and yet....

They were moving without oars.

These longships cut seamlessly through the water, making a direct line for the shore with no indication of how they were moving. Talbot looked for some sort of wake which might indicate their means of propulsion, but there was nothing apart from the small waves following in the boats' wake.

"Hey, Wes, I think we're in trouble."

"I know. I'm the one who told you, remember?"

"No. This is something else entirely. They're not using oars."

Wes's eyes narrowed against the early-morning glare reflecting from the water, understanding soon creasing his expression. He scanned the land behind them for a place to retreat to, but there was nowhere. The village had been placed in a crescent valley, sheer rock walls on three sides opening out onto the sea. This provided some protection from the elements, but also trapped them when attacked from the water.

There would be no retreat.

"Beaver," said Wes. "What about if we got the women to row, could we escape then? I mean, these things are called skei, which means they cut through the water, right?"

Talbot shot Wes a disgusted glance. Biaver didn't notice the look, merely nodded approvingly. "You know our ships, demon Wes. But we cannot use the women in such a way. They are not warriors, and it would shame us to use them as such."

"Well, if we don't use them, they're going to be dead, along with the rest of us. So you'd better decide quickly before those fuckers land their magic boats and have gratuitous sex with us on the beach here. Can you handle a bit of shame in order to keep an intact sphincter? We need to survive this in order to defeat the Aesir."

Biaver's face took on a look of torment as the decision was handed to him. He presumably only comprehended the basic outline of what Wes had said, but that was enough. Talbot understood the Viking's dilemma: he already felt disgraced for accepting the allegiance of Wes and Talbot, along with turning his back on his people's religious beliefs. Now he was being asked to run with women from an enemy he could not defeat.

"My shame is complete," he finally murmured, his eyes downcast. "We will gather the women and children and flee like cowards."

"Only for today, Biaver," said Wes, his expression grim. "There are other days."

The use of his proper name brought a shimmer of pride back into Biaver's visage, and he nodded resolutely. "It will be as you say," Biaver said before turning and relaying the orders to the other villagers. Several stared at their leader, shock erupting upon their visages. Others merely nodded, accepting the orders without issue.

Within moments one of the longships was loaded with as much as they could grab, the women and children seated on its central benches. Talbot guessed the seating arrangement was intended to give them as much protection as possible, but the reality was etched across the features of every warrior:

If they were caught, there could be no protection.

The four approaching longships potentially carried over three hundred Aesir warriors. Talbot had no way of knowing what sort of fighters the Aesir were, but if they were only *half* as deadly as the Titans – which Talbot thought might be overly hopeful – it would still mean the Vikings would be lucky to survive for seconds, no matter how doughty they were.

Pushing the thought from his mind, Talbot rushed to the shore to assist the Vikings as they launched the longship into the calm water. The warriors, along with Wes, heaved themselves effortlessly into the boat, but when Talbot tried, he found his Viking pants and sheepskin boots were so clogged with water he was unable to haul himself up. A Viking dragged him roughly into the boat where he tripped and fell straight over one of the benches. He swiftly rose back to his feet, but not before he saw several looks of scorn from the warriors as well as a couple of the women.

Only one set of eyes held no derision, and they were set within the face of an angel.

"Try not to embarrass us too much, Talbot," muttered Wes. "And stop staring at the hot Nordic chick. Chances are she's married to one of these goons, and he'll stab you in the face with a frozen trout. I'd hate to lose you after all I've gone through to get you back. Besides, the guys in the black boats are likely to chop off your nuts in a minute, so you won't give a shit about her – except maybe to go shoe shopping."

The truth behind Wes's words impacted Talbot's thoughts, and he wrenched his gaze away, staring at the approaching longships with dread. They had halved the distance now, and Talbot hurriedly stumbled over to a bench seat, dropping heavily beside an absolutely huge Norse woman.

"Just make sure Helga doesn't eat you before our enemies catch us, okay?" called Wes.

"Ah… Wes, these people can understand us; you remember that whatever Zeus did to you in Olympia seems to have somehow carried on, translating everything you say, don't you?"

Wes glanced over at the hefty woman beside Talbot, noticing for the first time that the scowl upon her face was directed straight at him.

Talbot had never seen Wes move faster as he leaped over the three benches and into the aft of the longship beside the warrior holding the steering oar. He sat down on the three-man seat there, closest to the port-side railing.

"G'day, mate," muttered Wes casually to the helmsman.

"Why aren't you rowing, Wes?" called Talbot.

"Because I can't shoot anyone with an oar in my hand," he replied, brandishing his Heckler and Koch, still avoiding the Helga's glare.

"How much damage do you expect to do with a handgun?"

"Shitloads," replied Wes with a wink. "It's me, remember?"

Talbot grinned in return, unable to deny the magnetic personality of the commando. He was still smiling as he turned sideways to see the huge Norse woman scowling down at him, at which point his grin disappeared in an instant.

His brother had been the historian, but in that moment Talbot tried as hard as he could to recall anything which might indicate if ancient Norse tribes actually ate people, because right now the bulky woman beside him seemed ready to bite his head off.

"Take up oars!" hollered Biaver, seated beside Wes at the rear of the vessel, a goatskin drum pressed between his knees and a rounded stick resting across the skin.

Talbot snapped to attention and grasped the oar in front of him.

As his palms wrapped around the wooden oar, Talbot immediately saw the flaw with this system, as did every warrior on board. By having the women safer in the middle of the longship, the greater poundage of the rowing was reliant upon them. In simple terms, the women had the most work, and the stronger warriors were on the outside, where they had less leverage on the oars.

Without a word, all warriors stood and motioned for the women to move to the outside position, and they moved to the center, gripping the oars once more. Talbot began to stand, but the Nordic woman placed a huge hand on his shoulder, effortlessly pushing him back down.

"I think you'll be better off where you are, outsider," she said, her voice rumbling like thunder.

Talbot nodded, unable to find his voice. Part of him felt deep shame, while commonsense told him the woman was right. Either way, he simply nodded, sat down, and silently assisted with guiding the oar into the water.

"NOW ROW, you wasted goat entrails!" roared Biaver. He hit the drum in a rhythmic percussion.

Talbot tried to haul back on the huge oar, but his efforts were stalled by the great strength of his rowing companion. In his eagerness, Talbot had forgotten about the timing beat; trying instead to heave manically on the oar without thought of the rhythm. If everyone did this the oars would clash and chaos would ensue. Helga – or whatever her name was – hauled the oversized oar backward in time with the beat, and the longboat surged forward in the water. Beyond the aft of the vessel, Talbot could see the Aesir longboats cutting effortlessly through the water, turning smoothly to intercept them.

Calming himself, Talbot timed his next stroke to correspond with the beat and felt a tiny twinge of satisfaction when he didn't screw it up. Of course, Helga's strength controlled the actions of the oar more than any real input from Talbot, but small steps were good steps, as long as they were in the right direction.

And right now the right direction was away from the enemy.

The Aesir longships drew closer than ever. Talbot could distinctly make out the warriors aboard each of the four boats, standing shoulder to shoulder, unmoving against the slight rocking motion of the water against the hulls of their longships. They looked more like robots than warriors....

Robots? No, that was impossible.

He peered at the warriors aboard the Aesir ships. They were definitely human, at least in appearance, each differing from his neighbor. So they weren't robots. What could they be? Cyborgs? Some kind of Aesir terminator?

Talbot shook the thought away; now was not the time to think stupidly. Any kind of machine was highly unlikely, so he weighed up other ideas. It could be hypnosis, maybe brainwashing. That was possible. Especially if the Aesir were as advanced as he suspected.

If these warriors were indeed brainwashed, it was likely they would be numb to fear, but they might also be more sluggish in their actions. They'd be more like drones than combatants fighting for their life. If only he could use this information somehow….

Gazing across the water, Talbot suddenly had it.

"Wes!"

"What?"

Talbot removed one hand from the oar and pointed at the mast of the closest ship. Wes followed where his finger aimed and looked back, confused.

"They're brainwashed and confused. They won't react to it."

Wes appeared thoughtful for a moment before nodding. Rising from the small seat at the stern, he turned and peered back at the pursuing boats, wordlessly drawing his sidearm. The distance to the closest ship's mast was around a hundred yards away, which Talbot thought was really stretching the range of the handgun. Maybe they should wait until they were closer, surely that would be smarter.

Wes calmly chambered a round by pulling back the slide and releasing it with a snap….

He rested his forearms on the railing of the ship to steady his aim….

Sighted his target….

And finally squeezed the trigger.

Talbot's gaze shot toward the longship just in time to see the bullet hit the side of the single mast and ricochet down to smack one of the warriors straight in the forehead, dropping him silently. None of the other warriors reacted.

"You missed!" shouted Talbot incredulously.

"Yeah, er… that was a practice shot, mate."

The warrior on the Aesir ship did not rise again. None of his companions gave the slightest indication they had noticed him getting killed. It was like a force of zombies.

Wes didn't mess around with his second shot. With a crack it echoed out across the water and Talbot could almost *see* the bullet fly straight toward its target – the large metal lantern halfway up the mast.

Being early morning, the lantern wasn't lit, but it was still full of highly flammable oil. It shattered as the bullet impacted, oil pouring down the timber mast, a spark from the bullet hitting the metal lantern and igniting the liquid. Within seconds the mast was on fire, the flames catching swiftly and hungrily feeding upon the wood.

The conflagration leaped to nearby crewmembers, who caught fire like kindling. Standing shoulder to shoulder as they were, the blaze crawled from warrior to warrior until the entire deck blazed, alight with human candles. No screams rang out across the glassy water, and the scene was somehow more sinister as a result.

Aboard the Viking ship, all eyes were fixed upon the burning vessel. Aghast expressions reflected the horror Talbot felt in his own heart at witnessing such an act, surprising upon the faces of hardened warriors. These were men used to slaying one another in battle, but what they now saw wasn't war, it was carnage. Soon the entire longship was engulfed in flames and swiftly came to a halt in the water.

"We are releasing them!" shouted Biaver suddenly. "They are bewitched by the Aesir and death is the only succor we can give them!" He saw some of the expressions become firmer as a result of his words, and others of the warriors nodded, but the women still quietly wept at the sight of helpless men being cooked alive.

Throughout the entire action, however, not one person had ceased rowing. Their distance from the other ships was still narrowing, but their pace was constant. Talbot saw Wes looking around, searching for something. Their eyes met.

"I can't do that again, mate," called Wes.

"I understand," replied Talbot, understanding the guilt the

warrior must be feeling.

Wes looked confused for a moment, and then shook his head. "What I mean is I can't replicate that shot. That thing was a miracle, and I can't believe it happened."

"Then what can we do?"

"Buggered if I know. I was hoping they might get scared off by my magic like these boys initially were. But if these goons are gonna just stand there and get cooked, there's no way a couple of dead guys will freak them out. I mean, you saw their reaction – or rather, their *lack* of reaction."

Talbot stared at the three remaining pursuers. Soon they would draw alongside the Norse longboat, and then the slaughter would begin. It didn't matter that they were like zombies; weight of numbers would see the Vikings killed within seconds, Wes and Talbot among them.

"I don't –" began Talbot, but cut himself off as a monstrous head broke the surface of the water far behind the Aesir longships. "What the hell is that?"

Wes spun around, looking behind, but now the head was gone, dipped beneath the surface once more. "What are you talking about?"

Talbot scanned the waters again, this time spotting the head breaching the surface behind the Aesir longships off to their left. "There!" he yelled, pointing.

At that precise moment, when Talbot was totally distracted by the serpentine head, his oar, propelled by Helga the Norse giantess, smacked Talbot straight in the jaw. The impact propelled him backward off the bench seat with his legs straight up in the air.

And Talbot sank into oblivion....

***

Wes heard the wet smack as the oar smashed into Talbot's face and the resulting thud as he crashed to the deck. He shook his head and chuckled softly, but didn't stop scanning the waters for sign of whatever it had been Talbot was so excited about. He peered beyond the longships following them, over to the left where Talbot had been gazing –

Holy shit!

It dipped back beneath the calm waters, but not before Wes got a glance of a domed cranium, covered in scales, which glinted in the early morning sunlight.

"Hey, Biaver, this lake isn't called Loch Ness, is it?"

The leader of the Vikings glanced at him oddly. "It is not a lake, it is –"

"I'll take that as a no," cut in Wes. The Aesir longships were only about sixty yards away now and swiftly closing; he had to think of something fast.

"Like I was saying, this body of water is known as Hvergelmir," said Biaver persistently, his beating of the drum remaining constant. "It is not a lake. It joins with the ocean many miles away."

"Are there any giant creatures which don't normally occur in nature swimming around in here?"

"What did you see?" Biaver's beating of the drum faltered slightly.

"Something broke the surface behind the Aesir longships. I didn't get a good look at it, but I think –"

Biaver cut him off. "Was it the head of a serpent? Enormous, like the giant fish we sometimes see in the deeper ocean, the ones spraying water?"

"Er, yeah, I guess. What is it?"

"Nidhogg," Biaver mumbled, his drum forgotten. The rowers carried on regardless.

"What the fuck is a nidhogg?" urged Wes, his eyes once more scanning the water.

"It is the worm which chews on the roots of Yggdrasill, the World Tree that supports all of creation."

"Well, of course it does. But the thing I saw looked more like a giant snake or dragon than a worm. I mean, I've seen worms. I'm not scared of worms. The thing I saw made me pee a little bit. It looked like a smaller version of Jörmungandr."

"You have seen Jörmungandr?"

"Yeah, I kicked his arse. But what can you tell me about this thing? Is it the nidhogg?"

"I have never seen the nidhogg, but that is the only thing it could be. This is the first sign that Ragnarok approaches," murmured Biaver, his voice barely above a whisper.

"That's fantastic. Maybe you should start playing your drum again so these guys don't completely fuck up." Wes indicated the rowers, who had started to lose their rhythm. Biaver resumed his drum strokes, somewhat faster now.

Wes scanned the water, searching for the faintest ripple, the tiniest indication of where this new menace might be. The giant head had disappeared once more beneath the waters of the Hvergelmir, but Wes's trepidation remained. In fact, it had more than doubled since Talbot had been –

Shit! Talbot!

He spun around and saw Talbot finally recovering consciousness, being nursed by the hot Viking girl he'd been ogling earlier. Well, he wouldn't be much use in the approaching confrontation.

Wes hefted his .45. He stared at the seemingly tiny gun.

We're screwed.

Without warning, an enormous serpentine creature burst forth from the tranquil surface of the Hvergelmir, like a moray eel surging up from a bathtub. A moray eel the size of two jumbo jets lined up nose to tail.

The scaled skin of the creature was jet black, tapering at the end into a giant fin-like tail similar to that of an eel. The head was the size of a Volkswagen Beetle, sleek and tapering smoothly into its neck while the horrifying jaws revealed jagged teeth the size of baseball bats.

Okay. So that's a nidhogg, thought Wes. *Fair enough.*

The nidhogg soared high into the sky, almost its entire length extending from the water and blocking out the early morning sun for just a moment. Crashing down on top of....

The Aesir!

The nidhogg smashed into the centermost Aesir longship, snapping it like a matchstick and dragging it, along with its seventy or so mindless crewmembers, beneath the surface of the water. The entire incident took only a second, but everyone on the Viking vessel – already facing backward on their rowing benches – saw it and froze.

The Aesir longships, however, did not.

Whatever macabre machinery drove the Aesir longships through the water silently continued pushing them toward the rapidly slowing Norse longship. The Aesir ships were now perhaps only thirty yards away. Wes shouted for the Vikings to keep rowing, and Biaver took up his drum once more, which he had dropped and forgotten completely upon seeing the nidhogg.

Wes aimed his .45 at the closest ship, trying to replicate the miraculous shot he had pulled off moments ago, but the bullet merely shattered the unlit lantern which dropped uselessly to the deck below without igniting. Checking his magazine, Wes realized he only had six rounds left.

Not enough to take down a gigantic worm.

The nidhogg heaved out of the water again, smashing directly up from beneath the next Aesir longship, lifting it high into the air, its huge jaws holding the vessel aloft momentarily, then snapping shut and crushing the boat in two. Just before the huge beast crashed down, Wes saw what appeared to be membranous wings folded flat to the nidhogg's body. Time froze, and for a moment Wes imagined the beast in full flight, like an airborne snake.

Both halves of the Aesir longboat fell, crashing to the water along with the nidhogg, a great wave exploding outward as they simultaneously struck the surface.

Wes stared in astonishment at the heaving wall of rolling water. The first time the nidhogg had landed, the wave had been more suppressed. This time, however, the surge was huge, perhaps because of the added force of the falling Aesir longship. Whatever it was, they were now facing a wall of water stretching almost as high as the tip of their mast.

"Brace yourselves!" he yelled, and at a barked order from Biaver all oars were lifted from the water. The wave came at them from the stern of their boat, lifting them high and heaving the longship forward like a surfboard. The remaining Aesir craft was not so lucky.

The wave emanated out in a ring, smacking into the side of their vessel which rolled like a log, instantly capsizing.

Wes's last sight before the wave lifted them out of view was of the Aesir warriors sinking into the dark water, not even trying to save themselves as their armor dragged them down like stones into the inky depths.

*   *   *

Talbot came out of his semi-conscious delirium to gaze up at the face of the most gorgeous creature he'd ever seen. It was the same girl he'd been gawping at when he'd first climbed aboard the longship, but she wasn't paying attention to him; she was looking beyond the stern of the vessel. A part of Talbot yearned to see what she was peering at so intently, but the greater part of him wanted nothing more than to rest against her breasts forever.

"Hey," growled Helga at the woman. "Your baby is awake." He snapped his gaze over toward her and the large woman chuckled darkly before gazing beyond the stern also. It was only then that Talbot realized the longship had stopped and all the oars were sitting out of the water. The drum was silent.

"What –?" He almost swallowed his tongue as the beautiful young Norse woman peered down at him intently. "What's going on?" he breathed.

"It's a miracle," she replied, her voice sounding like the tinkling of a crystal wind chime. Her delicate arm lifted, indicating he should look.

Despite an intense desire to remain where he was, Talbot stood unsteadily on the rocking deck of the longship. He followed the direction of the girl's pointing finger, and his jaw dropped.

The remaining Aesir ships were gone, only scattered debris marking the water where they'd previously been.

"Why the hell are we just sitting here?" roared Wes, and suddenly everyone sprang into action. The drum beat sounded out, strong and steady, and the rowers began to haul away on their oars. Something huge had obviously just happened and, with the pretty young lady scampering back to her place in the boat, Talbot looked for a source of information.

Firstly he glanced at Helga, hefting the huge oar more easily on her own than when he'd been hindering her. She frowned at Talbot, and he grimaced. He doubted she would be too helpful.

Skipping between the benches as lithely as he could, Talbot hopped back to Wes, who was still standing at the very rear of the longship, staring over the railing into the water, his .45 clenched tight in his right hand.

"So, you finally woke up," said Wes without turning. "You missed all the fun." Behind the jovial words, Talbot sensed a tension in Wes he'd only ever seen when combat was close.

"What happened?"

"We met the nidhogg. It's a big hundred and fifty foot worm which looks like a snake that humped a dragon. The bastard tore through those Aesir ships like they were tissue paper. I only have six .45 caliber bullets with which to kill it. Any suggestions?"

"Oh shit," muttered Talbot.

"That pretty much sums up the situation." Wes's eyes never moved from the water, scanning back and forth for any sign of movement from the murky depths.

"We have to make for the shore," suggested Talbot.

"No shit."

Talbot looked around and saw that the helmsman had now aimed the longship for the closest point of land, which still sat around a hundred yards away. Nervously, Talbot began to scan the water alongside Wes.

"Do you want to hump my leg as well?" asked Wes calmly.

"What can we do?"

"Don't panic, and try not to get eaten."

The commando's casual attitude exerted its usual affect on Talbot, and he gradually began to unwind. Wes was tense, but composed, and this always gave Talbot confidence. He was sure that, deep inside, Wes felt something akin to fear, but the commando kept it so well controlled that Talbot always drew reassurance from his attitude.

Moving to the other side of the longship, Talbot once again scanned the waters surrounding the vessel. The liquid was dark and gloomy, and he was unable to see more than a few feet down. Glancing back toward the bank, Talbot realized they had covered at least a third of the distance, and began to feel his pulse slow even more. After all, whatever it was couldn't be worse than anything he had seen in Tartarus or Olympia, or even the things he'd witnessed which had broken through to Earth. No, nothing could be worse than what he had already seen.

Talbot returned his gaze to the water... and his heart froze.

Cruising along a few feet beneath the surface was the creature Wes had just described. It was gliding on such an angle that its right eye was staring directly at Talbot, burning into him. Talbot made to yell out to Wes, but the nidhogg did something which instantly stopped him.

It winked.

Talbot hadn't imagined it. The enormous beast had pulled slightly closer had calmly lifted its head, breaching the surface slightly as it did so. The dinner plate-sized eyelid had flicked closed momentarily in an exact imitation of a human wink.

The strangeness of the moment caused Talbot to pause. The beast was not acting maliciously toward them... yet... but if he acted rashly – perhaps by calling out to Wes – the moment might be broken, and the nidhogg could attack them. Talbot held the gaze of the horrific creature, staring deep into its eye. The orb appeared to contain a great deal more than bestial cunning; more akin to intelligence. Talbot sensed this beast was different from those he had faced before; there was something less feral in the look it gave him, something much deeper.

He glanced away for only a moment to check how close they were to the shore, quickly flicking his gaze back to the underwater behemoth –

But it was gone.

There was no whisper of movement, not the slightest ripple; the massive creature had simply disappeared into the murky depths, leaving behind less evidence of its presence than a goldfish.

Talbot stumbled as swiftly as he could across the stern of the longship, clumsily navigating his way past the helmsman with his enormous steering oar, making his way over to Wes. Swiftly and without embellishment, Talbot told his companion about encountering the beast.

"You should have called me!" growled Wes, smoothly moving across to the opposite railing. Talbot followed him, somewhat more awkwardly.

"I would have risked upsetting the creature if I had," argued Talbot. "And there was something else." Talbot rapidly explained what had happened.

"So the fish-eel-dragon-snake thing winked at you? When are you guys going to set a date?"

"For what?" asked Talbot.

"For the wedding," snapped Wes. "Seriously, are you totally fucking stupid? That thing just tore through those Aesir ships without thought –"

"What if it *was* thinking, though? What if it's on our side?"

"What if it was Prometheus?" retorted Wes.

Talbot froze. He hadn't thought of that, and it made more sense than anything else. But....

"Could Prometheus make himself that big?" he asked.

"He didn't seem to have a problem turning into that giant dragon. What did he call himself? Fartner?"

"Fafnir?" suggested Talbot.

"That's the one. Well, Prometheus had no problem turning himself into Fafnir, did he? And that was one big motherfucker of a dragon, kind of looked a bit like that lizard-worm thing too. We simply can't trust anything or anyone on this, Talbot. That bastard already fooled us once posing as Poseidon; what's to say he won't do it again for shits and giggles?"

"For *what?*"

"Shits and.... It's a saying. It means he might just like messing with us because he can."

There was a possibility – a pretty strong possibility – that Prometheus had been the nidhogg. But even if he weren't, chances were the creature was doing what it did for its own reasons. They had no means to ascertain what those reasons might be.

The longship beached upon the shore, sliding up the sand with the momentum of the rowers. Immediately, warriors were leaping overboard to drag the vessel further onto the bank. Talbot turned to Wes, but the commando was already over the side, hauling on a rope.

"Damn it," murmured Talbot. "My boots were just starting to dry."

"You can stay up here with the women and children, if you like," bellowed the hoarse voice of the woman Wes had referred to as Helga. "Svetlana's goat will keep you warm while the real men work."

Talbot burned with embarrassment as the laughter of the Norse women echoed across the ship. The only one not joining in their mirth was the pretty girl who had nursed him after he'd injured himself. This memory in itself made his cheeks burn. In a society where strength was revered, Talbot had twice fallen short of the mark. He grimaced and moved swiftly to the railing of the longship, vaulting over it in a single graceful movement –

Landing directly on one of the Viking warriors.

Both men crashed into the water, Talbot coming up spluttering and wiping the salt water from his eyes. The warrior, a towering Norseman standing a good six inches beyond six-feet-tall, his red beard virtually bristling with wrath, surfaced a second later, fury burning in his startling blue eyes. He grasped Talbot by the tunic with his left hand and drew his right fist back to smash him in the face.

"Don't do that, buddy," sounded the casual voice of Wes, cutting through the commotion.

The Norseman looked over at him and scowled. "Your companion is a fool."

"Yeah, but he's *my* fool, and if you hurt him that means I'll have to repay you in kind. I don't think you want that, do you?"

The Viking released Talbot with a shove, and he fell back into the water. When he resurfaced, he saw the huge Norseman moving through the thigh-high water toward Wes. The commando stood casually, waiting.

"Wait!" yelled Talbot, scrambling to get his legs under him.

"What is it, you blundering fool?" growled the Norseman.

"I don't want anyone to get hurt because I made a mistake. Settle this with me instead. Wes, I forbid you to intervene."

"You *forbid* me?" Wes raised an eyebrow at him. "What the fuck…?"

"That's right," replied Talbot, hoping Wes understood how important this was. He had to regain some sort of respect if he were to travel with these warriors. These were a people who thrived on violence and masculinity. If they thought he were less than a man, they wouldn't listen to a thing he told them. And he needed to put a stop to it now, before things got any worse. Wes raised his hands in the air in a submissive motion, and the Norseman turned back to Talbot, striding through the water toward him.

Talbot had one chance, one card he could play in order to gain a modicum of respect from these warriors. He'd never been in a fistfight before, despite all the action he had seen with Wes, and he just hoped he didn't totally screw this up.

Stumbling upon hidden rocks within the churned-up water, Talbot backed away from the Viking and up onto the stony beach, kicking his sodden boots off and away as he did. The rest of the Norsemen also exited the water, several chuckling. The railing of the longship thronged with the Norsewomen. His nerves fluttered anew.

God he hoped this worked.

His opponent moved toward him, and Talbot raised his arms directly out from his sides, lifting his left knee into the air. Beyond the warrior, he saw Wes staring incredulously before covering his face with a hand and shaking his head, but Talbot was already committed. The warrior looked at him quizzically, wondering at this strange behavior. Seconds passed and the Norseman shrugged it aside, charging at Talbot with a murderous bellow.

And Talbot struck!

His left foot shot down as his right came thundering up, smacking the Viking directly in the nose and… and….

Had absolutely no effect at all.

The only reaction from his opponent was to pause and stare at Talbot with a disbelieving expression which seemed to say: *What the hell are you doing?*

Oh boy.

The warrior's fist thundered toward Talbot. He instinctively ducked out of the way, pushing the warrior back from him. The giant man overbalanced and tripped, falling face first…

… colliding with the only large protruding rock on the entire beach!

Talbot stared, amazed as the behemoth rolled and tried to rise to his feet once more, his strength suddenly giving out. He slumped back on the sand, blood running from a large gash in his forehead.

Holy shit!

Talbot glanced around, seeing astonished reactions reflected upon the faces of each and every warrior on the beach. Wes was openly laughing, and strolled across the sand to where he stood.

"The crane? That was the best you could come up with; the fucking crane? Does that make me Mister Miyagi? How the hell do you manage to survive tying your shoes each morning, man? It's a damn miracle, I tell ya."

"What was I supposed to do?" Talbot gasped.

Wes was holding his side. "Oh man, it hurts to laugh that much. What were you supposed to do? I don't know, but I never imagined the one person you would try to emulate would be Daniel-san. Who next? Fonzie?"

"It got the job done." Talbot glanced back at his opponent, watching his compatriots assist his unsteady rise to his feet.

"All jokes aside, you did well," said Wes, wiping tears from his face. "It had to be done, otherwise these guys would have never had any respect for you. You had to stick up for yourself… by smacking that guy in the face with the most useless martial arts move of all time!" Wes's laughter rang out once more, echoing off the nearby hill. "Why not Jackie Chan? Bruce Lee? Jet Li? No, you had to go for Daniel-san, and the crane. 'Hiyaaa!'" Wes replicated the stance, kicking his foot up into the air and laughing some more.

"We can't all be bad asses like you, Wes," said Talbot, his mouth spreading in a grin.

"You proved that today, buddy." Wes threw an arm companionably around Talbot's shoulders. "Now let's go and make peace with this big bastard before he realizes what just happened."

The two marched across the beach, unaware of the eyes staring down at them from the cliff above.

CHAPTER 7

A huge boulder crashed down, smashing into the middle of the camp, sending warriors sprinting for cover as they drew their weapons.

"What the hell was that?" gasped Talbot after diving behind a small outcrop of rocks alongside Wes.

Wes ignored him, peeking around the edge of their cover and searching for whatever was attacking them. It wasn't too hard, their assailant stood directly opposite them, not hiding at all, out in the open atop the edge of a nearby cliff.

"Somebody opened up a jar of ugly," he muttered.

Talbot looked around the opposite side of their cover and gasped. The thing that had thrown the Volkswagen-sized boulder was enormous, quite possibly the most hideous beast he'd ever seen. He heard a gasp from his left and saw Biaver also staring at the creature.

"It is a jarnvidjur!" gasped the Norseman. He turned and saw the incomprehension upon Talbot's face. "A woman troll!"

The jarnvidjur was large – almost four times the height of a normal man – though still small when Talbot compared it to the giants he and Wes had fought in Olympia. She stood on two legs like a human being, but that was possibly the only thing even remotely human about the jarnvidjur's appearance. All across the corpse-gray skin were huge weeping pustules which dribbled green ooze like horrendous acne. Naked and rotund, nothing denoted its sex apart from the huge drooping breasts – all four of them – which sagged down toward the ground like over-milked udders.

And then there was the face.

Talbot had seen piles of manure more attractive than the grossly deformed features of the jarnvidjur. Two long curving horns sprouted where the ears should have been, tiny ears sitting lower as a result, somewhere in line with the bottom of the thing's undershot jaw. Owing to the undersized jaw, the upper teeth seemed like a gross overbite, and were sharpened like fangs. Two vertical slashes flapped where the creature's nose should have been, crowned by jaundiced, beady eyes which blazed with rage.

"WHERE IS THE TRAITOR?" roared the beast in a surprisingly feminine voice. "WHERE IS THE ONE NAMED WES?"

"Well, that's interesting," muttered Wes.

"What are you going to do?" asked Talbot.

Wes grinned mischievously. "I reckon I'd better go and say g'day."

"Wes, no!" But it was already too late.

Wes strode directly into the center of the open area and leaned against the huge boulder the jarnvidjur had just hurled. The creature stared at him balefully, seemingly unsure of how to react to such boldness.

"Hey sexy," called Wes smoothly. "What's cooking?"

"YOU!" the jarnvidjur hissed. "How dare you act so casually after all you have done? I smelled your corruption the moment you set foot in Jarnvid."

Talbot shot a quizzical glance at Biaver who hurriedly whispered, "It is the name of this place. It means 'Iron Wood'" Talbot nodded silently.

"And what have I done, baby?" Wes asked the jarnvidjur loudly.

"You have betrayed all of the Vanir!" spat the creature.

"How so?"

"You have allied yourself with the Aesir after befriending us and learning the secret of our defenses! I have come for you, and will laugh as I eat your heart!"

Wes nodded calmly before turning his head and looking at Talbot. "Fucking Prometheus."

Talbot swore softly, rising to his feet, and stepping into the open to stand beside Wes, albeit much less casually. He stared at the huge rock the jarnvidjur had thrown and imagined such a thing landing on top of him; would he even feel it? He shook the nasty thought away.

"Who are you?" hissed the jarnvidjur.

"M-my name's Talbot, Talbot Harrison. What's your name?" He cursed to himself; a creature like this probably didn't even have a name.

The jarnvidjur appeared shocked by the question, and at first Talbot thought it would simply ignore him.

"My name… is… Barktooth," she finally replied, her voice slightly smaller than before.

"Well, Barktooth," began Talbot, unsure of how to proceed. "I can assure you that Wes is no traitor. I believe it was a Titan named Prometheus –"

"DO NOT SPEAK THAT NAME TO ME!!!"

"Okay…. Anyway, the one I was talking about can shape-shift into whatever form he likes. We've been battling him for a long time, and I think he might have disguised himself as Wes in order to trick you."

Barktooth sniffed the air, breathing in deeply through the two slits which served as its nostrils.

"His scent is the same," she hissed, though Talbot thought he detected a note of uncertainty in her tone.

"But…?"

The huge creature swayed its head from side to side in a bestial display of confusion. "This scent seems… cleaner. There is not as much corruption."

"Maybe Prome – I mean, maybe the traitor can alter his own scent. Is that possible?" asked Talbot, his hopes rising.

The jarnvidjur peered down at him, her gaze unreadable. "You will come with me to meet with Fenrir. He will know what to do with you."

It was not a request.

Talbot glanced at Wes who simply shrugged. "Who's afraid of the big bad wolf?" he said with a sly grin. "Nice work, by the way. You really managed to get us out of that shit quite well. I'm just glad you didn't resort to using the crane again. I mean, we don't want to kill the poor thing, do we?"

Talbot shook his head savagely and stalked off toward the jarnvidjur, a sudden burst of combined anger and embarrassment pushing aside any trepidation he might have. Wes's laughter echoed up the narrow path as he went.

Stupid Australian.

***

They crested the hill, and Talbot sucked in a huge gulp of air. The entire group had been following Barktooth for over an hour, and he'd found out the hard way how swift a pace the jarnvidjur could maintain over the rough terrain. Even the hardened Norse warriors were struggling to keep up, with only Wes able to maintain the pace without great effort.

Talbot looked over the group quickly, his mind wandering....

Upon reaching the decision for his warriors to follow Barktooth, Biaver had declared the greater part of the villagers would make camp in the caves near the bottom of the mountain. He had left a token force of six Norsemen to protect the fifty or so women and children while the rest had swiftly grouped together and followed Barktooth.

The surprising thing was the inclusion of the woman Wes had called Helga in the group of warriors. Actually, she hadn't really been included, but had merely joined them, and apart from a few odd glances between the warriors as she strapped on a Viking sword, hefting a shield and fastening it to her back, nothing was said. Talbot got the impression many of the men were too scared to refuse her.

He could understand why.

"What is her name?" muttered Talbot to one of the nearby warriors.

"My name is Tonna!" barked the huge woman from across the rallying point, the muscles of her forearm bulging as she tightened her sword belt.

"Nice hearing you've got there, Tonna," Wes had said with a sly grin. She'd glared at him harshly. "Man, are my balls still there after that look?" Wes had asked him.

Talbot knew better than to look around. A second later Wes was chuckling again as he refastened the button fly of his camouflage fatigues. "It's okay! Everything's still gigantic. You can relax, Talbot."

"Thank goodness for that."

"Look, just because your girlfriend's staying behind is no reason to get upset."

"She is not my girlfriend," snapped Talbot, rather more defensively than he'd meant to.

"I meant to ask you before," said Wes, suddenly seeming serious. "Whatever happened to that pretty thing you told me about when we were in Olympia. You know, the one you were going to tell you loved."

Talbot frowned. "I did. And she didn't."

"Ouch! That's really weird, though."

"What's weird?"

"That Zoe chick, the one who claimed to be your daughter," began Wes.

"You mean the one who fooled you into thinking twenty years had gone past?"

Wes snapped a worried glance around, making sure nobody else had heard. "Keep your voice down, that's embarrassing," he hissed.

"As embarrassing as what you just said about that Norse girl?"

"Good point," agreed Wes. "Anyway, Zoe knew about your liking that woman you worked with – Suzanna, wasn't it?"

Talbot nodded silently.

"How the hell could she know something like that? Only you and I knew about it, unless you had another confidant I don't know about. I thought we had a really special moment there." Talbot shook his head, his mind furiously trying to understand who this young woman claiming to be his daughter could be.

Standing at the crest of the mountain trail, Talbot felt a sharp whack on his butt, jolting him out of his reverie.

"Snap out of it, sunshine," said Wes, skipping down the trail in front of him.

Talbot grinned despite himself at Wes's childish behavior. It was always the same; the commando could make any situation seem more bearable, no matter how unbelievable it was. There was very little that appeared to cause him concern.

His boyish charm had yet to erode the mistrust of Barktooth, though.

The enormous jarnvidjur, what the Vikings referred to as a female troll, growled throatily and bared her teeth whenever Wes came close, and Talbot feared the unspoken truce between the two would cease at any moment. Wes seemed unconcerned, however, and would often throw a random question at the creature as though they were old friends.

"Tell me, Barktooth, is there a *Mister* Barktooth waiting for you back at the swamp?" Wes had inquired at one point, and Talbot was sure even the seemingly invincible Wes would be finished for good.

Barktooth had growled and snarled at him, saying several things even Talbot, with the talent of the Elder-tongue, could not understand, but she had not attacked.

"Very interesting," Wes had whispered moments later, ensuring they were far enough back to escape the jarnvidjur's highly tuned hearing. "It appears our swollen guide might not be allowed to attack me."

"Why would that be?"

"Why indeed?" mused Wes cryptically.

Talbot paused, gasping at the majestic view laid out before him. The climb up the mountain trail had been hard, but this almost made up for it… until he remembered they were on their way to meet a giant wolf more likely to kill them than listen to them.

Shaking his head softly, Talbot moved down the narrow trail, following the giant gray-skinned beast who was possibly leading them to their doom.

As he walked, his thoughts turned to Fenrir. Being an archeologist, Talbot had studied several aspects of mythology, but mainly things relating to architecture or items from a specific time period. These were an archeologist's bread and butter. He might study historical texts for hours, but in the end it was the buildings and artifacts which truly drove him on. From these things he was often able to discern what a people were like, what their lives revolved around. The problem he now had was there was not much archeological evidence leading back to Fenrir, and as such he knew very little about him. What he could remember was hazy and obscure.

He recalled reading somewhere that Fenrir had been birthed by a giant woman named Angerboda. His father had been Loki; described as both prankster and the Norse god of fire. Even taking into account the way a story could be twisted and misinterpreted over time, the pairing still seemed an odd choice for parentage. This had been the reason it had stuck in Talbot's head; he remembered wondering at the time how such a strange union and birthing could have ever been considered plausible. A god and a giantess have sex and nine months later a giant talking wolf pops out? Seriously?

But that had been in a more naive time for Talbot, an era before he knew the truth, at least partially, of the universe. The topic of Fenrir's birthing was not really the issue now, nor was his ability to speak. The main question was: what was Fenrir going to do when confronted with Wes, a man he had already claimed was his enemy?

Talbot had seen Wes bluff and cajole his way out of virtually impossible situations before, and when all else failed, the guy was seemingly invincible, so Talbot would never underestimate his skills, but this task seemed beyond even Wes's impressive range of abilities. How the hell could he fight a giant wolf – and Barktooth also, in all likelihood, along with who knew what host of other beasts – with only six bullets? He doubted any of the Viking weapons would do any damage to these creatures, so in all likelihood they were screwed.

He looked at Wes and chuckled.

Somehow, Talbot could picture the commando strolling into Hell itself just to ask someone to light a cigar. He'd probably saunter out moments later, his hair smoldering a bit, puffing on a Cuban, and making suggestive comments about the phallic symbolism. The guy was, for want of a better description, a freak.

Talbot looked ahead and saw the silhouette of what appeared to be an enormous hound on the opposite hill, off in the distance, its form outlined by the sinking sun. It might have been a crop of trees or an obscure rock formation, but somehow Talbot didn't think so.

Fenrir the Wolf was waiting for them, and Talbot felt his heart hammering with the unknown prospect of how the wolf would receive news that the man he had already labeled his enemy was walking directly into his den.

***

Talbot followed the immense figure of Barktooth through the ranks of both humans and non-humans, filled with apprehension. He avoided looking directly at any of the strange creatures which emerged from the thick forest on either side of them; creatures that came to see who dared approach their camp. Instead, Talbot walked with Wes straight down the middle, attempting to mimic the commando's straight-backed stance and confident forward glare. Still, every now and then, Talbot caught a glimpse of what looked like either incredibly stocky children or very short men lingering just within the tree line. He wasn't game enough to turn, though, lest his stride falter.

Biaver's Viking warriors had initially been refused admission to the camp, and only through some slick negotiation did Barktooth begrudgingly allow them to enter the grove. Part of Talbot wished they'd all been forced to remain behind, and felt his hackles rise as they walked through the camp.

"Whatever happens," Wes murmured to him, "don't let them see your fear. No matter what occurs in this place, stay strong!"

Talbot nodded silently and slipped his meanest sneer onto his face.

"What's that? Are you constipated?" asked Wes softly. "I said stay strong, not look like you're busting for a fart."

"This is my mean look."

"Wow. You're almost as terrifying as a puppy covered in soap bubbles."

"Well how am I supposed to look?" whispered Talbot.

"Just try to come across like yourself – *without* the strained look you get when you're scared."

"What strained look?" asked Talbot, dropping his expression.

"The one you've got on your face right now," replied Wes without looking at him.

Talbot gave up trying, and merely stared forward impassively. A huge cave opened ahead of them, and he felt his heart begin to hammer, but remembering Wes's advice, he ignored it, forcing the fear away. A deep, throaty growl reverberated from the shadows of the cave, and Talbot heard the nervous rattle of the warriors behind them reaching for weapons, but at a hissed order from Biaver they stopped.

"Wait here," Wes ordered the Norsemen. "This is something Talbot and I have to do alone." They gratefully complied.

Wes and Talbot followed Barktooth to the mouth of the cave, and once there, she waved them inside. Another growl echoed from out of the darkness. Talbot glanced nervously at Wes, who beamed one of his mischievous grins – the type which always made Talbot's stomach drop in fear –as he stepped into the darkness.

Damn.

Talbot moved into the shadowy cave, stumbling through the dim light and scenting the faint odor of mildew. A hidden rock smashed into his shin and shards of pain shot through his right leg. He cursed loudly.

The next instant a hand was clamped over his mouth, and Wes was hissing in his ear. "Understand this," whispered Wes urgently. "The thing in this cave will, in all likelihood, already be upset about us being here. If you carry on like a stupid schoolgirl it'll probably piss him off even more."

"Sorry," mumbled Talbot.

"Do not be sorry," rumbled a throaty voice from further down the echoing cavern. "Come around the corner so I may see you both."

Talbot tried to choke down his heart, which had leaped to his throat upon hearing the deep voice. He followed the sound of Wes's faint footsteps through the dark cavern. It was a long grotto, and as the voice had promised, they soon came to a bend in the natural rock formation.

They crept around the corner –

– and were abruptly bathed in a light so bright Talbot found himself unable to see, forcing him to squeeze his eyes shut. Hearing Wes cursing beside him, he guessed the same had happened to him. Talbot instinctively crouched low to the ground, and heard Wes do the same, but the commando seemed to be shuffling around on the floor of the cave, searching for the way back.

"There is no retreat from this room," stated the loud, raspy voice they'd heard moments before. "The exits are now sealed, and you are trapped." Talbot ceased hearing Wes's movements.

"What do you want?" asked Wes.

"I want to know if you are a threat to my people. Your previous actions – or the actions of the one you claim was Prometheus in your guise – almost destroyed us. I will not allow such a thing to happen again."

"Are you Fenrir?" asked Wes.

"I am known by many names, but yes, that is one of them."

"Are you the same Fenrir who appeared in our world; the giant wolf who tore apart the White House, and then snacked on a gryphon like it was a bucket of KFC?"

"I have no idea what those references are, but yes, it was I who visited and threatened you on your home world."

"How did you travel forward through time? It's not possible," asked Wes.

The brightness shut off with such suddenness Talbot was temporarily stunned. He slowly opened his eyes and saw the cavern was now bathed in a much more comfortable glow. Yet to call this place a cavern was a travesty; the room might have been carved from natural rock, but the walls, ceiling and floor were smooth, polished like granite.

Benches and shelving traced three of the walls, taking their shape from the natural rock, cut directly into the stone. A simple table adorned the center of the room, behind which was seated a man. Spinning around, Talbot saw a smooth rock panel had slid into place where the entrance had been, sealing the room. He quickly looked back to where the man was sitting.

"Who the fuck are you?" growled Wes. Talbot flicked a glance at the commando and saw he had his .45 out and trained on the mysterious stranger.

"I am Fenrir."

Talbot studied the stranger. He appeared around thirty years old, and seemed normal enough, although perhaps too neat considering the era, even to the point of being fastidious, especially when compared to the Vikings accompanying them. Yet on closer inspection there seemed something... feral... about the stranger, an untamed quality within the man, beneath the shoulder-length silver hair and eyes the color of ash. He wore a simple loose tunic of gray belted at the waist and dark gray pants.

"Bullshit!" snapped Wes. "I saw Fenrir. He's a wolf the size of an elephant that pops in and out of existence – when not threatening me, that is."

"You aren't the same," mused the stranger calmly, ignoring Wes's statement. "I had thought there was something different about you when we met in your time, but was distracted by that flying creature. What did you call it? A gryphon? Amazing beast. Are they common in your time?"

"Are you shitting me?"

"No, I am not shitting on you. That would be disgusting."

"I meant, are you kidding? You know, joking?" said Wes.

"Not that I know of," replied the stranger, steepling his fingers and peering intently at Wes. "But that is all beside the point. It seems I have been fooled by another, and I think you know who I'm referring to."

"Prometheus," said Talbot. Suddenly the frosty eyes of the man who had named himself Fenrir turned on Talbot with piercing power. A low growl sounded.

"It appears you both have knowledge of the traitor to whom I refer. And who are you?"

"I'm Talbot – Talbot Harrison. I'm the one with the Elder-tongue," replied Talbot awkwardly.

"Of course you are."

Talbot glanced over at Wes, who gave a curt nod, reminding him of their earlier conversation about not showing fear.

"So who the hell are you really?" snarled Talbot, more harshly than he'd intended in his attempt to compensate for his previous awkwardness.

The seated man smiled slightly and raised an eyebrow. "I see a bit of a lesson is required for you both to believe me, please have a seat."

The floor beside both Wes and Talbot shifted and thrust upwards, like a finger pushing through a balloon. But this floor wasn't rubber; it was granite. Within a second, the stone floor had re-shifted into two chairs complete with high-backs and arm-rests.

"Nice trick," said Wes casually, sitting down and crossing his legs. Talbot followed his lead and took a seat. The granite chair wasn't hard as he'd expected, it was actually quite comfortable. The oddity of this place just kept increasing.

"So what's going on?" asked Wes.

Fenrir stared hard at him as though appraising his ability to accept what he had to say. "Prometheus isn't what you think he is," he finally said.

"What do you mean?"

"I mean he isn't one of the Titans."

The enormity of the statement almost made even Wes's controlled expression crack. Talbot simply gaped at Fenrir in amazement.

"What is he then?" Talbot asked.

Fenrir turned his icy expression toward Talbot. "He is one of my kind; one of the Vanir. He fled over a decade ago after betraying us. He branched off, with his many followers, founding the race known as the Aesir. Prometheus has always been planning to claim dominion of our home world, a land called Vanaheim. We have been battling with the Aesir ever since, and that war has overflowed into this world."

"Is that why Prometheus can change his shape?" asked Wes.

The enormity of Wes's question hit Talbot like a bomb, and he wondered how he hadn't put the pieces of it together himself. If

Fenrir was of the same race as Prometheus, maybe this was why Prometheus was so invulnerable, and perhaps Fenrir would know of a way to finally kill their enemy.

"Well, what about it?" persisted Wes.

Fenrir sighed. "My race, the Vanir, learned long ago how to manipulate matter. We can restructure the molecules of an object, and remold it into any shape or design we wish; much as I did when creating the chairs for you. The light that flared when you entered this space was another example of my ability to control atomic material."

"That's amazing," gasped Talbot.

"No more amazing than the technology of your time," replied Fenrir. He grinned wolfishly as Talbot's jaw dropped. "Yes, I have walked the streets of your world and am equally amazed by such things as your televisions and jumbo jets. My race has simply evolved differently to yours, that is all."

"Zeus said something similar about the Olympians," said Talbot.

"I have never met anyone from Olympia, but there is a great likelihood of it. All worlds are derived from the same matter. As such, regardless how different our realities are, we are all somehow related. Understand?"

"So you're saying that even though we come from different dimensions and times, we're all linked?" offered Talbot.

"Close," replied Fenrir. "But to put it into clearer context, imagine three people starting out on a journey, each without knowledge of the other two. They all begin from the same point, but as they travel all three each take a different route to get to their destination. It is like that with our three races. Whereas the Olympians developed themselves more cerebrally, my race developed ways to manipulate substance through the vibration of atomic structure. Your people perfected the development of tools in order to aid in their journey. Finally, all three races arrive at a similar junction point, but with vastly different talents and abilities to overcome obstacles."

"So why was Prometheus trying to defeat the Olympians?" asked Talbot.

"The Olympians were merely an obstacle. His true goal was to use the technology of the Olympians along with your power of the Elder-tongue in order to bring his army of Titans – whom he had tricked into following him – through to Earth and from the gate on Earth into my home world once more."

"Holy shit, that's complex," breathed Wes. "But what exactly are the Aesir and the Vanir?"

"We are a single race of people, split down the middle," stated Fenrir. "The Vanir are the true inhabitants of the land called Vanaheim, whereas the Aesir are the supporters of Prometheus who escaped into this realm. We – my supporters and I – have come here to try to thwart whatever plans Prometheus has, before it is too late."

"Good luck with that," muttered Wes, crossing his legs in the chair and leaning back. "That son of a bitch is more slippery than a naked chick wrapped in eels and dipped in a tub of baby-oil."

Fenrir stared at Wes, his brow crinkled.

"So what you're saying," interjected Talbot, "is that the Aesir are the same race as you. Does that mean they're also able to manipulate matter?"

"Up to a point," replied Fenrir. "Only the most senior of them – like Prometheus – will be able to alter their physical shape. This takes many years of comprehensive study, along with a battery of tests, and the absorption of various, potentially lethal, chemicals. The manipulation of the environment, such as what I just showed you in this room, requires knowledge the Aesir do not yet possess."

"What about the point I made earlier?" cut in Wes. "How did you travel forward in time? It's not possible."

"All things in life are possible. Just because you do not know how to do something does not make it impossible. The main issue you have is that from the past the future hasn't been created yet. But through linking with the rift gates we found we were able to leap through time both forward and backward so long as there was an active rift gate open in the time we wanted to get to in the future. Time doesn't exist in the rifts, so they're like highways intermingling with each other, regardless of when they occur in our timeframe."

Comprehension swiftly dawned on Wes's face. "So the rifts are exempt from the theory of relativity!"

"Exactly. By leaping between rifts I was able to navigate my way into your time in order to threaten you."

"Nice job, by the way."

"Thank you," replied Fenrir with a toothy smile.

"So, could *we* do it?" asked Talbot, indicating Wes and himself.

Fenrir shook his head. "Your bodies wouldn't be able to withstand the pressure in between the rifts. You'd need something incredibly strong, powerful enough to penetrate it – like punching through that rock wall into the room beyond; you couldn't do it with your fist, could you?"

Talbot nodded in understanding. "Does the journey you mentioned earlier, the one that three races embarked upon, have something to do with the rifts?"

"Not at all; the journey is a metaphor for the quest for knowledge. Each of our races has an inbuilt yearning to know the intricacies of the universe, and we are all learning different aspects of it through various means. Your people's technology defies the laws of logic and reality on many levels, whereas my people's ability to manipulate matter at a cellular level would appear to be magic to another race. The Olympians managed to develop the knowledge of how to harness the power of the rifts into gates so that they could travel between dimensions without fearing the crushing effects which would otherwise see them destroyed. All three of our races are now approaching the same place in our quest for answers, but we have all traveled different roads to get there."

"On this journey, is there any chance we could get some lunch?" asked Wes. "I'm hungry enough to eat an otter covered in anchovies."

"What are anchovies?" asked Fenrir.

"Don't worry about it," replied Talbot, shaking his head.

Fenrir waved his hand over a small sphere on his desk, and suddenly the wall shifted and liquefied, like a melting candle, instantaneously reforming into the rough rock of the tunnel they had entered through, now dully illuminated. Talbot and Wes rose and followed Fenrir out into the open air, once more greeted by the Viking crew, all of whom seemed on edge, but otherwise unharmed.

Strange creatures which could only be the Vanir surrounded them, but Talbot hadn't fully realized what that would mean. He had heard of and read about these beings through fable, but had never imagined seeing them in real life.

Some of the Vanir were human, or at least *looked* human, but intermixed with them were short figures, their granite features and stocky physiques identifying them as dwarves. All the dwarves bore beards, making it impossible for Talbot to tell which were male and which were female.

Lithe, wraithlike figures stood closest to the trees, appearing nervous as deer. Elves. They carried no weapons, but Talbot sensed they possessed an unnatural swiftness, and something waspish about their nature indicated they were not as fragile as they might seem.

Several tall, bulky figures, twice the height of Titans, stood in the rear. Obviously these were giants, though they were much smaller than the ones Talbot had seen in Olympia. Some appeared human-like, but many were hideous, like Barktooth, and Talbot wondered if there were any difference between giants and trolls in this place.

It seemed whereas the people on Earth were split into races of color and ethnicity, the people of the Vanir were divided by a gap which almost created different sub-species among them. Talbot suddenly realized the stories of these creatures, tales which had spawned hundreds of legends about giants, elves and dwarves, had originally all sprouted from the Vanir, retold through the fables of Norse mythology.

"If Aragorn, son of Arathorn, turns up, I'm out of here," muttered Wes, staring around at the bizarre assortment of figures awaiting them. Raising his voice, he asked, "What are we eating?"

The question broke the tension in the group and suddenly there was activity everywhere. Food was brought out and within moments a camp full of life emerged. Biaver's Viking warriors visibly relaxed at the prospect of a meal, and tensions lifted further as they realized they weren't going to be the main course. Everyone was soon seated around the cook fires and within moments the smell of roasting meat wafted through the area, making more than one stomach rumble in anticipation.

Talbot suddenly thought of something and turned to Fenrir. "The creature in the water, the nidhogg, is that under your command also?"

"The nidhogg? Why do you ask?"

"Because it saved us from the warriors of the Aesir."

"They weren't warriors of the Aesir," said Fenrir. "They were the people of this land, but their minds have been warped in such a way as to make them veritable slaves of the Aesir. Mindless pawns in a war not their own." He shook his head sadly.

"Whatever they were, they were after us, and the nidhogg stopped them. Did you command it to do that?"

Fenrir laughed. "Nobody commands the nidhogg. She does as she sees fit; sometimes for good, and sometimes for ill."

"She?" asked Wes.

"Yes. *She.*"

Fenrir looked up and smiled, while both Wes and Talbot twisted around to glimpse who the speaker was.

"Son of a bitch…." muttered Wes, rising to his feet.

Talbot also stood, gasping slightly upon seeing the woman who had spoken. She was incredibly beautiful, long, black hair cascading down her back, surrounding a face of exquisite allure. Memories of the pretty Norse girl back on the boat were shredded in an instant as he gazed into the deep hazel eyes of the stranger. Part of him realized he was staring, but the rest didn't care.

"Who are you?" he breathed.

She ignored him, her eyes locked on Wes. The commando grimaced, his hand resting lightly on his holstered .45.

"Hello… Zoe."

***

"Y-you're Zoe?" stammered Talbot.

The ghost of a smile crossed her lips. "I'm sorry I had to lie to you, Wes, but it was the only story I thought might gain your trust."

"It gained my trust right up until I found out you were full of shit. When was that? Oh yeah, right before I met with the President of the United States of America, and a big fucking wolf turned up! No offence, Fluffy."

"None taken," replied Fenrir.

"Get over it, Wes," snarled Zoe. "I had a task to accomplish, and I'm sorry if I stepped on your fragile little toes while doing it. I transformed into a bird when you weren't looking. Fenrir sensed I was there and returned me here with him after he threatened you. I wish I'd seen your face."

Wes ground his teeth slightly before rubbing his jaw with the knuckles of his right hand. "So who are you really?"

Zoe glanced at Fenrir. He nodded slightly.

"I'm Prometheus's daughter."

Talbot's jaw dropped, and Wes spat a curse.

"Well, that's just perfect. Why wouldn't I trust you if I'd known you were the daughter of the guy who tried to kill us? You should have just said who you were in the first place." The sarcasm dripped like thick syrup from Wes's words.

"I'm sorry, Wes," said Zoe, her voice defiant despite her professed apology.

"Why are you fighting against your father?" interrupted Talbot, as much in an attempt to diffuse the hostility as anything else.

Zoe seemed to appreciate the distraction. "I grew up with my father, and he was wonderful, but as the years passed he changed. He became convinced that the Vanir deserved to be a stronger race. Our people knew of the rifts, but our leaders left them alone, fearing the risks involved, preferring to expend our resources on creating a better way of life on our own world rather than exploring the cosmos in the hope of finding something greater." Her gaze dropped down to her hands, which appeared to be trying to knot an invisible piece of rope.

"I remember my father arriving in our home one evening –" Zoe's voice grew quieter and more introverted. "He was furious at the Vanir Council's dismissal of his proposal for expansion into other realms, along with his suggestion to colonize these worlds at the expense of other species. My mother tried to calm him, but when this failed she flew into her own rage and accused him of caring more about his ambitions than his own family...."

"What happened?" asked Wes, his voice much gentler now.

"He murdered her," she said coldly, her eyes piercing Wes like daggers. "He transformed into the thing that crashed into Talbot's home and tore her apart like an animal. I remember her screaming at me to run. I've never run so fast in all my life, but he chased me. I made it to another home, which he destroyed also, killing everyone inside.

"By this time, the Vanir law-keepers had responded. My father fled. Nobody knew where he hid for many years. There were rumors he was building an army. I have since found out what you both already know – he traveled via the rifts to the land of the Olympians and beyond that to Tartarus in order to find a force powerful enough to conquer the Vanir.

"After you defeated Prometheus, he returned to Vanaheim and kidnapped me. I later discovered he needed my blood in order to recover from the grievous injuries inflicted by you, Talbot Harrison. Over many months of your time, with me being held captive, my father told me in incredible detail everything that had happened. This is how I was able to fool you, Wes, into thinking I was Talbot's daughter. He spoke constantly of it, iterating every detail, every fragment of his trickery – and his failure. He couldn't believe that the two of you, mere humans without any special attributes, were able to overcome his intricate scheming. It tormented him." She ran a hand through her long, dark hair, pushing it away from her face.

"And he planned. He never told me what he was setting up, but I knew him well enough by then to recognize what he was doing. Everything that has led up to this point is due to his manipulation, make no mistake. My father is insane, but I imagine you already know that, what with everything you have been through thus far."

Wes glanced at Talbot, who shrugged. "Sure, I guess so," said Wes. "Most of the time we were just trying not to get killed."

Zoe sighed. "He has become so obsessed with the idea of raising the Vanir to the status of gods that he has forsaken everything he once cared for. He has followers who have joined him in his insane dreams, and together they have set up in this world, during this period in history, calling themselves the Aesir. The people of this time are primitive, and the Aesir have become godlike in their eyes, turning many of the people of this land into slaves."

"That's incredible," gasped Talbot.

Wes nodded. "But why couldn't you just ask for my help? If I'd known Talbot was here, I would have come straight away."

"I couldn't take that risk," replied Zoe.

Wes suddenly remembered something. "How come Prometheus didn't recognize you? I mean, when he smashed into Talbot's apartment. You're his daughter, but he fell for the same ruse you were playing to me."

"I don't normally look like this," Zoe replied simply. "I have been in disguise."

"Damn. Don't tell me you're ugly, I was just beginning to enjoy the view," said Wes, grimacing. "I couldn't get excited about you before, when I thought you were Talbot's daughter, but while you've been spilling your guts I've been checking you out, and you're not half bad. And now you're gonna turn out to be some sort of grotesque bag lady? Well, let's get it over with."

Zoe's visage shimmered and shifted, much as the wall in the cave had done. Her black hair changed to blonde, while her beautiful face faded away and… reformed into features even more stunning.

Wes was speechless. He had thought Zoe attractive before, but now she was nothing short of stunning. Talbot abruptly nudged him in the ribs with his elbow, drawing him from his daze.

"Um…." Wes mumbled, snapping shut his jaw, trying to gather his thoughts. "Is – is your name still Zoe? Or is it something weird like the rest of these goofballs?"

"My birth name is Aedos, but I prefer Zoe, especially from you, Wes," she said with a small smile. "For what it's worth I'm sorry to have lied to you. If it were possible I would have never involved you in the first place."

"Why are we involved at all?" asked Talbot. "I mean, the last time was understandable, I had the power of the Elder-tongue, and Prometheus needed it in order to open the gate leading out of

Tartarus. But why does he need us this time?"

"The answer to that lies in what the Aesir are looking for," interrupted Fenrir.

Talbot and Wes turned as one to stare at the Vanir leader.

"Well? Don't leave me hanging here, Falfnar," insisted Wes.

Fenrir frowned at him slightly. "Prometheus is looking for the entrance to Valhalla."

"What does that mean?" asked Wes. "Is Valhalla a place, like Olympia or Tartarus? Or is it something else?"

"We have no idea," replied Fenrir. "From what we can decipher from the ancient scrolls, Valhalla is a myth: the realm of dead heroes."

"Could it be like Hades or Tartarus?" asked Talbot. "They were referred to as places for the dead also. Might it merely be another rift gate into Tartarus, with Prometheus simply trying to replicate what he failed before? I mean, he's in a different time now, so surely the Titans still exist in Tartarus; it would then be a simple thing for him to convince them to follow him once more. He did it once, after all, and we all know how persuasive he can be."

"It's possible, but we doubt it," said Zoe, moving over to stand beside Fenrir.

"Why?" asked Wes.

"Because my father, for all his faults, would have learned from the mistakes he made the last time. You found a way to defeat him previously, so he would never repeat tactics, including the tools – in this case, the Titans – that already failed him twice before."

"So Valhalla might contain something even more deadly than the army he used against the Olympians?" asked Wes, remembering with horror the beasts Prometheus had unleashed from Tartarus, alongside the terrifying army of Titans. "Who the hell could that be?"

"Not *who*," said Fenrir, casting a worried glance sideways at Zoe. She gave him a supportive smile and squeezed his hand. Wes noticed the gesture and felt the slightest twinge of jealousy. "More like *what* is Prometheus going to unleash upon the Vanir once he finds the gate to Valhalla?"

"That doesn't sound good," said Talbot.

Fenrir grimaced. "It's probably worse than anything you can

imagine."

Wes stared hard at the two Vanir. Moments ago he had felt a strange sensation as jealousy had flickered to life within him, and now another foreign emotion burst forth.

It was panic.

CHAPTER 8

Talbot awoke with a strong sensation of being watched. Peeling his eyelids open he stared straight into a face that was definitely not human. Startled, Talbot gave a short barking yelp of surprise, and the creature scrambled backward.

"No, wait!" he called, and the beast froze, its expression anxious, as though it might flee at any moment.

Now that he was more aware, Talbot had a chance to properly study his visitor. He had a strong suspicion it might be male, but wasn't positive. The creature's clothing was featureless – bland colors on something that back home might have simply been described as a sack – and neither they nor its features left him any wiser as to its sex. Its body appeared similar to one of the dwarves he'd seen earlier, though less stocky and slightly taller. He also noticed the ears of the strange being were pointed, like those of the elves he had met at the feast. The pink nose was like a button, tiny beneath the huge, dark eyes wide with fear. Whatever it was, it seemed produced through the fusion of dwarf and elf. Perhaps the two species could mate. Maybe this thing was the result.

He'd discovered, much to his surprise, dwarves and elves weren't really separate species. After talking to some of them after the dinner feast, he had found out it was more appropriate to say they were merely variations within the Vanir, rather than completely different genus as the folk tales and myths had always asserted. True, the elves were quieter, and the dwarves reputedly brasher, but apart from that, these creatures soon seemed merely people, albeit with vastly different appearances.

Talbot had also discussed other things with the Vanir at the feast, predominantly asking about shape-changers.

There were certain individuals within the Vanir who could alter aspects of their physical appearance at will. The ones he'd talked to had tried to explain the process to Talbot, but the specifics of it all flew over his head, and he soon gave up trying to comprehend them. What he did discover, however, was that the ability to modify some aspects of matter was a widespread thing among the Vanir, though much training was required before even the slightest amount of skill became evident.

This made him wonder at the power of beings such as Fenrir, Zoe and Prometheus. Their talents stretched far above the abilities of most Vanir. All three could morph into the forms of larger beasts, expanding their cellular structure well beyond its normal constraints. However, Prometheus's power to regenerate at will was unique, a skill even Fenrir had never mastered. None among the Vanir or Aesir were able to replicate identities as skillfully as Prometheus, either, not even his own daughter.

But all of this was secondary. Talbot concentrated instead on the creature before him. Could this be Prometheus in disguise? His heart quickened.

"Who are you?" he asked.

The creature appraised him nervously once more. "I am Kvasir." The voice was high and reedy, a slight sing-song note creeping in, intermixed with the quavering of fear. Talbot's suspicions that the speaker must be male became almost a certainty. The tone, while fearful, contained something strangely masculine.

"What do you want, Kvasir?"

The strange creature stared at him silently, head cocked to one side. "You will fight the Aesir."

Talbot couldn't figure out if it was a question, or merely a statement; there was no real inflection in Kvasir's voice to indicate what he truly meant.

Nodding slightly, he slowly sat cross-legged on the ground. This seemed to calm the anxious figure slightly. "Yes, we will fight the Aesir. Is that a good thing?"

"Fighting is never good," said Kvasir, shaking his head. "But sometimes we must fight in order to save what is good. Prometheus is searching for something we should all fear, something long buried. We must oppose him. But do not let hatred enter your heart, Talbot Harrison, lest it control you, and destroy you from within."

The words were spoken with great confidence, a stark contradiction to the timid being who uttered them. Talbot blinked rapidly and refocused on Kvasir, but the diminutive creature appeared unchanged.

"That's very sensible," said Talbot cautiously. "I'll be sure to heed your wisdom. But how is it you know my name?"

"A name is easy to discover. Intentions are not. I have watched you and your companion since you arrived in our camp, and know of the task you face. It will not be a simple thing; it is so much more than just fighting Prometheus. You must go deeper than that if you wish to succeed; you must find the roots of the issue."

"How do we do that?" asked Talbot, his eyes narrowing. What had initially been simple humoring had now turned into genuine interest.

"You must find what lies behind Prometheus's machinations. He has access to a power or a source of knowledge we have not yet discovered," chirped Kvasir. "From what the female you know as Zoe told us, he was grievously injured following your previous encounter, and yet is now back, stronger than before. It is true that he used her essence to recover, but there must have been more behind it, something even she does not know. Your past tactics will not work this time; he is invulnerable."

"So what do we do?"

"You must first stop him from opening the gate to Valhalla. We have spies within his slave camps who report he is getting closer to his goal. Only the power of the Elder-tongue can impede him – or aid him. Because of this we attempted to find you earlier, when the Aesir first captured you, but apparently those who caught you made a mistake and integrated you in with the digging slaves. If they had known who you truly were it is doubtful you would have been rescued so easily. Our last chance was to send Zoe into your time to fetch the aid of your companion: Wes. It was most fortunate –

doubly fortunate, in fact, for if she had failed, we would have been forced to kill you in order to stop Prometheus from using your power."

"Wonderful," said Talbot humorlessly. It wasn't nice hearing a stranger – especially such a *strange* stranger – pronouncing his expendability in such a detached fashion. Something suddenly hit him. "What about my brother?"

"We have tried to get people close to Thomas Harrison, but as yet they have been unsuccessful. We hope to free him before the gate to Valhalla is found."

"And if you don't free him?"

Kvasir's dismayed expression spoke louder than any words.

"Who are you to make that sort of decision?" snapped Talbot, his control slipping. "I mean, you're not even human. What the hell are you?"

Kvasir sighed. "There are many stories of my origin, Talbot Harrison. Some say I was born by mixing the saliva from both the Aesir and Vanir. This is amusing, but I suppose it holds some truth, up to a point. The simplest explanation is that I am a creature with above normal intelligence who has sided with the Vanir for the impending encounter. I am a combination of many things, but most of the Vanir simply see me as a voice which aids their hand in times of trouble. I can provide clarity when the mists of discord are thickest."

"What does that even mean?"

"It means I am not your enemy. I am merely trying to help you by showing the path you must take in order to achieve that which you desire most."

Talbot stood silently, contemplating what the diminutive figure had said. "I don't understand," he finally stated.

Kvasir stared up, his eyes pleading. "It means there is more at stake here than merely you or your brother. Our entire race will be placed in jeopardy, along with this world, *your* world, if you refuse to help us. There is something on the other side of that gate, something horrendous, and if Prometheus releases it we may all be destroyed."

Talbot was suddenly filled with remorse. Once again he had failed to see the big picture because of his own agenda. He had prided himself on his determination to stop Prometheus at any cost, but when something of his own had been threatened, he'd immediately balked.

"I'm sorry," Talbot apologized, the words feeling leaden and inadequate. "Tell me everything you know."

Kvasir narrowed his eyes, his expression once more tremulous. "Prometheus, or Odin as he is known among the Aesir –"

"Prometheus is Odin?" interrupted Talbot, causing Kvasir to jump slightly.

"Y-yes. Have you heard the name before?"

"Only in myth," said Talbot. "Please go on. I'm sorry for interrupting."

The short creature tugged nervously at the lobe of his right ear. "Odin commands the Aesir, along with many of the humans inhabiting this place. He has forced hundreds into slavery, as you well know, and uses those slaves to search for the gate to Valhalla. He seeks to unleash the forces contained within that realm."

"In order to invade your home world."

Kvasir nodded sadly. "His mind is cracked, and the only thing he thinks of anymore is revenge against those he believes slighted him and caused the death of his wife."

"But Zoe said it was Prometheus himself who killed her mother," argued Talbot.

"As it was, but in his mind he was driven to it by the closed minds of the Vanir Council. They denied his proposal to expand the empire into other dimensions. He cannot accept blame for his actions, and seeks to thrust judgment onto those who denied him what he desired most."

They were becoming sidetracked, rehashing facts, and Talbot began to suspect it might be on purpose. "But what is Prometheus seeking in Valhalla?"

Kvasir looked ready to flee, glancing around furtively. "He hopes to awaken an army," he whispered, as though to mention it might make it reality. "An army of giants."

"We've fought giants before," said Talbot dismissively. "They're tough, but not invincible."

"From what Zoe relayed to me, there were three giants in the battle atop Mount Olympus."

"That's right."

Kvasir gazed into his eyes seriously. "The army of Valhalla is said to be comprised of the better part of ten thousand giants. There will also be an assortment of other beasts, unlike anything you have seen so far."

"Ten – ten *thousand*?" gasped Talbot. "We can't fight that many – no matter how many shape-shifters like Zoe and Fenrir are on our side."

"I know. That is why we were contemplating such drastic measures with you and your brother. If that army gets through from Valhalla, nothing we can do will stop them. They will tear through this planet, and then on to our own world."

"What will Prometheus do with this army once he's conquered the Vanir?"

Kvasir shook his head. "I don't know. In truth I don't think Prometheus himself knows, but I'm assuming he doesn't care. His all-consuming drive is to see the Vanir destroyed, but beyond that, he doesn't mind how much destruction he creates."

"We have to stop him," agreed Talbot.

"And how do you propose we do that?" inquired Wes from the shadows.

Talbot looked up and Kvasir spun around as Wes stepped out from the darkness. "How are we supposed to defeat Prometheus, or Odin, or Mr. T., or whatever you want to call him? We've already killed him once – twice if you include the time Heracles did it – and the bastard just keeps on coming. He's kinda like the Energizer bunny. And who the hell are *you* anyway?" Wes asked Kvasir, who cringed from the Australian's accusing stare. "Well?"

"I am Kvasir."

"Kav… kevl…. I'm gonna call you Bob," said Wes. "Now, Bob, you look like a mix of dwarf and elf; would that be correct?"

Kvasir nodded. "I was a… an experiment."

"That's awesome. So why are you so smart and why should we

listen to you?"

Talbot moved to protest, but was cut short with an abrupt gesture from Wes.

"I know many things," replied Kvasir.

"Oh yeah, like what?"

Kvasir suddenly fixed Wes with a piercing gaze. "For instance, I know you are not what you appear to be."

"Yeah, I'm a regular porn star, but stick to the point. What's going on, apart from the shit we already know? An army of giants is pretty bad, but there's something worse in Valhalla that you don't want us to know about. It's either because you're embarrassed about it, or you're scared of it. Personally I don't give a shit either way, but it may end up fucking with my schedule, so stop the guru bullshit and tell it to us straight. What's going to happen if they open that gate?"

Kvasir looked to Talbot for support, but Wes had piqued his curiosity, and he now wanted to know what was being kept from them as well.

"I – I do not know –"

"You're lying to us, Bob," Wes pronounced calmly.

Fenrir's voice cut through the night air. "That is enough!" Wes turned, and the leader of the Vanir stormed toward them, his face flushed with anger. "How dare you –?"

"How dare I?" Wes cut in. "I dare because me and Talbot have been jumping through other people's hoops for too long, and I've had enough. Just once in this stupid game I want some answers!"

Fenrir stood defiantly for a moment, but finally nodded slightly, dropping his gaze. "You do deserve that. But I will not see Kvasir subjected to that sort of animosity again," he concluded, his voice hardening again, and his gaze becoming steadier.

"Yeah, sure. Bob's cool," replied Wes calmly. "When we get home we should hang out a bit, Bob. We'll pick up some girls... or guys, depending on what the hell you actually are."

Talbot suppressed a grin with difficulty. Glancing at Kvasir, however, he noticed a flicker in his expression, a sudden look of intense focus upon his misshapen face, and then it was gone, replaced once more with timidity.

"Hey, what's going on?" he snapped. Kvasir jumped nervously, but Talbot wasn't falling for it. "You're not meek and mild at all! What the hell are you up to?"

The look of apprehension immediately fell from Kvasir's face, and he drew himself up to his full height, staring calmly at Talbot's face. "I believed this would be the wisest approach to solicit your assistance. I was right, but hadn't planned on the interference of your companion."

"Welcome to the party, Bob," said Wes. "Nice of you to finally join us."

"Don't pat yourself on the back too much. It was merely instinct which led you to deduce that I was being fallacious with you." Several of the Vikings had awoken and moved over to see what the fuss was all about.

"Aw. Stop using them there big fancy words now, y'all hear?" drawled Wes cheekily. "And you still haven't answered my question; are you a guy or a chick?"

"I am male, as you very well know. You are very much a trickster, aren't you?"

"But I'm low key," replied Wes, with a wink.

"Loki? I do not understand," said Kvasir. Talbot gasped, glancing at Fenrir, who frowned. Murmuring broke out among several of the Vikings in the gathering audience.

"And that pleases me," replied Wes. "But all of this is off the point. What is Prometheus trying to bring through that rift?"

Fenrir appeared about to argue, but was silenced with a look from Kvasir. It was obvious Fenrir was still the leader, but in some things he seemed to submit to Kvasir.

"Odin, or Prometheus as you seem to prefer calling him, is seeking a weapon, a creature of terrifying power. The texts we have managed to obtain regarding this are obscure, but they all reference something so colossal it could consume this entire planet. This may be a figurative reference or quite literal, we're not sure yet. The information we have gathered leads us to believe the creature can drain the power of whatever it touches in such a way as to potentially turn worlds into ash. As I said, though, this wording may be symbolic or factual."

"Okay. Factual would be bad," said Wes. "Actually, symbolic doesn't sound like a Vegas hotel room full of hookers either. Where do you find out all this shit, anyway? Do you have a Stone-Age Google hidden around here or something?"

"We have obtained much information from ancient texts and writings from both this world and our own, other knowledge coming from local lore and mythology. A lot of it is conjecture, but deep within each parable lays a grain of truth."

"So basically you're relying on fairy tales, is that right, Bob?"

"I am unfamiliar with this phrase."

"Well that makes me all happy in my pants. What I'm saying is there isn't any real proof to what you're saying; you're just guessing. Correct?"

Kvasir frowned slightly, obviously annoyed. "That is exactly what I am saying… except for the information relayed to us from a slave we managed to release, of course."

"Why the hell are you so determined to piss me off?" grumbled Wes. "We can sit around here all night while you try to prove to me how sagacious and eloquent you are when you could have just said, 'There's a terrifying motherfucker coming who can suck the life out of everything. Some dude we saved from the slave pits told us.' Now wouldn't that have been easier?"

"But –"

"That's right. Now what did your slave boy say? And make it the condensed version, minus the section on how brainy Bob is."

Kvasir glanced at Fenrir.

"We need their assistance," said the leader of the Vanir.

It was obvious Kvasir was revered among the Vanir, but Talbot was beginning to understand what Wes was getting at. A lot of Kvasir's perceived wisdom came from the way he presented it to others, building it up so much as to increase other people's opinion of his intellect as a result.

Kvasir began to say something when a huge rumbling echoed from the far end of the valley. Instantly the small figure paled.

"It cannot be," breathed Kvasir, peering worriedly at Fenrir. "They cannot have found us."

Fenrir sniffed the air deeply. A breeze wafted from the direction of the sound, and Talbot soon realized Fenrir was trying to get the scent of whatever approached. It was such an animalistic reaction that Talbot had no trouble imagining Fenrir as part wolf.

Without looking down at Kvasir, Fenrir said, "Get our people out of here. Find somewhere safe until I rejoin you."

Kvasir nodded and scampered off, calling out high-pitched orders, his voice authoritative despite sounding like a child. Within moments activity had erupted, and soon dwarves, elves and others were moving swiftly from the camp, in the direction the rest of the Viking villagers had been left. Biaver strode over to Wes. "What should we do?" Talbot could see the tension in the man.

"Go with the Vanir and protect them as best you can," replied Wes. "Once you get to your people stay with them until we return. We'll figure out the best course of action from there. If we don't meet up with you... well... you'll know what to do. Give me one of your swords before you go."

Biaver called out and swiftly a Viking sword was presented by one of the warriors. He handed it to Wes who belted the scabbard to his waist, drawing the weapon and slicing it through the air, testing its weight and balance.

"Probably not as good as my old blade, but it'll be better than a gun with only six bullets... especially once the bullets run out."

The Norsemen gathered their things and hurried to catch up with the Vanir. Part of Talbot wished he could go with them.

Fenrir glanced at Talbot and Wes. "There is no need for the two of you to stay," he said calmly.

"I wouldn't miss out on this for all the boobs in Hollywood, buddy," replied Wes.

Fenrir nodded, though Talbot knew there was almost no chance of him understanding what Wes was talking about. His attention would be focused entirely on the coming threat.

"Both of you must stay behind me," ordered the leader of the Vanir. "I believe the thing approaching us is an Aesir named Surtr.

He has the ability to change shape, much like myself, though he is nowhere near as powerful as Prometheus. His chosen form is that of a giant troll, and our information tells us he has recently come into possession of a sword of enormous power."

"A sword?" asked Wes, his brow narrowing.

"Yes. Now move back, I must prepare myself."

Talbot and Wes moved behind Fenrir, and the Vanir leader let out an ungodly scream, making Talbot jump slightly. The scream swiftly turned into a deep throaty howl, similar to that of a wolf, only deeper and much more powerful.

The change happened so swiftly Talbot almost missed it. Fenrir's muscles doubled and then trebled, expanding astonishingly swiftly. His bones seemed to crack and flow into a new alignment as his clothing shifted and smoothed, altering again until it became thick gray fur. Within the space of several seconds he changed from a demure-looking man into a monstrous wolf.

"Whoa," murmured Talbot.

He had seen Prometheus under different guises, but Talbot had never observed the actual transformation process before. It was terrifying, almost as much as the sight of Fenrir as a giant wolf. Wes had told him about the wolf tearing apart the gryphon on the lawn of the White House, but a part of Talbot hadn't fully grasped how powerful Fenrir would be.

"Remember to stay behind me." It was the voice of Fenrir, slightly deeper, but definitely recognizable. "Whatever is approaching, whether it be Surtr or another, it is definitely large. I do not want to accidentally crush either of you during our clash."

"Thanks for your concern," chirped Wes with a grin.

Talbot suddenly realized he lacked a weapon. Either way, he really held no place in this conflict. He was an archaeologist who had managed to survive the last encounter against Prometheus mainly through Wes's protective prowess, along with bucket-loads of luck. Right now he felt like a powerless spectator.

And an idiot.

The rumbling neared, and Talbot glanced toward the head of the valley. Partially hidden in shadow, perhaps a hundred yards away, a colossal figure emerged. He heard Fenrir growl, and saw the giant wolf tense, readying to attack.

"Hold, Fenrir," called the huge stranger, his voice rumbling like distant thunder.

"What do you want, Surtr? You declared yourself an enemy of the Vanir a long time ago."

"You warned me back then, and I wish more than anything I had heeded your words, brother."

"I am no brother of yours, Surtr," replied Fenrir. "You gave up that right the moment you sided with the Aesir and the madman."

The shadowy figure moved closer, enabling Talbot to finally see his outline. Surtr was around twice the height of the female troll, Barktooth, and immensely thickset. Talbot wondered if this difference in size between the male troll form which Surtr had adopted compared to the female form of Barktooth was true to all trolls. Perhaps Surtr had just gone bigger to make himself more terrifying.

Talbot nodded appreciatively; it had worked.

"You were right, Fenrir," said the gargantuan figure. "He is indeed insane, and I should have listened to you."

"What do you want, Surtr? Speak swiftly, or we shall find out which one of us truly holds more power. You always wanted to know before, now may be your chance."

"No, Fenrir. I have come to make peace with you. I wish to join your force in battle against Odin and his insanity."

Fenrir laughed hollowly, the sound rasping from his canine throat. "I am not a fool, Surtr. You were always Prometheus's most loyal follower, always the one he would call upon to do his darkest bidding. Why should I believe you?"

"He killed my wife." Surtr's voice cracked, and he seemed to wrench the words from within himself. "The maniac murdered my beautiful Sinmara when she argued against his madness. I cannot defeat him on my own, but with your aid, I might one day have my revenge."

Fenrir stood silently, his wolf form heaving in deep breaths of air, as though trying to taste the truth of Surtr's words upon the breeze.

"What guarantee do I have?" he finally asked.

"I see the humans behind you, and recognize the taller one. I took this from him." He drew something from behind his back which flickered and glowed with power, and Talbot gasped as he recognized it. "I was with Odin while he attacked the place where the warriors fought with the strange weapons, and found that human –" He indicated Wes. "– who I thought was dead. I realized the power of this creation and took it from him, and have since devastated the Vanir with its might. I return this to him, as a symbol of my devotion in defecting to your cause."

Talbot gazed at the weapon. It was definitely identical to, though much larger than, the sword Wes had wielded so proficiently throughout their previous battles against Prometheus. Somehow Surtr had enlarged the blade to accommodate his vast bulk, perhaps through powers similar to those which Fenrir had used to alter into his wolf form. There was something scientific about these abilities, but it also bordered on what had always been classed as magic. To these beings it seemed merely a way of life; much like a subway was to residents of Tokyo.

It glowed with strange electricity. Yellow and orange lightning caught along its edge, licking, curling – controlled, but terrifyingly lethal to those who opposed it. Such was the arcane force trapped within the blade by the Olympian, Hephaestus, and Talbot knew it was one of the most fearsome weapons the fabled smith had ever created. Passed on to Wes by Chiron, the half-man half-horse leader of the centaurs, just prior to his murder by Porphyrion, the King of the Gigantes, the sword would be a welcome aid in their battle.

Surtr rapidly shrank, the giant sword clattering to the rocky ground. The process appeared much more painful than Fenrir's transformation. Bones cracked as they shattered and reformed, the muscles and tendons surrounding them contracting with horrendous squelching sounds. His skull crushed inward, the eyes tilting toward each other as the nose and mouth sank into the face like water sucking down a drain. No scream issued from Surtr's mouth, and yet his expression conveyed absolute agony as it sprang back elastically upon the newer, smaller, cranium. His eyes rolled down out of the back of his skull and with several whip-like cracks his jaw snapped into location. Tentatively testing the joints of first his arms and then his legs, Surtr finally knelt down, his palms lightly touching the hilt of the enormous sword.

The transformation of the weapon was much less dramatic than the shrinking of the Aesir, and within moments the Sword of Chiron became a blade the length of an English broadsword. Fenrir remained in his wolf form, tension palpable within him as Surtr approached. He obviously expected some sort of trick.

Surtr stabbed the sword into the hard stone of the valley floor, and it sank deep into the rock. Wes drew his Viking sword from its scabbard and passed the blade hilt-first to Talbot. He walked calmly past Fenrir, to the sword in the ground, and stood there, staring hard at the figure of Surtr.

The Aesir defector was lightly tanned, and perhaps forty years of age, though Talbot knew that age could be deceptive when dealing with these people. If Surtr could remold himself into the form of a giant troll at will, what was to stop him knocking off a few years or – as Zoe had done – reshaping his visage completely?

Regardless, Surtr now appeared weary, his hair streaked with gray, the skin of his face lined with more than just years. Grief hung palpably around him, and Talbot doubted even one able to manipulate molecular structure could recreate such convincing anguish.

"Please," he whispered, sounding as though he were on the verge of tears. "I must have my peace. He took the one thing in my life that meant something."

Wes easily wrenched the sword from the rock and raised it high. For a split second Talbot thought he was about to decapitate the Aesir traitor, and apparently Surtr thought the same, for he raised his chin slightly, giving Wes a clearer shot at his exposed neck.

Wes lowered the sword, walking back to Fenrir. "He's legit, I'd bet my left nut on it... if I still had one. Hey, can you make this scabbard a little bigger. My sword's too big... if you know what I mean."

A look of concentration passed over Fenrir's brow, and he lightly touched the scabbard with his wolf snout. The leather swelled and lengthened, and Wes sheathed the Sword of Chiron, nodding his thanks.

"I named the sword, in case it did not have one already," said Surtr.

Wes raised an eyebrow. "Yeah? What did you call it?"

"It is Laevateinn. This means: damaging twig."

"I already have a damaging twig in my pants," replied Wes, "but Laevateinn's a cool name. I think I'll keep it."

"How can you remember that name, but nobody you meet?" asked Talbot.

"I don't care about most of the people I meet," replied Wes with a shrug.

Talbot followed Wes down the valley in the direction the Vanir had fled. Some twenty yards into their journey, he turned and looked back, seeing Fenrir – who had now returned to his human form – talking quietly with Surtr. He couldn't hear their words, but something seemed to pass between the two, with Fenrir eventually stepping in and embracing Surtr, who finally released his anguish and began sobbing in earnest.

The moment touched Talbot, who had no idea what had happened to create such an enormous gulf between the two men. If two enemies could embrace, it brought Talbot a strange sense of hope that maybe the rest of the universe stood a chance as well.

Maybe....

***

"I hadn't realized how much I missed this thing," said Wes, gazing down at the blade sitting across his thighs. It had been designed as a short sword for the leader of the centaurs, but in Wes's hands it became more like a broadsword, though maybe slightly smaller. A constant coursing of energy glowed up and down the length of the blade, causing it to blaze in waves of yellow and orange, almost like the blade was on fire.

Talbot glanced across at Surtr, sitting out of earshot with Fenrir. He had no idea how the Aesir had been able to grow the blade to suit his own larger form as a giant troll. Obviously the powers of the Aesir and Vanir were not necessarily constrained to their own physical forms, much like when Fenrir had manipulated objects in the cave. He wondered momentarily about what else this ability could do which might be of aid to them, but pushed the thought aside. The fact the blade had returned to Wes was what mattered for now.

The Australian now gazed at the weapon with a slight grin on his face, like he had been reunited with an old friend. Finally he stood up and sheathed Laevateinn in the scabbard belted at his left hip.

"Now," he said, looking at Talbot sharply, "what are we going to do about all this shit?"

"How the hell should I know?"

"You're the brains of this outfit, buddy. I'm just here for my good looks."

Talbot shook his head, but swiftly gathered his thoughts, knowing it was pointless to argue with Wes. "We have to discover his plans and then stop Prometheus, or Odin – whatever he's calling himself. That's our primary goal."

"Goals."

"What?"

"You said we need to discover his plans and then stop him. That's two things," said Wes calmly. "Hence – *goals*."

"Okay. Whatever."

"So how do we do it?"

"I have absolutely no idea," replied Talbot. "That chanting thing I did to him in Atlantis obviously doesn't work. It was designed to destroy things unnaturally made from Olympia and Tartarus, not where these guys come from. It definitely hurt him, but Prometheus doesn't seem concerned about it at all anymore. Maybe it's got something to do with Zoe's blood… I don't know."

"You should have just saved that whole speech and stuck with 'I don't know'," muttered Wes dryly. "I guess the first thing we have to do is get these guys organized in order to oppose the Aesir, and then try to infiltrate one of those slave camps to find out exactly what we're up against. Not that I don't have faith in Bob's half-arsed predictions, but I prefer to see things for myself. Next thing is to develop an attack strategy based on the information we recover. We have no real idea what the size of the Aesir force is, or what they're made up of. We need to work out strategies with the Vanir for attacking their force and releasing the slaves they have. For this I need exact numbers and formations of their forces, including the guards, along with where the slaves are positioned."

"Can't we just sneak up and take a look?" suggested Talbot, realizing that most of what Wes said was passing over his head.

Wes grinned. "Sounds like a plan to me," he said happily. "Let's go!"

"What? *Now?*"

"No time like the present, cupcake."

"But how will we get there? How the hell are we supposed to find our way in the dark with no idea where we're going?" asked Talbot.

"We'll use a guide," replied Wes. "I think the new guy will do nicely."

"Surtr? How do you know we can trust him?"

"Just a feeling."

Talbot nodded. From anyone else, that statement might mean nothing, but to Talbot, whose life had been saved several times by Wes's intuition, it was more than enough. Wes's instincts were honed from years of action, and if he said he trusted someone, then chances were they could be trusted.

At least Talbot hoped so, remembering the size of the male troll Surtr had arrived as. Even with the newly named sword, Laevateinn, Wes would be hard pressed to vanquish such a creature should Surtr decide he didn't want to play nice.

Pushing the problem aside, Talbot rose alongside Wes, and together they approached Fenrir, who sat deep in discussion with Surtr. Talbot wondered if his musings about them being brothers had been figurative or truthful; chances were he'd never know.

Without preamble, Wes swiftly outlined their plan of action. It didn't take long.

"Fenrir, we're off to spy on the Aesir. This guy's gonna guide us."

For such an immeasurably risk-filled task, the words rang inadequate in Talbot's ears. Shrugging the feeling aside, he watched Fenrir's surprised expression turn to a frown. He glanced at Surtr, who nodded slightly. Fenrir turned back to Wes, sighing deeply. Talbot could almost sense his distress over the moment. He had only just been reunited with Surtr, who he might now be returning into the hands of the enemy, perhaps never to return again.

It couldn't be helped. They needed intelligence, and even though Surtr had only just defected, his information might still be limited. They would question Surtr while en-route to the Aesir site, and would then know better what else to search for when they reached the slave camp.

If they reached it.

As they moved from the re-established Vanir camp – the Viking warriors and villagers setting up in the southern sector, officially integrated into the group – Talbot couldn't help but feel nervous. They were heading into the veritable heart of the enemy's territory with six bullets, a seemingly bipolar shape-shifter, a glowing sword, an ass-kicking Australian....

And Talbot.

Part of his brain rebelled against the complete lack of logic to his presence here. He had mentioned this to Wes at one stage as they were preparing to leave.

"Are you scared?" asked Wes.

"Of course I'm scared, but that's not the point. I really bring nothing along on this expedition. Why do you want me to come?"

"Maybe I just like your company," replied Wes, checking the magazine of his .45 before snapping it back home and slipping the gun into the waistband of his pants once more. Laevateinn was in place in its scabbard on his left hip.

"Yeah, right." Talbot would have checked his equipment, but it hadn't changed since he'd strapped the Viking sword to his belt. He remembered how awkward it was to walk with almost three feet of straight steel hanging from his hip, stumbling almost every third stride.

Surtr led them through the darkness with an unerring sense of direction. Wes questioned the former Aesir about several things, but many responses resulted in very vague answers bordering on guesses. Surtr eventually apologized, explaining that for the past few months, he had become estranged from Prometheus – or Odin as he referred to him.

A fissure had developed between the two Aesir, even before Prometheus had killed Surtr's wife, Sinmara. For months, the Aesir lord hadn't divulged any of his ambitions to Surtr, who had once been his closest lieutenant. As such, Surtr knew nothing about what plans Prometheus was developing, or what tactics he already had in place. He could only pass on to Wes what they already knew: the digging had something to do with the search for Valhalla.

That Prometheus was insane seemed beyond doubt. He was now randomly accusing his closest followers of treachery; killing them without mercy. An attempt by some of his followers to assassinate Prometheus had gone awry, and Prometheus had impaled all twelve of them, leaving their corpses dangling until the limbs rotted apart as a warning to others.

Only Prometheus's most zealous followers were privy to his goals. He was, after all, an extremely charismatic and manipulative figure, and as such many were drawn to him, following without thought for his actions, no matter how horrific. Surtr had been one of them, and it had only been their difference of opinion, culminating in the murder of his wife, that had made him snap out of his unquestioning loyalty and leave the service of the mad leader.

"Is there anything you can actually tell us that might be of some help?" asked Wes, his patience beginning to slip in the face Surtr's frustrating lack of information.

"He is obsessed with his quest to wrench some sort of vengeance from the Vanir," said Surtr. "I don't think he even has a clear idea why he seeks revenge anymore; all of his energy is spent manipulating people and events to achieve his ultimate goal."

Surtr frowned. "We originally believed in what we were doing; we thought it was the right thing for the Vanir as a people, to expand our boundaries beyond our own world, to find new technology outside what we were used to. The Council denied Odin's proposition without regard for how it might influence our world for the better. Our land is severely overpopulated, and with our ability to manipulate the very atomic structure of things we have practically made disease a thing of the past, so even death beyond the ravages of age is rare. Within the next century we will have too many people for our world to sustain us.

"Odin's plan to resettle on other worlds was initially a peaceful one, but when the Council questioned him about what our reaction should be if indigenous inhabitants resisted, he responded truthfully. He told them we should take the lands by force if anyone opposed us, and the territory would then become the property of the victors – who would of course be the Vanir.

"The Vanir Council's refusal was the first step on his road to madness," continued Surtr, his gaze haunted in the moonlight as they walked. "None of us believed he had actually murdered his wife. His story was that the Council had ordered assassins to kill her as a warning to him not to stir trouble. I now know the truth. No man who had lost his own partner to assassins could so callously slay somebody's wife as he did my beautiful Sinmara. I will not rest until he is dead... or I am."

"Good to know," said Wes cheerfully. "Now when you've finished feeling sorry for yourself, could you try to remember something which might help us before we stumble into their camp and get killed? I know you wouldn't mind, with your death-wish and all, but it would break too many hearts if I didn't return."

Surtr stared aghast at Wes's casual dismissal of his anguish. Talbot almost felt sorry for the man... until he recalled Surtr had killed countless innocents, including Australian soldiers, in his blind acceptance of Prometheus. The fact Wes was actually talking to him was probably more than he deserved, especially considering he hadn't yet shown any sort of guilt for his deeds, merely remorse for his lost wife. The more Talbot thought about it, the less sympathy he felt for Surtr, and the more he understood Wes's reaction to the Aesir traitor's selfish grief.

They traveled the next hour in an awkward silence through the shadows. It was such an inhospitable land, Talbot had to keep reminding himself they were still on Earth, merely centuries in its past. He kept glancing up at the half-moon to reassure himself they hadn't somehow been transported to a land of cold rock and dead trees, the shadows seeming like skeletons in the dark. More than once, Talbot's heart leaped as he caught what looked like something moving from the corner of his eye, only to spin around and see it was simply a gnarled branch, clawing silently at shadows.

"It is over this crest," whispered Surtr, motioning with his hand at the hill they were approaching. "The main dig site lies beyond, though I have not been here for some time."

Despite the darkness, Talbot felt almost certain it was a different area to the one where he had been held captive. Suddenly his heart lurched as he remembered that his brother, Thomas, was still enslaved at one of these sites.

If Thomas still lived, that was.

At a silent signal from Wes, all three dropped to their bellies and shimmied up to the top of the hill. Once there, they hid within a clump of thick bushes, and Talbot peered down to the valley below, noting how much larger this site was than the one where he had been held prisoner. The entire valley floor was carved away so deeply he could only see the bottom thanks to large glowing domes placed at several intervals, presumably of Aesir design and origin. The clay and stone had been layered around the sides of the excavation, reshaped into roadways, and he could almost picture thousands of slaves having to trudge up that slippery slope carrying sacks of rock and dirt during all sorts of weather.

The main dig site was clearly distinguishable in the center of the huge excavation, glowing beneath the Aesir's odd light source. Scanning the area, Talbot suddenly gasped. Wes clutched him firmly by the shoulder, silencing him, but he couldn't halt the shock which washed through him.

In the deepest pit of the oversized excavation was a rift gate.

He'd known this was what they were searching for, but this gate was at least triple the size of any Talbot had seen before. The other gates were simplistic designs similar to that of Stonehenge, whereas this was circle upon entangled circle of standing stones, some with cross-stones re-set above them while others seemed to stand alone.

The Aesir must have discovered this gate soon after Wes had rescued him at the other site; either that or they'd exhausted thousands of slaves to get it prepared so swiftly. Otherwise Talbot's pit would have surely been shut down and the slaves... he didn't want to think what might have happened if they'd no longer had a use for him.

Looking down from this height, Talbot could see the intricate pattern the design made up. It reminded him of the code he'd learned to unlock on their previous mission.

They had found a similar pattern within a cave in Ayers Rock, Australia, where Talbot had managed to mentally convert Aboriginal dot-paintings into music using his innate talent – some elusive element associated with the Elder-tongue. Once he'd played the tune, the entire cave had dropped into the depths of the Earth, leading the way to a hidden rift.

Gazing down at the stone pattern, Talbot suddenly realized it was designed this way as a defense mechanism. The gate required either someone possessing the talent of the Elder-tongue or one of the original Olympians involved with designing such gates to activate them.

Hence the Aesir's desperation to gain Talbot's cooperation... or his brother's.

Aesir scurried around the fully excavated gate, and Talbot's pulse raced yet again when he realized they weren't working on the gate, it looked more like they were preparing to start the ancient machinery. But if that was the case, it meant....

Talbot frantically scanned the excavation site for the gate's primitive control board, his heart thudding against his ribs as panic threatened to set in. He finally spotted it on a small, slightly raised area of flat ground opposite the gate. Sure enough, standing at the controls was Thomas. He was rapidly touching symbols on the large stone panel, and Talbot could see them lighting up as his hand flickered over them. Standing behind him, hovering ominously, like a vulture over a man dying in the desert, was Prometheus.

Thomas hit the last of the symbols on the stone panel and suddenly the entire area flared with intense light, but the gate did not open as Talbot had expected. Every gate he had ever seen manipulated in such a manner had opened a rift in conjunction with the control panel sequence completing. This time, however, a high pitched squeal echoed out over the entire area. Talbot covered his ears as agony ripped through his brain.

He squeezed his hands tight over his ears and tried to focus on the gate. Prometheus appeared unaffected by the defense system, even as Thomas writhed on the ground in agony. Unconcerned, Prometheus motioned to someone Talbot couldn't see and soft lilting notes mixed in with the piercing screech. The power of the alarm tone gradually lessened as the plucked notes of a harp floated like a light layer of silk atop a blazing fire, but instead of being consumed by the flames, the notes lessened the conflagration. Talbot swiftly realized Prometheus must have been ready for such a secondary defense.

Defying physics, the prodigious stone blocks began to spin as though the expanded version of Stonehenge had been placed on a mammoth merry-go-round and flung by a giant. Within seconds the stones themselves became a blur, and a deafening crack sounded throughout the pit. An absolutely enormous rift unfurled in the air, at least ten-times the size of any Talbot had seen before, hanging vertically like a tremendous sail waiting to be filled by the breeze. This sail, however, was completely dark, reminiscent of a black hole, seeming to draw the little light from the surrounding area as it hung motionless. Shimmers of color, akin to miniature rainbows, skipped across the rift's surface resembling oil on the ocean, reminding Talbot again why this was referred to as Bifrost, the Rainbow Bridge.

From where they lay hidden, Talbot, Wes, and Surtr had a perfect view across the excavation. Prometheus stood before Bifrost, a huge grin of triumph spreading across his face. Talbot could almost sense the smug satisfaction radiating from Prometheus, the promise of his quest for power reaching its ultimate crescendo.

That look somehow sickened Talbot.

An arm the thickness of a school bus suddenly burst forth from the center of the open rift, seizing Prometheus around the torso, lifting the fourteen-foot-tall figure from the ground like a child's toy. The skin of the arm was deep crimson, growths all along it reminding Talbot of warts or moles, but each of these opened and closed like a hungry mouth. The fingers on the hand were long and thick, ending in a long black pointed nail extending like a sword blade beyond the tip of each digit.

Talbot instinctively began to stand, intent on sprinting down to aid his terrified brother. A hand grabbed his shirt just as he started to rise, and Wes pulled him effortlessly back down into the cover of the thick bushes.

"Wait," hissed the commando.

Talbot's gaze returned to the scene below. He watched as Prometheus battled uselessly against the giant hand which gripped him, battering his hands against the thick crimson fingers. A look of concentration momentarily crossed the Aesir leader's face and an instant later razor-sharp blades shot out from his body, piercing the flesh of the huge hand. It hardly reacted to the attack, its grip barely flinching. Desperately, the Aesir lord transformed his hands into battleaxes, and slashed and hacked at the skin of the thumb in an attempt to get loose. The blows barely marked the red skin, and the few which actually managed to cut the surface healed instantly.

The hand squeezed tighter, and despite their distance, Talbot could almost hear Prometheus's ribs shatter, his internal organs bursting from the incredible pressure. This in itself couldn't kill Prometheus, and he waited to see what the Aesir leader would do next.

A huge surge of yellowed liquid, molasses-like in its consistency, spurted from the puckering apertures of the giant arm, spraying out across the ground, covering the dig site in the blink of an eye. Guards who had been frozen in horror after the initial attack now tried to flee, only to find themselves stuck within the dense emulsion, their piteous cries echoing across the valley as they realized they were now trapped like flies in honey.

Thomas got covered in the same substance and once more Talbot tried to move, but Wes continued to restrain him.

"You can't help him by dying," hissed the Australian.

A crackling burst of radiance shot from the giant red hand. The lightning jolted through the thick substance, causing everything within it to freeze momentarily. The charge traveled all the way to the outer edges, becoming a voluminous web, finally snapping like elastic which had stretched to its limit. It shot back from all sides, retreating into the open pores of the horrific arm.

Everything within the excavation was instantaneously drained – that was the only explanation for it. Life was washed away in an instant, like a tsunami of soul-sucking acid had hit every being within the pit and emptied it absolutely.

One moment the figures were fully formed, fighting to break free from within the goo, the next they were empty husks, crumbling in the light breeze. Talbot bit his hand, preventing himself from crying out as he spied the drained and broken shell that had moments ago been his brother.

Prometheus wasn't drained, however. With his regenerative abilities, his life force wasn't sapped as easily as the mortals. He fought against the initial drain, and more emulsion poured over him, repeating the draining process, sucking even more life from him.

He survived again.

Seven times they watched the cycle repeat.

Talbot had known Prometheus was powerful, but nothing could have made him believe he might endure seven leeching blasts before succumbing. Each time it happened, he could see the life being sucked from the Aesir leader, but he managed to regenerate himself enough each time to survive the next blast. The sixth time had seen Prometheus's body broken and crumbling, more like a corpse than a living thing. At a shake from the red arm his leg broke loose and fell to the dirt floor of the site, shattering like pottery.

Instantly a budding new leg began to form, but it was too slow. The milky emulsion covered Prometheus once more, pouring down his throat and in through his empty eye-sockets. The last draining finally sucked Prometheus completely dry of energy, and after the flash of light, all that was left within the gigantic hand was gray ash, which soon blew lifelessly across the valley floor.

Prometheus was finally dead.

There was no time for celebrating – or mourning the loss of Thomas. The red arm withdrew only to see the rift stretch and grow until it filled most of the open pit, reaching a height almost level with the lip of the excavation. The skyscraper-high rift then shimmered once more, and the owner of the massive arm stepped through, ducking slightly as it emerged.

Talbot had seen giants before, but nothing could have prepared him for what crossed through the rift. The giants they had fought in the battle between the Olympians and the Titans had been perhaps a hundred and fifty-feet-tall – tiny in comparison with this behemoth.

This giant was so grotesquely muscled its movements almost appeared troubled, but it was the skin which drew Talbot's attention most. The nodes he had seen on the hulking arm were all across the giant's naked torso, its skin the same deep crimson color. The puckering lumps reminded Talbot of thousands of hungry baby mouths, each looking to suckle. The troubling thing was he had just seen what they liked to suckle upon –

Life.

His gaze traveled up to the giant's head, and Talbot gasped. It was not human, not even close. Eyes sprouted all around the hairless cranium, granting the beast all-encompassing vision. Ears bent and turned like a cat's high upon the scalp, and its nose formed flat against the giant's face, with only two slits in the skin for nostrils. A lipless mouth held rows of serrated teeth, each as long as Wes's sword.

"We have to get out of here," whispered Surtr, his voice close to panic.

"Not yet," replied Wes. The Aesir defector ignored him and rose from the bushes, running off down the hill in the direction from which they had come, possibly hoping that in his human form he could escape undetected.

He was wrong.

The rift giant turned with a swiftness that defied its colossal size, leaping effortlessly from the deep excavation site, up and over the hill. Surtr attempted to dart aside, but the giant landed in front of him, completely blocking the pass. The monstrous head glared down at the Aesir defector with its many beady eyes, promises of horror burning within its gaze. Surtr sprinted to the left, but a huge foot crashed down in front of him once more.

Then Talbot noticed the second giant. It had emerged unnoticed from the rift while they were engrossed watching the hopeless plight of their companion as he tried to flee.

This second giant was different from the first, more like those they'd seen before in the battle between the Olympians and the Titans, it simply seemed an enormous version of a very ugly, white, human male. Everything was in proportion, right down to the loincloth the giant wore around its waist. Apart from this scrap of cloth, the creature was naked.

Seeing he was cornered, Surtr began shifting and altering his body into the form of the huge troll he had used earlier, his bones and ligaments popping like firecrackers as his body expanded. But against the two monstrous behemoths confronting him, the troll's forty feet of height seemed insignificant, and the larger of the two, the red-skinned one, began to laugh, a sound deep and ominous.

"You think to stand against Hrungnir? We will destroy you before feasting upon this pitiful world. Your children and your children's children will forever remember this day as the one you all became slaves of Valhalla."

The words hung ominously in the air for a moment before Surtr leaped high, his boulder-sized fists smashing Hrungnir directly in the groin. Instead of upsetting the giant, this action seemed to amuse him immensely, and his wicked mouth stretched wide in a malicious smile as he caught Surtr by the arms, lifting him high and dangling him there, helpless.

"I suppose we can do with one less slave."

The milky resin-like substance poured from Hrungnir's skin and flowed swiftly over Surtr while he thrashed and writhed. Even though Talbot had just seen the action of Hrungnir leeching the life from his victims in the valley below, he was still shocked as the bolts of power shot through the liquid. Again the entire mixture withdrew with a snap, along with the life force of Surtr. Seen up close, the incident proved even more horrific, as Talbot witnessed the exact moment when Surtr's life was drained from him, and the horrified expression he shot back at Talbot right before turning to dust.

"Holy shit," breathed Wes beside him as they both crouched even lower in the thick bushes.

The giant named Hrungnir appeared to scan the area with its many eyes before turning back to the other giant and barking something Talbot couldn't hear properly. Immediately, his companion bowed and leaped back into the pit. It stepped through the rift only to return moments later, marching up the hill to where Hrungnir waited. Another giant emerged, followed by another, and another. Soon, a steady line of giants was pouring out, filling the pit.

Talbot lost count of their numbers after the first hundred or so, but they continued on for several hours until the sun finally crested the horizon, bathing the host of giants in its early-morning light. Rather than making them seem less threatening, the sunlight made the army of behemoths even more real, and Talbot constantly found himself holding his breath as more and more of the gargantuan creatures emerged from the rift.

In between the enormous humanoid creatures, Talbot watched various flying beasts appear. Some were serpentine – he guessed they were a type of dragon – while others were like winged humans, grossly malformed, but recognizable in form. Dragging through his memory, Talbot concentrated on what these beings from Norse mythology might be. He finally concluded they were creatures called valkyrie. From what he could recall, though, the valkyries were described as angelic creatures who guided the souls of fallen heroes from the battlefield to Valhalla. But there was nothing angelic about these things. Almost demonic in their appearance, they stretched perhaps twice the height of a human being, with wide, bat-like membranous wings sprouting from their backs.

The giants far outnumbered the dragons and valkyrie, and soon these other creatures were lost within the mass of gigantic bodies. Talbot glanced over at Wes several times while the assorted creatures were gathering, amazed to find the commando silently sleeping. He frowned, wishing he could remain so calm in the face of such calamity.

Finally the stream of giants ended, leaving a force of thousands standing around Hrungnir, who barked an order, leading them away. The ground thundered as the incredible congregation marched off in the direction Wes and Talbot had come from – straight toward the Vanir camp. Glancing over at Wes, Talbot saw the commando was now alert, his eyes narrowed as he watched the army rapidly disappearing into the distance.

"We have to warn the Vanir," said Talbot, clambering to his feet and moving from the cover of the bushes. Wes did the same.

"We can't warn them," said Wes, his voice bereft of emotion. He brushed dirt from his chest. "Those giants move way too fast for us to even keep up, let alone get in front of them. The Vanir are gonna be alone for this one; hopefully they're smart enough to run and not fight. We have something else to do first."

"What?"

He looked below them at the rift gate still hanging suspended in the air. "We have to destroy that gate before anything else gets through."

Talbot looked back at the rapidly disappearing force of giants, feeling hopelessness sink in as they headed unerringly toward the Vanir camp.

"Wes, if they kill off the Vanir, there's nothing in this time to oppose them. This is Earth, it's not some foreign plane of existence where we can just say, 'Oh well,' and keep on going. If they conquer the world during this time, chances are our entire planet is doomed."

"Don't you think I fucking know that?" snarled Wes. "But we can't do anything about the giants yet. All we can do is try to prevent more bad shit getting through from Valhalla."

Talbot's heart wrenched, but he knew Wes was right. He followed the commando down the winding paths cut into the sides of the excavated site, avoiding the yawning footprints left by the invading giants. It took them a while, but eventually they approached the unearthed control panel. Talbot froze, remembering what had happened.

Thomas was dead… *really* dead.

Talbot had gone through the mixed emotions before when searching for his brother beyond the rifts which led to Olympia,

Hades, and Tartarus, but never before had he faced such definite evidence that Thomas was gone forever. From where he stood, he could even see the remaining pile of ash which marked his brother's demise, and Talbot felt suddenly choked with emotion.

"No time for that, princess," snapped Wes. "We've got work to do. Do your bawling later when we've got time."

Despite the callousness of Wes's words, they instantly cut through Talbot's remorse, and he moved forward, only to be waved back by the commando.

"On second thought, stay out of the way. Go cry over there for a while." Wes drew Laevateinn and strode forward. He studied the panels momentarily while Talbot stepped back, confused.

Suddenly, Wes swung Laevateinn and spun a full three hundred and sixty degrees on his heel, bringing the blade crashing down hard on the main stone control panel. The heavy block exploded outward as though hit by a missile. Wes repeated the motion three more times, smashing the secondary panels into tiny fragments as easily as if he were carving through snow. The entire action lasted less than a few seconds, and in the end all that was left was a pile of rubble, Wes standing in the middle, sheathing Laevateinn smoothly.

"Sorry about your brother," he said quietly, looking Talbot directly in the eye.

Before Talbot could reply, a deafening thunder filled the air, and they both spun to look at its source. The surface of the rift was cracking. Before, the rift had looked like a pond of ink, shimmering colors flowing across its surface, but now it looked like a choppy whirlpool.

"Uh, Wes. I think we'd better go."

"I think you're right."

The two ran straight up the angled side of the pit, which was set at about forty-five degrees. The going was tough, but both had the distinct feeling they didn't have enough time to take the long winding route they'd descended.

And they weren't a moment too soon.

The rift began sucking in the air around it. A low flying bird with the misfortune of swooping in front of the rift at exactly the wrong moment was dragged in with the sudden influx of air, disappearing with a twittering screech. Soon the suction became so great that bushes along the rim were torn out by their roots.

They were only halfway out of the pit.

Talbot scrambled up the steep clay sides, often slipping and clawing his way up on all fours. Panic roared through him, wind crashing all around him.

They were just cresting the top of the excavation when trees began flying past them; full-sized trunks torn from the earth and sucked into the swirling vortex of the collapsing rift. The forest edging the dig site already revealed several patches where weaker trees had been torn loose, but the larger ones were starting to sway alarmingly; their bending loosening the dirt holding their roots. Talbot gazed at the forest in horror, imagining thousands of trees flying toward them with nowhere to hide.

"Run, you stunned mullet," yelled Wes, snapping Talbot into action. He began sprinting for the illusory safety of the trees, knowing they could tear loose at any moment, smashing into his head like a baseball bat hitting a cantaloupe.

But they didn't.

The rift imploded instead.

Wes grabbed Talbot and thrust him to the ground just as the air crackled. The sky itself seemed to shatter, the vibration stinging his cheeks as the vortex detonated. Talbot glanced back and saw the rift collapsing in on itself; the gravity too strong for it to hold shape without a gate. The entire process happened swiftly, and only a few more trees were dragged across the ground before the rift closed completely with a momentous clap. Wes warily rose to his feet and helped Talbot to stand.

"How cool was that?" gasped the Australian.

"*Cool?* My brother was just killed!"

Wes's grin dropped. "Not that part; the bit with all the trees flying around. I told you I was sorry about your brother."

"It doesn't mean I'm over it, Wes. I'm not like you."

"What does that mean?"

"It means I can't just shut off my emotions to deal with them when it suits me. I can't stop thinking that right now the Vanir are probably being slaughtered –"

"There's nothing we can do about that!" protested Wes. "You saw those things! What the hell are we supposed to do? You want me to swing in like Tarzan on a vine and scoop them all up? Hang on, I'll just go and change into my loincloth."

"It doesn't mean we shouldn't care, Wes."

"That's just stupid. We can't do anything, but we should feel *guilty*? What should we feel bad about; not getting killed with them?"

"We should feel bad that they're dying. It's that simple."

"I'll worry about that when the issue at hand is resolved," said Wes.

"What issue?"

"The tiny issue of an army of around ten thousand giants strolling across our planet during a time when we have absolutely no means of fighting them."

Talbot realized what he meant, but coming from Wes it sounded so much worse. He'd always felt confident when Wes had said he'd take care of a problem, but now Talbot realized the opposite was also true. Talbot felt terrified as he looked at Wes, because when he looked into the commando's eyes he saw something he'd never seen there before –

Doubt.

CHAPTER 9

Fenrir gasped as he struggled on, stumbling for what seemed like the thousandth time. Zoe reached out and grabbed his arm, preventing him from falling. He gave her a tired smile of thanks and looked back at the stragglers, both human and Vanir.

They were pitifully few.

It had been a miracle any had escaped at all, especially considering the speed and ferocity of the giants' attack. The Vanir lookouts had been killed, leaving Fenrir with no warning of the approaching force until they were upon them, tearing his Vanir followers apart, limb from limb.

The enormous one named Hrungnir had made a swift speech on how they would be dominated, laughing hollowly at their feeble attempts at defense. He had brushed aside Fenrir's wolf form as though he were a puppy, and Fenrir had only survived because of Barktooth. The jarnvidjur had launched an attack on Hrungnir's back, and he had flung Fenrir aside before grasping Barktooth and absorbing her essence. Whatever the foul substance flowing from the giant's arms was, it seemed to suck every ounce of life from its victims. All that had been left of Barktooth was ash.

Fenrir lost his footing once more, and this time Zoe slipped his arm over her shoulders, gripping him around the waist to help support him. He started to argue, but realized he had no energy for it. After his easy defeat by Hrungnir, Zoe had grabbed Fenrir and dragged him away from the battle, followed by these pitiful few, and they had escaped into the hills. The giants seemed happy to let them go, gorging themselves instead on those who couldn't escape.

Out of the force of thousands he had led into this land to stop

Prometheus, only twenty or so now survived, along with about a dozen humans from the Viking camp.

Their dying screams still sounded within Fenrir's head....

For days the Vanir and Norse stumbled on, lost and bewildered. The Vikings hunted for small game, and the group lived in fear. At one point a faction of eighteen Aesir had approached them, their eyes full of horror, their skin covered in the blood of their comrades. Fenrir had questioned them at length before agreeing to let them join their group of survivors.

After two weeks of stumbling around the countryside, the group of survivors came across an Aesir slave camp – or rather, what remained of an Aesir slave camp. The site was big enough to hold several hundred slaves and their guards, but none remained now. The telltale sign of giant footprints trampling the muddy ground told the story of what must have happened.

Strangely, the mindless warriors, the ones brainwashed by the Aesir to unquestioningly obey orders, were killed, but left untouched. They had neither been absorbed by Hrungnir, nor had they been eaten by the other giants; the bodies were simply discarded like unwanted trash. Fenrir wondered if the process Prometheus had employed to make them fearless had somehow corrupted their flesh as well, making them unpalatable for the giants.

Someone shouted a warning of strangers approaching. Shielding his eyes against the sun, Fenrir spotted two figures walking directly toward them, not hiding their approach in any way. The figures wore swords at their hips, but their hair appeared to be cut short, lessening the probability they were Norsemen. Even before they became distinguishable, Fenrir had already figured out who the two were, and for the first time in weeks his heart lifted.

"Did you miss us?" called Wes, striding forward and shaking his hand. Talbot merely nodded.

"Where is Surtr?" asked Fenrir.

Wes shook his head, his eyes dropping, and Fenrir's uplifted mood plummeted. His first instinct was to let his emotions loose and rail against the heavens for taking his brother from him so soon after reuniting them, but too many years as a leader had left Fenrir with the knowledge of what losing control in such a way would do to those who followed him. A leader needed to appear strong during the fragile times, a beacon of hope when all else seemed lost. So Fenrir held back his emotions and merely nodded.

"What happened?"

Wes recounted what had occurred after they'd left the Vanir camp and gone to scout the dig site. His report, clinical and detailed, brushed over embellishments and stuck to solid facts.

"So Prometheus opened the gate. I suspected as much," said Fenrir at the end of the tale. "Are you sure he's dead this time?"

"Considering he looked like barbequed potpourri when he blew away, I'd say, yeah, that fucker's toast."

Fenrir nodded. "I shall have to tell his daughter."

Fenrir's gaze crossed the camp to where Zoe was aiding one of the injured Norsemen. She looked up and met his stare, and he was suddenly unsure about how she would react to the news.

He motioned for her to come over, and then recounted the story to her. Zoe's gaze shot to Wes for confirmation, and the commando silently nodded. A strange look came over Zoe's face and she wandered away to the edge of the camp and sat alone, staring out at the horizon.

"I should go talk with her," said Fenrir, but Wes placed a restraining hand on his arm.

"I'll go," he said.

"Wes, are you sure that's a good idea?" asked Talbot.

"Trust me," replied Wes, and before either of them could argue the point he was heading over to Zoe.

"Was that wise?" asked Fenrir.

"We'll know in a minute," replied Talbot.

***

"Hey, how's it going?" asked Wes, sitting down beside Zoe.

"I'd rather be alone at the moment."

"No you wouldn't. Why are you upset?"

"Who says I'm upset?" she countered.

"Your sad face says so. Why? Come on; spit it out like a bad porn star."

Zoe thought for a moment, contemplating telling Wes to leave again before realizing she really did want to talk. "My father is dead."

"Yeah, I know. Isn't that a good thing?"

"I thought it would be. For a long time his death was all I could think about. I thought I might be happy when he finally died; I imagined my mother's spirit might know some peace."

"And now?" prompted Wes.

"Now? I just seem to feel all... hollow... inside. There's nothing in the place where my anger used to be, just emptiness."

Wes nodded. "That's because you're confused."

"What do you mean?"

"Your brain is telling you your father's death is a good thing, but your heart is realizing that a big part of your existence is gone forever. For good or bad, he was still your father, and with him gone, a major part of your life has just ended. It'll probably get worse as the years go by; you'll forget all the bad stuff and just end up missing him."

"He killed my mother."

"But he didn't kill you," countered Wes.

"Are you saying I should regret his death? Do you think he was somehow good?" asked Zoe incredulously.

"Me? Nah. I thought he was a piece of shit and wish I could have killed him myself. But then again he wasn't *my* father. We're talking about you, and the reality of what will happen. Prometheus was an arsehole, but I don't know what he was like as a father – he might have been awesome."

"He killed my mother," Zoe repeated. "He tormented me and used my blood."

"Yeah, that is a good point. So why do you give a shit about him dying?"

The question totally disarmed her and for a moment Zoe had no answer. "I guess because of all those things you said. I just don't know what to think at the moment. I keep remembering him telling me stories when I was a kid; not the ones about you and Talbot, they came later after things went… bad. But when I was a child he used to hold me and tell me about such fantastic places and creatures, and he'd change his appearance to look like them. I was totally in awe of him back then; he was like a god to me."

"And that's the part of your heart which is now mourning; the part that remembers the good dad, not the bad one. Eventually that part will take over, rounding the edges of the pain until you can look at the whole thing without hurting."

Zoe began to cry, feeling walls inside her breaking down. She never noticed Wes's arms fold around her, nor did she realize it when she returned his embrace and huddled her face into his chest, her body shaking with the strength of her sobs as years of pain were unleashed. The crying went on for several minutes before ebbing, and when it finally stopped she sat back and wiped her eyes, staring at Wes as though seeing him for the first time.

"Thank you," she whispered.

"No worries," he replied, giving her a wink.

Something passed between the two of them, but before Zoe had time to realize what it was, the moment was gone, leaving her confused. Wes noticed it too, and with an awkward grin he muttered something inane before rising and moving away on his own.

Zoe tried to understand what had just occurred, but the memory of it was like a greased fish, and kept slipping out of her grasp. She could only remember one thing.

It had excited her.

***

Talbot walked over to Wes as the commando wandered through the simple camp of refugees.

"Is she okay?" he asked.

Wes turned his head. "Huh? Oh, uh… yeah, I guess. She's a tough chick."

"That was nice of you."

"What was?" asked Wes vaguely.

"Talking to her. I wouldn't have expected it from you."

Wes frowned, his eyes narrowing as he regarded Talbot. "Why? Because I'm a dumb monkey?"

"No, of course not! It's just a side of you I've never seen before."

Wes relaxed. "Sorry, mate. My head's all messed up at the moment, that's all."

"What's wrong?"

Wes paused in his walking, spreading his arms wide. "This! All of this shit!" he spat vehemently. "I have no idea what the hell we're going to do, and every time I turn around, I see in somebody's expression that they expect me to figure everything out and make it all alright again. If it's not you, it's Fenrir. If it's not him, it's Zoe staring at me with her big blue eyes."

"Oh," said Talbot, suddenly understanding.

"What's that supposed to mean?"

Talbot shrugged. "I never realized you cared about her like that."

"Like *what*, exactly?"

"Like... as in you *like* her," Talbot replied.

"Of course I like her. She's a cool chick."

Talbot shook his head slightly. "That's not what I mean."

Wes stared at him quizzically for a moment before letting out a barking laugh. "You think I – With her – You've got to be joking!"

Talbot shrugged. "I just say it how I see it, Wes."

"Well you need glasses, nerd boy! I – I'd never – I.... Shit!"

Talbot nodded, patting Wes on the shoulder. "Yep. That's about it, buddy. Good timing too, by the way."

Wes sat down, covering his face with his hands. "This can't be happening," he muttered.

"You're in love," said Talbot, grinning despite everything else that was weighing down on them.

"I think you're right," groaned Wes.

Talbot chuckled, sitting down beside his friend. "So what now?"

"Fucked if I know," replied Wes, dropping his hands. "But all of a sudden an army of giants seems much less daunting."

Talbot's laughter echoed out around the camp.

***

Two weeks passed without further wrath from the invading army. Wes had constantly seemed distracted, avoiding Zoe whenever possible, but when forced together the two seemed uncomfortable, which sometimes led to arguments.

Talbot could understand why. They were in the early stages of a war – or rather they were fleeing for their lives – and Zoe and Wes had both just come to the realization they were attracted to each other. A relationship under such circumstances was a ridiculous idea, and Wes and Zoe understood this. So their desire remained unfulfilled, knowing that if they were to succumb it could only distract them.

This was logical. Talbot had hardly even known the pretty young Norse girl who had nursed him when he'd injured himself back on the longship. When he and Wes had reunited with the Vanir and surviving Norsemen, Talbot had discovered she wasn't among them; she'd been killed by the giants. He'd never even found out her name, and the knowledge he never would hurt Talbot like a kick in the guts. Wes knew that such a feeling of loss would be worse, much worse, for him if he allowed himself to let his emotions loose regarding Zoe.

The end result was a snappier, grumpier Wes.

Both Vanir and Norsemen swiftly learned to tiptoe around the crabby Australian as he continually fretted over the issues they faced each day. First and foremost was their need to survive. The army of giants from Valhalla was swiftly making the land a charnel-house, destroying anything in their path as Hrungnir absorbed almost everything he could get his hands on. Men, women, children, and even livestock were all fodder for the leader of the giants, but scouts had now begun reporting that people were also being herded alive, like cattle. Talbot guessed this might be what Hrungnir had been referring to when he'd boasted about creating slaves for Valhalla.

He pushed the concern aside. It didn't matter. The only thing of importance at the moment was surviving. That in itself was becoming more and more difficult with all forms of wildlife being either eaten by the giants or scared off by their movements. The Vanir knew of many roots and plants which they could eat, but food like that left Talbot and many of the others feeling increasingly weak and lethargic each day. Despair was becoming prevalent among the survivors, and fights often broke out, especially among the Norsemen. The number of humans in the group had swelled, survivors from destroyed villages finding them and being incorporated into their faction. There were close to two hundred Vanir and human survivors in total now.

And Wes's mood worsened each day. He was snapping at people when they failed to break camp quickly enough each morning, or he'd set an incredibly fast pace as they hiked across the broken land. Everything he did was plausible up to a point, and most of the Vanir and Norse accepted his mood simply because they didn't know Wes too well.

But Talbot knew him.

"We need to get these guys on an even playing field," stated Wes one morning.

"What do you mean, Wes?" Talbot asked.

"I mean we're only delaying the inevitable right now. Running away from these guys is not a long-term solution. You said it yourself; this is Earth during our past, and if things go to shit here we've got nowhere to go back to – providing we even *find* a way back to our own time."

"So what do you suggest?"

Wes frowned and looked down at his hands. "I think we need to find a way to travel into the future – the same way Fenrir came through to threaten me. We need to get home and… and…."

"And what?"

Wes brought his gaze up, staring Talbot directly in the eyes. "And somehow lure the army of giants into following us there," he said softly.

Talbot almost swallowed his own tongue.

"Well… you… I mean… you can't!" stammered Talbot. "What

the hell will happen if you take them through to our time?"

"Your time. I'm from *your* future, remember?"

"Then why don't we take them to your future with all the futuristic weapons and stuff?"

"That's not an option," Wes replied cryptically. "If things are the same as when I left then we definitely don't want to take these bastards there." His steely, slightly haunted gaze left Talbot with no doubt it was not open for discussion.

"Okay, why take them through to my time, then?"

Wes sighed. "At least in your time there are weapons which might actually be able to defend against these guys. With the Aesir and Vanir already decimated during this age, the planet doesn't stand a chance. If the giant army from Valhalla destroys humanity during this time, things will go to shit back in ours – I mean yours. You understand?"

"Not really," replied Talbot.

"Good. Now you know what's been going through my head for the past few weeks."

"Is that it? I thought it was because…." Talbot trailed off.

"Because of what?"

Talbot sighed, glancing around before he answered. "I thought it was because of Zoe."

"Zoe?" Wes sputtered. "Why would it have anything to do with Zoe?"

Talbot shrugged. "I thought it could be because of the way you felt about her."

"That's got nothing to do with this," snapped Wes defensively, casting a quick look around. "Well… not really. But I can't afford to worry about it at the moment. Our main concern has to remain with beating these gigantic motherfuckers, and that's the best idea I can come up with. Can you suggest something better?"

"Well, of course not, but –"

"Then it's decided. We shall call it Operation Tea Kettle."

"Why?" asked Talbot.

"Because it's probably the only time in human history I'll ever get to name a strategic global military campaign. What's wrong with it?"

replied Wes with a straight face.

Talbot chuckled. "Nice to have you back, Wes."

"Nice to *be* back, cupcake," replied Wes. "Now let's go and see Fenrir."

They strode through the camp, finally coming to the tent of Fenrir and entering it. The leader of the Vanir had recovered well from his encounter with the giants, at least physically, but Talbot doubted he would ever be the same. There was a wariness in Fenrir's gaze now that had not been there before, and Talbot guessed this was due in part to a small niggling measure of self doubt which had wormed its way into Fenrir's heart following his easy defeat by Hrungnir. His self-confidence seemed shattered, and Talbot wondered if the Vanir leader had ever experienced anything so demoralizing before.

"Hey there, Fluffy," said Wes with a sloppy salute to the seated Vanir. "How's it going?"

"Are you joking?" replied Fenrir, a subtle growl in his voice.

"Still sulking, huh? Anyway, we need your help."

Fenrir shot Wes a venomous glare. Wes grinned.

"What do you want?" asked the Vanir coldly.

"How do we get back to the future? Not in a Michael J. Fox kinda way, more like the way *you* did it. Mainly because I don't have a Delorean big enough for what I want to do, otherwise that'd be really cool."

"What in the world are you yapping about?" asked Fenrir, frowning up at Wes. Talbot had to suppress a grin; he'd seen that look before when people had to deal with Wes.

"Oh, didn't I tell you? We're gonna take the giants to our time where we can blow the hell out of them with bombs and crap."

Fenrir stared, mouth agape, at Wes. "You can't be serious," he finally said.

"Now you see why I can't do it with a Delorean," replied Wes. "We'd have a serious problem with legroom."

"Do you have any idea what kind of power transporting an army of ten thousand giants would require? And that's not even including the dragons or other flying beasts!"

"Is it one point twenty-one gigawatts?"

"What?" snapped Fenrir.

Wes sobered slightly. "Can it be done, Fenrir?" he asked seriously.

"It could be done, but –"

"Don't worry about any butts, yours is pretty enough. This is the only option left to us, Fenrir, apart from throwing rocks at them – which I'm pretty sure wouldn't work."

"You would need to gather the entire Valhallian Army together in one place. How would you do that?" asked Fenrir, climbing to his feet.

"With my special charm, of course," replied Wes cryptically.

Fenrir seemed far from convinced, but he moved across the tent and pulled out a rough map, sketched on goat hide; obviously a creation from one of the various Norse tribes now gathered with them. Scanning the document swiftly, he jabbed his finger down on a point toward the east.

"There," Fenrir said.

Talbot and Wes stared down at where he had pointed. Talbot had very little experience reading maps of this kind, but it was simple enough to understand. The place Fenrir had indicated appeared to be a vast box canyon situated up in the mountains bordering this inhospitable land.

"Looks good," agreed Wes. "We'll begin preparations tomorrow." Fenrir nodded, returning his attention to the map while Talbot and Wes exited the tent.

"Right," said Wes once they were outside. "I'm going to need your help for something."

"What's that?" asked Talbot.

"I need you to figure out how the hell we can get all those big bastards into the one place at the same time."

Wes strode off into the night, chuckling while Talbot spluttered and cursed.

**

Sveinn crept up to the outskirts of the enemy's camp – if it could be called a camp. The giants seemed to merely drop where they were at the end of their daily march, sleeping wherever they wanted. There were no toilet holes dug, nor were there any cooking fires; the giants seemed to prefer eating people raw – quite often while they were still alive. They defecated toward the outskirts of their 'camp' and more than once over the past two days Sveinn had almost been caught by one of the terrifying figures wandering toward where he hid and urinating the equivalent of a river nearby.

The man named Wes – the strange outlander with the glowing sword which he had taken from the fire god named Surtr – had given this task to Sveinn personally, and several of the other Norse warriors had looked at Sveinn with jealousy in their eyes upon seeing him bestowed with this honor. The warrior named Wes was regarded as something of a demigod since joining the clan; some claimed he was actually Loki in mortal form. At the very least it would explain his closeness to Fenrir, leader of the Vanir. To be given a task directly from him was a great prize; it spoke of his faith in Sveinn being able to achieve what needed to be done.

He would not fail.

The morning sun began to crest the mountains and, still lying prostrate, Sveinn checked his bearings to make sure he was in the right place. Lining up the mountain peak which looked like an axe-head on one side, he turned slightly to the right and saw the tree on the ridge which was blackened like ash. Even further to the right was the lake shaped like a woman's hair between her legs, something which usually brought a grin to Sveinn's face, but not today.

Slowly rising to a crouch, Sveinn ran, doubled over, to a large rock about twenty yards from the nearest giant. The gargantuan form lay unmoving, snoring, the noise like that of a small avalanche. Gathering his nerve for a moment, Sveinn thought through what he had to do once more and steeled his rattling nerves.

Rising and moving slightly from behind his cover, Sveinn glanced around for the source of his objective. Amid the enormous sleeping and barely stirring giants, he could not see what he was after. Maybe if he climbed onto the rocks....

Clambering onto a nearby pile of boulders, Sveinn scrambled to the top where he crouched and once more scanned the thousands of bodies stretched out for miles in every direction, searching for the leader, the one with the red skin.

"What have we here?" boomed a voice behind him.

Sveinn spun around and tripped, falling backward....

... only to land in something cushioned and red.

Glancing around hurriedly, Sveinn recognized crimson fingers attached to his landing pad and with gut-wrenching dread he realized his mistake. He managed to draw his sword and unsteadily clambered to his feet. The house-sized hand he'd landed on rose to an astronomical height, almost level with the most horrifying face Sveinn could have imagined.

It was the leader of the giants – Hrungnir.

Dozens of black emotionless eyes stared at Sveinn, and the lipless mouth clicked loudly while the two nasal slits breathed in, pulling Sveinn closer in the process. His weapon seemed pitiful when compared to this behemoth, but he would not fail. These creatures had killed his people... his wife... his daughter....

'What are you doing, little man?" queried a booming voice.

"I... I have nothing to say to you, you... *murderer!*"

Hrungnir chuckled, the sound like boulders rumbling. "It is better that you tell me, for I shall know it in the end anyway. It is a talent I have, along with drawing in the power of the things I absorb. When I leech things, especially you pitiful beings, I retain your memories; this is how I am able to speak your language. So whatever you are holding within your mind will eventually be mine anyway. You might as well tell me what it is and save yourself the anguish of the extraction." Several other giants had roused and were now gathering around.

Sveinn hawked and spat a large glob of phlegm across the short distance, striking directly into one of Hrungnir's many lidless eyes. The multi-eyed beast roared, and Sveinn thought he would be dashed to the rocks below, but Hrungnir controlled himself and grinned maliciously.

"I had hoped you would see reason," said the giant. "Oh well, it seems this was inevitable."

Liquid exploded out from the open nodes in the red giant's skin and covered Sveinn in an instant. He drew back his sword arm, intending to hurl it at the face of Hrungnir, but his body froze, unable to move within the solution as it contracted around him. A burst of energy passed into Sveinn, tearing through him like tiny daggers, but he kept repeating the same phrase over and over in his mind, just as he'd been taught to do. Even when it felt like insects were scrabbling over the inside of his skull, he repeated the words as Kvasir the wise one had instructed him, allowing nothing else in. Finally it felt as though a clawed hand had clasped his heart, and with a wrench he felt his life tear loose.

His wife's face flashed before his face, but it was not a memory. She carried his beautiful daughter in her arms, and they were both reaching out to him....

***

Hrungnir let the ash drift free from his hand, frustrated at the minimal information he had gathered from the human. It seemed as though the man had only one thought running through his mind as his life drained, only one tiny morsel for Hrungnir to devour. One phrase, repeated over and over.

Don't tell him about the survivors in the caves! Don't tell him about the survivors in the caves! Don't tell him....

But the man *had* told him, despite his best attempts to keep it secret. The only other information forthcoming from the captive had been the image of a rough map with a mountainous location on it, along with the impression of thousands upon thousands of people hidden within a warren of caves.

More food.

More slaves.

Hrungnir swiftly roared orders, and the thousands of giants

snapped into motion. He had proven himself the strongest among them since defeating their former ruler in combat, and now none challenged him lest they feel his wrath. The most recent to confront him had been many turnings of the suns ago; Laftrol had attacked him when he was not prepared. The hulking giant had been the equal of Hrungnir in size and strength, but had not possessed his ability to absorb the essence of his foes.

Laftrol had not died well.

As he had told the stupid human, he not only absorbed energy from his victims, he also soaked up all their memories and knowledge – except when such memories were stunted and broken like this Norseman's had been. Such things annoyed him incalculably. With his army moving off in the direction of the high mountains, Hrungnir vowed to torture some of those he found in the caves merely for the pleasure of it. Looking at the wooden cages containing the hundred or so human prisoners, Hrungnir contemplated torturing one or two of the pathetic creatures to release his frustration, but pushed the urge away with an effort. Those slaves were needed to raise Valhalla, his home world, out of the decay into which it had fallen.

Valhalla had once been the jewel within the realm of Jotunheim, but since the rule of Thrym, it had descended from supremacy into weakness. The slaves he would cultivate from this world would help bring them back to their former glory. The army he led was the last of the great forces of Valhalla, their other forces having been defeated in every major battle in recent history. The War Clave had once consisted of fifty armies such as the one Hrungnir now led, but had been decimated to the point where there were only two left: the one he led and the one which had remained in Valhalla to retain order.

The male and female human slaves would be forced to breed, the offspring manipulated genetically in the womb in such a way as to create more giants. This method always destroyed the female, as growth far exceeded what the human body could contain, but he didn't care. The females in Valhalla had been long since killed off, and they desperately needed to replenish their warriors.

Nobody remembered how the wars had started; they had simply

existed since the dawn of memory. Hrungnir cared nothing for the history of such things; all that concerned him was victory, and he would achieve it at any cost. It had been a miracle when the mysterious gate had reopened after centuries of being closed, but he had leaped at the opportunity. As a result, he'd been able to absorb the essence of the one who called himself Prometheus. The man had held other names, other names to go with other faces, but his memories told Hrungnir that Prometheus was always the one he'd felt most comfortable with.

Hrungnir remembered the ecstasy which had shot through him upon absorbing the leader of the Aesir. The creature had held considerable power for a hominid, and had almost sated Hrungnir's near-bottomless appetite for power.

Almost.

Nothing would ever fully satisfy his hunger, which was why Hrungnir yearned for war and death. With them he had an almost never-ending supply of sustenance for his craving. If what the memory of the human scout had shown him was true, if the caves were still full of unsuspecting victims, their mission might be over sooner than anticipated. Thousands of captives could be sent back through the portal....

The portal!

In his euphoria after absorbing first the one named Prometheus, and then the other powerful one named Surtr, Hrungnir had completely forgotten to protect their only means of returning home. He swiftly barked orders, and a hundred warriors broke off from the main force, sprinting back toward the portal. Cursing inwardly, Hrungnir couldn't believe such a basic detail had escaped him, but upon recalling the exhilarating burst of power he'd received from Prometheus, he understood.

Absorbing the essence of his foes was the ultimate elation, better than any other sensation in existence. The breeders had apparently experimented with his embryonic fetus in ways they hadn't dared before, stumbling upon a way to create this skill in him. Such a thing had never been replicated, however, because when he had been delivered he'd inadvertently absorbed every single living thing in the area, including the ones who had created him.

Their knowledge had died with his birth.

This uniqueness pleased Hrungnir. He enjoyed being the only one of his kind, and it gave him an advantage over foes who would seek to overthrow or defeat him; he consumed them utterly and sent a message to all other potential rivals. This had swiftly deterred many would-be opponents to Hrungnir's position. As warriors, they were bred not to fear death or defeat, but being drained of everything was a different story altogether. Otherwise brave foes had been daunted without Hrungnir ever having to waste time or energy fighting them.

As he marched along in the middle of his force of giants, Hrungnir suddenly had a memory swim up from the recesses of his mind. It took him a moment to determine which victim it had come from – with so many different memories from different sources, it was difficult to keep track of which ones belonged to whom – but it was definitely one of his more recent foes.

Prometheus.

In the memory, Hrungnir saw vast, overpopulated cities full of humans just waiting to be harvested. With crops such as these he could build an army of millions of giants with which to retake Jotunheim, and crush his enemies beneath his heel once more. He focused on the memory, evoking the name of the place. It was an odd land, sounding bizarre within Hrungnir's mind, and took him a few moments to understand how it should be pronounced….

Amr…. Arim….

America.

CHAPTER 10

Sweat dripped down his brow, stinging Talbot's eyes for the hundredth time, and he angrily swiped it away. He'd never been patient before, but at the moment he felt like he could wait forever; at least it would prolong having to meet what was coming.

Talbot stared up at the sheer cliffs towering around them and tried to push away the intense sense of guilt pressing in on him. Wes had asked him to develop a way to draw the entire force of giants to this place, and the only idea he had managed to come up with had been the use of a dupe, a means to make Hrungnir believe a large-scale contingent of survivors was hidden away here.

Apparently it had worked.

The scouts Wes had placed on the hills at the entrance to the canyon had reported a billowing cloud of dust on the horizon, indicating the army of giants was on its way, hence Talbot's growing unease. The nerves and guilt seemed to combine in his gut, creating a horrendous emptiness within him – emptiness laced with pain. Sveinn had been chosen by Biaver after conferring with Wes, and the warrior had readily accepted the task put to him. Talbot had been present when the plan had been outlined, and had been amazed as Sveinn grinned, but behind that grin seemed to be a deeply hidden sadness, covered by layers of grit.

And now Sveinn was dead.

It was Kvasir who had speculated that Hrungnir might actually draw something more than mere sustenance away from those he drained. It had been a risk, but it had worked. Now Talbot hoped Fenrir could indeed do as he had said, and transport the entire group of around ten thousand giants from this place into the rift. Once in the rift they would somehow 'jump' into a parallel rift, leading them all back into Talbot's time and world.

The entire enterprise seemed impossible. It felt like they were about to attempt to juggle a dozen knives while cooking a four-course meal.

It had always seemed harrowing enough to Talbot to simply travel through a normal rift gate. Now Fenrir was suggesting that by manipulating matter they could somehow jump into a rift – much like digging into the earth to connect with a mine shaft – regardless of where they were, or the absence of a gate. The power required to drag the entire invading force of ten thousand giants into such a thing along with them would be mind-boggling, but Fenrir had promised he could do it.

Talbot hoped the Vanir leader could deliver. The last place they would ever want to be without some route of retreat was in this box canyon, surrounded by walking skyscrapers with a penchant for eating people.

Looking up, Talbot saw Biaver approaching him, the remaining Norse following close behind. Wes rose to meet them, and Talbot moved to stand beside him.

"I must protect my people," said Biaver, "and cannot aid you in this endeavor. I am sorry."

"There's no need to be sorry, Biaver," admonished Wes. "They're your priority, we're nothing to you guys."

"On the contrary, you will feature in our tales forever." He waved one of the other Vikings, a short, timid-looking man – especially for one of the Norse – to stand beside him. "This is our saga-keeper, Snorri Sturluson. He shall record your tale, your battle of Ragnarok, so our descendants will also know of your valor."

"I'm sure that'll turn out to be completely spot-on with the facts, too," said Wes with a wide grin. "Especially considering this is the first time I've even seen Snorri."

"I have heard several recounts of your actions, Lord Loki," said Snorri. "Too many of our tales are warped by superstition and fable. The fact I have met both you and your son, Fenrir, will aid me immensely in keeping things accurate."

"My son Fenrir, eh? Well you're off to a great start," replied Wes, patting him on the shoulder. He turned back to Biaver. "Seriously though, get your people somewhere safe, and we'll get these idiots out of your hair... which looks much nicer with the braids, by the way."

Biaver frowned slightly at the comment, finally nodding and moving to grip wrists with Talbot in a warrior's shake. "Good luck," said Talbot, feeling awkward with the grip.

As the Norsemen moved away, Talbot turned to Wes. "Do you realize who that guy was?" he asked, pointing at Snorri, the Norse saga-keeper.

"Why would I care?" replied Wes. "I've got other shit to worry about. But by all means get a boner over it for me."

Wes chuckled and moved away, leaving Talbot grinning slightly and shaking his head. The grin vanished as he turned and saw the entrance to the canyon suddenly filled with dust.

The army of Valhalla had arrived.

Talbot's heart leaped into his throat, and he seemed unable to swallow it back down. He remembered the size of the giants, and the power of their leader, the one who had called himself Hrungnir. Alone, that giant would cause devastation, but combined with the ten thousand or so giants with him…. What could possibly stop them?

Wes had the idea of taking them forward in time. The future would have weaponry which could combat them, but what could possibly defeat an army such as this without destroying the planet as well? He vividly remembered the first time he'd encountered a gryphon, flying in a marine helicopter on the way to Quantico. The marines had hit the gryphon with everything at their disposal, and they'd barely affected the beast. From what Talbot could tell, a gryphon was little more than a pigeon compared to these behemoths.

And Wes was going to unleash them on the USA.

Shaking away his trepidation with effort, Talbot reinforced his faith in Wes. Through skill or perhaps blind stupid luck, the commando had managed to see them through each and every dilemma which had crossed their path thus far.

Zoe stood silently beside him, concern evident upon her face, and Talbot followed her gaze back toward the rising dust plume, wondering if this time Wes had bitten off more than he could chew.

***

"Where is Hrungnir?" shouted Wes calmly.

The monstrous assembly of giants towered around him. The commando leaned casually on a large rock with Talbot, Fenrir and Zoe standing slightly behind him. Zoe and Wes had argued briefly about her joining them, but when she had blatantly pointed out that Wes couldn't stop her, the Australian had simply shrugged his shoulders and submitted.

The giants looked confused at Wes's demand, but slowly parted to allow the enormous figure of Hrungnir through their ranks. None of the giants carried weapons, their sheer size and strength being daunting enough. Standing in front of them, Talbot doubted the best fighting force in his own time could stand against them without using something as devastating as nuclear weapons.

Hrungnir gazed down at them, hunger seeming to glint within his gaze. "Where are your hidden people?" he demanded, his voice booming.

"You realize you can't get home, don't you?" countered Wes, stalling for time while Fenrir gathered the power required to transport them all into the rift.

Hrungnir's face glowered with rage, and Talbot thought they were done for. The giant could simply wring the information out of them as he drained their minds and bodies, but for some reason he calmed himself.

"My warriors have told me as much when they returned from checking the ancient gate. We will find another way to return home when the time arrives."

"Sure you will," replied Wes. He calmly examined the mass of giants surrounding them. "So am I right in assuming all your guys are with you now?" The question was asked innocently, but Talbot tensed in anticipation of the answer.

Hrungnir frowned, suspicion evident upon his horrific face. "Yes. Why?"

His many eyes scanned the mountainous crags surrounding them on three sides as though expecting an ambush within the expansive box canyon. The greatest ambush ever devised would have no hope of impacting such an army, though, even confined as they were within the mountainous canyon, thought Talbot. The weapons of this time were useless, and the Vanir, though mighty and godlike to the Norse, were near powerless against such a force.

"I just wanted to make sure we didn't have to make two trips," said Wes. "You know, one for you guys and another to pick up any stragglers."

"I grow tired of this discussion! Tell me where the hidden survivors are and I might let you live... for now."

"Let me live? What for? To become some sort of slave for you bunch of perverts? Are you gonna try to use me as a penis puppet, Hrungnir? If so, I think you're vastly overestimating my physical flexibility."

The leader of the giants stared down at Wes disbelievingly. "You dare defy me?" he growled, looming over the four figures.

"You ready yet, Fenrir?" muttered Wes. "I think I might have pissed this guy off."

"I am ready."

"Then do it!"

Time itself seemed to slow around Talbot. Hrungnir's right hand swooped down, the liquid already oozing from the enlarged pores of his skin. Fenrir's body burst outward, covering the entire valley like a spider web of epic proportions. The entire host of giants was encompassed within the trap, along with the small group of humans in the middle. A flash of energy exploded, blinding Talbot with its intensity. Everything blurred, and the entire scene faded.

An instant later Talbot found himself re-materializing in a somewhat familiar location. He was traveling through a rift. He had no physical body to speak of as his form moved at what he guessed was an atomic level. He had a sense of Wes nearby, along with Zoe and Fenrir, and barreling on through the vortex behind them all was the army from Valhalla. Vibrations thudded through the rift, and Talbot guessed energy was being stretched to the absolute limits of its molecular structure. Part of him wondered what would occur if the rift was torn apart due to the sheer size of what now traveled through it, but he swiftly pushed the uncomfortable thought aside.

There was no limbo within this rift, unlike the one they had used to get into Olympia. Perhaps this was due to Fenrir's ability to leap directly into the rift without requiring any sort of gate; a trait seemingly unique to the leader of the Vanir. The limbo had not been a pleasant experience, Wes and Talbot barely surviving it.

The rift suddenly shifted and contorted, and Talbot realized Fenrir must have thrown them sideways into the rift from Talbot's own time as he'd said he would have to. How Fenrir had managed to uncover such reserves of power after transporting them all into the rift to begin with was beyond Talbot's comprehension, and he worried that the stress might prove too much for the leader of the Vanir.

Such thoughts were torn from Talbot's mind as the rift suddenly bucked, and he felt himself picking up pace. He sensed they were coming to the end of the rift and braced himself.

This was never fun.

Talbot broke free of the rift and felt his body become corporeal once more. He caught a glimpse of what looked like a vast desert before everything flashed once more, throwing him back into a rift and almost instantly spitting him out again. He landed heavily on grass, knocking the wind out of him.

Gathering his senses, Talbot glanced quickly around, seeing Wes kneeling close by, holding Fenrir's head. Zoe was just rising to her feet. Behind them stood a building Talbot couldn't fail to recognize, its pristine white walls and distinct architecture making it one of the most identifiable structures in the free world.

The White House.

Scrambling to his feet, Talbot rushed swiftly to the rest of his group. "We have to get out of here before those giants emerge!"

Only then did he notice how frail and insubstantial Fenrir looked, like he had somehow been drained of all life. Not in the way Hrungnir did it; this was somehow different. The leader of the Vanir opened his eyes with an effort and peered up at them.

"The giants have been abandoned in a desert in another country," gasped Fenrir, the effort of talking making him weaker by the second. "It was the best I could do. I must leave you here, as I knew I would. The drain from transporting such a mammoth amount of molecular structure has destroyed me, but I was able to keep you separate for the time being...." Fenrir sucked in a huge gasp of air. "Do not waste time; you must prepare your world for the evil we have unleashed upon it. You may have only delayed the inevitable by bringing Valhalla's army to this time, and may have in fact aided Hrungnir's plans. He hopes to gather humans for whatever warped design he has in mind. I fear Prometheus's evil will pale in comparison to what you now face."

Talbot noticed Zoe's face flicker with some unknown emotion at the mention of her father's name, but it was gone before anyone else realized. Sounds of yelling were echoing from the White House, and he saw what he assumed were Secret Service agents running toward them. He glanced at the building, noticing for the first time the crumbling hole in the side of the iconic structure – evidence of Fenrir's last trip to this time. He looked back down.

Fenrir was gone.

His body still lay there, propped up by Wes, but the spirit of the Vanir had fled, and he finally looked at peace. Wes placed him almost reverentially onto the ground, closing Fenrir's eyes with his free hand as he did so.

"Get down on the ground!" shouted one of the approaching Secret Service agents, and Talbot moved to comply.

"Relax, Special Agent Delafore, it's only me," said Wes casually, still looking down at the body.

"But you...," said the agent uncertainly, "you only just left... didn't you?"

"Yeah, probably," replied Wes. "But that was a different me. We've gotta see the guy in charge again. Things have gotten worse, much worse. And get somebody to take care of Fenrir's body. You guys don't have to worry now; I don't think he'll turn into a wolf again."

"That was the wolf?" spluttered Special Agent Delafore. "But it threatened to kill you!"

"Shit happens," said Wes. "Turns out he was a pretty good bloke. But let's get moving. I've got a feeling a really big problem just appeared in the Middle East."

Special Agent Delafore led the way, and Wes, Talbot and Zoe followed silently behind him. He guided them swiftly through the White House, moving to the East Wing, where they all piled into a secure-looking elevator flanked by two Secret Service agents – one on either side outside the doors. The elevator quickly dropped down, and when they emerged, Talbot was confronted by a thick steel door, a sign above it reading: *Presidential Emergency Operations Center*.

"Lucky that sign's there," muttered Wes, "otherwise anyone might just wander in."

Special Agent Delafore pressed his palm flat against the scanner beside the door, and it slid open sideways. He then motioned for them to enter while he waited outside, the door closing once Wes, Talbot and Zoe had entered. Sitting opposite a big timber desk was potentially the most recognized face in the free world. The President of the United States of America.

"I heard you were back," said the President to Wes without preamble. "And considering I just got confirmation you took off with Poseidon from Dulles International Airport about five minutes ago, I have to assume this is one of those little discrepancies in time we've spoken about before. Correct?"

"That's right, baby," replied Wes, causing the President to raise an eyebrow. "All sorts of shit's about on rain down on us, and it's partially my fault, but it was either bring it back here or let the whole world get screwed up in the past. So I figured we'd drag the whole colostomy-bag full of marvels here and deal with it the best we could during this time."

"What's happened?" asked the President, his tone instantly more business-like as he sat down.

Wes sat in the chair opposite the President and rested his booted feet on the polished timber desk, launching into a full retelling of everything that had happened to them since the two had last met.

The President seemed unsurprised by Wes's conduct, and Talbot guessed he was somehow used to it. Then again, figured Talbot, the man *was* the President; he was probably used to watching foreign dictators wiping their ass on the American flag in front of him and pretending it didn't affect him.

As the tale trailed to an end, however, the first cracks began to show in the President's composure. He stared at Wes incredulously as the former SAS commando calmly recounted how an army of around ten thousand giants was now somewhere on the planet, probably intent on destroying everything, and how they wanted to enslave as many people as possible to take them back to Valhalla – a mythical realm in the President's mind until this moment.

All in all he took it pretty well.

"Are you shitting me?" snapped the President at the close of Wes's tale. Wes laughed, but when he saw the President was serious his expression dropped.

"No joke," said Wes. "I wish it were. This is some bad shit we're facing, but it's much better we oppose it here and now than back where Talbot and I were. Trust me on this."

The President sat silently for a moment, glaring across the desk at Wes before shifting his gaze to Talbot, and then on to Zoe, whom Wes had avoided any direct reference to throughout his narration.

"Who is this?" asked the President.

"Er... that's Zoe," said Wes noncommittally.

"The same Zoe who disappeared right before our last meeting?" Wes nodded. "And who exactly *is* Zoe? The last time you were here – around thirty minutes ago by my time – you had no idea who she was, Wes. Can you identify her now?"

Talbot saw Wes bite his lip lightly before answering. "Yeah, she's Prometheus's daughter."

If Talbot was expecting surprise from the President at this revelation he was sorely disappointed. The man merely stared at Zoe more intently, who returned his gaze without tension.

"Can you vouch that she can be trusted?" asked the President, never shifting his piercing gaze.

"Yep," replied Wes without pause.

"Okay," said the President, as though that were all he needed. "Before we go any further, I need to get the Secretary of Defense in here."

"He'll still be traveling back from dropping me and Poseidon off at the airport... not that it really was Poseidon, mind you. Damn Prometheus," muttered Wes.

The President pressed the intercom located on his desk. "Get me General Shannon."

"General *Robert* Shannon?" asked Wes.

"Yes. Do you know him?"

"Yeah, we've met once or twice. I'm pretty sure he hates me."

The President smiled humorlessly. "Why do I get the feeling he's not the only one?"

"As long as you love me, baby. That's the only thing that matters."

The President shook his head, but Talbot saw the grin he bore was now more natural. "You do realize I could have you shot for talking to me like that, don't you?"

"What would you do without me?"

"As long as you don't talk to me like that in public. I'd hate to lose you now, after all the crap I've had to put up with from the people you've pissed off over the years. It's only because you're one of the few people I can rely on to be honest with me that I put up with you."

"That and the fact that I come from the future and can help you out with all sorts of futuristic shit like my technology and stuff."

The humor instantly dropped from the President's face, and his gaze snapped back at Talbot and Zoe.

"Don't worry about them. They've seen too much shit to care much about our little arrangement. I mean, seriously, Zoe's dad was a shape shifter from another dimension who manipulated members of our government – including you – into opening gateways into other dimensions. And Talbot, well he just got caught up in a whole hay-bale full of elephant crap when we found out he could talk an ancient language nobody else could. So I think your secret's pretty safe for now, no need to call out the CIA sharpshooters on the grassy knoll."

The President tensed once more, but finally relaxed, chuckling softly. "You sure have a set of balls on you, Wes."

"Do you want to see them?" offered Wes, standing up and making to undo his belt.

The President waved him away, laughing. "No, that's fine; I'll take your word for it." Wes sat down, grinning.

The door to the Presidential Emergency Operations Centre opened and a very stiff-looking army general marched in, stopping and crisply saluting the President as the door closed behind him with a soft hiss. His heavily starched uniform appeared as though it might crack if he relaxed in the slightest, but despite the paunch beginning to show around his middle, General Shannon still looked to be a fighting man. His silver hair was cut short and neatly parted to the left while his leathery face remained hairless.

The general's gaze wavered momentarily as his eyes were drawn first to Wes's boots – once more on the President's desk – and then slowly up until the two men's eyes met.

The general did not look at all impressed.

"YOU!" he snarled.

"G'day, Shirley," said Wes amiably.

The general visibly reddened. "What is this... buffoon... doing here, Mister President?"

The President gave General Shannon a stony stare. "He is doing whatever I ask from him. Is that a problem?"

"No, sir," replied the general. "It's just that the last time we met... well... he made me look like a fool."

"Don't take it personally, Shirley," drawled Wes. "It's part of my special charm."

"We don't have time for pissing contests, so you two need to get over this right now," barked the President. "Now, General, we have been informed of a large-scale force of foreign origin which may be of threat to the United States."

"Foreign? Terrorists?"

Wes chuckled, but the President waved him to silence. "There is an invading force somewhere on the planet which we need to locate and monitor while strategizing a plan of action to defeat them."

"Who are they, Mister President?"

The President looked sideways at Wes, as though momentarily questioning the believability of the situation.

"The information I have been given leads me to believe it is a force of –" He paused, taking a deep breath. "It is a force of giants; potentially ten thousand strong."

General Shannon stared uncomprehendingly across the desk at the President, and Talbot could tell from his expression he couldn't believe what he'd just heard.

"I'm sorry, Mr. President, I must have misheard you, I thought you said giants."

The President nodded.

"Is this some kind of joke? Did this man put you up to it?" The general pointed at Wes.

"Do I look like I'm joking?" demanded the President stonily, his gaze piercing. "There is much more information available than I can brief you on at the moment, but rest assured that this is a real and tangible threat to our nation, if not the entire planet."

"But… *giants*? How can this be real, sir?"

The phone on his desk buzzed and the President hit the intercom.

"What is it?"

"*Mister President, I'm sorry to interrupt, but you've been sent a Code Alpha security message. It's a video feed coming through live from the Al Jazeera news network,*" advised the female voice on the other end of the line.

"Thank you," he replied.

The President plucked the remote control off his desk and flicked on the widescreen LCD attached to the wall of the Operations Centre. News footage instantly appeared, showing what appeared to be carnage-filled streets where flames billowed and cars were exploding. The caption at the bottom of the screen said the filming was taking place somewhere in Qatar. Smoke filled most of the picture, and Talbot couldn't understand anything the reporter was saying – not because of the language, Talbot should have been able to decipher that; rather it was from the terrified babbling of the man as he rapidly reported on the situation. He was too petrified by what was going on to make any sense.

A second later Talbot didn't need words to understand.

A gigantic foot smashed down on the reporter, and the camera dropped to the ground. From the tilted angle the camera landed at, pointing slightly skyward, they saw a second screaming man – possibly the cameraman – lifted high into the heavens by an enormous hand. A grotesque head came into view, lingering momentarily before clamping oversized jaws around the man's torso and wrenching him in half.

"Oh, sweet Jesus!" gasped General Shannon.

"Nah, I don't think that's Jesus," said Wes casually. "Jesus had a beard."

The general stared open-mouthed at Wes for a moment before turning back to the President. The news feed had severed and returned to the anchors. The President turned the screen off and silence filled the room.

"Mister President, I'm sorry for doubting you," said the general softly. "You say there are ten thousand of those things?"

"Around that many," cut in Wes, answering for the President. "And that bugger on the screen was one of the small ones. The others range from one-fifty to two hundred-feet-tall. The leader is a big red bastard called Hrungnir who can spray out this shit which sucks the life from whatever it touches. He's about two-hundred-and-fifty-feet-tall and has more eyes than a spider."

"I need you to develop a strategy against this threat," said the President to General Shannon. "I will open up a dialog with the foreign nations involved as well as the United Nations, and we will pool our resources in order to face this danger and defeat it swiftly and with minimal casualties, both civilian and military."

"What sort of weaponry do these… um… *giants* have?" asked the general.

"Wes will brief you fully as soon as we are finished here. For now I want you to organize strategy and troop deployment. You will have overall seniority on this operation, General, with the air force and navy under your command along with the full strength of our army and marines. Make no mistake, this is not an enemy we can take lightly, and they must be defeated at all costs."

"Understood, Mister President," said the general, saluting crisply once more before spinning on his heel and marching out the door.

"That dude really needs to get laid," muttered Wes.

"And you need to ease up on him a bit. He is quite possibly the best tactical general at our disposal, and I will not have you distracting him with your usual shenanigans," ordered the President.

"Come on, the guy's more tense than a garbage bag full of blue testicles. Get him a blowjob at least. If you ask nicely I'm sure Talbot here would help you out."

"What –?" gasped Talbot.

"I mean it, Wes," said the President sharply. "You might think everything's a joking matter, but the rest of us don't have that luxury. I need General Shannon to be focused, and you too, while we're at it."

"Me? I'm always focused, baby. I'm like a magnifying glass above an anthill."

"As long as you don't burn down my anthill. I know you like being this warped, enigmatic figure who wafts in and out as he pleases, but not this time. The stakes are too high. You will toe the line on this one, Wes. Is that understood?"

Talbot glanced at Wes, seeing him adopt the dangerous expression he sometimes did, and Talbot swallowed heavily, his heart beginning to hammer.

"And if I don't?" asked Wes with menacing softness.

The President stood and leaned over the desk, his face thunderous. "Then I will have you dragged through the streets with a small Norwegian waffle maker spanking your bare ass."

Wes's expression cracked, and he burst out laughing, lifting Talbot's tension. "Is that supposed to deter or encourage me?"

The President grinned in turn. "Probably a bit of both."

"Okay, okay. You've sweet-talked me enough; I'll go easy on General Grumpy Fat-Guts."

The President sat back down. "Good. Now go and brief him on everything, I want to talk to your companions for a moment."

Wes muttered something good naturedly under his breath as he took his booted feet from the President's desk and rose to his feet, whistling as he strolled from the Operations Room. The President waited until the pneumatic doors hissed closed before fixing Talbot with a steely glare, all traces of humor gone from his face.

"Doctor Harrison, I know you are still suffering from the loss of your brother – for the second time, from what I can recall – but in your opinion, what are our chances?"

Talbot was taken completely off guard. "Er... Mister President, sir... I'm no tactician. I don't know what you want to hear."

"You witnessed the battle in Olympia against the Titans," said the President crisply. "Is this army more dangerous to our world than either of those forces?"

"Absolutely!" replied Talbot without hesitation. "We faced three giants when fighting alongside the Olympians, and that was with their enhanced weapons. *Three* giants almost proved too much for us then, and now we're facing as many as ten thousand, not to mention their leader, who may actually prove to be invulnerable, if what I fear is true."

"What do you fear?"

Talbot looked sideways at Zoe before continuing, returning his gaze to the President as he did. "He consumed Prometheus before my eyes. I think the process was much more than just absorbing his essence; I think he took what made up Prometheus into himself."

"What does that mean?" asked the President.

"I'm only guessing, but he might be able to do what Prometheus was capable of doing. He may be able to manipulate his own bio-organic matter in such a way as to make himself virtually invulnerable. At this stage we have no idea how tough these giants are, but imagine one who is two-hundred-and-fifty-feet-tall and can regrow his own head."

"I see your point," said the President, concern evident upon his face, though absent in his words. "From the reports I managed to read after the last incident, the creatures from Tartarus were almost completely invulnerable to our weapons anyway, weren't they?"

"That's right, sir."

"But the Olympian weapons – weapons like that sword Wes

wears – are able to hurt them."

"Yes, Mister President. Through some technology alien to us, Hephaestus was able to create weaponry charged with a type of force not from our realm. This energy enables their weapons to be effective against the creatures from Tartarus."

Talbot was confused. Why was the President asking him things about Tartarus when they were facing an army from Valhalla?

"If these giants are more powerful than the creatures of Tartarus as you say, our weapons will almost certainly prove ineffectual against them. We may very well be defenseless in the coming clash." The last words were spoken softly, and the President's expression took on a faraway look.

Talbot finally grasped at what the President was saying, and suddenly felt awkward. He wasn't supposed to see something like this, where the most powerful man in the world took on an expression not unlike that which any normal man might adopt under the circumstances.

He looked afraid.

CHAPTER 11

Europe was a charnel house.

They were seven months into the worst war the planet had ever seen. The Middle East was gone – simply gone. Countries which had battled against each other for centuries had died fighting side by side against the threat of the giants, but it had all been in vain. Asia had been next, but even with the terrifying armies and weaponry of China, they had fared no better than countries such as Iran, Iraq and Afghanistan.

Even China's nuclear strikes had proven useless.

The nukes had been China's attempt to stave off the imminent invasion of their country after millions died in South East Asia, but the missiles had probably decimated the land and people more than they'd deterred the giants. After a total of four nuclear strikes on the Valhallian force as it crossed the mountainous region of Nepal near the southern border of China, a grand total of about forty giants had been killed, with reports of between five and six hundred giants injured.

That was not a good ratio considering the monumental damage wrought to the surrounding countryside.

Needless to say, the People's Liberation Army did not fare well against the remaining force of giants – still numbering nearly ten thousand. The fighting lasted little more than a month, with additional nuclear strikes as the force of giants pushed north-east, pausing to raze the cities of Chengdu, Xi'an and Hebei before continuing on to the capital.

Beijing was utterly annihilated, every building obliterated, every child consumed or enslaved. A city which had stood for over three thousand years was gone in days.

News reports were sketchy, as were intelligence updates – even to the White House and Pentagon, where the primary logistics took place for the United States as they prepared for the coming offensive. China had refused aid from the US, claiming they would crush the invading force using their superior army, including close to ten million troops.

Ten million more dead or enslaved.

After they had decimated China, Valhalla's army then carved a path up into Russia, staying close to its southern border, easily cutting through into Europe – the Russians apparently learning from China's mistake and retreated beyond the invading force's reach. The giants had seemingly targeted their weapons bases, somehow finding them unerringly within the vastness, and destroying their stockpiled nuclear missiles… at least all the ones the United States knew about. Their major cities along this route of desolation, including Moscow, could not evacuate swiftly enough, and the giants left only rubble in their wake.

After crossing the border into Belarus, the Valhallian force had markedly slowed. Not because of any great military threat, more that there was such a concentration of people in a relatively small space, and so the giants took their time moving from city to city – leaving nothing in their wake. China had been vastly more populated, but the giants had progressed so swiftly because of the great spaces between population centers. With nothing to kill or enslave, they had seldom paused, even for sleep. Europe was different, more like an all-you-can-eat buffet for walking skyscrapers, and so they practically strolled through, stopping completely at times to gorge upon foreign delicacies.

Talbot spent much of his time during the early parts of the invasion trapped within the Pentagon War Room, hearing reports coming in directly to the President, or in his absence those delivered to General Shannon. A small part of him figured he should feel honored at such close access to the hub of the action, but he wanted nothing more than to return to the way things had been before, when he was just a lowly college professor. Unfortunately, owing to his vast experience with the situation, along with his talent for the Elder-tongue, Talbot had been thrust into a role as an advisor to the President. He was now privy to a wealth of information the general public had no knowledge of, and it terrified Talbot more than he could admit, even to himself.

The Government had no idea how to handle what was coming.

If Talbot had been sitting at home, ignorantly watching the news, seeing all the incredible and terrible things happening on the other side of the world, he would have been concerned, but his faith in the United States' military probably would have left him feeling secure at night. The fact that such a military giant as China was decimated so easily would have concerned him greatly, and the millions of deaths would have seemed horrific, but he would have slept soundly knowing that his country had plans in place for something of this magnitude, they were simply waiting for the right time to strike.

Talbot was no longer safe within such ignorance.

The absolute power of nuclear weapons had failed; they had nothing to fall back on. The military ego-heads who puffed themselves up so proudly would normally be all for flying straight over and blowing the hell out of the enemy. Those same braggadocios were now sitting back and preaching a course of trepidation. Up until the Chinese had unleashed their nukes against the enemy with such astounding failure, these same military advisors had indeed been advocating strategies based on attacking the enemy.

Now they were at a loss for what to do.

In a world where military might was based on having a formidable offense, they were suddenly screwed. The United States no longer held the biggest stick in the playground, and without it, the men put in charge of protecting America had no idea what to do. Politicians; men who would normally throw young, brave soldiers straight into any conflict they chose without thought for the loss of their lives, were scared senseless as their own demise loomed closer by the day.

They had witnessed China, the second most powerful nation on the planet, brushed aside like an annoying insect by a group of mythical giants, most of whom carried no weapons apart from primitive clubs made of metal or broken trees, and wore little more than loincloths. Without the power of their weapons to back them up, these fearless warmongers proved little more than witless fools, and more than once Talbot found himself wishing he was back in his ignorant little world, watching these events unfold on CNN.

Talbot saw Zoe and Wes so rarely now they were almost strangers to him. Wes was always in the strategy room, aiding in developing tactics against the invading force. The last time Talbot had seen him he had seemed worn thin from frustration and lack of sleep. Zoe was also separated from him, working with the country's top scientists, aiding them in molecular reconfiguration research... or something like that. He wasn't privy to such information.

He, too, found himself tired, so desensitized to the horror. Each morning he saw new images of the depravities these giants were capable of. His mind had no choice but to switch part of itself off. Stress mounted each day as the course of the Valhallian army was monitored, but everyone knew where they would eventually end up, of that there was no delusion.

Initially, they'd held hopes the oceans might be able to stop the giants, but that hope had been dashed when the invading army had easily swum across the English Channel to invade the United Kingdom. The United States had sent troops to aid them, of course – Britain had long been an ally of the USA – but it was all in vain.

Everything in their path was decimated.

Talbot felt sure there were people alive; small towns were left largely untouched, but capital cities and any municipalities of substance were crushed. Like a plague of locusts, the Valhallian army had swept across everything, leaving only rubble in their wake.

Time and again, Talbot was reminded of the strategy of Alexander the Great as he had fought his way halfway across the world. But instead of converting those defeated over to their cause as Alexander had, the invading giants merely killed their enemies or enslaved them. Talbot tried hard not to think about what those slaves in the makeshift cages hauled by the giants were fed in order to keep them alive. The giants lived mainly on a diet of raw human flesh, and Talbot couldn't see them diversifying their habits merely to provide their slaves with food which was more appetizing. These thoughts often gave him nightmares, and in them he saw families forced into the cages and fed meat which still screamed....

Wrenching his mind away from such dark imagery, Talbot concentrated instead on the issue at hand. He flicked on the television sitting atop his desk in the war room, watching for the fiftieth time footage of the horrific images of the giants effacing the city of London. He was searching for something, *anything*, which might be of use. The footage was the clearest and most comprehensive they'd received to date, and he needed to feel useful.

Hundreds of tanks rolled into view on the screen, unleashing a hail of incendiary rounds at the giants, but to no avail. The huge creatures seemed more annoyed by the blasts than injured, and their ferocious retaliation was terrifying to behold. Tanks were picked up, their fifty-caliber machine guns still pounding at point-blank range, but their efforts proved hopeless. The giants treated the tanks like toys – hurling them into buildings or simply smashing them to the ground, their gargantuan bodies impervious to the ensuing explosions.

As his eyes glazed over at the horrors unfolding on the screen, Talbot's mind began to wander. He recalled yet again the path Valhalla's army had taken since arriving on Earth. There seemed a strange pattern to the movements of the giants and after a few more moments of watching the devastation on the monitor, Talbot stood up and moved over to the huge world map splayed across the entire back wall of the War Room.

Staring at the map, Talbot traced the route the giants had taken since they'd materialized in the middle of Qatar. At first it appeared random, but on closer examination there seemed to be a method to the course they were taking. Their route had cut through the countries and regions which would be of most threat to the army from Valhalla, carving a swathe through China and Russia – two of the world's strongest nuclear threats – before heading through Europe and taking out the United Kingdom.

In essence, the invading force had neutralized any effective aid to the United States, barring that of Australia, which was far away and small enough to be considered negligible. The giants had avoided

Africa to instead travel through China and Russia – a strange course to take according to the so-called 'experts'. Clad as they were, many claimed they should have been attracted to more temperate climes, so why head into Russia? This act alone had led many to believe they were merely acting randomly, but staring at the map, Talbot didn't think so.

Something niggled at the back of his mind.

He stared at the map, hoping the answer would somehow emerge. Why would the giants –?

And then it hit him.

Talbot raced through the War Room to the President's desk. The President himself was surrounded by other advisors and people vying for his attention, but Talbot didn't have time.

"Mister President, I know why they're traveling the way they are."

The statement brought silence to the President's desk, and all eyes turned to Talbot. Many of those standing there seemed annoyed at the interruption, but Talbot only cared about the man sitting down behind the desk.

"What do you mean, Doctor Harrison?" asked the President.

Talbot swiftly gathered his thoughts, scanning his ideas for any major holes in his theory. "They're coming here next," he said quickly.

Several of the President's advisors scoffed at what Talbot said; others merely narrowed their eyes, staring at him intently. Talbot could almost hear their thoughts: Who was *he* to come up with such a radical statement?

A couple of years ago these men's opinions might have meant something to Talbot, but he was beyond all that now. All that mattered was that Talbot *knew* he was right, and he had to make the most important man in the room know it too.

"Many of my other advisors tend to disagree with that idea, Talbot. What makes you believe it, and why should I trust you over them?"

Talbot pointed at the map. "Think of Alexander the Great. As he progressed across the continent of Asia he made sure there were no enemies left to attack him from behind. He did this by conquering and wooing the countries and cultures involved – even so far as to getting himself declared Pharaoh in Egypt. He did this, not out of ego, but rather to ensure he had no strong enemy at his back as he pushed on across Asia – or the Persian Empire, as it was known back then."

"You think these brainless beasts are recreating Alexander the Great?" scoffed one of the advisors. "Stop wasting the President's time; he has more important things to do."

"I think you need to shut your damn mouth," snarled Talbot, lifting his gaze from the President to stare balefully at the advisor. "I'm talking to your boss. Your yapping just makes noise, and solves nothing other than to ease your own terror."

The advisor became almost apoplectic with rage, but the President forestalled his outburst. "What *are* you saying, Talbot?"

Talbot took a deep, calming breath. "The giants are making sure nobody of worth can attack them from behind. Look at the path of their conquest so far, it's shaped almost like a horseshoe, and would appear random except for the fact they've hit every significant city or military installation along their route. Barbaric behavior doesn't explain how they've managed to knock out every significant nuclear missile stockpile outside of the United States. The only country with nukes which hasn't been hit is North Korea, and let's face it, those guys are only going to look out for themselves anyway."

The President stared up at the map on the wall, his expression a mask. "You're right," he said softly.

"So every major force of arms in the world that matters, apart from us, is now crippled. I'm no strategist, but it seems to me like they're cutting off the limbs before they go for the heart," continued Talbot.

"What does that even mean?" sneered the same advisor Talbot had upset moments ago.

"It means," said the President, cutting in before Talbot could answer, "any country which could potentially aid us in the upcoming battle is now off the grid. We're on our own when the giants get here."

"But surely the ocean –"

"It didn't stop them crossing the English Channel," said the President.

Something nagged in Talbot's mind. "Mister President, why would they want to come here anyway? I mean, they can get food and people for whatever they want in Europe and Asia, why go through all the hassle of getting here?"

The President stared hard at Talbot, and then dismissed his advisors with a softly spoken order. When they had gone he looked at Talbot once more.

"There is a chance they know what we have here," said the President in a low voice so as to not be overheard.

"What are you talking about?" asked Talbot.

The President appeared reluctant to say more, but answered regardless, almost as if he had wanted to get it off his chest for quite some time. "We transported the gate – the Syrpeas Gate, the original one that used to be located in Atlantis – back here so we could study it. Your brother helped us get it working again once we'd brought it back. I think the giants may be intending to get their hands on the gate."

Talbot's mouth hung open, and he closed it with a snap. "You brought the Syrpeas Gate to Washington? Are you out of your mind?"

"It was agreed –"

"Who agreed? All of this shit has happened because of that damn gate," whispered Talbot hotly. "You guys said you were going to dismantle it after you recreated the events leading up to us beating Prometheus the last time."

"It was decided upon by a joint crew of academics, along with the most senior government officials, that it was in the nation's best interests to investigate the phenomenon further," defended the President.

"Yeah, great. Well your research has led to this shit," snapped Talbot, pointing to a board with images of the giants in action pinned across it.

"I could argue that your actions in the past led to this, but I'm not that petty. Now get a hold of your emotions before you say something you'll regret," said the President stonily. "We can sit here all day whining about whose fault it is or just deal with the situation as it stands."

Talbot suddenly realized the foolishness of arguing over blame – recognizing too, who it was he was abusing – when the bigger issue of how to combat the coming threat was still looming over their heads.

The President continued. "Let's assume they know about the Syrpeas Gate and are headed here next as you fear. What can we do to fare better than any of the other nations who have tried to oppose them thus far?"

This put Talbot on the spot, and he was momentarily stunned. He hadn't been prepared for such a direct question and had no idea what to say.

And then it came to him.

"We need the help of the Olympians," he finally replied.

Surprise spread across the President's face. He obviously hadn't expected this to be Talbot's answer. "How do you propose to do that?"

"The Syrpeas Gate leads to Tartarus, and from there we'll have to travel to Olympia through their rift gate."

"*If* it still exists," said the President. "Remember that their time runs separately to ours. A thousand years might have passed since you were last there, there's no way of knowing."

"I know, but there's really no other option, is there? You said it yourself, Mister President: only the weapons from Olympia had any effect on the beasts from Tartarus when ours did not. The giants have shown they are impervious to anything we can throw at them. The Chinese hit them with the most devastating weapons our planet has ever known and they barely sprained an ankle. We *need* the weapons of the Olympians in order to survive this conflict."

The President seemed to contemplate his words momentarily before nodding. "I think you're right. When can you leave?"

And the reality of the situation crashed down upon Talbot. Nobody could take his place on this mission. Talbot had just volunteered to put his head back in the mouth of a lion with allergies who kept sneezing, and the worst thing was, he knew there was no other way.

This was his only option… and it sucked.

"I need Wes," he said resignedly, his eyes downcast.

"Done. Who else?"

Talbot shook his head. "That's it. Any more would just weigh us down and draw unnecessary attention. We won't have time to babysit anyone through the things they're likely to see in Tartarus, either."

"Will you have to travel through Hades?"

"No. We'll take the Syrpeas Gate directly to Tartarus. From there we'll find a way to sneak through their rift gate – it opens directly onto the plateau behind Mount Olympus."

"What about the Titans?" asked the President.

"I'm not sure how detailed your reports were, but the Keres – the strange creatures which could somehow alter their phase of being, or whatever it was – were brought through into Olympia by Heracles to aid us in the final battle. They drove the Titans back through the rift, intent on killing them all, so I'm hoping the city of the Titans will be empty when we arrive there."

"But you can't know for sure," said the President.

"Nope," replied Talbot. "But I have to hope it's like that, because if it's not, our quest is going to be much shorter than we'll be planning."

"Why is that?"

"Because we'll be dead."

The President smiled humorlessly, and Talbot saw the nerves behind the gesture. He understood it, and worse, felt exactly the same way.

He was going back into the one place he'd hoped never to see again.

Beyond Hades.

***

Talbot slapped his hand down on the final symbol. A loud crack echoed, indicating the opening of the rift. This rift was similar in shape and appearance to the one his brother had opened from which Hrungnir had emerged, except for its size. The rift which now opened in front of Talbot was much more modest, but still reached the ceiling. The underground lab, situated far beneath the Pentagon, seemed to dim as the very light appeared to get drawn into the rift.

A cold hand closed around Talbot's heart as he gazed at it. After the events leading up to the conflict between the Titans and Olympians, he'd never wanted to see another rift again. The universe had since conspired against him.

"Kind of hurts your balls to look at, don't it?" muttered Wes beside him.

Talbot chuckled. "Yeah. I'm just glad you're coming with me."

"Why? Do you need me to hold your sore balls?"

Talbot grinned and mutely shook his head, turning back to gaze at the rift once more. His smile rapidly disappeared as the icy hand clutched his heart once more.

"I'll go first, then," said Wes, and before Talbot could stop him the commando ran and leaped headfirst into the rift.

Talbot glanced around behind him, shrugging at the President. What could he say? Turning back to the rift, he pushed down his trepidation and moved forward, pausing momentarily before closing his eyes and stepping forward, painfully away that his encoding of the control panel would cause the gate to snap shut behind him like a steel trap.

Color exploded around him as the rift sucked him at incredible velocity toward Tartarus. All other thought was ripped away as his body dissolved into the trans-dimensional gateway and traveled to another world. The journey was eternal and immediate at the same time, but Talbot was finally shot out to land flat on his back on the spongy ground, gasping for breath. One day he would figure out how to land properly, but not today.

Drawing himself slowly to his feet, Talbot sucked in a breath and looked around. As he could have predicted, Wes had Laevateinn drawn and was braced against any sort of unexpected attack, but upon initial inspection Talbot thought it was a highly unlikely prospect.

This place looked lifeless.

For a moment Talbot wondered if the rift had dumped them in the wrong place and they had somehow ended up in Hades instead of Tartarus. The last time he and Wes had arrived in Tartarus, they'd traveled through the Pit, but this time they had emerged in the middle of a desolate landscape. Ebony clouds swirled overhead despite the seeming absence of wind, and the ground had the same fleshy, sticky texture he remembered from their last visit. Peeling up his right boot it felt like he was lifting his foot from an enormous tongue.

Yep. They were in Tartarus.

"Where do we go?" he asked Wes.

"I reckon we need to head in that direction," replied Wes, pointing off in the distance.

Talbot squinted, but could see nothing. "Why?"

"See those things circling in the sky?"

Talbot focused hard and could barely see something moving in the sky just beneath the backdrop of ashen clouds. "What are they?" he asked.

"No idea," replied Wes. "But if they're there something else should be as well, don't you reckon?"

Talbot shrugged. Wes's idea seemed plausible enough, but Talbot remembered that everything they had come into contact with on this plane of existence the last time had tried to kill them.

"Okay, but be careful," he told Wes.

"Yeah, right," replied Wes. "What would be the fun of that?"

Talbot suppressed his trepidation, following Wes across the sticky surface toward the strange creatures circling in the sky high above, barely scraping beneath the ominous clouds. There were no trees anywhere, barely any hills in any direction, and Talbot found it difficult to track their progress except by their distance to the flying creatures.

Like Wes, Talbot was now decked out in a complete set of desert-camouflaged fatigues, and his legs began to chafe slightly from the constant march across the dull landscape. Time trickled by as they walked, and Talbot drew his water canteen from the pouch attached to his belt, taking a small sip. On his opposite hip was a holstered Glock 39, which Wes claimed was the most powerful Glock handgun ever, but still felt pitifully small when Talbot considered what they might encounter here.

He gazed toward their target. Strangely, the closer they got to the flying creatures, the further away they seemed to get, as though they were –

"They're luring us somewhere," said Wes suddenly as though he'd read Talbot's mind.

"Where?"

"Maybe a trap, maybe something else."

"What does that even mean? What else could there be?"

Wes looked at him solemnly. "There's always something else, never forget that."

With few other options, they moved on, traipsing across the bleak landscape. Hours seemed to pass, but Talbot couldn't be sure – his watch had stopped as soon as they'd passed through the rift. Checking the sun didn't help, it was completely hidden behind the black clouds. Even if they could see it Talbot had the distinct impression it would be traveling at a different speed to the one back on Earth.

The ground lurched, and Talbot stumbled forward, only to be abruptly hauled back by Wes, the commando's left hand snaking out with lightning alacrity and grabbing Talbot by the collar of his military fatigues before he could fall. Talbot glanced at Wes and saw the commando drawing his sword, Laevateinn.

"What the hell was that?" gasped Talbot.

Wes raised a finger to his lips, motioning for silence while his eyes scanned the area for signs of danger, staring specifically toward the ground. Talbot was abruptly reminded of the attack on the beach by enormous crab-like creatures, beings which had emerged from beneath the sand without warning. Examining the ground here, he could see that even though it felt spongy, the land itself was very much solid, not like the sandy beach had been.

What the hell could have –?

The ground cracked, split apart with a jagged zigzag pattern, and a hulking figure casually stepped forth, like a man entering a room through sliding doors. This was not a man, however, and Talbot instantly recognized him for what he was.

He was a Titan.

Standing taller than most others Talbot had seen of his race, the Titan was dressed simply in cotton-like pants and a sleeveless shirt with no shoes. He was around seventeen-feet-tall and had prodigiously wide shoulders. In fact, he was extremely muscular all over, reminding Talbot of a taller version of Heracles. Unlike Hercules, he sported a salt and pepper beard, and masses of silver hair cascaded down around his muscular shoulders, making him appear older than the Olympian son of Zeus.

And of course there were his eyes.

Like Prometheus – or rather Prometheus's guise as a Titan, Talbot reminded himself – this Titan's orbs appeared to be filled with a swirling mist. But where Prometheus's eyes had been black as pitch, this figure had eyes of the most brilliant azure Talbot had ever seen, which seemed to peer deep into his heart.

Wes stepped protectively in front of Talbot, Laevateinn in his right hand, ready to strike. Talbot realized he hadn't even drawn his weapon yet and quickly fumbled the Glock out of its holster before chambering a round and aiming around Wes toward the Titan.

"Who the fuck are you?" snarled Wes.

The huge figure considered Wes before grinning humorlessly. "If I did not know better, I would say you were the two humans who almost destroyed my race," he said, ignoring Wes's question. Talbot prepared himself, certain the Titan was about to attack.

"And what if we are?" asked Wes.

"Then I would have to compliment you on defeating that fool, Prometheus."

"Well then…. Huh?" said Wes.

The Titan chuckled. "I was banished from my people when I opposed Prometheus's plans to attack Olympia. He turned my fellows against me, and I have been left for many turnings of our world to live out here in the wastelands of Tartarus."

"How did he turn them against you?" asked Talbot, intrigued.

"Prometheus told them I was in league with the Olympians, conspiring against my people. He said my work on terrestrial manipulation was at Zeus's bidding."

"What's terrestrial manipulation?"

The Titan pointed at the jagged hole in the ground through which he had just emerged. Peering past the lip of it, Talbot saw smooth steps leading down into the ground, beyond which was a flickering light, possibly from lanterns or candles.

"My work among my people was learning how to balance the resonance of atomic matter. I attempted to discover ways to modify its structure however we saw fit. I was only ever able to perfect this against solid, unmoving objects, whereas Prometheus somehow managed to find a way to do it with living matter, primarily himself, something no other Titan has ever accomplished."

"Well that's because Prometheus wasn't a Titan," said Wes.

The towering Titan's brow crinkled. "What do you mean?"

Wes scratched his chin. "Talbot can probably tell it better, but basically he was from a race known as the Vanir, who are from a different realm altogether. He was using your people, trying to raise an army to attack the rulers of his own world. Olympia was just a place he was trying to get through. He needed to use their gates to get into our world and from there back to his own... or something like that. In between all that was a lot of time travel, and some trolls, and a hot chick who gave Talbot a boner, but none of that really matters. It's all really complicated, and for most of it you'll just have to trust us. Essentially, your people were being duped into fighting a war which wasn't theirs."

The Titan stared hard at Wes, and then glanced behind him to Talbot, who nodded.

"My people were decimated because he wanted to use them as *tools*?"

"Yeah, that's about it," replied Wes, still wielding his sword, ready to strike at the Titan.

"He will pay for this!" raged the enormous figure.

"He already has," said Talbot. "After his plans with your people failed, he looked elsewhere for help, opening a gate into a realm called Valhalla. Prometheus released giants – actually, an army of them – and their leader destroyed him by consuming his power."

"You saw this happen?"

Talbot and Wes both nodded. "Yes, he's gone," said Talbot.

The Titan frowned. "Don't be too sure about that," he murmured.

Glancing skyward at the creatures still circling there, the towering figure motioned for them to follow him down the stairs. "We had best talk inside lest the harpies discover their trap is no longer working and decide to attack us here instead. Such beasts are not usually a problem when dealt with individually, but in groups they can prove dangerous."

Talbot looked at Wes who shrugged.

"What is your name?" asked Talbot as they followed him down the stairs.

"My name is Atlas," replied the Titan without turning.

Talbot gasped at the name, but Wes didn't react.

With a shuddering groan, the terrain resealed behind them, locking them in like a tomb. They were now below ground with the Titan who Greek mythology claimed was charged with supporting the heavens, and Talbot couldn't help but wonder how they would get out if Atlas turned out to be an enemy.

He glanced back at the sealed entrance once again with more than just a little apprehension.

***

"What did you mean before?" asked Talbot.

They were seated within Atlas's simple abode. Apart from being underground, it was more or less a conventional dwelling, albeit with furniture twice the size of anything human. The flickering light came from a giant insect-like creature, similar to a large glow-worm, which Atlas had trapped in a clear cabinet. The light from the creature easily illuminated the single room and its stone furniture.

"What did I mean about what?" asked Atlas.

"Before we came down here you said we shouldn't be too sure about Prometheus being gone. What did you mean?"

Atlas bit his lip lightly as though contemplating what to tell them, his swirling blue eyes staring at the fluttering bug and its glowing butt of light.

"Prometheus has been killed before, many times, but he has always managed to come back."

"Yeah, I know," said Wes. "Talbot and I have both killed him at different times."

Atlas nodded. "As have I. In fact, I think at last count there had been almost twenty attempts to kill Prometheus, all unsuccessful. Perhaps that's why Kronos finally acquiesced to his wishes and invaded Olympia the first time; he could find no other option other than to do as Prometheus wished."

"But we saw Prometheus's body turned to ash after Hrungnir absorbed his essence," protested Talbot.

"And that is what worries me," said Atlas. "It terrifies me more than you know. Tell me all of what has happened from the point where the Keres turned on my people and chased them back here from Olympia."

Talbot recited the tale to Atlas, Wes interrupting occasionally with relevant pieces of information. When they finished updating him, Atlas shook his head, his expression even more worried than before.

"This does not bode well, my friends."

"Why?" asked Talbot, frowning.

Atlas stared at him, his swirling eyes unsettling to look at, but Talbot forced himself to return the Titan's gaze.

"Prometheus is more than just flesh and blood. We tried everything to destroy him, but his power was beyond even *my* skill, and I am the foremost developer of matter manipulation among my people. He brushed aside my efforts to destroy him at an atomic level like I was a child."

"And Talbot hit him with some sort of chant which fucked him up before he chopped off his head. Bastard still came back."

Atlas stared hard at Talbot. "Do you possess the Elder-tongue then?"

"Yes I do. Why?"

"Because it goes to show how powerful Prometheus actually is. If you had to behead him *after* using that chant and he still endured, then there's a strong chance he has also survived his encounter with that giant... somehow."

"How can we know?" asked Talbot.

"The army of giants you have spoken about, have they adopted seemingly informed tactics, knowing things they should have no possible way of knowing, becoming more organized in some way?"

Talbot felt his stomach drop, remembering the course the giants had taken upon the war map; they had effectively destroyed every single nuclear installation along their looping route. The President's military advisers had counseled that these were just random acts, but Talbot knew better. Only someone with complex awareness of the whereabouts of those nuclear locations could pinpoint them so accurately; there was no chance involved. With cold dread, Talbot realized Prometheus had infiltrated the Government on such a level as to possess the intimate knowledge of those locations needed to find them.

Talbot could have argued within himself that Hrungnir had merely absorbed the knowledge from Prometheus, but he would never really have believed it. The truth of the matter was that somehow Prometheus had survived...

...and now was in control of the body of Hrungnir, the most powerful giant in a nearly-indestructible army of giants, leading them all toward Washington DC.

Glancing at Wes, Talbot could tell by his concerned expression that the commando was deducing things in a similar fashion. Despite his nonchalant manner, Talbot knew Wes was certainly not stupid, and if he could figure things out then Wes most undoubtedly could also. Wes finally looked over at him and nodded, silently confirming what he already knew.

Prometheus was back.

CHAPTER 12

Gaining control of the giant, Hrungnir, had taken Prometheus longer than he'd anticipated, but the power now at his disposal made every tortured second worthwhile. Never before had Prometheus possessed such a potent form, and he could tell he hadn't even tapped the latent core of strength the huge creature contained within it. The ability to absorb other life forms was an advantage Prometheus would have never dreamed of, and with it, he felt utterly invincible.

They would all pay, every single person or creature to have ever opposed him. *They* had killed his beautiful wife and blamed it on him, but it couldn't have been him. It couldn't.

They'd lied to him, made it look like he'd murdered her so as to discredit him. Prometheus could never have hurt her. The last thing he remembered that night was her beautiful face shouting....

Or was she screaming...?

He pushed the false memory away, it was absurd. He could never do that. Never.

Gazing out over his monolithic new army, Prometheus grinned maliciously. London lay a smoldering ruin around them, its people dead or enslaved. He'd had to keep up the pretense of collecting humans as slaves so as to ensure the army of giants didn't become suspicious of him. Several curious glances had confirmed the monstrous creatures were not as dim-witted as they had originally appeared. He had to be cautious.

Examining his own monstrous body once more, Prometheus felt another surge of elation. Hrungnir had not been easy to mentally overpower, but Prometheus had done it so discretely and with such a lack of haste that by the time the leader of the giants realized it wasn't just random memories coercing his every action it was too late.

And now this incredible form belonged to Prometheus!

Thus far, he had not learned how to manipulate the molecules of Hrungnir's hulking frame, and as such could not change his form yet, but Prometheus had no doubt he would discover the process in time. He'd struggled enough managing such simple things as walking and moving his new body around. He didn't need to attract more attention by trying to change its shape as well. It would be near impossible to explain to the other giants if he suddenly dissolved into a quivering ocean of goo after making a mistake.

And he needed them on his side. This army was crucial for Prometheus's plans; they would head to the United States, crushing any opposition, eventually destroying Washington and gaining access to the all-important Syrpeas Gate.

Those foolish humans thought the Syrpeas Gate was only useful for traveling directly to Tartarus, but Prometheus knew better. He'd learned the secret directly from Hephaestus during his infiltrated time within the ranks of the Olympians. The Syrpeas Gate was the key.

After he was done with this world, he would destroy the Olympians for their effrontery, and then move on to Vanaheim, the world of the Vanir. He would release his people from the tyranny of the Vanir, bringing new freedom through the way of the Aesir.

And then he would bring back his beautiful wife….

Movement to his left broke through his thoughts, and Prometheus turned his bulky head. The many eyes scattered around his cranium had initially posed a daunting challenge, as he'd never experienced such a range of vision before. Even now, when he was getting used to such sight, Prometheus still found himself unable to stop from turning his face toward whatever object drew his attention. Such little things were the hardest habits to change.

Two giants were fighting. He had swiftly discovered this was a normal practice among the ferocious creatures, mainly over issues involving jealousy or greed. In many ways they were like children.

Prometheus strode toward the two colossal creatures, stepping easily over the broken remains of what had once been Buckingham Palace as he did.

"What is it?" he snarled viciously.

Prometheus had found this the best way to coerce and control these creatures – through sheer bullying. Hrungnir had become the dominant male due to his size, but also through cunning and aggression. The two smaller giants stopped their clash immediately, swiftly parting, staring down at the ground in what Prometheus recognized as a display of submission.

One of the giants, the one to Prometheus's left, held out his hand, dropping the contents into Prometheus's outstretched red palm. Glancing down at what the giant had just given him, Prometheus began to laugh, the ominous sound booming out over the battered and broken palace grounds.

It was a dead corgi.

***

"We must act swiftly," stated Atlas.

"And…?" asked Wes.

The Titan looked at him quizzically. "And meet with the Titan council, of course."

"Oh no. No, no, no, no, and no," said Wes, shaking his head vigorously. "Those bastards will stick a giant toothpick up my arse and make me a pimento after the last time I met them."

"They were under the influence of Prometheus. They will realize that now."

"And how many are left?" asked Wes.

"How many what?"

"Titans. How many Titans are left after the Keres sliced and diced them?"

Atlas grimaced. "I understand what you mean, but you must realize my race is unlike yours. We are warlike, and the Council will bear you no grudge for your previous victory. They will listen to what you have to say without seeking retribution. What other choice do you have? You are trapped in Tartarus with no hope of escape unless you seek the assistance of the Titans. There will be no way for you to infiltrate the city without being caught, and if you are caught they will kill you immediately. If you go there openly, they will listen to what you have to say."

"And then they'll kill us."

"Possibly. But the alternative is to wander around this wasteland or try to creep inside to use the rift gate. Better to face your fate head-on than scurrying around in the shadows."

Talbot could tell from the look on Wes's face that Atlas had just about sold him with that line, but the Australian wasn't about to admit defeat to the Titan yet.

"And what makes you so friendly with the Titans again? You just finished telling us how they kicked you out, and now you're suddenly willing to face them again? What's the deal with that?"

Atlas looked discomfited at the question, and Talbot instantly knew Wes had struck a sore point, something the Titan had been trying to avoid.

"My people were misled by Prometheus about me. With you both beside me to validate my story, they will accept me back. At least that's the outcome I hope for."

"Finally, some honesty. You want us to walk through the gates of a city full of Titans, who will probably want to exfoliate our balls with sandpaper, and see the Titan Council, just so you can sleep in your own bed again. Is that about right?"

Atlas dropped his gaze, staring intently at the floor. "I am sorry. It has been many seasons since I lived among my own kind instead of simply existing out here among the filth and the harpies." The huge Titan sighed before straightening once more, his cloudy eyes steady. "I will help you in any other course you deem appropriate, of course."

Wes grinned. "Well, lucky for you I reckon your course is pretty damn sexy. What do you think, Talbot?"

Talbot smiled, though in his heart he felt dread at the prospect of walking into that city once more. "I think I trust your judgment. Both of you," he added, looking at Atlas.

Surprise lit Atlas's features, and his cloudy eyes darted between Talbot and Wes, seemingly waiting for them to shatter his hopes once more, before he broke into a wide grin and leaned forward to encompass them both in a bone-bruising hug.

"You will not regret this decision," gushed the Titan, releasing them.

"Just don't start dry-humping me, okay?" muttered Wes, rubbing his bruised shoulders.

"Dry *what?*"

Wes grinned mischievously. "Don't worry about it. When do you want to leave?"

"Well, now of course."

"Of course," replied Wes softly, giving Talbot a look and shrugging. Talbot smiled in return.

One day they would sleep….

But not today.

***

"Open the gates," boomed Atlas.

They stood outside the Titan city, having followed the gargantuan Atlas across the strange desert-like land to get here. The harpies had hovered overhead, much like the scavenger birds they reminded Talbot of, but they kept their distance. Atlas advised his companions that the harpies had indeed been drawing them into a trap before they'd inadvertently stumbled across his abode. Talbot was immensely happy for that coincidence; he'd been through enough drama on this journey already.

"I said OPEN THE GATES!!!" roared Atlas, thundering the end of his imposing staff into the ground.

The land rumbled and a prodigious crack fractured the earth from the base of Atlas's staff all the way to the thick gates. The gates burst inward with tremendous force, scattering the Titans who had gathered there.

As they entered the city, Talbot got the distinct impression Atlas had once been revered among the Titans, possibly even feared, with many throwing themselves facedown before him as he strode inside.

"Nice fan club you've got here, Atlas," muttered Wes, his hand never leaving the hilt of Laevateinn, even though the sword remained in its scabbard at his hip.

The many shocked faces were quickly turning to snarls upon recognizing Talbot and Wes. Talbot gripped his Glock 39, but followed Wes's lead and refrained from removing it from his holster.

"I was once held in high regard among my people," said Atlas, striding through the crowd and heading for a huge building Talbot recognized from the last time he and Wes had ventured through the Titan city, 'until that charlatan turned them against me."

"That's awesome," said Wes. "Now these guys aren't going to go nuts against me and Talbot, are they? I mean, the last time we were on this street I kind of… chopped one of Cerberus's heads off."

"You defeated Cerberus?" asked Atlas incredulously, looking sideways at Wes.

"Well, no. Technically it was Talbot who killed him in the battle on Mount Olympus. I just made a point of chopping off his head when we were here."

"Incredible," muttered Atlas, glancing down at Talbot. "I had thought that creature was invincible."

They marched up the main street toward the towering central building – a four-storey structure built of the same dark stone-like material as the houses which lined either side of the street. Being four-levels high in the Titan city meant the building towered the equivalent height of a ten-storey dwelling back on Earth.

Atlas didn't pause, mounting the oversized steps and pulling open the wide double doors, striding inside, leaving Talbot with a sudden sense of déjà vu. The last time they had been here, Prometheus had done exactly the same thing. Talbot just hoped this quest finished differently from the last one.

They entered the sizable hall, a huge single staircase facing them. Atlas ignored the staircase, turning right instead and heading toward the doors Talbot remembered housed the Titan Council.

Before they had covered half the distance, the door to the Council Room slammed open and Kronos stormed out. The King of the

Titans sneered at Atlas, barely containing the fury simmering just below his surface. Talbot felt sure the mist within his eyes swirled more frenetically. Several other tall figures flowed out from the assembly hall and huddled behind Kronos, whose graying beard practically bristled with rage.

"What do you want here, *outcast?*" spat Kronos. "How dare you bring our enemies through the gates of my city and into my very home? Why should I not kill you all right now?"

Wes's sword was out in an instant, its power glowing down the length of the blade as he leaped forward, but Atlas stopped him with a swift but gentle hand upon his chest. Their Titan companion then surprised both Talbot and Wes by turning back to Kronos and dropping to one knee with his head bowed.

The King of the Titans seemed just as surprised as Wes and Talbot, and he paused, confused. Whatever he had been expecting, this obviously wasn't it. Talbot swiftly glanced at Wes who shrugged before sheathing Laevateinn and kneeled alongside Atlas. With no other real option, Talbot followed suit, and soon all three were on one knee before Kronos.

"Well?" asked Kronos, but Talbot could hear the edge was now gone from his voice, replaced by curiosity.

"My Lord," began Atlas, "I have come to beg from you the lifting of my banishment. You now must realize the deceitfulness of the one known to be Prometheus. As these two humans will attest, his treachery spreads much further than you can possibly imagine, and we have all been ensnared in his web."

"So *you* say. And who are these two murderers to endorse your claims. Prometheus aided our people in many ways; it may be that he has merely been cast in a darker light since our defeat by the Olympians."

Atlas's head shot up. "Then why did he not return here with you to aid against the Keres. If Prometheus were so loyal to the Titans he would have thrown himself forward to receive their vengeance instead of cowering and allowing his people to suffer at the hands of those whose rage was only against *him*. Is it not true that once they arrived here among you and realized Prometheus had not followed they allowed the rest of you to live? Does this not indicate the level of his treachery?"

Kronos opened his mouth to answer, but Talbot cut in. "We were all manipulated by him. When we finally returned to my world we discovered he had been influencing people in ways which made no sense at the time, but they do now. And then there is the fact he isn't even a Titan –"

"NOT A TITAN? What lies are these?" roared Kronos.

Talbot looked up at the King. "Didn't you ever wonder why he had the power to change his shape at will when nobody else from your race could do such a thing?"

Kronos paused. "He told me he had experimented upon himself using the blood of a hydra."

"That's what we thought as well," said Talbot. "But he's much more than that."

"I saw him born, I watched him grow...." said Kronos, but now his voice was not so certain.

"Was there a time when he disappeared? And when he returned did he seem different?"

Kronos nodded. "When he came home he had the power to regenerate and alter his shape. He acted unusually also, something deep inside him seemed fundamentally altered, but I thought it was simply due to his experimentation."

"Prometheus also impersonated people in our world many times, during many eras. And now it seems he has managed to possess the body of the most fearsome beast in existence. He currently leads an army of giants from a realm called Valhalla across my planet, destroying everything in his path."

"Prometheus *lives*?" gasped Kronos.

Talbot watched as the Titan King's surprise slowly turned into something else, something darker. "And he has not returned to us? His actions saw our race decimated... and yet he strode free to continue his deceit elsewhere. A mere tenth of the Titans to venture through that gate managed to return, and that... *traitor*... has since discarded us; left us here to rot."

Rage now flowed freely through Kronos, the Titan's storm-gray eyes swirling maliciously. "We *must* have revenge!"

"We can help you with that," said Wes swiftly. "We're on our way to Olympia to ask Zeus for help to defeat the Val... Van Halen... Valentinian... their army, the one from Valhalla, you know, the one Prometheus leads. We need all the help we can get to stop them, and you guys are more than welcome to tag along."

All four of them were now standing, Kronos towering over Wes and Talbot. He glowered down at them, his features unreadable. "You expect us to aid you after what happened the last time?" he demanded, his voice coarse and full of suppressed emotion. "Why would we assist you when you participated in the near destruction of our race?"

"Don't cry, princess," taunted Wes casually. "You guys are the ones who attacked the Olympians. Don't get all whiney now because you got your arse handed to you on a platter."

Talbot almost choked on his own tongue, but glancing back to Kronos he was surprised to see the Titan King grinning slightly.

"My people have a saying," said Kronos calmly, all traces of his former rage now receded. "If your enemy can look you in the eye and insult you without flinching, then it shows your own true strength."

"I can piss on you too if that helps," replied Wes.

Kronos's expression broke into a wide smile. "You are indeed a worthy enemy. But I think that today you are our friend. Your army defeated ours fairly, though I might point out that without the unexpected aid of the Keres we would have decimated you and the Olympians."

"Woulda, shoulda, coulda. It doesn't matter how you got your arse kicked, it still got kicked."

Kronos nodded. "This is true. We shall discuss our new friendship over a feast tonight. Themis will show you all to your rooms where you may rest until summoned."

Talbot glanced behind them and saw the female Titan he had met during their previous encounter. "Isn't she related to Prometheus?" he asked, suddenly worried. "He called her his cousin."

"We all refer to our fellow Titans as cousin; it is a term of respect," said Kronos.

"Yeah, right," muttered Wes, too quietly for anyone but Talbot to hear. "Sounds more like incest; a game for the whole family."

They followed Themis up the oversized staircase, each step three times the height they were used to, turning right before she led them through a bewildering series of corridors. She finally indicated three doors and, without a word, turned and departed.

"Thanks for your help," Wes called out after her.

Opening the door to the first room, Talbot saw it was simply furnished, containing a single Titan-sized bed, table and chair.

"They could have given us a ladder to get up on this damn thing," said Wes, entering the room and struggling onto the huge bed. The top of the mattress rose almost six feet off the ground. Wes punched the mattress, wincing slightly and holding his hand. "It's like concrete. I have a feeling we're gonna need to get some rest before Kronos's wonderful feast tonight, but how the hell am I supposed to do that when the bed's as hard as a Zumba coach's butt? Talbot, come up here, check this shit out."

Talbot clumsily climbed up onto the bed while Atlas closed the door and silently moved over to the single chair, sitting down. The Titan had a strange, slightly bemused expression upon his face.

"What's up, Atlas?" asked Wes.

Atlas glanced up at them both. "I thought I would feel differently."

"What do you mean?" asked Talbot.

The Titan sighed. "I have waited for this moment for... well, a very long time. In my dreams I always envisioned it would be different, somehow... *better*. I had thought Kronos would embrace me as his brother once more, but he hardly even glanced at me except when he was angry."

"These things take time," said Talbot. "Perhaps he just feels awkward."

"Perhaps. But I can't help but feel there is something else."

"Sexual tension," said Wes suddenly.

"*What?*" gasped both Talbot and Atlas at the same time.

"Um... nothing," replied Wes swiftly. "Maybe Kronos still holds some sort of resentment toward you."

"I don't think so," said Atlas. "My race may be many things, but discreet is not one of them. When I heard about the subterfuge involved in fooling you both, I was amazed they were able to pull it off. The fact Prometheus was the main perpetrator helped me to understand better, because usually my people are very straightforward in their dealings, especially ones involving antagonism or resentment such as what you insinuate."

"Damn. You use a lot of big words," said Wes. "Is that to make up for your little –?"

"*Wes!*" cut in Talbot. "I think what Atlas is saying is he expected a different reaction from Kronos due to the Titans' natural way of dealing with each other. Right?"

"Yes, that is correct," said Atlas. "As I said before, Kronos and I were once like brothers, but that was before the poison of Prometheus had seeped into his veins."

"I think he just needs some time. He seemed more intent upon the revelation of Prometheus being a traitor than anything else. He's probably just in shock."

Atlas's face seemed to lighten at that prospect. "You might be right," he agreed, nodding slightly to himself.

"Let's hope so," muttered Wes.

Atlas rose from the chair and moved back to the door. "I think I shall get some rest."

Atlas left, shutting the door behind him. Moments later they heard the door to the room next door open and close.

"That dude's got issues," muttered Wes, dangling his legs over the edge of the huge bed.

"No, he's just been alone for a long time and has forgotten that others don't care for him as much as he remembers."

"But what about those guys bowing and shit when we entered the city?"

"I think that was more adoration than actual caring," replied Talbot. "It's like hero worship – you can tell in the way Atlas responded to what they did. He was used to it, and as such didn't notice. But what he truly wanted was to be welcomed back by Kronos, and that didn't happen."

"Well boohoo. Megalump needs to get over it."

"Didn't you ever have anyone you respected, Wes?"

The commando appeared thoughtful for a moment and for just a second Talbot saw something flicker across his face; some sort of emotion, gone almost as soon as he noticed it. Talbot wasn't sure if Wes had even recognized it before his mind closed it out.

"Nope. Unless you count *me*, of course. I always kind of liked me."

"Not even me?" asked Talbot.

"Oh no," protested Wes, holding up his hands. "I'm not entering that conversation, no way, no how."

"What do you mean?"

"I mean, we start talking like that, and then all of a sudden we're all deep and meaningful and you're telling me how your uncle with the hairy back touched you in your special place. No sir, I will not discuss that sort of stuff with you."

"Then how about this; do you miss Zoe?"

For the first time since Talbot had met Wes the Australian seemed dumbfounded. All barriers seemed to come crashing down for the tiniest instant, and Talbot saw an expression on his face which had never been there before.

"Er… what do you mean?"

"I mean, do you miss her? Seemed you two might have something going on between you."

"What the hell is this, twenty fucking questions? She's Prometheus's daughter, Talbot, how could I possibly have anything going on with her? Besides, with the way she can change her shape, who's to tell what she really looks like? She might actually be Prometheus's son; did you think about that? Yeah, she might have a big ol' John Holmes eighteen-inch one-eyed anaconda hidden in there somewhere just waiting to pounce."

Talbot fought to keep his face serious. "That's not a no."

"No, that's a go fuck yourself. Anyway, we've got bigger problems. What's our next step in getting back to Olympia? Do you reckon you can open the gate these guys have, or will Zeus have locked it off?"

Noticing Wes's not-so-subtle change of subject, Talbot let the issue go, but he couldn't completely forget that instant where Wes's expression had changed.

"I think I should be able to open the rift again. You and I need to go through first just in case the Olympians have implemented that defensive thing they had when we took the rift under Ayers Rock, remember?"

"How the hell could I forget?" asked Wes incredulously. "I almost didn't make it through. And you left me behind when you got to the other side, if I remember correctly."

"What choice did I have?"

Wes chuckled. "Yeah, I can see how Briareus could be persuasive."

Talbot laughed too, remembering the massive Hecatonchires – one of three brothers – who had arrived and escorted Talbot across Olympia to meet Zeus atop Mount Olympus. Briareus had around a hundred arms, with fifty heads perched atop his huge body, standing some fifty-feet-tall. Briareus had been the sole survivor of the three Hecatonchires brothers in the battle against the Titans, and Talbot wondered how he had fared since they'd last seen him. Shaking himself out of his reverie, Talbot focused instead on the task ahead of them.

"It's not going to be easy convincing Zeus and the others that the Titans are now on our side," he said.

"I know," replied Wes, his tone serious, "but the opportunity was just too good. I'll have a hard time trusting these guys too, but we're going to need all the help we can get. We both know how well these Titans can fight."

Talbot nodded. "I wish we could find the Keres, too. I reckon they'd make short work of those giants."

"I don't think it would be a good idea to unleash those guys on Earth. Remember what Charon said about the ones who had been there before?"

"Oh, right. That's where the stories of vampires and werewolves come from."

Wes nodded sadly. "If we took them to our world, they'd never recover."

"What do you mean?" asked Talbot, frowning.

"Well, all the stories about vampires these days have them turning metrosexual. I just couldn't live with myself if we turned the Keres into simpering, sensitive dudes more worried about their hair and wardrobe than sucking the life out of people."

Talbot hooted with laughter, the sound bouncing off the walls. He continued howling until tears were streaming down his face, only gradually reining the sound back in.

"You're a funny guy, Wes," he said, gasping for breath. "Has anyone ever told you that?"

"Once," said Wes, "but I didn't listen to him."

Talbot wiped the tears from his face. "Why's that?"

"Because he was carrying a manbag; I'm pretty sure he was a vampire."

Talbot's laughter rang out once more….

***

Talbot entered his own room in the Titan building, finding it almost identical to the one Wes was now asleep in. The feast was fast approaching and he needed to grab whatever rest he could. He clambered up onto the bed and stroked the flickering bug-light attached to the wall above. It had taken him and Wes an age to figure out how to dull the light created by the huge, insect-like creature, the same kind they'd seen in Atlas's underground dwelling. Wes had finally lucked onto the answer when he'd swiped at the outside glass-like cover and a hidden darkening sleeve had slid into view. It was really very simple; in fact it was the light's uncomplicated design which had confused them for so long.

As he lay in the darkness, Talbot wondered what was to come. They were making the most of the rooms to get a bit of sleep while they could, but the feast that evening would be decisive, and Talbot knew he'd be walking on eggshells. One wrong move or misspoken word could see them both killed.

The sheets of the oversized bed felt odd, like no material he had ever known, and in place of a pillow there was merely a raised section of the mush-like mattress. As such, Talbot had a hard time getting comfortable, and it seemed only moments before Wes was shaking him awake, the commando perched on the edge of the bed, and the bug-light exposed once more.

"Get up, sleeping ugly," said Wes, giving him another shove.

"Wh-what?" mumbled Talbot.

"Time for dinner with the in-laws. I hope you've got your game face on."

"Huh?" muttered Talbot, but then he remembered the situation and realized what Wes was talking about: it was time to go and break bread with the Titans. His stomach instantly tightened, and not because of hunger.

At that precise moment a terrifying thought occurred to him: what if they were only invited so they could be the main course? Shaking aside the nasty idea, Talbot cast off the strange bedcovering and leaped down the short drop to the floor, stumbling slightly. Wes dropped down beside him, landing like a cat. Without a word, Talbot gathered his composure and reached up, grasping the handle and opening the door.

Atlas stood in the hallway outside his room, his seventeen-foot frame appearing even larger within the cramped confines of the narrow corridor. He nodded in greeting, but said nothing. The nerves between the three were tangible, and part of Talbot felt slightly relieved he wasn't the only one feeling anxious about the upcoming dinner. Despite what Kronos had said, Talbot found it difficult to believe the Titans would simply let bygones be bygones.

Glancing to his left, he saw Wes was striding with his left hand on the hilt of his sword. Through his own experience, Talbot knew that such a thing was necessary in order to walk without getting tripped up by the sword, but there seemed more tension in Wes than normal.

As if reading his thoughts, Wes glanced at him and winked.

Okay then, it was his own nervousness projecting onto his companions. He should have known better than to suspect Wes of being anxious; on a slow day the guy had dealt with things which would make brave men weep. He glanced at Atlas, but couldn't determine anything of the Titan's mood.

Talbot sucked down his doubts and put his faith in his companions; hopefully they would find a way through the evening ahead without getting killed. He'd just try to shut his mouth as much as possible and hope nobody spoke to him.

***

"So, Doctor Harrison, I believe you killed our protector, Cerberus."

Oh shit.

Talbot's mind turned completely to jelly as he fumbled for an answer. What could he say to something like that? The entire dinner had gone well so far, the Titans providing higher seats for Talbot and Wes; chairs he suspected were designed for children, but were comfortable nonetheless.

The main discomfort at the feast had involved some of the dishes; Talbot had struggled to identify a single thing the Titans had bought out. One of the courses had consisted of something closely resembling a lower intestine, but when the server had cut off a section for a Titan, Talbot distinctly though he heard a low screech, as though the thing was somehow still alive.

He'd avoided that dish.

But there was no avoiding this question. His mind raced, hoping for something, anything, to distract the multitude of swirling eyes now scrutinizing him.

"Um…." mumbled Talbot uncomfortably. Glancing at Wes, he saw the commando raise an eyebrow.

He was on his own, then.

"You *do* remember Cerberus, don't you?" asked the Titan once more. Talbot had met him earlier, along with the dozen or so other Titans at the long table, and recalled his name was Iapetos. He was grinning slightly at Talbot's discomfort, his green eyes churning maliciously.

Anger boiled within Talbot. He was being deliberately baited, and he knew it, but in that instant he didn't care.

"Of course I killed him. I charged into that bastard while I was riding a unicorn and skewered him like a shish-kebab. I don't remember seeing you, though; were you hiding here in the city doing laundry with the women?"

Wes's choked laughter was the only sound as Iapetos's expression dropped from one of derision to shock.

"I – I *was* there," sputtered the Titan.

"You must have been at the back of the group. It's a shame; I would have liked to have met you there."

Stunned silence followed this comment also until Kronos stood, his face unreadable. The King of the Titans stared at Talbot for what seemed like an eon, and Talbot's anger quickly washed away. He had just done the one thing he had been scared Wes would do: he'd picked a fight. The Titan King's eyes kept drilling into him, but Talbot forced himself to meet that stare. He'd dug himself a hole, and now the only way out of it was to stick by what he'd said.

Kronos began to laugh, long and loud.

Talbot looked around, surprised as the other dozen or so Titans at the table, including Iapetos, joined in the laughter. Wes finally released the guffaws he'd been holding back, and Talbot giggled uncertainly.

"Well played," said Kronos once the laughter died down enough. "Well played indeed." The leader of the Titans sat down once again and took a huge mouthful of something gray and blue, which looked like gelatin, but crunched like gravel when he bit into it. Activity around the table returned to normal, and Talbot sat back in his chair, confused.

Wes leaned over. "Well done," he said quietly in Talbot's ear, chewing loudly on something green which hissed every time he opened his mouth.

"What just happened?" whispered Talbot.

"They were testing you. Wanted to see if you had the balls to stand up to one of them."

"Why?" asked Talbot quietly, trying to make it look like he was moving his squishy food onto his oversized fork.

"They're a warlike people – don't ever forget that," hissed Wes. "Why would they follow a cauliflower into battle?"

"A *what?*"

"A pissy-pants, a wuss, a soft cock. Whatever you call it, it amounts to the same thing: a coward. They're not going to help us if they think we're scared."

"Do you really think that's why they did it?" asked Talbot as whatever it was he'd been pushing around began crawling off his plate.

Wes gave Talbot a scornful look before raising his bowl-sized goblet toward Kronos, who was engaged in his own quiet conversation with Iapetos. The King of the Titans raised his goblet in return and smiled.

"They tested you and you passed, that's all you need to worry about for now." Wes took a deep swallow and winced, covering the reaction up with an effort. "Man, that stuff tastes worse than goat piss."

"Have you tasted goat's piss before?" asked Talbot with a chuckle.

"Yeah, not something I'd recommend." The statement was uttered so candidly that Talbot was left with no doubt as to the honesty of what the commando said. He silently pushed his own goblet further away.

"Do you think it's over? The testing, I mean," whispered Talbot after a while.

"Look at Atlas."

Talbot glanced over at the Titan. He was easily the largest figure at the table, and at the moment he looked as though every muscle in his body was tightened to its breaking point.

"What's going on?" Talbot murmured to Wes.

"Now it's his turn."

Atlas surged to his feet, his chest heaving and sledgehammer-like fists clenched. "YOU PUSH ME TOO FAR, COEUS!"

It was only then that Talbot saw who Atlas was staring at across the table. A Titan with a closely-trimmed chinstrap beard tracing his square jaw and short-cropped black hair glared back at Atlas through swirling red eyes. A female Titan sat upon his lap, his plate-sized hand clasping the side of her buttock. She flicked her head around, her gaze panicked.

It was Themis.

Several things suddenly slotted into place. When she'd shown them to their rooms earlier, Talbot had thought the female Titan had remained silent because of him and Wes; he'd never suspected her behavior owed anything to Atlas's presence. And then there had been Atlas's awkward explanation of his melancholy after arriving. Atlas had passed it off as related to Kronos's lack of reaction to his return, but now Talbot knew it was the lacking response of another Titan which had upset him so much.

And that Titan had been Themis.

Talbot had paid no heed when Coeus had pulled Themis onto his lap – several of the Titans had done it with the other serving maids. However, Atlas had clearly seen it, and from his reaction he evidently did not approve.

"Don't get involved," Wes hissed into Talbot's ear. "This is *his* test, and if we interfere they might kill us all."

Coeus calmly pushed Themis off his lap, and she shot a distressed look at Atlas before scurrying from the room.

Kronos stood. "Do you challenge Coeus, then?" he asked, and Talbot could hear the eagerness in his voice.

"I do," growled Atlas, his swirling eyes never leaving his opponent.

"Then we shall go from here to the Dome of Reprisal," declared Kronos. "No enmity shall be left when we leave."

Talbot sensed a great deal of ceremony in the whole affair, and he guessed this was possibly a common occurrence among the Titans.

As the entire group rose from the table and started departing the food hall, Wes nudged him and they joined the procession. The Titans marched through the huge building and out the front doors. Their path headed directly toward another immense structure, this one with a high vaulted roof. Apparently this was the Dome of

Reprisal which Kronos had spoken of.

"I guess that's the Dome of Daffodils, right?" murmured Wes. Talbot coughed heavily to cover his laughter. One look at Atlas, however, and all thoughts of mirth subsided.

The enormous Titan strode angrily ahead of Talbot and Wes, his fists still clenched at his sides, tension rippling through him like the bolts of power charging Wes's sword. Talbot didn't know the details of the relationship between Atlas and Themis, and he didn't need to. He supposed he should have foreseen what approached. Atlas had been expelled from a community of warriors; how else would they allow him to reenter their ranks?

Word must have spread swiftly throughout the citadel as several hundred Titans were rapidly moving toward the Dome, coming to watch the spectacle. Kronos strode between them and pushed open the heavy doors, marching inside. The congregation waited for the main party of Titans – including Wes and Talbot – to enter, shuffling in behind them.

One moment it was as dark as pitch, and the next the entire place lit up like they'd stepped into the center of the sun. The dome flared so brightly Talbot yelped and even Wes instinctively covered his eyes with one hand, his other impulsively flashing down to loosen Laevateinn in its scabbard. The brightness dulled somewhat after a moment, rather like someone adjusting a dimmer switch, and Talbot was able to peer around the interior of the enormous structure without difficulty.

The flaring light had apparently not affected the Titans, with several giving the duo curious glances at they filed past on either side of them. Not one of the towering figures appeared the least discomfited by the intense light from moments before, although many seemed displeased at the presence of the two humans. If rumors spread as swiftly as word of the combat between Atlas and Coeus, then most of these Titans would know exactly who Wes and Talbot were, along with their subsequent parts in the failed invasion of Olympia by the Titan army.

Talbot felt a sudden need to keep moving. He followed Wes into the Dome and they soon found themselves on a circular raised outer section – like the external rim of a wheel – which completely surrounded a depressed arena, its diameter the length of a football field. Rising high behind this circular section was a series of tiered benches, like steps. It took Talbot a couple of seconds to realize these were for spectators to sit on, to provide a better view of the pit below – kind of like NASCAR.

But this was definitely not NASCAR.

Judging from the bloodstains on the walls of the arena, Talbot guessed this was more like the Coliseum in Rome. Staring around the structure, Talbot wondered at the similarity between this and the actual Coliseum, which he had studied intensely at one time in his career. It seemed the lower rows, the ones closest to the arena floor, were reserved for the higher-ranking Titans such as Kronos and the members of the Council. There were others from among the crowd who sat here, but the majority of what looked like simple inhabitants without any kind of rank moved higher up into the Dome of Reprisal.

Wes sat down in the very front row, in a special raised section reserved only for the Titan Council, choosing the position right next to Kronos. Talbot glanced nervously at the surrounding Titans as they started murmuring among themselves. Whether Wes realized it or not, in the breakdown of Titan culture, he had just claimed equal status to the King of the Titans. Talbot's heart raced as he stared hard at Wes, noting the lack of strain upon his features and his relaxed bearing. The commando yawned as he scratched the back of his neck, for all appearances completely oblivious of the social statement he was making.

Yep, he knew *exactly* what he'd just done.

Trusting Wes's judgment of the situation, Talbot awkwardly navigated between Titans and colossal, stone-like steps, finally making his way over to Wes. He sat on the bench beside him, promoting himself to equal status as both Wes and Kronos, and glanced around nervously, trying hard not to *appear* nervous as he saw several glowering stares aimed in their direction. This would certainly test their host's patience.

All of that was forgotten as Atlas leaped over the railing and easily dropped the twenty yards or so down to the arena floor. On the opposite side of the Dome, Coeus appeared. It seemed there were no exits anywhere inside the arena, the only way out evidently being with the aid of those positioned where the two combatants had entered the arena. Neither could leave until the issue between them was deemed resolved, and Talbot guessed that decision would be made by one Titan, and one Titan only.

Kronos.

The surface of the arena seemed similar to that of the land outside the city walls; the horrible spongy, slightly sticky ground which reminded Talbot so much of a tongue.

Atlas and Coeus moved toward each other. Both were unarmed, and Talbot wondered how the combat would play out, whether weapons would be introduced or –

And then it was over.

The action had been so fast Talbot had missed it completely. His jaw hung down as he stared at the single figure remaining. One minute Coeus was there, and the next thing he was gone. *Literally* gone.

"What happened?" he hurriedly whispered to Wes.

Even the normally composed Wes appeared astounded by the outcome, along with the entire assembly of Titans in the Dome.

"Holy shit!"

"Wes, tell me."

Atlas was calmly striding back across the arena floor toward the edge he had entered from. Muttering was now sounding through the Titan spectators as they discussed what had just occurred; obviously Talbot wasn't the only one who had missed it.

"I'm really glad that Atlas guy wasn't with them when they invaded Olympia," said Wes quietly to Talbot, making sure Kronos didn't overhear them.

"Why?"

"He kicks arse!"

"Tell me what happened."

"Coeus came for Atlas, who didn't move a muscle, but the ground opened up beneath Coeus's feet, and he just dropped into it. The surface snapped shut like a Venus Flytrap. That motherfucker's gone."

"Whoa," murmured Talbot, looking toward Atlas. The Titan appeared somewhat melancholy, as though what he'd just done had sucked away his previous rage, leaving him hollow. The Titan was hauled up by his fellows at the railing, and he trudged over to the raised dais, finally standing before Kronos.

"It appears your powers have grown since you left us, Atlas," said the King of the Titans.

"I had a lot of time on my hands," replied Atlas, his voice cold.

"So it would seem. How is it you are able to affect the stability of the ground without your staff?"

"The skill is now ingrained within me. I have no need to focus it through an external device."

Kronos cast his gaze out at the arena floor, its surface unblemished by Coeus's death. "A shame about the demise of your cousin," he mused quietly.

"Coeus made his own choice when he decided to lay his hands upon my wife," growled Atlas, his blue eyes swirling maliciously.

"But he did that at my order, as I think you know."

"Would you have me put you in the same place as he now is?" asked Atlas, his voice dangerously low.

Kronos regarded the Titan momentarily, the question hanging in the air. Despite the low volume, the sound of the conversation had traveled, and every ear in the Dome strained to hear the king's reply. The moment stretched on for what seemed like an eternity, and Wes shoved himself and Talbot indiscreetly along the front bench – away from Kronos.

Finally, when the pressure was so thick in the air Talbot thought it might shatter completely, Kronos began to laugh. It was not a derisive sound, merely one full of cheerfulness which rang crisply in the still air, cutting through the tension. Talbot released the breath he had been unconsciously holding and heard Wes chuckle. Glancing at Atlas, he saw the Titan was still ominously angry, but he no longer appeared ready to attack the leader of the Titans.

"Well done, Atlas," said Kronos. "It is good to see you are still a

Titan despite having been isolated for so long. I am glad these humans haven't corrupted you either."

"Here we go," murmured Wes. Talbot leaned closer to ask what he meant, but Wes gave his head a tiny shake. Talbot closed his mouth, though curiosity tore within him.

"What do you mean?" Atlas asked Kronos.

"I mean these pathetic creatures." Kronos indicated Wes and Talbot. "Their weakness is palpable. How could you have…?" His voice trailed away as Wes stood and, without looking at anyone, walked calmly down from the raised dais and over to the arena railing. He leaped over it, dropping the distance to the floor of the arena without issue and landing like a cat, boldly striding toward the middle of the area, stretching his muscles as he went.

Nobody moved, a stunned silence filling the Dome once more. Wes sat down cross-legged in the center of the arena floor, patiently waiting… but for what?

Kronos appeared disgruntled, as though Wes had just spoiled the surprise he'd been preparing. "Pallas!" he called.

A huge Titan, bigger even than Atlas, strode into the Dome through the main entrance. He entered fully garbed for battle, leaving no doubt in Talbot's mind this entire affair had been orchestrated.

"My Lord," gasped Atlas, all signs of his former wrath now gone, "you cannot match him against Pallas!" Kronos merely grinned.

Peering down at his companion, Talbot realized Wes had been expecting something like this. The Titans had tested Talbot's bravery at the table; tested Atlas's powers moments ago, and now they would test Wes… or kill him.

Pallas was easily the tallest Titan Talbot had yet seen, his immense barrel chest covered in a black breastplate, the rest of his body also clad in Titan armor. Conceit seemed to ooze from the Titan, and Talbot could almost taste his haughtiness, even before he glimpsed the smug face glaring out from within the open-faced helm. Pallas carried a gigantic double-handed sword, longer than Wes was tall. As the Titan jumped into the arena, Talbot noted how graceful his movements were despite his enormous bulk. The mere sight of him terrified Talbot.

The two met in the center of the arena. Wes rose and drew Laevateinn, moving forward warily. Pallas darted in, his actions smooth, the flashing blade deceptively quick despite its bulk. His weapon shone black as polished ebony, seeming to drip malice. The two combatants came together, their blades cracking like thunder as Pallas swung a devastating overhead blow which Wes smoothly parried. Wes's riposte almost connected with the breastplate of Pallas's armor, but the Titan leaped nimbly backward.

The two swordsmen circled each other, more warily now. Suddenly, they rushed together once again, their blades flashing in a flurry. No other sound rose above the crackling of Wes's sword and the ominous thunderous crackling Pallas's sword made as it cut through the air. When the two swords clashed, it seemed the opposing forces fractured the air like a sonic boom, and the atmosphere itself vibrated with each impact.

As Talbot watched, he could not help but feel that Wes was going to lose. Despite the awesome abilities of the Australian, his opponent was almost his equal in skill, but also much, much larger, stronger and heavier. Wes was deflecting the Titan's blows on an angle rather than managing to block the full force of the strike, and it was rapidly tiring him.

The contest carried on, their pace unrelenting. Again and again they clashed, and each time the two warriors parted Wes seemed slightly more exhausted, his sword dropping fractionally lower. Talbot really began to worry as he saw Wes trying to suck in more oxygen. The Australian backed away from Pallas, his sword held double-handed and drooping closer to the ground, sweat pouring from his forehead.

He was done for.

Pallas sensed it too, and a malicious gleam crossed his features as he moved in for the kill. He feinted to the right, and Wes fell for it, clumsily trying to block the move as Pallas's sword swung toward the weary Australian's neck.

And in an instant everything changed. The formerly exhausted Wes easily spun in a full circle, away from Pallas's sword, swinging Laevateinn with tremendous force. Having missed the killing blow,

Pallas became unbalanced, stumbling forward. Wes's sword slashed down on his upper right arm, cutting through it like a laser. The arm, still holding Pallas's sword, fell twitching to the ground. The Titan stared incredulously at it.

"And that –" said Wes casually, all traces of fatigue now gone, "–is called the rope-a-dope, you motherfucker. You can thank Mister Muhammad Ali for inventing that, and say hello to left-handed masturbation."

The ruse had been perfect, and Pallas had fallen for it, as had Talbot, Kronos and the entire Dome full of Titans. Silence filled the auditorium as Wes sheathed his weapon and began to casually stroll to the arena railing.

Kronos, finally recovering from his shock, stood up. "You cannot leave until your opponent is dead."

Wes paused, glanced back at the kneeling form of Pallas, clutching desperately at the stump of his right arm, trying to stem the bleeding, and then turned back to Kronos. "You're shittin' me, right?"

Kronos looked momentarily confused. "You must kill him."

"Get in here and help him before he bleeds to death, you idiot," snapped Wes coldly, once more moving toward the railing. "He's done. I won. Somebody get me a fucking ladder so I can climb out of this bunghole."

Atlas moved to the railing, leaned over and gripped Wes's wrist, easily hauling him up. Kronos appeared almost apoplectic with rage, and he strode to confront Wes, Talbot following close behind.

"YOU MUST –" he began. But he was cut off, almost literally.

Wes had whipped Laevateinn out in a flash and swiped it directly up between Kronos's legs, the tip of the blade slicing the material of the king's pants and causing Kronos to abruptly reconsider his next words.

"Unless you want to be the tallest soprano in history I suggest you back the fuck up," growled Wes. "I said it was done, and it's done. He fought well and deserves to live." Kronos's crotch was almost level with Wes's shoulder, and the point of Laevateinn was practically sitting on the Titan's….

Talbot's thoughts were broken off by Kronos's laughter, and the odd sound of slow clapping as the Titans began to applaud. Kronos started to clap too. Talbot suddenly realized what had happened. Wes's test had not been whether or not he could kill Pallas, but whether or not he could stay his hand from the killing stroke.

These bastards and their stupid tests.

He could tell from Wes's quizzical expression that the commando hadn't realized what was happening, so Talbot moved over to him and whispered it in his ear. He let his sword drop before sheathing it, glancing back to where Pallas was being assisted from the arena before shaking his head and stalking from the Dome.

Talbot gazed around at the still clapping Titans, wondering if they were applauding Wes's restraint, or the blood already spilled.

CHAPTER 13

Talbot shot out of the rift, smashing head-first into grass. Why the hell couldn't he get the hang of these things? At least he hadn't winded himself this time.

Climbing to his feet, he saw Wes about ten paces away, staring toward a distant city. He stared around, distinguishing the landmarks; they were standing upon the vast plateau behind the great Olympian city of Mount Olympus.

Sucking in a huge gasp of air, Talbot breathed a sigh of relief. He'd successfully managed to open the rift gate and bypass the security features the Olympians had put in place. It had almost been too simp –

"Move and you die," said a strangely familiar voice behind him. Talbot felt the point of a weapon prodding him warningly in the back. He raised his hands in submission.

Despite the threat, or maybe because of it, Wes turned around casually and grinned. "Heya Gigantor. How's it hangin'?"

Talbot heard a chuckle from behind him and the point of the weapon was removed. He cautiously lowered his hands before turning around.

It was Heracles!

Talbot's relief was palpable, though he guessed it shouldn't have been a surprise to be greeted in such a way. Heracles stood with about thirty Olympian warriors, all with weapons drawn. "Hello, Heracles," he said. "How's it going?"

The Olympian's grin disappeared. "I have a feeling it's about get decidedly worse."

"Why's that?"

"Because you two are here, and I doubt it's for a social visit." Heracles turned and barked out an order. The rest of the warriors swiftly ran to their horses and mounted, riding back to the city. "We can discuss your arrival while we walk back," he said grimly.

Talbot grimaced, glancing toward the Olympian city. The wall surrounding the city had just started being repaired after the damage caused by the invading force of Titans during their last conflict. Remembering how each realm operated on a completely separate time system, Talbot swiftly realized it was possibly only days or weeks since the last battle had occurred. No wonder Heracles looked unimpressed to see them again.

"How did you know we were coming?" he asked the Olympian.

"As you have obviously determined, we were unable to close off the rift linking our realm directly with Tartarus. My father implemented defenses such as those you encountered when coming here from your home world, but when you managed to bypass these they triggered an alarm which gave us forewarning of your arrival." Talbot thought he could detect a note of criticism in Heracles's voice.

But why shouldn't Heracles be upset? The last time the two of them had graced this world they had heralded what was possibly the worst battle this world had ever seen. The Olympians were only just starting to rebuild after their losses and, lo and behold, here came Talbot and Wes once more.

He had every right to be pissed.

Staring at Heracles, Talbot marveled anew at the Olympian's size and power. Standing just under seven-feet-tall, he looked every inch the figure from Greek mythology – apart from the fact his dark hair was cut short in the warriors' fashion. Heracles wore a sleeveless flowing robe, belted at the waist, exposing the bulging musculature of the Olympian's upper body. Talbot knew that several Titans, including Atlas, were more muscular than Heracles, but none seemed to exude as much raw power as the son of Zeus did. He truly looked immortal.

However, Heracles was just a mortal, albeit an incredibly powerful one. He could die just like anyone, as could all of the Olympians, despite the exaggerated tales of their godlike natures through Greek folklore. The myths were exactly that: myths. Though they were based upon actual events and people, the stories had been blown out to astronomical proportions by a primitive society which had no other way to explain the things the Olympians could do.

"What has happened?" asked Heracles as they made their way toward the city.

"All sorts of shit," commented Wes amiably. "But you're looking well, still bulging in all the right places."

Heracles stopped walking. "Tell me what is going on," he said seriously. "What terror follows you both this time? Is it the Titans again?"

"Funny you should say that," replied Wes. He then shrugged at Talbot before launching into the tale of how they had come to be back in Olympia. At the close of the story Heracles's expression still hadn't changed.

"You are fools to believe the Titans," he spat. "How much evidence do you need of their treachery?"

"We don't have a choice, Heracles," said Wes. "We need their help in order to stop Prometheus and his army of giants from destroying us."

"So you would trade one conqueror for another? What makes you think the Titans will be any different to these giants?"

"They're finished, Heracles. Their society is in a shambles after their battle with you – with *us* – right here. The Keres decimated them, and there are probably only a thousand Titans left."

"Then what aid can they possibly bring to your people?"

"Their weapons, like yours, are hopefully able to wound these giants," said Talbot. "Ours are useless, and only end up destroying the land. We need help from outside our own realm."

Realization filled Heracles features. "And so you have come to ask us, a people trying to come back from the brink of destruction, for our help to vanquish an enemy, one we don't even know, from your world."

Wes grinned. "Pretty much."

"The Titans weren't your target for aid at all, they were merely a happenstance. What makes you think we can aid you?"

"Poseidon," said Wes, "or rather Prometheus masquerading as Poseidon, made reference to how there were many more settlements in Olympia than just this one. He spoke of a city by the coast – I can't remember the name of it."

"It is called Artemisium," offered Talbot.

"Yeah, whatever. I don't really care," replied Wes, "The point is there're bound to be heaps of people we can call upon to come and help us."

"And *why* would we help you?" asked Heracles incredulously. "Or don't you care about that either?"

"I care about that; I care very much in fact. That's why we're here having this conversation instead of me sitting in Bangkok getting a beer and a blowjob."

"A blow... what?"

"It doesn't matter," interjected Talbot hurriedly. "We need help, Heracles. We need it because they're on their way to seize control of the Syrpeas Gate, and then who knows what they'll do?"

"They are trying to get to the Syrpeas Gate? But that is in Atlantis, far beneath your ocean, isn't it?"

"Not anymore," admitted Talbot. "Our government transported it to Washington D.C. in the United States of America."

"I am unfamiliar with this land."

"Trust me, mate, you're not missing out on much," said Wes. "Think of it as a modern Athens; the contemporary hub of everything commercial, political and artistic; where everyone's trying to screw everyone else – although possibly less literally than the Athenians."

"I see," said Heracles.

"The point is," said Talbot, "an army of around ten thousand indestructible giants led by Prometheus is heading there in order to take control of a gate which may be able to lead him here."

"The Syrpeas Gate does not lead to Olympia," argued Heracles.

"Not directly. But how do you think we got here?"

This silenced Heracles, and Talbot could see the Olympian musing over what had been said. The fact they couldn't seal the gates completely was enough to give him pause, along with the proof of Talbot and Wes standing before them. Their defenses were hardly impregnable, and if an army of Titans had brought their land to the brink of ruin, what would ten thousand giants from Valhalla do to it?

"We must talk to my father," stated Heracles, leading them swiftly toward the city.

An hour later, they were standing within the Olympian Council Hall, in front of the enigmatic leader of the Olympians: Zeus. He appeared the same as when Talbot had last seen him: perhaps fifty years old, his light brown hair streaked with gray and hanging almost to his shoulders. A trimmed beard framed his handsomely tanned face, a face whose features were now furrowed with concern.

"This is dire news indeed," he said. "Not just what you have said about Prometheus and his army of giants, but also the news about the Titans. Do you truly believe they were not just manipulating you? Could they just be doing this in order to attack us once more?"

"I can't see how they could," replied Wes earnestly. "They're finished. You can see it in everything they do. Even that bullshit test they set up for us was easy to see through. Prometheus was the real brains behind those guys, and as we already explained, he was using them as much as everyone else."

"I find it almost impossible to believe the Titans would have agreed to aid you without some ulterior motive," stated Zeus.

"Oh, they've got one, for sure," confirmed Wes. "But at the moment the main thing is that we need their help, and they're pissed off enough at Prometheus to help us."

"Which brings us to the main reason for your visit; Heracles informed me of your request for support."

"We need it. These huge bastards have taken our strongest weapon like a lubed up kabana and asked for more."

"I have no idea what that means," said Zeus, frowning slightly.

Talbot intervened before Wes could elaborate. "It means our weapons are ineffective."

"And you believe ours will be able to stop them?"

"We hope so. They were able to work against the creatures and giants from Tartarus, so I can't see why they wouldn't be effective against the giants from Valhalla."

"But you don't know for sure," said Zeus. "You haven't tested this theory for yourself?"

Talbot's heart sank. "No. We haven't had a chance," he said, his eyes downcast.

"Then I'm afraid I will have to decline your request," said Zeus. "I am very sorry, but I cannot risk the safety of my people – a people already devastated by a war we have only just begun to recover from – just on the hope that our weapons *might* prove effective."

Talbot moved to argue, but felt Wes's hand grip his shoulder and held his tongue.

"He killed your brother, you know," commented Wes nonchalantly.

"*What?*" hissed Zeus, his stare suddenly intensified.

"Prometheus killed Poseidon. Didn't I mention that before? He was gloating about it to us."

Something feral glinted in Zeus's expression, and for the first time since he'd met him, Talbot thought he was going to see the Olympian leader lose control. Rage bubbled just beneath the surface, but with what must have been an incredible amount of self-control he managed to mask his anger.

"Prometheus killed Poseidon?" he grated between clenched teeth.

"Yeah," replied Wes. "I'm not sure when he did it, but he reckons he did."

"And you are sure he now leads this army?"

"Yes," replied Talbot.

Zeus raised his head, and Talbot saw how enraged the leader of the Olympians still was. "You will have your aid. My brother will be avenged."

"Cool," replied Wes, turning and striding out of the Hall. Talbot followed him, catching up outside.

"That was a bit harsh."

Wes glanced at him, nonplussed. "What was harsh?"

"The way you broke the news to Zeus about his brother; you could have been a bit more subtle."

Wes paused. "Our world is under attack. Every second we spend here might see the Earth destroyed, and you want me to be *subtle*?"

Damn. Talbot had forgotten about the differing time systems.

Back on Earth a hundred years might have passed, or perhaps not even a second; they had no way to tell. Even without the conflicting times, the fact their world was under attack should have motivated him enough to do whatever was needed to stop Prometheus.

"Sorry," muttered Talbot.

"So you should be," replied Wes cheerfully, resuming his stride. "Let's go and get something to eat… and then I might go and jerk off."

Talbot's eyes shot wide in their sockets, and he coughed loudly to cover his shock. Wes glanced around at him and grinned. "I love fucking with your head."

"Thanks a lot," sputtered Talbot. "I should be used to it by now though, I guess."

"What? Me jerking off?"

Once again Talbot began coughing uncontrollably, and Wes's laughter rang out through the streets of Mount Olympus.

***

"How long have we been waiting?" asked Wes testily, lying on the reclining chair in the andron. The villa they were staying in within Olympia was beautiful, and Talbot had been fascinated with its design and construction, but Wes had been pacing since they'd arrived, impatience palpable in his every movement.

"By my count it's only been three Olympian days," replied Talbot. "But our time systems work separately from each other, and it might be longer than that by our time… or shorter," he concluded lamely.

"How long does it take to gather an army anyway?" muttered Wes.

Talbot knew the question was rhetorical, so he ignored it. "I'm just glad the Titans have been behaving themselves," he said, hoping to change the subject.

"Of course they're behaving," snapped Wes. "They only sent five hundred warriors through. What the hell can five hundred Titans do?"

"You know they promised more once we can establish a linking portal directly from Tartarus to wherever we choose to make our stand back on Earth," said Talbot.

"Yeah, I know. I just don't like the idea of marching into battle against those fucking giants relying on the Titans to back us up."

"But you told Zeus –"

"I told Zeus exactly what I needed to in order to get him to help us," snarled Wes.

Talbot knew the venom wasn't directed at him. Wes was a man of action, and he detested sitting around just waiting for something to happen.

"The truth of the matter is I don't trust Kronos and his elongated buddies any more than I could throw them," Wes continued. "They're about as honest as a basket of cobras on crack. But the thing is: we need them. If they can bring something to the battle which will help us then it's worth the risk. I mean, look at that shit Atlas did in the arena; that was seriously cool. At least *he* came through with the first group. Bit of a shame Zeus declared they all have to remain under guard while they're here." He shrugged. "But I can't blame him. I don't trust the bastards much either. What about you? Do you reckon you can do the linking rift thingy Zeus mentioned?"

"I hope so," muttered Talbot.

"Do more than hope, buddy. If you screw that up, this entire venture is for nothing."

"No pressure though, right?" said Talbot sarcastically.

"None at all… as long as you don't mind playing the role of prison-bitch to ten thousand guys with cocks the size of blue whales."

"Nice visual," muttered Talbot. "Thanks a lot."

"You're welcome, princess," replied Wes with a grin. "I'm always happy to be of assistance."

"At least you're smiling again."

"Not for long if we have to wait here much longer."

"Zeus said it would take a while. We have to wait for all the other Olympian cities to be notified, and then they have to get here."

"That's another thing," said Wes. "When they get here, how the hell are they supposed to get up the mountain? I remember that climb the last time when I was following you. You got a nice piggyback ride from that big bastard with all the arms –"

"Briareus," said Talbot.

"Yeah, that guy. Well while you got carried up, I had to climb the old fashioned way… and it sucked. How the hell are thousands of dudes in armor supposed to scale it?"

"I honestly have no idea," admitted Talbot. "But I'm sure they've got a way. I mean, they must have some method to get up and down, otherwise what would be the point?"

"They've probably got an escalator hidden somewhere. I tell you what: I'll be really pissed off if I climbed up and missed an elevator call button or something simple like that. That climb just about killed me the last time."

"If it's any consolation, getting carried up by a giant thing with fifty heads and a hundred hands wasn't exactly relaxing."

"Yeah, ah, nope. No consolation. Try again, Regis."

Talbot's mind thought furiously. "At least we didn't have to do it again this time."

Wes seemed to consider this. "Hmm. Okay, fair enough."

An unexpected knock came from their door. The Olympian named Hermes opened it and stepped inside. True to mythology, Hermes was indeed the Olympian herald due to his fleetness and ability to retain the minutest details of any message.

"Lord Zeus requests your presence," said Hermes without preamble.

"We could have been all up and sexing things on in here, you know," snapped Wes to the herald. "Maybe you should have waited until we cleaned up the oil and vegetables first."

Hermes, unused to the Australian's sense of humor, stood frozen in the doorway with an expression which looked like a cross between horror and confusion upon his face. "Wh-what?" he gasped.

"I said we'll be there presently," Wes lied smoothly.

Now Hermes seemed completely confused, but merely nodded and stepped from the villa, closing the door behind him.

"You are such a prick sometimes," said Talbot, chuckling.

'Hey, we could have been doing that stuff. He wasn't to know."

"The guy's got a job to do," replied Talbot.

"And next time he barges in on someone he'll think twice. Now stop trying to seduce me and let's go."

"What? Where exactly do these weird things you say come from, Wes?"

Wes grinned widely. "All part of my special insanity, Sally."

Talbot laughed loudly and followed Wes out the door. Once outside, they both headed directly up the hill toward the Council Hall. The walk was easy enough and Wes strode up to the double doors, swinging them open, striding inside.

"They could have been sexing things on in here, you know," muttered Talbot.

"Shut up," replied Wes. "His godliness is here."

Zeus turned from the large desk where he was discussing something with Heracles and two other Olympians, a man and a woman, neither of whom Talbot recognized.

"Ah, welcome," said Zeus. "Let me introduce you to my kinsmen and fellow Olympian leaders, Artemis and her brother, Apollo."

At mention of the names, Talbot paused. By now he shouldn't have been shocked at meeting figures straight out of Greek mythology, but each time he did, it seemed somehow unreal. He stared at the two mythical figures before him; Artemis, the goddess of hunting, standing tall and beautiful, her golden hair cascading down past her shoulders, her bow looped over her shoulder, glowing with Olympian power, and Apollo, the Greek god of prophecy, his piercing stare aimed directly at Wes, eyes seeming to bore into him.

"Hey, how you doing?" said Wes casually, nodding in their direction. "So where's the army?"

"They are camped on the plateau, and will come through when the time is right," said Zeus.

"Uh huh, well, the time *is* right. It's right now, actually," said Wes. "How many are there?"

"Just over seven thousand," replied Zeus. "But we have weaponry for three times that many warriors in your world."

"That's fantastic," said Wes. "Let's go."

Apollo glanced at Zeus. "You were right. I thought he'd be different, but he's exactly the same."

"What's that mean?" asked Wes.

Apollo smiled, the expression warming his face greatly, and Talbot suddenly realized how incredibly handsome he was. "Zeus told us you were… exuberant. I can now see that his description was well chosen."

Wes's eyes narrowed. "Damn straight. Now let's go."

Zeus nodded. "I will link the gate we have here," he indicated the panel of wall which Talbot and Wes knew concealed Mount Olympus's own rift gate, "with the rift which opens out on the plateau. That way we do not need to bring the warriors through the city. The Titans will meet you out there."

"You mean you can link the rifts to open in different places?" asked Talbot.

"The rifts are able to be manipulated in various ways – such as the one which brought you back from the past in your own world. It is also how we were able to transport Apollo's and Artemis's troops up to the plateau from the plains below."

"Damn it!" snapped Wes. "I knew there had to be an easier way than climbing."

Apollo and Artemis stared at him incredulously. "You *climbed* Mount Olympus?" gasped Artemis.

"Last time we were here. I had to, I didn't know about the stupid rift escalator thing."

Artemis shook her head disbelievingly, her expression showing she was impressed.

"At any rate," continued Zeus, "I will link this gate to the one on the plateau and realign the coordinates so that it takes us to your home city."

"Huh?" grunted Wes.

Zeus shook his head, glancing at Apollo, who stood smiling. "Let's just go out to the plateau. We'll ride out there to meet up with the rest of the army."

"Hell yeah," replied Wes.

After Zeus had recalibrated the control panel, they left the Council Hall and strolled down the hill toward the breach in the rear perimeter wall. Talbot instantly recognized the route they took, even though the last time he had traveled it they'd been fleeing in terror from a horde of Titan invaders. He focused on the large building near the still standing gates. That building housed the Olympian stables, home to some of the most incredible mounts Talbot had ever seen.

They arrived at the stables, and Wes almost sprinted inside, like a child scared of missing out on the best toy. As Talbot approached the stable doors, he heard the clatter of hooves, jumping out of the way just in time as Wes rode out atop a majestic pearl-white palomino pegasus. The incredible creature flattened its enormous wings against its flanks as it emerged from the stable, but spread them wide like an eagle upon reaching open ground, flapping them several times before folding them away once more.

"I wanted a red one," shouted Wes as he hauled on the reins and turned the beast around, "because red goes faster. But they reckon they've run out." His maniacal laughter sounded, and he rode through the open gates of the city, trotting out onto the plain leading to the plateau. A second later he lifted up into the air, his laughter trailing behind him.

"Same as always," muttered Apollo, grinning. When he saw Talbot looking at him his grin dropped and he addressed Zeus. "I mean, he's the same as I heard him described. He seems like an absolute maniac."

"He definitely is the perfect man for the task." Zeus glanced at Talbot. "Is it just my imagination, or has he gotten crazier?"

"It's hard to say with Wes," replied Talbot with a shrug.

He moved inside the stable and chose his own mount: a glossy brown-coated unicorn stallion. He still couldn't believe such creatures actually existed.

Each unicorn – and there were six in total here – stood at least twice the size of the pegasus Wes had just flown away on, and the pegasus was larger than a big horse from Earth. Talbot preferred to stay on the ground, and the added size of the unicorn made him feel more like he was riding a tank than a horse. It had been while riding a similar mount that he had killed the illustrious Cerberus during the battle against the Titans on the plateau outside.

The same Titans who were now their allies.

What a weird rollercoaster ride this was. What was going to happen next? Was Hades going to magically materialize along with the Keres –?

The Keres!

"Hey Zeus," called Talbot across the stable to where the leader of the Olympians was mounting his own unicorn – a caramel mare bearing a horn as long as a broadsword. Apollo was in the stall beside him ready to mount a chestnut stallion pegasus while Artemis was climbing atop a chocolate-colored mare.

Zeus turned. "Yes?"

Talbot recalled his conversation with Wes on the subject, but still couldn't shake the thought. "Whatever happened to the Keres?"

"I have no idea. We haven't heard anything about them since they pursued the Titans through the rift at the close of our battle here the last time. I guess if you didn't see them in Tartarus they could possibly have returned to Hades. It seemed the perfect world for them." He shuddered. "Such creatures are not for the realm of the living."

"Don't you think we could use their help?" asked Talbot, recalling the ferocious efficiency with which the Keres had torn through the ranks of the Titans.

"Oh no!" said Zeus emphatically. "You would not want their assistance, not if you could help it, at any rate. Do you not remember what they did to my son?"

Talbot recalled the joining when Charon the Ferryman had consumed Heracles, and he shivered. "Okay, good point. But still, you have to admit they'd be handy."

"Don't travel down that road of thought, Talbot Harrison," interjected Apollo. Talbot turned to face him. "It would be *handy* if we had another two hundred thousand warriors, and it would be *handy* if they were all twice as large as the giants we are about to face, and it would be very *handy* if our weapons were ten times stronger. Well, we don't, and they aren't. What we have is what we have, and no amount of wishing will change that fact." Apollo mounted his stallion and looked back at Talbot, his gaze piercing.

"Point made," replied Talbot. "I'd better get out there before Wes decides to do something stupid."

"I will return to our gate and manipulate the rift to open on the plateau," advised Zeus.

Talbot nodded, turning and clambering atop the huge unicorn with difficulty, his legs stretching wide, circling the broad back of the beast as he kicked the stallion into a trot. Once outside the stable, Talbot navigated his way through the open gates, urging the unicorn into a canter.

The great beast strode smoothly and powerfully across the field, and Talbot marveled at the incredible power of the animal, feeling his heart racing in his chest as it raced across the plain. The unicorn's hooves, as large as a Clydesdale's, pounded away at the ground, effortlessly tearing up the distance to the waiting army comprised of Olympians and Titans. Talbot could see the tiny figure of Wes flying high above the gathered assembly of warriors, and as he watched, the very air seemed to rip open, revealing a massive rift which hung vertically, unsuspended in the sky. The entire army appeared to step back in shock at the appearance of the rift, and seconds later Talbot understood why.

A detonating crack echoed, almost causing him to lose his seat upon the unicorn.

Regaining his balance, Talbot realized what the noise had been. He'd forgotten the sonic boom-like blast which sounded whenever a rift appeared. No wonder the troops had been shocked; he'd almost crapped his pants too.

Wes came in for a perfect landing at around the same time as Talbot reached the edge of the amassed army and hauled on his mount's reins. They met up somewhere in the middle of the throng, the Australian commando grinning wildly.

"I love this shit," called Wes.

Talbot shook his head, but smiled. "What do you think? I mean about our chances; what do you think about our chances?"

Wes glanced around at the impressive-looking warriors, and

Talbot followed his gaze, taking in the bronze breastplates and reinforced leather kilts worn by the Olympian soldiers, as opposed to the full-body ebony armor worn by the towering Titans. Even their weapons stood in marked contrast. The Olympian swords, spears and arrows were imbued with the mysterious power created by the smith named Hephaestus. The Titan weapons, Talbot knew, had been charged with a similar energy, but theirs appeared like unrefined oil running over their ebony blades, seeming to drain the light around it. Nonetheless, they were just as devastating as the Olympian weapons.

"I think we're screwed," said Wes softly.

"Why do you say that?" asked Talbot, surprised by Wes's uncustomary lack of enthusiasm.

"We're going head to head against an army of *giants*," replied Wes, turning his impassive gaze toward him. "Ten thousand of the bastards. We don't even have equal numbers to the Valhallian Army, let alone equal stature. Those fuckers took out China, Russia and most of Europe, chomping on nukes like they were pills at a rave party. We've got about as much chance of going head to head with them as an army of gerbils has against a mass of deviants. Prometheus will love it; he'll just bend over and –"

"Okay, I get the idea," cut in Talbot. "But surely we have a chance."

"Of course we have a chance. They might all drown while crossing the ocean. They reckon you shouldn't swim for half an hour after eating, well those guys have been munching on Chinese food… along with Indian and French. They'll probably all cramp up and sink, leaving us with no problem."

"But we have all those extra weapons from the Olympians," argued Talbot, ignoring Wes's sarcasm.

"More needles for the gerbils to stab the perverts in the arse with. That should really annoy them. And then there's the fact our troops, the ones on Earth, have never used swords or spears before."

"You sound like you're giving up."

Wes sighed. "I'm just being realistic, that's all. I saw the video of when the Chinese hit them with their nukes. Nothing should have survived it. *Nothing*. But those giants strolled out like they were all just picking daisies. Nuclear weapons, Talbot. They hit them with enough explosive force to potentially crack our entire planet in half, and only managed to kill a token amount of them. Now we're going up against them with pointy sticks and flying horses. Sure, our pointy sticks make cool noises and sparkle, but these are *giants*, man. How the hell can we kill *giants*?"

"You've done it before," said Talbot.

"That was just luck."

"Then bring your luck on again. We need to kick the hell out of these guys, and that isn't going to happen if you're moping around being all sad and realistic!" snapped Talbot, his patience running out.

Instead of Wes snarling back as he expected, the commando began to laugh. "I knew that would get you fired up."

"What are you talking about?"

"You rode over here all scared, but while trying to convince me everything was okay, you managed to convince yourself instead."

"You tricked me?" asked Talbot incredulously.

"Yep. You don't have to thank me; it's all part of the service."

"You really are an asshole sometimes, Wes. I was worried you'd somehow lost your confidence."

"No way!" replied Wes. "I live for this shit." He pranced his pegasus in a circle, allowing it to flap its gorgeous wings lightly.

"I most certainly believe you do."

"Now let's take these pretty little soldiers home and kick some gargantuan booty. What do you reckon?"

Talbot chuckled. "I reckon you might be right. Let's go."

The two rode through the ranks to the head of the army where they paused.

"Let's go, ladies!" yelled Wes, and he plunged into the rift.

Talbot had a fleeting moment of trepidation as he rode his unicorn into the rift. He suddenly wondered what might happen if something went wrong, and the creature he rode somehow melded with him whilst disembodied within the power of the rift. But it was too late; the rift grabbed them, and the next thing he knew he was hurtling through dimensions without control. He lost sense of everything around him for a time, but soon became aware of other bodies hurtling through nothingness nearby. He couldn't see them, but he sensed the Olympian and Titan warriors were in the rift as well.

At least they'd followed.

Caught up in Wes's exuberance, Talbot hadn't thought to wait for Zeus, Apollo or Artemis. He'd caught a brief glimpse of Heracles grinning at them as they'd jumped into the rift, and then he was gone. The Olympian had probably ordered the warriors to follow them in.

The rift abruptly ended, and Talbot suddenly realized the unicorn he rode was still beneath him as its hooves clattered across the tarmac.

Tarmac?

Deep in his thoughts, Talbot hadn't even noticed the end of the rift. He was so used to landing clumsily that the unicorn's impeccable exit had left him unaware of the passing. Talbot shook his head, clearing his thoughts, and kicked his mount into a canter, riding to where Wes sat atop his pegasus, some twenty yards to the side, a wise position given that an entire army was about to materialize out of the rift behind them. As he rode, Talbot recognized where they had emerged:

Dulles International Airport.

He wondered how much of their placement was luck, and how much owed to Zeus's coordinates. The Olympian leader had previously shown an ability to tap into their thoughts, perhaps he'd plucked this location directly from their minds. Regardless, they couldn't have asked for a better place to emerge with an army.

The sun beating down on the tarmac was becoming oppressively hot. Glancing up at the sky, Talbot saw they were rapidly approaching midday.

A loud crash sounded, and Talbot spun around atop his mount. A dozen Olympians had smashed into the ground as they literally spewed forth from the rift. Part of him felt a strange sense of satisfaction that he wasn't the only one affected in such a way when emerging from the rifts, while another part flared with panic at what was soon to pour out behind them.

"Get out of the way!" he yelled, the unicorn's hooves clattering as he rode toward them. "The entire army is coming through, keep moving!"

The Olympian warriors, showing their discipline, immediately leaped to their feet and moved aside as more and more soldiers poured through. As each new wave emerged, the others shifted them aside so the way was clear for the rest of the army.

Wes rode up beside Talbot, his smaller mount seeming somewhat more skittish, flaring its wings out slightly as it approached the unicorn.

"That was really gross," said Wes.

"What was gross?"

"I saw that guy's balls when he fell over and his kilt flew up."

Talbot looked down at Wes, disgusted. "What the hell...?"

"It was like two pickled onions covered in hairy elbow skin."

"Are you sure you're not gay?" asked Talbot. "I mean, I don't have a problem with it, but you seem kind of obsessed with penises and stuff."

"Why don't you give me a kiss and find out?" yelled Wes. Several Olympians turned around. "Sorry guys, I didn't mean that. Keep your skirts on."

"If I remember correctly," commented Talbot, "you seemed to enjoy wearing a kilt the last time we were in Olympia."

"True, but I've got the legs for it," replied Wes. The grin suddenly dropped from his face as he stared beyond Talbot. "Well, here comes the welcoming party. At least we know Prometheus hasn't won yet."

Talbot turned and saw several emergency services vehicles, police units, along with various military transports screaming toward them. They reached them in seconds, several theatrically spinning their vehicles sideways, screeching to a halt. Wes turned toward the Olympians near the rift.

"Just continue with what you guys are doing, we'll handle this."

"How exactly are we going to do that?" asked Talbot quietly as the army and cops set up a semi-circular offensive position, waving the emergency services crews back.

"I'll use my charm," replied Wes, riding his pearly-white pegasus toward the waiting Americans.

"Oh no," murmured Talbot under his breath.

"G'day fellas," called Wes. "I don't suppose the President called ahead, did he?"

"FREEZE!" yelled a soldier wearing the stripes of a sergeant-major. Apparently he was in charge. Talbot heard several weapons being primed.

"You need to call your superiors right now," ordered Wes, all traces of humor instantly gone from his voice. "Tell them Wes is here with Doctor Talbot Harrison and a combined army from Olympia and Tartarus. If they don't know anything about it you are to speak to their superiors, and then their superiors until you reach someone high up enough to know what the hell I'm talking about. Call the President directly, if you can, he'll sort all this shit out in an instant. Is that understood, Sergeant-Major?"

"Um…," replied the soldier uncertainly. "Stand by."

Talbot understood the man's predicament; instinct told him to mistrust what had just appeared – and continued to appear – from the rift, but fear of screwing up made him question himself. Moments later he was speaking hurriedly into his two-way radio. The conversation went on for several tense minutes, during which Talbot was sure the man got transferred at least two times, until he finally nodded and passed the radio to another soldier and approached them warily.

"Sir, you have been identified," he said to Wes, "as have you, Doctor Harrison. I've been ordered to assist you in any way possible."

"Sure," said Wes. "We've got about another… er…," he glanced at the Olympian warriors emerging from the rift. "There are about five thousand more of these guys coming through – along with some weird-arse creatures. Try not to piss off the fourteen-foot-tall guys with weird eyes, and if you have any problems let us know. Also, I need you to organize transport for everyone, and find them somewhere to bunk down until we need them." As he spoke, Zeus, Apollo and Aphelion emerged riding their respective Olympian mounts. Heracles and the towering Atlas followed, both on foot, but equally impressive nonetheless.

The sergeant-major stared at the horde gathering on the tarmac and appeared immensely flustered with the orders Wes had given him. "W-where are you going to be, sir?"

Wes grinned. "We'll be at the White House introducing the President to some Greek gods."

***

The President retained his composure remarkably well considering the individuals he had just been introduced to. It could be argued that the man was used to meeting some of the planet's most powerful figures on a daily basis, but these were personalities from mythology. Granted, he had already met Poseidon and encountered Fenrir, but this was different.

For a start, there was Heracles, who looked every inch the figure of lore. Bulging muscles rippled with every move his seven-foot-tall frame made, and Talbot saw the President staring, awestruck, at him more than once.

No less spectacular was Atlas. The enormous Titan was truly a sight to behold. His muscular form, while not quite equivalent to Heracles's, stood some seventeen-feet-tall! For anyone who had not encountered one of the Titans before, the sheer size of Atlas was shocking. The fact the President knew about what the Titans had almost accomplished in Olympia must have certainly made Atlas appear even more terrifying.

And finally, there was Zeus. Of all the figures from Greek mythology, he was arguably the most legendary; for him to be standing in the White House was indeed an amazing moment.

Yes, the President handled himself very well indeed.

At least he managed not to faint.

CHAPTER 14

"The enemy has crossed the North Atlantic Ocean and landed on the Island of Newfoundland, just off the coast of Canada," reported General Shannon.

The group had assembled in the Presidential Emergency Operations Centre; a bizarre assortment of humans, Olympians and Titans. Zeus, Apollo, Heracles and Artemis were seated along one side of the enormous boardroom table, the opposite side accommodating the President, Wes, Talbot and Zoe – who had been extremely happy to see Wes and Talbot again, hugging them enthusiastically. Various White House staff and advisors, along with the Secretary of Defense and others Talbot didn't know rounded out the boardroom attendees. Atlas sat on the floor nearby, as none of the furniture was able to sustain his bulk. Getting him down here had been a challenge in itself, but the Titan had insisted. Even seated on the floor, his head still towered high above those arrayed around the table.

General Shannon continued. "During their crossing, the giants were set upon by an enormous beast which, from descriptions supplied by the Australian –" he pointed at Wes "– would appear to be the same one he supposedly battled whilst onboard the Olympian vessel."

"Its name was Jörmungandr," amended Wes casually. "The World Serpent. You can Google it if you like."

The general glared at him. "Regardless of what it was called, the creature inadvertently managed to aid us by attacking the giants, killing three of them before the enormous red one called – what was it…?" He shuffled through his notes.

"That one's Prometheus, but he used to be Hrungnir," called Wes, grinning. Talbot nudged him slightly, recalling the President's lecture on getting along with General Shannon.

Wes glanced at Talbot. "What?" he asked innocently. "I'm just trying to help."

"Well, the leader of the giants," continued General Shannon, ignoring Wes, "destroyed the serpent using his absorption power. Soon after it died, the Olympian vessel appeared. Was that at your order?" he asked Zeus.

Zeus shook his head, his brows narrowing slightly. Everyone's attention was caught in that instant. Each person present was waiting for information on how the Olympian weapons – weapons they were relying upon to defeat the Valhallian Army – had fared against the giants.

"Then it was either merely coincidence or else they saw an opportunity and decided to strike." The general appeared uncomfortable. "They were unsuccessful," he said quietly.

There was a moment of silence. "What the hell does that mean?" snapped Wes.

General Shannon's gaze shot up, pinning Wes with his vehemence. "It means they were destroyed before they got a single shot off. They came in too soon and were caught on the edge of Prometheus's sapping energy as he attacked the serpent. Satellite images show they immediately sank, disappearing into the ocean."

"Damn," muttered Wes. Talbot glanced over at the Olympians. Each wore grim expressions, but they appeared even more determined than before.

"When can we expect them to cross into the United States?" asked the President.

The general frowned. "Based on their previous land traveling speed, I'd guess no longer than a week; maybe two if they encounter some sort of delay."

Wes stood, walking over to the large map set up next to the general. It displayed the route the army of giants had taken through the Middle East, Asia, Russia and Europe before crossing the North Atlantic, pinpointing their most recent reported position on the

Island of Newfoundland.

"Where do you reckon they'll cross?" asked Wes.

"It's most likely they'll swim across here," the general said, eyeing Wes warily as he indicated the strip of water south of the area on the map labeled *Mouse Island*. "And that will slow them down slightly."

"Can they access the border using the Trans-Canada Highway?" asked Wes, pointing to a narrow strip on the map stretching from the Chanel Port aux Basques across the water to North Sydney on Cape Breton Island, north of Nova Scotia. "That would cut down their traveling time significantly."

General Shannon leaned forward, his brow furrowed, glancing from the point on the map back to Wes. Talbot could imagine he was waiting for some sort of barbed comment from the commando, but when nothing materialized, he straightened up.

"I suppose it is possible," conceded the general, "but due to their size they'd have to navigate it single-file. It might possibly prove faster for them to travel through the actual water. Either way their traveling time should work out the same."

Wes nodded. "If their line of movement continues as it has, they'll enter the United States through Maine."

"That's what we have determined," agreed the general, still looking at Wes skeptically, no doubt wondering at his change in attitude.

Wes stared even closer at the map, examining it intimately. Not a sound could be heard in the room apart from the heavy breathing of Apollo. Wes grabbed a long ruler and a thick pencil, lining up Washington D.C. with where the giants were currently located in Canada.

"Hey, Zeus, come up here," said Wes without looking away from the map.

The leader of the Olympians raised an eyebrow, but moved to stand beside Wes without question.

"Along this line, where would you be able to open one of those gate thingies you told me and Talbot about? You know, for the rest of the Titans, the ones Kronos is going to bring through."

"*If* he brings them through," replied Zeus, hesitantly.

Talbot glanced at the general and saw a look of incomprehension cross his face. It took Talbot a second to realize that General Shannon apparently couldn't understand a word the Olympians or Titans said. The President face also held a quizzical expression, though his appeared somehow different, as though he could understand the words and worried at their potential meaning. The President caught him staring and instantly the expression changed, becoming an unreadable mask.

"Don't worry about that," said Wes testily, cutting into Talbot's thoughts. "Just look at the map and tell me where the best place would be, the one with the greatest concentration of cosmic resonance, or whatever it is you need."

Zeus grinned slightly and looked at the map.

"It would be a center of congregation," he said. "A place people are drawn to for no other reason than that the energy of the universe resonates strongly there. Some use it to prosper, while others wither under its influence and fail dismally."

Zeus paused, taking the pencil from Wes's hand before moving to the table and scribbling something down on a notepad. He glanced back at the map several times while continuing to scribble frenetically. Talbot couldn't see what the Olympian was writing, but he guessed it had something to do with the latitude and longitude required for the placement of a rift gate. They wouldn't be creating an actual gate like the Syrpeas Gate, but Zeus would open a tear in the rift, which needed to occur in the place with the most natural energy. Finally Zeus moved back to the map, stabbing his finger down on a location Talbot couldn't see. Wes and General Shannon could see it, though. The general gaped at Zeus, while Wes merely frowned.

"Are you sure?" asked Wes softly.

Zeus nodded. "There can be no other place along this route. The coordinates I set up are for this general area, and this is the only place where a stable rift will be possible."

"Damn," Talbot heard Wes mutter.

"What's wrong?" asked the President. "Where is it?"

Wes bit his lip, and turned around until he was fully facing the

President.

"It's New York City," he said. "The only place we can release the Titan army is in the middle of New York City. And we need them to fight the giants. "

"What does that mean?" asked the President.

"Say goodbye to Wall Street," replied Wes dryly.

***

The streets of New York were, possibly for the first time in history, deserted.

Well… deserted wasn't entirely accurate.

The streets saw no civilians whatsoever. No bankers, no businessmen, no hotdog vendors, no muggers, no hookers. They were all gone. On the other hand, they practically thronged with activity as troops moved into position.

The trap was set.

Wes had put aside all animosity with General Shannon, and together the two had devised a strategy. And boy was it a strategy.

New York City had been destroyed. Every single building not essential to the upcoming conflict had been razed, the rubble from them heaped to help block off areas which needed to be secured. The protests had been intense, but with martial law being declared the moment the army of giants crossed the border into the United States from Canada, people began to realize how serious the danger truly was. This was no longer just something they were watching on CNN, it was coming to them, entering their backyard, a veritable tsunami of impending death. Civilians fled south in droves.

New York City was going to be America's first, and possibly last, stand.

From what Talbot had overheard, Wes and General Hammond both agreed that the natural land was their greatest ally for the looming confrontation. As the Valhallian Army swarmed toward New York, the land funneled in, tapering on both sides. The demolished buildings, piled high between outer perimeters of still-standing towers, emphasized this channeling effect, and the hope was they could constrict the advance of the army so as to stop them from encircling the defenders. Arguments had blazed for days, hoping to keep the metropolis alive, but the end result had been the same: New York City had to die.

Gazing at the rift, floating like a vertical oil-spill within the devastated city, Talbot's doubts flared for the millionth time. Zeus had worked furiously to open the rift using the controls of the Syrpeas Gate in Washington, but the Olympian leader had admitted to being at a loss at one point, and had turned to Talbot for help.

Talbot had stared at the monitor within the confines of the secure base, the scene displaying where the rift was to open, seeing the crumbling buildings amid the undamaged ones, bulldozers and cranes still reinforcing the barriers, cement being poured by every construction crew available. The towering structures had suddenly called to Talbot in a way he couldn't understand, but he let it lead him, following the call until he understood there was a resonance playing between the structures, a similar language to the dot-painting inside Ayers Rock so long ago. The resonance had bounced from rubble to walls, unseen but still there, hidden to all but Talbot. Understanding had slowly bloomed within him. In the same way a singer intuitively knows which notes work best with a song, Talbot knew how to translate what flowed across that screen, and swiftly moved to the Syrpeas Gate controls. His hand touched panels instinctively, tapping out a silent melody, instructions even Zeus did not understand. Zeus had appeared as though he wanted to interrupt Talbot at one point, but Talbot had viciously shaken his head, unable to stop lest the rhythm shatter. He sensed a tremendous power flowing through the gate, power which might detonate at any moment. The rippling rift had cracked open on the monitor after what had seemed an eternity of manipulation, but there'd been no time to savor his accomplishment; a chopper had immediately rushed them both here from Washington. Now all they had left to do was wait for the Titans to arrive.

There was no way to tell exactly *when* the Titans would appear, even though Talbot and Zeus had already opened the rift in the middle of the Financial District, right outside the Federal Reserve Bank of New York. The Titans had to emerge within the city. If they arrived outside the newly-formed perimeter, they would be useless, and the defenders desperately needed their numbers in order to make any sort of stand against the giants.

During another time, the Government might have listened to the multitudes complaining about the destruction of one of America's most important and influential cities. This was not that time, however. Everyone involved in the defense strategy had seen the footage from London, the spy-satellite imagery from China, along with reconnaissance video and sporadic news coverage. The loss of a city seemed a small price after what had happened to half of Europe and Asia.

Talbot shuddered at the memories, and pushed the images from his mind, staring at the desolation from atop the observation platform of the Empire State Building. The strategists had argued against keeping the iconic tower intact until Wes had casually pointed out that as the tallest building in the city it was also the best observation post. It now sat forlornly within the near-wasteland, like the arm of a city-sized sundial.

Part of Talbot mourned the loss of something as incredible as New York City. The place was so symbolic of everything American, nothing could ever hope to replace it, but with the fate of the entire planet potentially resting upon the outcome of this battle, he knew the loss was necessary.

One of the President's advisors had argued back in the War Room at the Pentagon that they should just allow the giants passage directly to the Syrpeas Gate. If their primary objective was merely to pass through the Gate, then why should humanity risk warring with such a potentially devastating enemy? The President himself had spoken up, his quiet words reverberating with emotion and conviction: "This is no longer an issue of negotiation to avoid war; we are already at war, and the time for allowances has passed – if it were ever a possibility. We do not negotiate with terrorists who kill our people in order to get what they want, nor shall we allow the effrontery of these invaders to pass unhindered.

"I am plagued by memories of what has occurred in the short time since these foes arrived on our planet, but one vision sticks out in my mind each time I worry about what is to come. It is an image I saw on one of the news feeds of a small child, no more than four or five years old, wailing over the corpse of a woman in China. I have no idea if this woman was her mother, but such a thing is irrelevant now."

The entire War Room had fallen silent, every person entranced by the President's resonating voice.

"This babe was murdered right there, screaming in terror and sorrow. A giant – one of the multitudes of such creatures from the Valhallian Army – casually picked her up and bit her in half before chewing and swallowing. And then it laughed." The President's eyes had held a strange, haunted glaze.

He'd snapped back into focus, looking around at the assembly of advisors, soldiers and politicians. "We *must* fight this enemy with every single breath left in us. Not because they want something from us. Not because they threaten our way of life. We must fight them simply because they constitute something so evil it should not be allowed to pass through our land unopposed. We need to fight for that little girl whose cries were cut off so violently when she was already mourning the loss of her mother." Everyone had stared at him, stunned by the powerful speech.

"I tell you what," Wes had whispered in Talbot's ear. "If I voted, I'd vote for that motherfucker."

The memory bolstered Talbot somewhat as he gazed around at the desolated landscape of what had previously been one of the most dominant cities in history. In the distance, he saw yet another building come down silently as the explosives beneath it were detonated.

Yes. They were doing the right thing. It was a small price to pay.

Wes's voice sounded right behind him, making Talbot jump slightly. "They used to have a sex museum right over there," said the commando, pointing south.

"How do you know that?" gasped Talbot.

Wes looked mildly confused. "I have no idea. I just know stuff like that. It's part of my special charm." He grinned boyishly.

Talbot resumed his assessment of the destroyed city. "Will our future generations understand why we have done this?"

"At least this way there'll *be* some future generations. A large portion of Asia can't say the same, along with most of Great Britain. These big bastards sure do like to eat."

"I know, but look at this." He indicated the depressing vista which had once been a bustling metropolis.

Wes shrugged. "It's only bricks and concrete. They can rebuild it."

"But what if that politician was right? What if we had just moved everyone out of the way and let them all the way through to the Syrpeas Gate in Washington? That's what they really want."

"And what about when they come back?" asked Wes.

"What do you mean?"

"I mean, if we just let these guys through this time, what happens when they come back to finish us off?" asked Wes. "We've both dealt with Prometheus the Walking Dildo before, and you know he won't just be happy with getting revenge on his own people. He'll will come back here with all his buddies and chomp down on people for one simple reason: he's an arsehole. Arseholes have one purpose in this universe, and that's to dispense shit. Prometheus is a perfect shit-dispenser. The other thing you're forgetting is that he's heading through the Syrpeas Gate."

Talbot frowned. "Yeah, so?"

"The Titans are on the other side of that rift, and while we may have had our differences in the past, they're our allies now. I know they're kind of annoying when they try to kill us, but we're relying on the Titans to save our butts – which they're doing free of charge. If we just let Prometheus and his eclectic bunch of psychotic fuckheads through without a fight, the Titans will get chewed up like puppy kibble."

"Oh," said Talbot. "I see…."

"And let's not forget about the Olympians; Prometheus's second least favorite species of humanoid behind the Vanir." Wes grinned without any sort of humor. "He'll have to head there at some point on his magical mystery tour whilst en route to Vanirdom or whatever their place is called."

"It's called Vanaheim."

"I wonder if they've got their own Disneyland there," pondered Wes. "But that's beside the point. Once these arseholes are done in Tartarus – which we both know is a fun-filled place anyway – they'll trot over to Olympia and eat their way through there too. Finally, they'll find a way into Vanaheim, where Prometheus can extract his revenge on a people who opposed his original wish of going into other dimensions in order to kill everyone."

"I see your point," admitted Talbot.

"After he's killed everyone and everything in Vanaheim, we should expect another visit from this wonderful army. By that time they will be much more organized and powerful, and those slaves they keep collecting might have been turned into whatever the hell they're planning on creating. So we'll still be trying to clean up the mess left behind when they reappear and screw us over again, probably finishing us off for good this time."

"But they won't be able to navigate the rift gates without the Elder-tongue," argued Talbot.

Wes gave him a disappointed look. "How do you think Prometheus has been getting around for all these years? I don't know how he does it, but he seems to be able to jump around wherever the hell he wants. I know he needed you to open the gate in Tartarus, but that might have just been because the Olympians did something to it. Regardless, I really don't think our defensive strategy should be based upon the hope that Prometheus, the guy who just keeps on giving, screws up or becomes complacent."

"The guy who keeps on giving us a headache, more like," muttered Talbot.

"That's right. Arseholes like Prometheus don't just go away because you give them what they want, and the President knows that. That's why we've destroyed one of the most important cities in America in order to create this trap."

"We're really screwed, aren't we?" asked Talbot.

Wes shrugged. "We're still breathing, so nothing's decided yet. But I wouldn't make any plans for Christmas if I were you."

"Can you explain this plan to me again? Maybe that will reassure me."

"It's not like it's complicated," said Wes.

"Just humor me, will you?"

Wes chuckled. "Okay, but try to keep up. They're gonna come from over there –" He indicated the desolate area to the north. "– and as they get closer those walls…." He pointed to the buildings along the Hudson River several miles to their left and right. The spaces between the buildings still standing had been jammed with the rubble left over from the demolished buildings, piled high and secured with tons and tons of concrete. "They get funneled in narrower and narrower as they move further south."

"Won't Prometheus know something's wrong as soon as he sees we've destroyed New York?"

"That's possible, but I'm hoping by the time he realizes it he'll be too committed. Also, our intelligence reports indicate the giants are of below average intellect and, unless Prometheus stops them early enough, they'll wander in here regardless. Given that their ability to withstand nukes was proven in Asia, Prometheus will feel invulnerable, so even though he'll know we're up to something, it'll be too much hassle to go around."

"But what makes you so certain they'll come this way?" asked Talbot.

"It's New York," replied Wes. "Everyone comes to New York, haven't you heard the song? Plus they'll want to resupply for the journey ahead of them."

"You mean people, right?"

"No, I'm talking about cotton candy. Of course I mean people!" snapped Wes.

Talbot shook his head. "Sorry, it's just…."

"Yeah, I know. The end of the world is nigh and all that crap."

"I never said that!"

"But you were thinking it," replied Wes. "It's hard not to worry about that sort of stuff when you look at what we've done here. I mean, we've razed New York City! That sure as hell wasn't *my* New Year's resolution. But the land is perfect here, the river is on either side – not that that'll deter them, but the buildings there are nice and high to take in the views and the gaps between them are now filled with rubble – and it also forms a natural funnel as we head south. We'll just chop the fuckers down one at a time."

"Do you really think it'll be that easy?" asked Talbot hopefully.

"Of course not," scoffed Wes. "Have you seen those guys? Nah, we'll give them a bloody nose and hopefully hold them off long enough for the Titans to come through. With any luck the Titans will have something special with them, some way to really hammer these giants in the butt, or else we'll either die here or have to retreat through the Brooklyn Battery Tunnel."

"You're not filling me with faith, Wes."

"Would you prefer it if I lied to you like the rest of those sheep? You'd see through that in a heartbeat, and I don't want to insult you."

Talbot felt momentarily lifted by the strange sideways compliment. "But won't the President see through it?"

"Of course. He'll see through it like a pane of glass in Amsterdam's red-light district. It's more to give a bit of hope to those whining sycophants who are latched onto him. We've got a chance here, buddy; nothing more than that."

Talbot remained silent for a moment, forcing away the hopelessness that threatened to fill his heart. "Tell me again about the whole funnel thing," he said.

Wes chuckled and launched into the description once more.

CHAPTER 15

"Oh, Christ help us. HERE THEY COME!" hollered the call over the radio.

Wes climbed slowly to his feet from where he'd been dozing, and gazed out toward the north, leaning on the railing of the Empire State Building's observation deck. It didn't take long to discern the Valhallian Army's location; they filled the entire northern horizon. He scratched his balls, thinking.

The call had come from the northern observation post, but they'd been receiving updates from the various airborne scouts deployed. The pilots of the jets and the few military helicopters they had as outer scouts needed to be extremely careful. The beasts accompanying the giants, the ones Talbot had described as valkyrie, could tear through an F/A-18E fighter jet like it was made of tinfoil, and their speed over short distances was almost comparable to the fighters. The only area where the F/A-18E excelled over the creatures from Valhalla came in their ability to perform at higher altitude. The thinner air stopped the creatures from pursuing the fighter jets above forty thousand feet, but surveillance ability at such a height was severely limited. The result had seen almost a dozen of the jets destroyed before any viable intelligence on the enemy had been gathered.

Helicopters were close to useless; they were simply too slow. As such they were used primarily as scouts for the absolute external boundary of the area. Some military advisors had argued that the maneuverability of the helicopters would compensate for their lack of speed, but they'd quickly been silenced when Wes had offered for them to prove their assertions by accompanying one of the choppers in the field.

Sycophantic idiots; they held no place in combat. Wes had no time for them.

But that was not an issue for now. The Valhallian Army was possibly twenty miles distant and marching steadily toward them. Wes loathed the fact he had to abandon the Empire State Building, but it would be like sitting atop a small island during a volcanic eruption if he stayed. Others would remain and relay what information they could to those in the field; he had cooler plans for Talbot and himself.

Much cooler.

He grabbed his radio. "Okay, ladies. Let's stop sunbathing and regroup at Assembly Point Alpha 2."

Wes heard footsteps behind him and turned, expecting to see Talbot. However, it wasn't the archaeologist, it was someone else entirely.

"Hello, Wes," said Zoe, somewhat shyly.

"Er... yeah, hi," replied Wes. "What can I do for you?" They hadn't spoken since he'd returned from Olympia and Tartarus.

"Why have you been avoiding me?"

Wes glanced back at the line of marching giants. "Is this really the time to be chatting about this?"

"When else is there?" she countered.

"Good point. The truth is I haven't been avoiding you, at least not intentionally. In case you hadn't noticed we're in the middle of some serious shit here."

"How could I forget? My father, or rather the creature that used to be my father, is leading them."

"So why come to me now?" asked Wes testily. "You've had weeks."

"I was too scared. I didn't know what to say to you."

"And now?"

"Now I don't care what you say, but I have to know. If we're going to die here, I want to know how you feel about me."

"How I feel about you really doesn't matter right now, does it? Chances are we're all going to end up as puppy kibble pretty soon, and whether or not I give a shit about you is pretty low on the universe's list of problems."

"The universe's list of problems?" said Zoe. "Or yours?"

"Either… or both. You decide. At the moment I have to worry about stopping the extinction of the human race, so if you'll excuse me…." He moved to walk past her.

"I love you Wes," she said simply, and he closed his eyes, cursing inside.

"*Why?*" he whispered without turning. "Why did you have to say that?

"Because it's true!"

"How the hell am I supposed to do my job with that hanging over my head?" Wes asked, finally turning to see her standing, staring at him with tears glistening in her eyes. His heart gave a wrench, but he steadied his nerves.

"I have to know how you feel," Zoe breathed. The desperation in her voice tore at Wes.

"I don't… I don't have the luxury of feelings here. I'm responsible for not only this world, but others too. These guys –" he waved a hand toward the Valhallian Army "– aren't going to just go away because of how I feel."

"Do you care for me?"

Wes tried to look everywhere but at Zoe's face, but in the end he stared into her eyes.

"Of course I care." The words sounded like they were being torn from him, something jagged stuck in Wes's throat, and he coughed as his eyes began to sting. "I have to go."

"One last thing," said Zoe. "I'm not an idiot. I know what's likely to happen here. But if we're going to die, I don't want my last wish to be that I'd kissed you and not asked."

"You want a *kiss?*"

"Yes." Her voice was small, her body timid.

Wes felt something within him he was unused to, a clenching in his stomach which bespoke a sensation alien to the commando.

It was trepidation.

If he took the next step, he was potentially opening himself up in a way he hadn't allowed for longer than he could remember. But gazing out at the horrifying army approaching them, Wes realized he no longer cared, and Zoe's words suddenly made sense to him. He didn't want his last thought as he got chewed on by a giant to be regret that he hadn't kissed this beautiful woman.

He stepped forward, trembling slightly as he took Zoe in his arms and gently dipped his head to meet her lips. Suddenly, like a tsunami washing over him, he realized that rather than weakening him as he'd feared it would, he now felt somehow stronger, more ready for the terror that was to come. He drew back and gazed into Zoe's eyes, feeling his own emotions well up once more. He pushed them aside roughly, replacing them with something else, something much more rigid.

Determination.

He was determined to defeat these creatures, to crush them absolutely, ensuring their threat would never again return to terrorize this planet. Releasing Zoe, he stepped back, more confident than he had been before.

"I have to go," he said softly. "But I'll be back to take up where we left off."

Zoe smiled, her face becoming even more beautiful as a result. "I'll hold you to that."

He turned and moved down the stairs, not seeing the way Zoe's expression dropped as her tears fell once more.

***

"I hate riding these things!" shouted Talbot over the noise of the wind.

"You could always get off," Wes called over his shoulder.

Talbot glanced down, the ground dropping further and further away as the pegasus rose higher into the sky. "No, I think I'll stay."

"Good idea," replied Wes.

"Why the hell are we doing this again?"

Wes grinned maniacally. "Because it's cool."

Talbot shook his head, and then realized what a futile gesture it was when sitting behind Wes on the back of the pegasus. "No, what I mean is, what do we hope to achieve?"

"Well, if you hold me any tighter, *I* might achieve a bit of a boner," said Wes. "But apart from that, we're doing reconnaissance."

Talbot ignored the sexual innuendo. Even if he had taken offense to the comment, there was no way he was going to let go of Wes. Despite the freezing wind rapidly numbing his hands, and the wetness of the clouds making them slick with moisture, he refused to even contemplate releasing the commando.

"Why do we have to do reconnaissance; weren't the jets doing that?" Talbot asked, hoping to change the subject.

"They were, but I need to see things for myself," replied Wes enigmatically.

Talbot shifted the Olympian sword which sat uncomfortably in its scabbard at his left hip. He still couldn't get used to the damn thing. Wes seemed to wear Laevateinn like an extension of his body, but Talbot's seemed to dig into his skin no matter how much he adjusted it. He finally gave up, deciding instead to just try his best to ignore the discomfort.

The rift drifted by beneath them, the image of its shimmering surface distracting Talbot from his annoyance and returning his thoughts to their current situation.

He knew better than to question Wes further about what they were attempting. He'd seen Zoe go out onto the observation deck right after Wes called for the evacuation, and knew the real reason the Australian had asked Talbot to join him out here flying around on a mythical horse. Talbot just hoped Wes's thoughts weren't so clouded with feelings for Zoe that he'd forget to focus on keeping the two of them alive out here.

As if in answer, a sudden movement from the corner of his vision caused Talbot to turn slightly – a flurry of bat-like wings had materialized heading directly for them.

It was one of the valkyrie!

Before Talbot could warn Wes, the commando had thrown their mount into a steep dive, and all Talbot could do was hold on. Clouds whipped past them as the pegasus dropped straight down. Talbot felt his fingers beginning to lose their grip from around Wes's chest. All thoughts of cold and discomfort fled as panic roared through him.

Glancing behind, he saw the valkyrie plummeting through the air right behind them. Further back a second valkyrie also took up the chase. The beasts were gaining on them.

Horrifically demonic in appearance, the valkyries had black skeletal heads sporting gaping maws, which seemed to be sucking and stretching ever wider the closer they got. These cavernous mouths contained no teeth, no gnashing fangs, and Talbot was reminded of Charon, the Ferryman in Hades who had consumed Heracles as payment for crossing the River Styx. Membranous, black wings remained folded tight to their bodies, making their dives as swift as possible. Two curving claws hung from each stalk-like leg, dangling from beneath the creatures like razor-sharp hang pincers.

"Hang on tight!" yelled Wes.

Talbot bit back a snapping retort and tried to tighten his grip with already numb hands. He brought his gaze back forward and terror flooded through him as the ground rushed toward them with terrible speed. Wes hauled back on the reins, but there was no way they could pull up in time, they were just too close, their speed far too intense.

Luckily, Wes didn't believe in impossibilities.

The pegasus lifted its head and slowly began to angle away from the ground. Talbot's heart was in his mouth, and he still felt certain they were done for, but with a wrenching pounding of its wings, the pegasus barely pulled out of the suicidal dive, its hooves scraping on the rubble-strewn ground of what had once been New York City.

The two trailing valkyries, however, had no such luck.

Talbot glanced behind just in time to see dual horrific splats impact the ground. The valkyries smashed into the earth at tremendous velocity, dust clouds spraying high into the sky, intermixed with something resembling green bug-guts. Talbot stared back for as long as he could, but nothing rose from where they crashed. Apparently, though they had proven able to survive a nuclear blast, they couldn't endure crashing into the ground.

Interesting….

Talbot had no time for pondering, however, as an enormous red creature rose up in front of them, seemingly out of nowhere. At first glance, Talbot thought they were done for, certain it was Prometheus in Hrungnir's form, regardless of the fact they were still twenty miles from the main body of the Valhallian army. A second look made him realize it wasn't Prometheus… but it might be just as bad.

It was an enormous dragon, some seventy-feet-long, its wings the width of a Boeing 747. The great head looked roughly like that of a deformed horse – warped and molded out of form in some giant melting pot. The brow was heavily boned, and it had a dominant, dog-like jaw filled with fangs the size of Wes's sword. Lifeless black eyes – similar to those of a great white shark – stared back at Talbot.

They were done for.

If this were anything like dragons of legend, there was a high likelihood they were about to get barbequed.

As if answering his thought, the dragon spewed forth an enormous eruption of blue flames from its mouth, and Talbot cursed. Wes, his reactions sharp as ever, hauled the reins to the left, and the palomino pegasus responded beautifully, banking sharply, the flames passing harmlessly to their right. Despite its size, the dragon sped after them with a swiftness that defied its bulk. Talbot never imagined something of such size could match the speed of a gryphon, but this dragon not only kept pace with their pegasus, it proceeded to reel in the distance between them, drawing inexorably closer.

Talbot glanced forward over Wes's shoulder, spotting the shimmering rift in the middle of what had once been New York City, hovering vertically in the air almost directly in front of them. Its base rested evenly with the ground, the apex rising high into the air. As he looked at it, the rift suddenly bulged outward, like a bubble cresting the surface of an oil slick.

What could it be?

The abnormality settled back again, the surface resuming its shimmering bleakness with occasional ripples of intense color. Wes banked the pegasus to the right as the dragon let forth another burst of blue flame, and Talbot lost sight of the rift. The pegasus flew faster and faster, its wings beating powerfully in order to gain more altitude at Wes's direction before dropping suddenly, trying desperately to shake their enormous hunter.

But nothing worked, and Talbot knew, as the pegasus rapidly tired, that it was now only a matter of time. He glanced back at the dragon. Apparently it also sensed the end of its chase was imminent. The crimson beast seemed to grin maliciously in anticipation.

He was still watching when something hurtled out of the sky. The sun hanging behind the newcomer made it impossible for Talbot to discern what it was, but it shot down like an enormous bullet from the stars, colliding with the dragon and smashing it from the sky. Wes turned the pegasus once more, and Talbot lost sight of the two flailing behemoths as they hurtled from sight.

"Wes!" he yelled into the commando's ear. "Something's attacked the dragon."

Wes glanced behind before pulling the pegasus to the right in a wide looping turn. The dragon was nowhere to be seen, but a billowing dust cloud rose from the ground, and Wes angled the pegasus down toward it.

"What are you doing?" hollered Talbot.

"I want to know what happened." Wes's tone was cool, his posture relaxed.

Talbot wished he could emulate such calmness.

His heart was hammering when they came in to land, and as the pegasus's hooves clattered on the broken stones, Wes smoothly dismounted and swiftly drew Laevateinn. Talbot fell from the saddle of the winged best and clumsily dragged his Olympian sword clear of its scabbard, his hands almost as numb as his mind.

The dust cloud eddied ahead of them, and Talbot still couldn't see anything within it. If the dragon emerged, they'd have no cover from its flames, and would be dead before either of them knew it. And yet Wes still strode confidently forward, his black leather boots traipsing easily across the uneven ground while the same boots did nothing to help Talbot as he stumbled and tripped, certain at any moment he would twist his ankle and be left as an entree for the beast – after it cooked him, of course.

The dust cloud swirled, an enormous shadow slowly emerging within it. Talbot's breath caught in his throat as he waited for the flames he was sure would erupt and consume them both, but Wes merely chuckled and sheathed his sword.

"What are you doing, Wes?" gasped Talbot.

Wes turned around and grinned lopsidedly at him. "Put your sword down, cupcake. We won't require your death-dealing skills just yet."

Talbot squinted, peering into the dust, unable to discern what the shape was no matter how hard he tried, but he trusted Wes's judgment, and warily sheathed his Olympian blade. The figure in the dust moved closer, its outline becoming more distinct.

Whatever it was, it stood roughly the same size as the dragon, but seemed much thicker through the body, less serpentine. Where the dragon had seemed like an enlarged lizard, the creature in the dust was bulkier, like an enormous… cat!

In that instant, Talbot knew what was in the dust cloud, and his hopes lifted slightly.

"Hey there, Kronos," called Wes.

The towering King of the Titans finally emerged from the dust, brushing dirt and tiny bits of debris from his broad shoulders before turning his swirling eyes on the duo. He rode atop a large gryphon, its eagle-like head screeching loudly upon sighting them, but without an order from Kronos to attack, it remained semi-docile… for now.

"Nice reception you had waiting for me," said Kronos dryly.

Wes chuckled. "Well, if you'd told me when you were coming…."

Kronos scanned the destroyed city. "And we thought Tartarus was desolate," he muttered.

"Where are the rest of your people?" asked Wes.

"I believe they are currently arriving through the rift. I came first as is befitting my rank as king."

"Of course," agreed Wes, still grinning.

"Unfortunately – or fortunately for you, I suppose – I arrived to see my newest allies being pursued by that strange creature. It was only proper that I intervene; I hope you don't mind."

"Yeah, well, I had him on the run, you know."

"Your definition of that must be very different from the Titan version," replied Kronos emotionlessly, but Talbot thought he saw a glimmer of humor in his swirling eyes, though he found it difficult to read any emotion there.

"Whatever," muttered Wes. "It's about time you guys got here."

"And where is our enemy?" asked Kronos while his mount eyed Wes's pegasus suspiciously.

"Oh, over there," replied Wes casually, pointing northward.

Kronos shaded his swirling eyes – a movement Talbot found strangely human – and stared toward the north. His entire body stiffened, and Talbot turned to look at the advancing army of giants, instantly understanding why the Titan king had reacted as he had.

The Valhallian army was simply awesome to behold.

Stretching across the desolate ground, as far as Talbot could see, the giants marched relentlessly forward, deceptively fast, like a river of lava. They varied greatly in height, but none more so than the towering figure of Prometheus in the form of Hrungnir. Talbot couldn't see his face from where they were, but he knew that the multitude of eyes must all be fixed forward. Prometheus must have known the humans would be laying in wait for him; he'd spent enough time hiding within the human race to know what New York City was supposed to look like, and the only reason for such an irrational action by his enemies led to one simple conclusion: a trap.

Prometheus was not a fool, and to Talbot's eyes the landscape just screamed out at what it was, but the Valhallian Army advanced forward regardless. There was something in the way they marched which bespoke invincibility. It wasn't merely the knowledge they had survived nuclear weapons, it was something more. Ten thousand giants, along with various flying creatures, flowed toward them, like a flood of towering death. Their opposition was comprised of around one hundred thousand human troops, many potentially useless without Olympian weapons, seven thousand Olympians and….

"Kronos," he said. "How many warriors did you bring?"

"I have managed to gather another thousand warriors."

"Shit," muttered Wes.

"Did you bring any spare weapons?" asked Talbot.

"We have some, but not many, perhaps enough to replace the weapons of one thousand warriors, but these will still be too large for your human hands," said Kronos. "I brought them in case my own warriors needed replacement weapons. If I had thought your people could wield them I would have brought enough for everyone; we have many more back in our own city."

"Damn," murmured Talbot. "I hadn't thought of them being too large; we could have used those weapons. With a hundred thousand swords, spears and arrows hitting those bastards we might have had a chance."

"Shame we don't have Surtr with us," said Wes.

"What do you mean?" asked Talbot.

"Well, remember what he did with my sword? He made it bigger to go along with his larger body, and when he gave it back to me he reduced its size again. I'll bet he could have done something similar with the Titan weapons in order for our guys to be able to use them."

Talbot thought about it, a tiny tremor of excitement rising within him. "It was something to do with the molecules, wasn't it?"

"Something like that, I think," replied Wes. "Why?"

"Because we have another individual here who has displayed an ability to disrupt the molecular constitution of solid objects."

"You speak of Atlas," interrupted Kronos. "He was once our leading mind in such matters."

Talbot looked at Wes, and saw a small grin beginning to spread across his face. "Are you pondering what I'm pondering?"

"Atlas can resize the Titan weapons!"

Wes appeared shocked. "Oh, right. Actually, I was wondering what a lap dance from a Titan chick would be like, but your idea is pretty good, too."

Talbot frowned slightly, shaking his head in wonder. He turned to Kronos. "We need as many of your weapons as you can bring through, as quickly as you can do it."

Kronos studied him intensely for a moment, his cloudy eyes swirling before he nodded. "It shall be done."

He turned his gryphon and swiftly rode back toward the rift.

With the dust now settled around the crumpled form of the dragon cradled deep within a crater, Talbot could clearly see a thin row of Titans emerging from the rift, some riding gryphons as Kronos had. Talbot's heart leaped at the sight of them, both from fear and hope.

Kronos rode straight up to another Titan – one Talbot hadn't met – and spoke to him. The Titan nodded to his king and leaped back into the rift, presumably returning to Tartarus with new instructions regarding the weapons.

For a moment, the tiniest moment, Talbot's heart lifted with the hope they might just stand a chance in this conflict.

And then he looked back at the Valhallian Army, still several hours distant, and pictured ants defending against lions.

***

"Hurry up! I need you men to hide behind what's left of the Ed Sullivan Theatre over in Times Square – or what used to be Times Square," ordered General Shannon. The soldiers leaped into several armored vehicles and took off in the direction the general had ordered.

The main issue in swiftly deploying troops arose when they discovered they'd destroyed every useful landmark within New York City. It was no longer an issue of telling troop commanders to go to Tenth Avenue or something similar and await further orders. There was no longer a Tenth Avenue… or First or Second. Now they had to find visual landmarks within the rubble. Inside the city itself, apart from the Empire State Building, there were a few undamaged buildings which could still be identified, and as such these were used to deploy troops to various points throughout the ruined city.

Sitting on a large block of broken concrete, Talbot gazed down at the Olympian blade in his hand. Almost all of the human soldiers had been issued Titan weapons – a variety of swords, spears and bows, each bow complete with a quiver of Titan arrows. The armaments seethed with the same dark energy Talbot and Wes had witnessed during their battle against the Titans in Olympia. Each weapon seemed to shift in and out of sync with the world around it, allowing them to cut through things with little or no friction, and utterly terrifying to behold. The soldiers had been given rudimentary instructions on how to properly use the weapons. Talbot hoped these were enough.

What was he talking about, hoping they'd be alright? *They* were soldiers, trained to fight and kill. Granted, they had never faced anything quite like what they were going up against, but the reality of it was they were much more suited to the task than he was. Just because he'd fumbled his way through their last encounter with the Olympians and Titans didn't mean he would survive this time.

Every kind of luck has its limits... even dumb luck.

He suddenly thought of his brother. So strange that he would think of Thomas at a time like this, but the image of him curled up as Hrungnir's power enveloped him, sucking the life from his body, would not leave Talbot's mind. He supposed he should feel some sort of hatred toward the enormous red giant, but he couldn't summon even a shade of the emotion. The fact he had been taken over by Prometheus had something to do with Talbot's ambiguity, but didn't explain it entirely. The truth of the matter was that Thomas was dead, gone forever, and no amount of retribution could ever bring him back.

The idea of traveling back in time to save Thomas as he had done once before flashed through Talbot's mind, but he discarded it instantly. They'd already played with time enough, and look at where they had ended up: sitting in the crumbling ruins of one of the greatest cities of all time.

Maybe one day in the distant future an archeologist like Talbot would stumble upon this site and try to discern what exactly had happened here. Talbot grinned mirthlessly and wondered if anyone had thought the same thing during the decline of Rome or Cairo or –

"Hey, Talbot! Stop playing with your nuts and come do something useful," yelled Wes. "Those bastards will be crossing the first skirmish point soon, and we have to be ready."

Talbot shook aside his thoughts, slowly climbing to his feet and moving to stand beside Wes. "What's up?"

"It's a pain in the arse coordinating the Titans and Olympians with our guys. Nobody understands what anyone else is saying. I asked Zeus if he could do the same thing to everyone that he did to me, but he just looked at me like I was an idiot, then said the effort would kill him."

Talbot nodded. "I'll go over and help Heracles."

"Great. Go tell him I think his legs look awesome in this light," said Wes with a chuckle.

Talbot made his way over to Heracles, who was practically yelling at a rather nervous-looking marine gunnery-sergeant. The marine had absolutely no idea what the powerfully-built, seven-foot-tall Olympian was saying.

"Can I help you, Heracles?" asked Talbot.

The huge Olympian sighed heavily, evidently relieved Talbot had appeared. "Can you please explain to this... person... that he is not to attempt to order my warriors whilst on the battlefield? They do not understand his words and may stab him in frustration, the gods know I almost did."

Talbot chuckled at the fact that Heracles – himself deemed a demigod in Greek mythology – was citing his own gods while frustrated. Maybe Olympians weren't so different from humans after all.

He turned to the confused gunnery-sergeant. "Don't order the Olympians around or else he's likely to chop your head off," he said casually, pointing at Heracles.

The gunnery-sergeant sneered. "And who the hell does he think he is?"

"He's Hercules. You know, the son of Zeus?"

The gunnery-sergeant's jaw dropped slightly. "You're shitting me," he muttered, gazing up at the muscular figure.

"Not at all, so try not to piss him off. Call him *Heracles* if you have to. He almost killed Wes when he kept calling him Hercules while we were in Hades."

The marine's eyes bugged out of his head. "He fought Wes? *Our* Wes?"

"Yeah, but it was because of the River Styx."

"Are you… Talbot Harrison? Doctor Talbot Harrison?" asked the gunnery-sergeant. By this time several other troops had gathered around.

"Er… yeah. Why? Have you heard of me?"

"Only scuttlebutt, sir," replied the gunnery-sergeant. "Gossip has been running rampant around here since… well, I suppose since the giants appeared overseas."

Talbot grinned uncertainly, knowing he should be doing something more productive, but dying with curiosity just the same. "What have you heard about me?"

"We heard that you and that Wes guy – the one who seems to order everyone around even though he doesn't have a rank – have dealt with things like this before. They reckon it was you two who brought those Titan guys here to help us. Is that right?"

"We needed their help. Our weapons can't hurt the giants."

"Oh we know that, sir. We all saw that news thing where they said the Chinese hit them with nukes, but they done nothing. How could nukes not hurt them, Doc?" Several of the other marines and soldiers now gathered, murmuring their own curiosity as well.

"I'm not sure," replied Talbot. "But I remember the first time I saw a gryphon – one of those big cat-like things with wings and a head like an eagle and a tail like a snake. It got hit by four AIM-9 sidewinder missiles and didn't even get a scratch."

"Holy shit," muttered the gunnery-sergeant.

"These things seem to live and die by a different set of rules," said Talbot, louder so that the troops – around fifty of them gathered now – could hear him. "That's why you all have been issued either Titan or Olympian weapons." He indicated the swords, spears and bows the troops now carried.

"But these things are ancient!" shouted a young corporal. "How the hell are we supposed to take down one of those giants with this? It's like trying to kill a rhino with a pocketknife!" There was a murmuring of agreement.

Talbot nodded. "I understand, and that's why you've been instructed to aim for their Achilles tendons at the rear of their heels.

They go down pretty quickly if you do. Then you need to swarm them and hit them in the arteries in their neck or groin."

"That's impossible," said the same corporal.

"Nothing is impossible," replied Talbot. "Wes and I managed to kill some atop Mount Olympus by using the same technique a while back."

Stunned silence received this comment, and Talbot suddenly realized how many must have heard rumors similar to what the gunnery-sergeant had heard.

"Anyway," he said uncomfortably, "I know you'll all do your best out there… and… and…."

"AND GO KILL YOURSELVES SOME GIANTS!!!" roared the voice of Wes from right behind him, magnified by the bullhorn he carried.

Talbot jumped around and saw several others in the group do the same before nervous laughter overtook them.

Wes chuckled. "Hope I didn't make you pee." Talbot gave him a reprimanding glance, and then turned back to the troops.

If Talbot had seen respect in their eyes when they'd found out who he was, there was absolute awe in their expressions as they gazed at Wes. Muttering rose among them, and Talbot saw several other soldiers and marines running over as they heard who was speaking.

"Alright you soft cocks," drawled Wes, his Australian accent slightly thicker as his language became rougher. He spoke directly to the soldiers and marines, rather than through the megaphone. "What Talbot just said is exactly right; these weapons are all you need in order to fight these bastards. You're better off with one of these –" he held Laevateinn high for them all to see, "– than the best nuke available. Do you wanna know why?" Several heads nodded, and others called out for Wes to tell them. "It's because these pocketknives will kill those fuckers. Nukes won't."

"But there's so many of them," argued a sergeant in the second row.

"Only about ten thousand," replied Wes. "And combined with the Olympians and Titans we've got around a hundred and twenty thousand bodies on the ground. We outnumber them by over ten to one, so what's your problem?"

"He's army, that's his problem," shouted one of the marines, followed by spattered laughter.

Arguments swiftly began to break out between the soldiers and the marines before Wes whistled shrilly into the bullhorn. All eyes shot back, fixing on him once more.

"Shut up with that petty bullshit," shouted Wes without the aid of the loudhailer. "From now on you're all brothers, because our enemies are out there, and they want to eat us – literally! The shortest one of them is about a hundred-and-fifty-feet-tall and could decimate us all if we don't band together like steel. I say we can kill these bastards, and I'm not known for lying."

Wes paused before continuing. "These giants can bleed. How do I know? Because me and Talbot killed three of them. *Three* of those big bastards between the two of us. And take a look at Talbot; he looks like he just escaped from the nerd lab!"

Nervous laughter rippled through the troops.

"What I'm trying to say," continued Wes, "is that we can win this thing. If Talbot and I can kill three giants, then what can a hundred and twenty thousand of you crazy bastards do to them?"

A roar answered Wes's question as the troops bellowed and whistled.

"That's not how it happened," Talbot whispered in Wes's ear. "We had a lot of help taking those giants down."

"I never said we didn't," replied Wes. "But they don't need to know that right now, do they?"

Talbot looked at the troops grinning and slapping each other on the shoulder. "No, I guess not," he agreed.

Wes raised the bullhorn to his lips once more. "NOW GET TO YOUR UNITS AND PREPARE TO KICK SOME ARSE!!!" Another roar sounded from the troops, and they began to disperse.

"Nice speech," said Heracles, striding over to where they stood.

"You understood that?" asked Talbot, knowing that he and Wes often mixed languages without realizing it.

"Not a word," replied Heracles. "But I understand their reaction. Those men will die for you now."

The words impacted heavily on Talbot. "I don't want them to die for me."

Heracles shrugged. "Regardless, they will. Besides, it wasn't really you, it was Wes. They will fight like lions now because of what he said."

"But it wasn't all true," argued Talbot. He turned to Wes. "I mean, you didn't even mention about Briareus taking out that last giant when we were in Olympia."

"Would that have helped them?" asked Wes.

"Well… no, but –"

"But nothing. A lot of these men, possibly all of them, are about to die fighting to defend our planet. They don't need to hear that we needed help from a freak like Briareus. They need to hear that they can defeat the enemy, no matter how daunting it might appear."

Talbot moved to argue, but Heracles forestalled him. "Wes speaks the truth. Deep down, those men know the reality of what they are facing, but Wes managed to change the invincible to the mortal with a few words. Now those soldiers will enter the battle with hope in their hearts instead of dread. If we are to defeat this horrendous enemy, this is what we must all carry into this fast-approaching clash."

Talbot bowed his head. "I'm sorry," he said, "I guess I'm just not a warrior."

Heracles stepped forward and laid a huge hand upon Talbot's shoulder. "You care about those men; that is what makes a leader great. You wish to protect them, just as they wish to protect your land. Your heart is strong, Talbot Harrison, even though you doubt this in yourself at times."

"I hate to break up the foreplay, guys," cut in Wes, "but there's a big fucking army of extremely large arseholes heading our way, so if you don't mind, let's get organized." Wes's grin took any sting from his words, and Talbot nodded, glancing toward the line of giants now looming ominously close. He gritted his teeth and gripped the handle of his Olympian sword in its sheath.

Be strong, he told himself. *Please be strong.*

CHAPTER 16

The gigantic figure lunged down and, more from luck than anything else, Talbot's mount skidded out of the way of the blow. Riding the unicorn, he hacked and slashed at exposed ankles, trying with all his might to avoid being crushed.

Things were not looking good.

Talbot had the sudden understanding of how ants felt when attacking an elephant who'd stumbled upon their nest, except this was more like a herd of elephants, and the number of ants was diminishing by the minute. The alliance of humans, Titans and Olympians might have the superior numbers, but they were swiftly getting annihilated. At least Prometheus wasn't able to use his absorption power, not when in such close proximity to his own troops.

A gigantic foot suddenly emerged out of nowhere, and Talbot instinctively threw himself from his mount onto the rocky, broken ground to avoid being pulverized. The huge foot swept over his flat body, smacking into his unicorn, kicking it like a football. The poor beast soared high into the air with a strangled neigh. Talbot didn't see it land, but imagined it would be messy.

And now he was on foot.

Nice.

Staring high above, Talbot saw a battle taking place among several gryphons, ridden by Titans, against various valkyrie and three huge dragons. He thought he saw a smaller figure amongst the melee – Wes perhaps?

"Sir!" called a voice, and Talbot turned to see the gunnery-sergeant he had spoken to earlier. The marine had a large gash above

his brow which was bleeding profusely, but otherwise seemed okay as
he held his Titan spear ready. "What are your orders, sir?"

Talbot stared incredulously at the giants surrounding them. The
plans so meticulously laid out had gone to hell as soon as the enemy
had engaged, and communication had swiftly broken down as chaos
erupted.

"I think maybe we should kill some of these guys, what do you
reckon?" suggested Talbot.

"Yes sir," replied the marine, saluting Talbot. He seemed
somewhat relieved to have someone telling him what to do again.

"Where is the rest of your team, Gunny?" asked Talbot, using
what he hoped was the appropriate abbreviation for the man's rank.

"They're all dead, sir," he replied, staring around at the colossal
legs surrounding them like a thousand-year-old forest.

"Jesus," whispered Talbot incredulously to himself. "I guess it's
just you and me for now then, Gunny," he said louder.

"Yes, sir."

"Remember to aim for the Achilles tendon."

"Not to be pessimistic or nothing, sir, but I can't even *reach* the
Achilles tendon on these guys," replied Gunny.

Oh shit.

Talbot suddenly realized the truth of what the marine was saying.
Both men stood around six-feet-tall. The height of the giants'
tendons was at least seven feet. He supposed they could jump up in
order to hit the tendon, but doubted they'd last longer than a second
using such a tactic. They needed something....

His eyes traveled around, finally stopping as they fixed on
something. The ghost of a smile crested his lips.

"Look out!" yelled the gunnery-sergeant, shoving Talbot out of
the way as an immense foot smashed down.

"Thanks!" shouted Talbot hurriedly as the foot lifted away once
more. He guessed it wasn't a deliberate attack – more likely the giant
just hadn't seen them and was walking across the battleground. There
was no time to dwell on it, though. "Let's use that," he said, pointing.

Gunny's gaze followed where he was pointing, and Talbot saw a
reflection of his own smile flash across the marine's face, but it was

gone in an instant. "It won't protect us against these for long," Gunny observed as they moved swiftly across the debris.

"It'll last longer than our skin," replied Talbot.

"True," agreed the marine, following Talbot across the uneven ground.

Upon the broken stone, an M1A2 Abrams battle tank, the primary workhorse involved in most US offenses, sat silently, awaiting them.

Or at least half of it was.

The revolving turret had been completely torn away. All that was left now was the armored base, complete with thick, bulldozer-like treads which could easily traverse the ruined terrain. The missing turret would be a surprising boon, as it now provided a perfect platform from which to slice and dice seven-foot-high Achilles tendons.

"Let's see if this thing still works," said Talbot, climbing up the side of the vehicle, cursing as his sheathed sword clanged against the metal body. He'd never get used to the damn thing.

They jumped into the tank, Gunny leaping into the controller's seat and turning the ignition. The thundering Honeywell diesel engine turned over smoothly, sending 1500 horsepower through the metallic beast, making Talbot grin again despite their current chaos. He'd always been a fan of these things, and imagined Wes's comments about him being a war nerd.

He glanced up at the sky once more, wondering how his friend was faring….

***

"Fuck you, you fucking-fuck!" roared Wes as the headless ebony body of yet another valkyrie dropped away from him, its green blood dripping from Laevateinn.

His pegasus pounded its wide wings mightily, and Wes surged through the air once more, this time heading toward one of the

Titans riding a gryphon, who was battling valiantly against a enormous black dragon. Almost in sync, the huge flying beasts hurled volatile bursts of caustic flame at each other, each somehow managing to avoid the heat of the other's flames. The Titan was a fantastic rider, angling his mount in such a way as to protect it each time the dragon sprayed a burst of flames.

Wes saw an opening, and urged his pegasus in under the bulging ebony belly of the dragon. Darting beneath it, he slashed his Olympian sword deep into the exposed abdomen, driving his mount forward through the air. The dragon's entrails spewed out through a great, long gash, twisting and flopping like immense blue sausage links as they dropped through the sky behind Wes.

The dragon cried a hideous shriek and slashed at Wes with the sword-like claws on its forelimbs, but he swerved his pegasus just in time and dropped away from the hideous talons. The beast remained airborne for several heartbeats, but then its wings began to falter. It dropped from the sky like a filleted rhino pushed from an airplane, its guts spraying the horizon as it plummeted through the air, crashing heavily on the cracked and broken ground below.

Wes gave the Titan a thumbs-up, noting the quizzical glance which crossed the warrior's face before he tentatively and awkwardly returned the gesture.

"I sure hope I didn't kill anyone in his family the last time," murmured Wes to himself.

He swiftly spotted another embattled Titan and directed his pegasus toward the warrior, suppressing a grin as he kicked the beast forward through the air. There was a feeling of ecstasy as he soared through the air, and Wes knew he was born for battle.

He loved this.

***

"I hate this!" yelled Talbot.

The very ground shuddered as the M1A2 roared across the debris-littered streets at full speed – a chugging thirty miles per hour – the towering giant pounding after them. Granted, the giant wasn't so much running after them as hobbling, a hunk of skin carved out of its ankle, just below the Achilles, but it still covered the distance quite swiftly.

Talbot, perched atop the damaged tank, had been on target, but at the last moment the giant had started to lift its foot, and Talbot's Olympian sword, its blade hissing with the mysterious power their weapons contained, had glanced off the bone of the giant's heel, taking a huge slice of its gray skin along with it.

The giant was not pleased.

"How the hell are we going to get out of this?" muttered Talbot. Gunny's eyes remained fixed on the viewing screen as he drove the tank expertly between different giants' feet, each almost as long as the tank itself. Their pursuer didn't try to go around the other giants, he simply shoved them out of the way, barging through their ranks as he chased after them.

On the positive side of things, as they swerved across the battlefield that was once New York City, Talbot saw several other giants had been brought down by their troops. Still, at the moment all he wanted was someone to take out the building with feet trying to stomp them into the earth like a bug.

Then, like a prayer answered, *he* emerged through the haze of the battlefield. The silhouette was huge, though not nearly as large as the surrounding giants.

Talbot yelled at Gunny to adjust their direction toward the hulking figure. It in turn had spotted Talbot's frantically waving form and was now sprinting toward them.

One hundred muscular arms sprouted from a massive torso.

Fifty heads spun and swiveled in a myriad of different directions.

Briareus, the last of the Hecatonchires, entered the fray.

Gunny hit the brakes at the same time as Briareus took a running leap, flying straight over the tank and smashing directly into their pursuing giant's midriff in a startling impersonation of a rugby tackle. Unprepared, the giant instantly folded, crashing to the ground. Briareus didn't allow it time to recover, dashing around, stooping behind its head, clutching the scalp and jaw. The giant dazedly raised its own hands, but it was too late. Talbot saw Briareus's immensely muscled arms tense, and with an enormous display of strength he wrenched backward and slightly to the side.

CRRRAAAACCCKKKK!!!

The noise of the giant's neck snapping sounded like a oak tree being broken in half, and it reverberated ominously across the battleground. Briareus stared at the giant for a moment, and Talbot wondered if he were remembering his brothers, both killed by a giant in the war against the Titans.

Snapping out of his reverie, Briareus spun toward Talbot and several of his heads silently nodded before he ran off, swiftly disappearing back into the thick of the fighting. Talbot grimaced, part of him praying the Hecatonchires would be okay. Glancing down at the controls, he saw Gunny staring back at him, waiting for instructions.

"Let's try that again, shall we?" said Talbot.

The marine grinned, slamming the half-tank into gear and hitting the throttle once more, aiming for a giant who was using a huge steel girder as a club.

"Oh boy," muttered Talbot.

***

"Oh... *shit!*"

Wes gazed down at the broken body of his pegasus laying motionless across the cracked stones and other rubble. Its head lay twisted at an obscure angle, and its blank gaze stared at nothing.

Ah well, at least it had helped him kill the last valkyrie they'd encountered – the very beast which, in its death throes, had lashed out with its foot, catching his pegasus's wing with its claws, slicing through the poor beast's muscle and flesh. The flying horse had managed to land heavily on its hooves, but had immediately collapsed, forcing Wes to leap clear as it cart-wheeled forward, the loud snap indication enough of what had happened to the pegasus's neck.

Wes swiftly climbed a high pile of rubble and stared around. From this elevated position, he noticed some giants had been brought down and now lay motionless on the ground, but there were nowhere near enough of them defeated. Through his discussions with General Shannon, they'd decided to try tactics such as tripwires and had also dug hidden pits, hoping to make the giants stumble, and then cut them to pieces using troops hidden nearby. These ambushes had obviously failed – there should have been thousands of giant corpses spread out across what used to be New York City, not just the scattered bodies he could perceive.

Glancing up, Wes saw a Harrier jump-jet flash overhead, but seemingly out of nowhere a valkyrie crashed heavily into it; the terrifying beast smashing its clawed fist through the reinforced glass of the canopy and tearing loose the pilot's head before leaping clear and flying away. The smoking jet crashed and exploded into the midst of a troop of marines about a mile west of Wes's current position.

The enemy had lost perhaps a couple of hundred warriors. Scanning the battlefield, Wes could tell the Human-Titan-Olympian alliance was suffering badly.

Very badly.

Allied corpses were strewn everywhere. Some had been wrenched apart, others simply crushed into the ground like insects. They were swiftly being annihilated.

Wracking his brain, Wes stared hard at the scene before him, hoping for inspiration, but nothing was forthcoming. He glanced around, spying the rift still open many miles to the south.

Something suddenly emerged from within it.

He initially thought he must have imagined it, and then another disturbance seemed to break the surface of the inky rift, colors rippling away like oil on water.

Maybe the Titans were retreating?

But these things were coming out, not entering the rift. To confirm, Wes glanced skyward and saw several Titans still flying gryphons, alongside the pegasus-riding Olympian warriors, steadfastly battling the dragons and valkyrie. He looked back at the rift, now noting a steady emergence of bodies from within it.

The flapping of enormous wings made Wes spin around, Laevateinn up and ready to strike, but he swiftly lowered the sword as he recognized Kronos atop a gryphon.

Kronos climbed down to stand beside him. "We must soon sound the retreat, my friend," he stated.

Wes ignored the comment, pointing instead toward the rift. "What's coming through there?"

Kronos shielded his swirling eyes against the afternoon sunlight and gazed toward the rift.

"I do not believe it," the leader of the Titans murmured.

"What is it?" asked Wes.

"Salvation," replied Kronos.

"Is it the Keres?"

Kronos stared at him incredulously, and Wes suddenly remembered that the Keres had almost annihilated the Titans during the battle in Olympia. "Sorry," he muttered.

Kronos turned his attention back to the rift. "Before I brought my people here, I sent an emissary out into the wastes of Tartarus, requesting aid from the denizens there. It seems our request has been answered."

"Who by?" asked Wes.

Kronos paused before answering. "All of them."

Wes suddenly realized what Kronos meant, and his heart leaped in his chest. The creatures of Tartarus, much like the gryphons the Titans rode, were almost impervious to human weapons, and as such it was possible they might prove effective against the Valhallian Army.

"Let's go see," said Wes hurriedly.

He swiftly climbed atop the gryphon, automatically taking the front, controlling position. Kronos stared at him for a moment before shaking his head incredulously and climbing up behind him.

"You do know I'm a king, don't you?" he said sharply.

"Yeah," replied Wes, "but I won't hold it against you."

Kronos chuckled lightly, and Wes kicked the gryphon into

motion, hauling up on the reins. It swiftly lifted off the ground, its wings beating heavily, its eagle-like head screeching a fearsome cry.

His hope renewed, Wes could understand how it felt, and let forth a battle cry of his own.

***

Talbot swung his Olympian sword wildly, feeling a rush of satisfaction as the blade bit deep into flesh. The sense of accomplishment rapidly dissipated, however, soon replaced by terror as he heard the bellow of the giant.

Had he missed again?

He glanced at the deep wound he'd inflicted on the giant's Achilles, and then he looked up.

Like a soaring tree chopped at the roots, the giant swayed slightly, glaring at Talbot as he stood awkwardly atop the mangled M1A2 Abrams tank. The giant roared once more and lunged down to crush them with the steel girder in its left hand, but at the same moment it pitched forward, the ankle Talbot had injured splitting even further as the unsupported leg failed, and the giant fell forward.

The giant caught itself with its hands before it crashed fully down, but several hundred soldiers set on it, hacking and slashing with their own weapons, trying to get it to drop further. The giant resiliently held itself high, its neck out of reach of their killing blows.

Talbot yelled an order to Gunny, and the marine raced the broken tank directly between the giant's legs, as far up as the tank could go. But it still wasn't far enough.

Dropping to the ground, Talbot ran toward the face-down giant's crotch, his mind flooding with Wes's insinuating taunts as he did so. The giant was getting its uninjured leg beneath it and would soon rise again. He had no time to waste. Sprinting in with his Olympian blade held double-handed, Talbot swung with all his strength, slicing deeply into the femoral artery located in the giant's groin.

The blade easily pierced the giant's flesh. Before Talbot could retreat he found himself hit with a horrendous spray of blood as the artery spurted thousands of gallons of the giant's life fluid. He tumbled end over end as the tsunami of crimson liquid hurtled him away from the creature's groin, halting only when he smashed into a semi-crushed Humvee. Clearing the gore from his eyes in time to see the giant slump forward, sigh heavily, and then lay still, Talbot watched several soldiers continuing to chop and hew at the top end of the body, terrified the beast would rise once more.

"Nice work, sir," yelled the voice of Gunny from the M1A2, safely parked away from the rush of blood. "But do you really think we have time to rest?'

Biting back curses, Talbot retrieved his Olympian sword and cleaned as much of the giant's blood off himself before climbing atop the tank once more.

***

Wes sat, legs astride the gryphon, stunned amazement plastered across his face.

"How did you get so many beasts to come to your aid?" he asked Kronos, who still sat mounted behind him as they soared through the air.

"I… asked them…." said Kronos hesitantly.

"And?"

Wes couldn't see Kronos properly, but had the feeling the Titan king had just shrugged. "I promised them food. It tends to get scarce on Tartarus."

"But they know not to eat our guys, right?"

"I advised them who our allies are and requested they refrain from attacking them."

Dropping his gaze to the ground, Wes wondered if they had just unleashed something even more dangerous than Prometheus and his army.

"What the hell is *that?*" Wes pointed toward the creature which had just emerged from the rift.

"Oh no," Kronos muttered behind him. "That is Ladon; I had no idea he was still alive."

Wes stared hard at the huge creature. "What are those things hanging off it?"

"They are his heads, he has over one hundred of them."

"A *hundred* heads?" gasped Wes, seeing them more clearly now as they grew closer. "What the hell is a Ladon anyway; another one of your experiments?"

"NO! He is one of the rare Hesperian Dragons – possibly related to the Lernaean Hydra."

"Is that good or bad?" asked Wes.

"He killed many of my kind."

"Uh huh…. So is that good or bad?" repeated Wes. "Nah, just kidding. But you talk like he's smart; is he more intelligent than the other creatures from Tartarus?"

"He is able to communicate as adeptly as you or I, but I fear he will not give us a chance to talk."

"Let's go find out," replied Wes, dipping the gryphon's head into a steep dive before Kronos could argue. He brought the beast's head up and landed smoothly perhaps thirty yards in front of Ladon. Dismounting, he dropped lightly to the ground, confidently approaching the dragon.

As he approached the multiple-headed dragon, Wes began to wonder if he'd made a mistake. From the air it had seemed such a simple matter, but now that he was staring up at a monster, he feared his logic was flawed. Ladon stretched twice the size of the gryphon Kronos rode and, unlike a normal dragon, it was without wings. Perched at the ends of long, sinuous, serpentine necks, each head resembled that of a komodo dragon, though larger, with thick powerful jaws which looked strong enough to crush his skull in an instant. The solid, muscular body was more like that of a huge wolf; its long legs appeared capable of great speed in long, loping strides. The scaled skin of the beast, however, was definitely reptilian, thick and tough-looking, shimmering with a gray-green tinge. Several of the creature's heads stared balefully down at him, a dark intelligence glinting in the black eyes.

"Hey, how's it hangin'?" called Wes, his mind racing to remember the creature's name. "You're Laid-on aren't you?"

A growl resonated deep in the many throats of the dragon. "I am Ladon," it responded, pronouncing the name *La Don*, like two separate words.

"Awesome. I'm Wes, and he's...." Wes pointed at Kronos, still sitting on top of the gryphon, and then thought better of it. Judging from the Titan's description of this thing they probably weren't exactly best friends. "Well... don't worry about him right now. Can you help us?"

"You presume much, human."

"Well, you're here, aren't you? It must mean you're concerned about what's going on."

"Perhaps I was merely bored," countered Ladon. "Killing Titans can become tiresome."

Wes glanced back at Kronos. "Yeah, I used to do that too, but some of them turned out to be okay. How'd you know I was human...? Actually, how do you even know what a human is?"

"There was much talk after the Titans were forced back through the rift into Tartarus by the Keres. And a lot of that talk was focused around a *human* who fought like a demon. His name was also Wes. He killed many of the creatures of Tartarus during that battle. I had thought to come here and find him for myself."

"Oh... shit," muttered Wes, loosening Laevateinn in its scabbard.

"And here you come and find me instead, saving me the trouble of an intensive search." Ladon's tone was conversational, though Wes was sure its eyes were glinting maliciously and several of the heads looked hungry. "I am indeed impressed."

This wasn't going well at all. Wes's instincts were screaming at him, and every moment they continued this meaningless conversation saw more soldiers dying on the field. He needed to find out where Ladon's allegiances lay... if it had any.

"The Wes you're looking for is me."

Ladon's many eyes narrowed, fury showing on several faces. "Then it would appear you are my enemy."

"Come ahead and die then, pin-dick," snarled Wes, swiftly drawing Laevateinn and dropping into a fighting stance.

At that moment, the most unexpected thing happened to a man used to being able to read almost any situation.

Wes was wrong.

Ladon began to laugh. The deep, rolling chuckle emerged from each and every one of the dragon's heads. Wes stood rooted to the spot, unsure of what to do.

"You do not remember me, do you, my old friend?" asked Ladon once its laughter had petered out.

"Wha...?"

"It is of no matter, and I am sure you will remember in your own time. For now you must forgive me my selfish joke, but I simply could not resist taunting you for old-times' sake."

"Huh?" asked Wes.

"Trust me, my friend. It is better that your memory returns in its own time."

Wes suddenly recalled his amnesia after waking in the ruined base in Australia. He'd thought he had recovered from any ill effects, but obviously not. Still curious, he began to form another question in his mind when a huge explosion jolted him back to what was happening around them.

There was a war going on.

"Does this mean you can help us, Ladon?" he asked hurriedly.

The giant beast chuckled deeply. "Of course. Come, ride upon me once more."

Wes glanced back at Kronos and shrugged before moving cautiously toward the monster, sheathing his sword as he did. Without warning, two of Ladon's heads shot down, one grabbing Wes by the back of his shirt, and the other firmly clasping the hand which flew across to draw Laevateinn once more. It gripped his arm without piercing the skin, merely preventing him from attacking.

"You truly haven't changed," chortled Ladon through several of its other heads. "But you may relax, I mean you no harm."

Wes felt himself lifted lightly off the ground and easily placed upon the back of Ladon, at which point both heads released their grip on him. He felt his knees sink into the flanks of the gigantic dragon with a familiarly which deeply disturbed him, and he wondered yet again what the hell this creature was....

***

"What the hell is that?" whispered Talbot upon spying the mass of creatures pouring out of the open rift. They could only be coming from –

Tartarus.

They'd left the damn door open and now the creatures of Tartarus, monsters they hadn't been able to combat before, were invading Earth once more through a portal which Talbot had helped open.

Damn.

But upon watching them, Talbot saw a horde of... something. It appeared to be an entire pack of sphinxes – large, lion-like mutations with the heads of women, wings of eagles and snakes for tails; yet another genetic mixture conjured by the Titans. The pack instantly assailed one of the giants, swarming over it like termites. They tore huge chunks of flesh from the immense figure, and Talbot witnessed the giant flailing its arms like a man caught within a swarm of bees, swatting its palms against the sphinxes.

Talbot had dealt with a sphinx before – or rather Wes had, and he'd laid witness. They were much like the stone they were carved out of in Egypt, and even Wes's sword, Laevateinn, had not been able to kill the single creature they'd had to face. Talbot doubted the giant would have much luck against the multitude now swarming all over it.

True to his prediction, within moments the giant stumbled to its knees, blood pouring from thousands of wounds inflicted by the sphinxes. They continued to rip and tear at the flesh of the giant until it crashed face-first to the ground. Even then they continued feeding upon the dead beast, and Talbot was eventually forced to look away.

"Um… what now, sir?" asked Gunny from the controls.

Talbot turned, witnessing similar scenes of carnage all around him. Away to the left a herd of minotaurs were haranguing another giant while harpies and other winged beasts battled with the valkyrie and dragons above. The tide had definitely turned, and while the battle was far from over, the focus had certainly shifted. The arrival of the beasts from Tartarus had gained them some breathing space, and their odds were much improved as the giants shifted their attention from the feeble humans to the far stouter creatures from beyond the rift.

Movement to the left caused Talbot to spin around. His jaw dropped. After everything he'd seen, Talbot had begun to think he was immune to any further surprises, but yet again he was proven wrong. Gunny followed his gaze and swore.

The creature came bounding across the cracked and uneven rubble like a huge reptilian cat. Where its head should have been sprouted scores of necks, too many to immediately discern, each bearing a head like that of a giant lizard. Its gray-green scaly skin glinted slightly in the sunlight, and the muscles beneath rippled gracefully as it soundlessly sprinted toward them.

Talbot readied his sword and was about to tell Gunny to get them rolling when the creature came to a smooth halt. A dozen scaly heads lifted toward the heavens and released a multi-voiced roar. Talbot's voice disappeared in that instant as he stared, mouth agape, at what was certainly the bringer of his doom.

Suddenly laughter rang out; a strangely familiar sound Talbot initially thought was coming from the beast. He stared quizzically until the necks parted, and he saw who rode the creature.

Wes.

Laughing his head off.

"I told you he'd shit himself!"

Before Talbot could answer, the beast Wes was riding spoke up, its voice deep and rumbling. "I have to agree with you, it was very amusing."

"Wes," said Talbot tremulously, "what's going on?"

Wes chuckled again. "This is Ladon," he replied with a self-satisfied grin. "He's my buddy."

Talbot began to form another question in his mind, and then thought better of it. Whatever was going on could wait.

"The creatures from Tartarus are here!" he gasped, knowing as soon as the words passed his lips that it was a stupid statement. Wes was *riding* one of the creatures from Tartarus.

"Yeah, but don't worry. Kronos reckons they're on our side."

"Do *they* know that?"

Wes sniggered. "What do you reckon, Ladon?"

"Do not worry, little man," said several heads, all in that same, rumbling voice. "My brothers and sisters will not eat you… at least not this time."

"That's good to know," replied Talbot with a forced grin. He glanced down at Gunny and saw the marine staring in disbelief at the display screen within the damaged tank. It clearly showed the huge beast Talbot was conversing with. If Talbot had been surprised by the arrival of such a creature, he couldn't imagine what the gunnery-sergeant was thinking.

"Kronos organized the creatures of Tartarus to come through and help us," said Wes seriously.

"Just like that?"

"I'm sure it was a lot more complicated than that," snapped Wes, "but right now it doesn't really fucking matter, does it?"

Talbot gazed around, hearing the screams of dying men, numbing his heart to the scenes of carnage. "I guess not," he replied wistfully. "What do we do now?"

Wes also surveyed the battle around them, his face emotionless. "The arrival of the guys from Tartarus has definitely thrown a spanner in their works," he said, pointing at several giants succumbing to the newly-arrived beasts, "but I don't know if it'll be enough. I think we need to pull back into the narrower pass and implement our secondary plan."

"There's a secondary plan?" blurted Talbot. "Why didn't you tell me?"

"Just in case Prometheus got you," replied Wes bluntly. "I

couldn't risk him finding out what we had devised."

"Nice to know you had faith in me surviving."

"You're alive, so don't bitch about it; we don't have time for you to whine. Has that thing got a working radio?" Wes pointed at the tank.

"What? Uh, yeah, I think so," replied Talbot sullenly.

Wes leaped down from the back of the giant serpent-lizard-dragon thing and strode casually over to the tank. He climbed up onto the guard covering the continuous tracks and sat next to Talbot on the edge of the large hole where the turret should have been.

He looked the tank over quickly and glanced at Talbot. "My ride's cooler than this piece of shit."

Despite still feeling annoyed at Wes's previous statement, Talbot chuckled, feeling his emotions lift as he did. Shaking his head, he took the proffered two-way radio handpiece from Gunny, passing it on to Wes.

"Thanks, sweetheart," said Wes.

"What frequency, sir?" asked Gunny. Wes told him, and he tuned it in. "Good to go, sir."

"General Shannon, can you hear me?" said Wes into the handpiece.

There was a moment's silence, and then the tinny voice of the general came over the radio. "*Go ahead.*"

"We're a go for Bravo. Repeat, go for Bravo."

There was another pause, during which Talbot could almost picture General Shannon pondering whether to argue the decision. "*Roger that,*" came the eventual reply. "*Will commence withdrawal of deployed troops immediately, but... er... what are these other things attacking the enemy? Are they... allies?*"

"Yes, General," replied Wes. "Tell our troops not to attack the creatures from Tartarus until further notice."

"*Understood,*" came the curt reply from General Shannon.

Wes let go of the radio's handpiece and the spring-cord shot it back into the M1A2, almost crashing into Gunny's head. "Oh shit! Sorry mate!" gasped Wes, but as Talbot looked at him he gave a wicked grin and winked.

"Hey, be careful! I need him," said Talbot, returning the smile.

"Okay, kiddies. This has been a fun recess, but some of us have work to do." Wes climbed off the tank and strode over to his beast. "Ladon, if you please."

The dragon-like creature promptly reached down with one of its many heads and easily grasped Wes by the back of his pants, lifting him high, ignoring his yowls of discomfort before promptly dumping him on its back.

"That amused me greatly. Thank you," said Ladon through one of its other heads, a third giving Talbot a wink. "But I can't say I enjoyed the taste."

"Hey!" snarled Wes. "My arse tastes great, thank you very much. Now can we get back to the war or do you guys want to screw around a bit longer?"

Wes, impatient as usual and riding atop the incredible Ladon, took off, not waiting for them. Ladon, with its enormous wolf-like body, could pound across the crumbled city as though it were a racetrack. Talbot grinned as he watched Wes go, imagining the terrifying creature on a greyhound course.

Gunny revved the M1A2, and they set off across the battlefield, Talbot staring wistfully as they rumbled past a broken Starbucks sign leaning at an obscure angle. "I could really do with a coffee," he mumbled.

What the hell are you doing?

His brain suddenly snapped back to reality. They weren't out for a joyride. Thousands of people were dying all around them, and here he was thinking about coffee and giggling like a fool. He glanced nervously down at Gunny, expecting the marine to be staring up at him with a look of disdain on his face, unable to believe Talbot could be acting in this way amid such horror. But Gunny remained oblivious, his eyes glued to the viewing screen.

Corpses lay everywhere, some human, some not so human. Many appeared to have been half-eaten, others mashed beyond recognition. Every now and then they came across the body of a giant, many of which appeared to have been fed upon by the creatures of Tartarus, their carcasses strewn about like misused toys.

So much for their invulnerability. The defenders had definitely turned the tide from a slaughter into something they might conceivably win. At a guess, Talbot figured maybe a third of the Valhallian force was now dead or out of action, but it simply wasn't enough.

And Prometheus still hadn't entered the fray. What surprises would he bring?

Coming over a low hill, Talbot suddenly saw Wes charge Ladon toward a giant. Talbot glanced down, ready to tell Gunny to change direction, but the marine had already seen the incident and was turning the tank around to support them.

It swiftly became evident, however, that their assistance was not needed.

Ladon barreled into the back of the giant's legs, knocking it over like a bowling pin and sending the giant flying across the wrecked ground. Before the enormous figure could gather itself it was too late, he was dead.

The whole thing had occurred so quickly Talbot literally rubbed his eyes to make sure he hadn't imagined it. But there stood Ladon casually tossing aside the enormous head of the newly decapitated giant, blood spurting from the exposed neck like sewage from a broken pipe.

"O-kay," said Talbot uncertainly as Gunny brought the tank to a halt beside Wes. "What just happened?"

"Did you see that?" shouted Wes excitedly, jumping around atop Ladon's wide back. "How awesome was that shit? I'm riding the coolest donkey ever!"

"That *was* pretty awesome," yelled Gunny, his voice tinny, echoing from within the confines of the tank.

"I think I blinked or something," said Talbot to nobody in particular. "What happened?"

"The giant was alive, and now it is not," said Ladon simply.

"But –"

"Hang on a minute!" ordered Wes suddenly.

"What is it now, do you need to pee?" joked Talbot.

"Do not urinate on me!" boomed Ladon.

"Will you two just shut the hell up?"

"Okay," agreed Talbot, but snuck a wink at Ladon who grinned mischievously. "What's the problem?"

Wes turned and glared at him, his expression decidedly serious. "The time for games is over."

"Why?"

"Because of that," replied Wes, pointing.

Talbot, still grinning slightly, looked to where Wes was pointing, and his expression dropped. "Oh shit," he murmured. "What the hell is *that*?"

"I think it's Prometheus," said Wes, his tone now conversational. "Looks like he's decided to enter our little fracas. It also seems like he's figured out how to manipulate his new body."

Talbot stared at the unbelievable vision filling the horizon to the north and guessed Wes was right. Prometheus looked to have finally managed to transform the horrific form of Hrungnir into something similar to a centaur.

But this centaur had no horse as a lower body. Oh no. This creature was nightmarishly superb in its design, spectacularly unique in its creation. Segmented black, hairy legs – twelve of them, each as thick as a Valhallian giant's torso -- sprouted from the dark body of the bloated arachnid, a body which would have dwarfed the largest aircraft carrier in any fleet, the length and breadth of the combined thorax and abdomen large enough to land a 747 on.

The torso sprouting from this nightmarish invertebrate was roughly human, but a horrific parody, as though Prometheus were mocking the mere image of those he fought against. Two monstrous arms sprouted from a grossly muscular trunk, the skin of which Prometheus had chosen to keep the same red as Hrungnir had been. Both hands sprouted seven fingers, each of which ended in a sickle-like claw the length of a helicopter blade and black like the weapons of the Titans.

Talbot's gaze rose to Prometheus's head, and he recoiled in revulsion. Forcing himself to focus upon it once more, whereas the face of Hrungnir had been horrible, what now resided atop the bestial shoulders looked like something a crack-addict had designed in Play-Doh to embody one of their night terrors.

The head was flayed, the skin appearing to have been torn from the skull in great gashes, and yet the exposed bone flexed and moved as expressively as an undamaged face would. Hollow cavities filled with gore were situated where two human eyes would usually reside, their lidless gaze staring blankly at the battleground. The ripped and savaged lips exposed a cavernous mouth ringed in serrated, saw-like teeth the same shade as the beast's claws.

Prometheus's new and improved upper body bore the same strange protrusions Hrungnir had displayed, like puckering baby lips, yearning to suckle. Talbot cringed, knowing what those things suckled on, terrified what the result would be if Prometheus released the absorptive power he had previously shown. As the human troops began to withdraw to the more constricted section of the demolished city, such an action would devastate them, possibly annihilating them, along with their allies the Olympians, Titans and creatures of Tartarus.

"You ever see anything like that in your text books?" asked Wes.

Talbot shook his head. "I don't think it's from anything in Greek mythology… and I've never heard of anything so horrific being related to Norse mythology either."

Ladon spoke up. "You must remember that Prometheus was in charge of several of the… *experiments*… during his time among the Titans. Many of the mutations you have witnessed are direct results of his work. He used to think himself quite the artist."

"I think he's quite an arsehole," Wes muttered. "Let's go and kill him."

"Er…. How do you propose we do that?" asked Talbot. "He's a giant zombie-spider-thing with regenerative powers, which can also exude a resin that sucks the life out of you."

"I never said it would be easy."

"Seriously, Wes. We need a plan for this."

Wes grinned haphazardly, causing Talbot's heart to lurch with dread. He wasn't going to like this.

"Okay, here's the plan: you take him from the left, and chop off his legs as you go, and me and Ladon will hit him from the right.

Don't stop to take photos, just keep going. Once you've done one pass, come back and do the same thing, but in the opposite direction. Keep doing this until you're level with his eyeballs – or what passes for eyeballs on that ugly bastard – and then piss in them before chopping the rest of him up so tiny he won't be able to put himself back together again. Then we call him Humpty Dumpty and go crack open a beer."

Talbot stared at him. "You're not serious are you?"

"Okay, you can have a Shirley Temple."

"I mean about the plan," snapped Talbot.

"Do you have a better idea?"

"No, but –"

"Then that's our plan. We cut him down to size," said Wes simply.

"His legs are thicker than buildings. How the hell am I supposed to cut through them?"

"With great difficulty," replied Wes. "Now do you have any more questions, or can we go and save the world?"

Talbot threw his hands into the air in frustration. "Do I have a choice?"

"None at all, my little peppermint cupcake. So let's shut up and get our chopping arms ready."

Ladon theatrically reared up like a horse in a Wild West movie, albeit a horse some ninety-hands-tall with a gray-green, scaly wolf's body and a hundred heads. Wes, caught unprepared, scrambled wildly for a handhold, but the reptilian skin offered no purchase. Luckily Ladon was prepared for this, and adeptly threw one of its heads backward and grasped Wes's shirt between its teeth.

"After all these years, you still haven't gotten used to that," said another head as Ladon landed on his front paws once more.

"I'll take your word for it," replied Wes. Talbot longed to ask what they were talking about, but unfortunately it was too late. Ladon leaped forward, surging away across the broken city at a phenomenal rate, leaving Gunny scrambling for the controls of the M1A2, trying to catch up.

***

The wind stung Talbot's eyes as they raced past retreating troops and bands of strange creatures from Tartarus, recoiling from the figure of Prometheus as he dispensed carnage with his every step. The mutated giant would lunge down, and with one enormous sweep of his clawed hands kill a hundred soldiers.

Talbot watched something flying through the air toward Prometheus. Focusing closely, he realized it was an arrow. Glancing at the ground he saw several hundred Titans beneath the colossal spider's belly, loosing arrows almost directly up into the arachnid underside of the abdomen and thorax. Several moments passed before Prometheus realized there was an enemy below, at which point he promptly lifted all twelve of his enormous legs into the air and dropped his spider body straight down on top of the Titan warriors.

The ground shuddered with the impact, enormous fissures snaking across the earth, gaping open beneath rubble, and absorbing tons of stone.

With only a hundred yards or so between them and their target, Talbot glanced at Wes and Ladon, expecting them to slow down and become slightly more elusive in their approach. In his usual fashion, Wes did the exact opposite of what was logical and shouted at Ladon, the words lost to Talbot over the distance between them, but Ladon immediately increased his pace. They peeled away to the left, leaving Talbot and Gunny a direct line toward the legs on the right side of the gargantuan arachnid.

Readying himself, Talbot focused on the rapidly approaching limb, while Gunny revved the Honeywell engine to its maximum, straining every last ounce of speed out of the near-crippled tank.

Prometheus had now raised himself back up onto his twelve massive spider-legs, blocking out the sky. Talbot gaped at how daunting their opponent was. It didn't appear as though he had spotted his tiny enemies approaching, but Talbot knew that would change all too soon.

The first leg was going to pass on the left hand side of the tank, so Talbot prepared for a backhanded swipe, hoping against all odds that the Olympian sword didn't slip out of his overly sweaty palms. Adversely his throat and mouth felt as though he'd swallowed a gallon of dust which, after drying up all his spit, had traveled down, and emptied like a sponge, filling his bladder until it felt ready to burst.

Swiftly wiping his palms on the sides of his fatigues, Talbot gripped his sword once more just in time to swipe –

And missed!

He frantically clutched at the open rim of the tank as he almost fell off, catching it at the last second and hauling himself back. What the hell had just happened? One second the huge leg was looming almost directly in front of him, impossible to miss, and the next it was gone. Glancing back he saw the reason: Prometheus had taken a step forward, and the leg had lifted almost directly up at the same moment as Talbot had swung. But there was more to it, as loathe as Talbot was to admit it, even to himself.

He'd closed his eyes.

Right at the last moment, in his excitement and fear, Talbot had closed his eyes and swung blindly. Thus when the leg had been lifted away, he hadn't realized, and his swing had pulled him completely off-balance, almost throwing him to the ground as a result.

Idiot!

There was no time to recriminate himself fully, though, as they hastily rumbled toward the next leg. This time he would not flinch, and Talbot focused intently upon the horrifying hairs protruding from the appendage, each as thick as his wrist. The limb's girth was huge, and Talbot wondered what would happen when he hit it. Would Prometheus kill them instantly, or would he take a few moments to react?

Talbot's palms felt like he'd dipped them in baby oil....

The Olympian sword suddenly doubled in weight....

He really needed to pee....

Talbot swung the blade with all his might just as the leg began to lift from the ground, but this time he didn't close his eyes. Instead, he followed the rising arachnid limb and adjusted his aim accordingly. His sword bit deep, the energy of the blade hissing and crackling as it carved through the hard outer casing of the leg like a thirteenth century Japanese katana slicing through ice cream.

And then they were clear!

Glancing back, Talbot saw a section of the leg – the pointed tip of the limb – fall clear, green gore spraying from the open wound. A few moments passed, and then a tremendous roar echoed through the air, seemingly from the very heavens. Apparently Prometheus didn't like his body parts – parts which had possibly been hard for him to produce – being chopped off like a… like a…. What would Wes say?

Like a Jewish kid's foreskin.

Talbot grinned at the analogy, but his smile soon dropped as he saw the next leg looming.

Only four more to go, he told himself. And then he glanced back, wondering how many times they could go back and forth before Prometheus would retaliate. He figured it wouldn't be many, but focused instead on the task ahead of him.

Chopping down the tree….

CHAPTER 17

Wes angled Ladon in close, Laevateinn held loosely in his right hand as they galloped at a furious pace. Despite the speed of Ladon, Wes knew they would be second to strike Prometheus, and began to get nervous when there was no reaction from the huge figure, wondering what had befallen Talbot to have not attacked yet. So it was with some relief he witnessed Prometheus bellow in pain and rage, indicating Talbot had finally struck and survived... for now.

Ladon's wolf-like paws padded almost silently across the rubble, and Wes firmly gripped the wide beast tightly with his thighs, his knees sitting in that unnervingly familiar position. It was like they were designed to be there, or had previously spent many long hours sitting atop this same creature. The mere texture of the gray-green scales seemed familiar to Wes, and every now and then he caught a scent, not unpleasant, but one which triggered half-memories hidden deep within his mind.

He had no time for that now, though.

The first tarantula leg stood like an ancient Roman pillar before him, and as Ladon raced past it, Wes swung Laevateinn with all his might, easily slashing through the meat and carving a deep gouge into it. The leg itself was far too thick to cut all the way through except at the tip, but if all its limbs were crippled there seemed a chance they might bring the monstrous beast down.

Of course there remained the issue of Prometheus's regenerative abilities.

Wes shrugged aside the problem in his usual fashion. That was an issue for later, if and when it even came up. He hoped with all his might that there was somehow a limit to Prometheus's powers;

otherwise he might as well be a true god, instead of just a mythological one.

Without pausing, Ladon powered on, rampaging past the next enormous leg, and Wes obligingly carved another chunk out of this one also. A kind of double roar sounded from high above them, and as Wes flicked green goo from his blade he hoped the noise was because Talbot had managed a similar feat on the other side.

Something told him it wasn't; the initial roar had sounded different.

Somewhat… triumphant.

**

The tank swerved wildly as Gunny fought to regain control. Talbot valiantly clutched at the rim of the destroyed turret as the huge leg hovered over them again. It was sure to stomp them squarely this time, not just a glancing blow like the first had been.

Prometheus's malicious roar of elation swiftly turned into a second bellow, this time one of pain, distinct despite the height it echoed down from. Talbot guessed Wes had managed another hit on a leg; the reverberating howl sounding just as pained and frustrated as the one they'd heard only moments before.

And the arachnid limb above them paused.

It was just enough time for Gunny to maneuver out from beneath it before the spider-leg crashed down with shocking force, causing rocks and other debris to scatter in all directions. Talbot actually had to duck into the tank in order to avoid being struck by flying debris.

"This job sucks," he muttered.

"Hoorah to that, sir!" bellowed Gunny, still battling with the controls. He finally got the tank back under control, and Talbot climbed out once more to perch on the turret edge, somewhat uncomfortably. One leg now hung within the hole created by the missing turret, while his other boot supported him on the guard surrounding the continuous track of the tank.

"To hell with this," murmured Talbot to himself, anger rising up within him, dwarfing his trepidation. "I'll teach this bastard to try to stomp me like I'm a bug."

Gunny seemed to have the same idea, and the tank cut through the space toward the next leg in a much more aggressive manner.

Talbot felt like growling as they closed the space between them and the fourth spider leg. Such was his anger at having come so close to being crushed beneath the proverbial boot of his footless enemy.

Gripping his Olympian sword loosely as Wes had shown him, Talbot felt the power of the blade thrumming lightly as he prepared to slash the gigantic hairy limb. He yearned for it, all thoughts of his bursting bladder now gone as he prepared to unleash all his rage with his strike.

The leg loomed ever closer.

Talbot's focus grew intense.

Every detail seemed to slow down around him as they drew alongside the gargantuan leg. Talbot swung the sword with all his might, intense satisfaction coursing through him as the Olympian blade passed through the thick exoskeleton like it was a thin layer of ice...

... and flew from his grasp, slicing clear of the leg and flipping through the air end over end. It finally struck the uneven ground, hitting point first, stabbing straight into the broken concrete directly beneath Prometheus's spider belly, embedded in the stone, the blade quivering.

Shit.

Talbot's heart froze in his chest. He didn't hear the pained roar of Prometheus as yet another of his arachnid limbs was damaged, didn't register Gunny asking him what was wrong.

He'd dropped his sword – the one weapon in his possession which could damage the legs – beneath the very place he *really* didn't want to go. The image of those Titans getting crushed moments ago flashed through his mind.

Crap.

Crap, crap, crap, crap, crap.

Hollering at Gunny, Talbot waited for the tank to stop before climbing tenuously down off the track guard, almost rolling his ankle as a piece of debris skidded away beneath his foot. Luckily the combat boots braced his ankle, and he avoided injuring himself, but cursed the incident nonetheless.

His sword stood fifty yards away… it might as well be a hundred miles. In fact Talbot wished it *were* a hundred miles away – that way he wouldn't be forced to wander under the massive belly of a gigantic spider.

Stupid sword.

Talbot clambered over the uneven surface, his gaze darting between the Olympian sword jutting from the ground like an Arthurian legend, and the arachnid leg gushing with green blood.

He had to get that sword. He was useless without it.

Creeping in what he hoped was a stealthy manner, Talbot focused utterly on the sword, blocking everything else out. He scurried forward, slightly hunched, moving as swiftly as he could toward the sizzling and crackling blade.

Forty yards….

His lower back ached, and Talbot realized hunching over the way he was probably didn't make him the tiniest bit less visible from above.

Thirty yards….

His right foot skidded on the loose rubble, but Talbot managed to adjust.

Twenty yards….

Not far to go now, his breathing came in ragged gasps; torn away as much by his nervousness as the short run.

Ten yards….

Talbot reached out, the Olympian sword seeming to almost leap from the ground and into his hand –

He was hit so suddenly from behind that Talbot almost lost his grip on the sword. The blow hurled him forward, and for a moment he thought he was being attacked. A fraction of a second later, however, the monstrous leg of Prometheus crashed down where he had been moments before.

"Sorry, sir," grunted Gunny, hurriedly getting to his feet and helping Talbot up. "I tried to yell, but you didn't hear me."

He'd blocked everything else out. Probably not a good idea.

"Thanks! Let's go," said Talbot, sheathing his sword and sprinting across the ground, around the spider's leg – which was still spurting gore –

Something caught his attention and he turned back.

It was right *there*.

Talbot pushed Gunny forward and twisted back, sprinting at the leg right as it started to lift up from the ground. He got there just in time and grabbed a hold of the thick hairs sprouting out from the limb, climbing furiously like they were rungs on a huge, moving ladder.

"What are you doing?" yelled Gunny.

Talbot ignored him. He really had no answer. It was a spur of the moment decision, but somewhere inside he figured they'd probably run out of fuel in the tank before making a mark on the giant creature Prometheus had transformed into – and that was only *if* Prometheus didn't work out how to regenerate his new body before they were done. Here Talbot had a chance....

A chance for what?

The answer continued to evade him, but for once Talbot didn't care. He continued to climb higher, acting without thinking. He would figure things out as he went along.

Wes style.

***

"You hairy whore!!!" roared Wes as he sliced through his fourth leg... or was it his fifth? Glancing forward, he saw only one leg left on his run and concluded the one he'd just chopped into must have been the fifth.

Lining up the sixth leg, Ladon sprinted past it, and Wes's right arm swept forward, Laevateinn easily slicing through the last limb on his side, and he grinned at the resulting roar. Strangely, he hadn't heard any reaction to indicate what Talbot might be doing, and his brow furrowed in concern. Despite anything Wes said to the contrary, Talbot was probably the best friend he'd ever had, and he worried about the little archaeologist when he was left on his own.

Shaking aside the apprehension, Wes spun Ladon around and prepared to commence his next cutting run when he saw the half-tank thundering toward them from around the back of the giant spider-like body.

"What is it now?" he muttered. "Hold on for a minute, Ladon."

Ladon had apparently already seen the M1A2 and was drawing to a halt even as Wes gave the order. The tank rumbled as swiftly as it could toward them, and within moments was drawing to a halt on the rubble. Wes noticed a problem immediately.

Talbot wasn't on board!

Wes controlled his panic with difficulty, his face blank as the gunnery-sergeant awkwardly climbed up from within the tank.

"We have a problem, sir," gasped Gunny.

"What is it?"

"Doctor Harrison is gone."

"What are you talking about?" growled Wes threateningly.

Gunny pointed toward the closest spider-leg. "He climbed up one of those legs before I could stop him."

Strangely, the first thing Wes felt was relief. At least Talbot hadn't been killed as he'd first feared, but for him to climb up one of those…. Wes's eyes stared hard at the leg, swiftly noting how easy it would be to scale using the oversized hairs as a ladder.

"That's a great idea," he muttered.

"Sir?" squawked Gunny uncertainly, and even Ladon seemed to be eyeing him suspiciously.

"Get me over there, Ladon," said Wes. "I'm going to meet Talbot at the top and hopefully we won't both get killed. I need you two to run distraction detail down here on the ground, so this big bastard doesn't realize what we're up to. Can you do that?"

Ladon nodded several of its heads, and after looking momentarily terrified, Gunny seemed to swallow down his fear and also agreed.

"Good!" said Wes chirpily. "See ya!"

Easily leaping the short distance between Ladon's back and the thick spider's leg, Wes momentarily perched there, making sure his sword was secure before climbing effortlessly up through the tangled mess of wrist-thick black hairs. The movement of the arachnid-like limb made the going slightly more difficult than if it'd been stationary, and every now and then the hilt of his sword would catch on the hairs of the leg, but otherwise he made good progress. Soon he reached the first out of five limb joints, and he paused to look down, instantly wishing he hadn't.

The ground spun dizzyingly away below him, not because of how far he'd climbed, but because Prometheus was walking forward once more and this limb was midway through a step. Wes suddenly realized he was around a hundred and fifty feet in the air, and the only thing he had to hold on to were the bristles sprouting from the leg.

Don't look down again!

Shaking away his vertigo, Wes continued climbing, albeit on a slightly more angled plane, until he reached the next joint. This time he paused, but did not glance down, not even when the spider's leg touched the ground once more and he felt a shudder pass through the limb. Instead, Wes stared out at the ruined landscape, the collapsed buildings creating an ominous canvas. Bodies were scattered everywhere; human, Titan, Olympian, and giants – death didn't discriminate. Smashed vehicles lay useless across the rubble, several smoldering or on fire in a scene reminiscent of the Apocalypse. He gritted his teeth again, resuming his climb, determined not to falter.

The spiky hairs began to thin out somewhat, making it more difficult for Wes to reach the next joint, especially when the leg lifted high into the air once more. He had to grip them tightly in order to stop from slipping and falling to a rather grisly death.

"I sure hope you didn't wax your bikini line, Prometheus," muttered Wes.

Once he passed the third joint of the spider's leg, Wes found the going somewhat easier as the angle of the limb leveled out slightly. He wasn't climbing directly up anymore, more of a forty-five degree angle. Wes was now pretty much level with the thick black body of the spider, and he risked a glance down, seeing Ladon dart in toward one of the forward limbs, appearing to take a bite out of it.

Seconds later an enormous roar sounded from above, and Wes looked up to see the hideous skull-like face twist in pain. The howl itself sounded like words, but he couldn't make them out. He wished Talbot were here. Maybe with the power of the Elder-tongue he would be able to understand what Prometheus was yelling.

***

The roar shocked Talbot so abruptly he almost lost his grip on the spider's leg. Luckily, he'd already made it past the last joint of the leg and was now headed back down toward the thick thorax of the body. If he fell from here, at least he wouldn't plummet all the way to the ground – unless he slipped over the rounded edge of the body, but with the thickness of hair on the thorax he felt confident he'd be able to hold on. Talbot was more worried one of the hairs would impale him if he fell. Despite being flexible, the hairs had the composition of hardened rubber. If he fell the last twenty feet there was a chance one of the pointed ends would skewer him completely.

Not a very pleasant thought.

Once he overcame his initial shock, Talbot realized the roar itself was not actually so bestial; it contained definite words which, when he focused hard enough, became clear.

"PUNY BEAST! I GAVE YOU LIFE AND THIS IS HOW YOU REPAY ME? I WILL CRUSH YOU!!!"

The giant torso of Prometheus thrust toward the ground, the horrific claws of his right hand grasping toward some unseen target. When he straightened, however, there was no evidence he'd captured his quarry. Talbot guessed Prometheus was beginning to see the awkwardness in the size of the latest guise he had adopted, and wondered whether the reason he persisted on using it was because he could not, as yet, change himself back. Either way, something much smaller on the ground was beginning to really piss Prometheus off.

With no way of knowing what Prometheus was bellowing about, Talbot pushed the issue from his mind and concentrated on descending the last twenty feet. He moved rapidly down the hairy limb until his feet finally touched down on the somewhat more stable surface of the beast's thorax.

Glancing around quickly, Talbot saw the huge abdomen of the mutated beast rising high and round, but ignored it. If he wanted to do some sort of damage to Prometheus he'd have to aim higher, and he brought his gaze around to the enormous humanoid torso sprouting from the spider's body.

What the hell was he going to do?

Talbot shook his head, not knowing what action he would eventually carry out. He checked his sword was still in place at his hip and sighed. He'd figure something out, even if it just meant hacking chunks out of Prometheus's back until he –

Until he reached the spine!

In an instant, Talbot had decided on his course of action and set out across the arachnid body toward the waistline of the giant. He could even see the point he wanted to hit; directly above the thick hairy line which denoted the ending of the spider's body and the beginning of the humanoid one. The muscle was thick to either side of the spine, but he could actually see the knobby bones of the vertebrae jutting out between the dense muscles in such a way as to provide a perfect target.

A voice, faint upon the breeze, but distinct all the same, floated to him, and Talbot paused, glancing around. A figure rose up atop the fat abdomen of the spider and waved.

It was Wes!

The Australian was grinning from ear to ear, and seemed to skip slightly through the knee-high mass of hair along the spider's back until he reached Talbot's side.

"How's it going?" asked Wes casually.

Talbot grimaced. "How do you think?"

"What's wrong?"

"I just climbed up an oversized spider's leg in the midst of a warzone full of giants battling upon the ruins of what used to be New York City. What could possibly give you the impression something is wrong?"

Wes reached into the pocket of his cargo-pants. "Do you want some gum?"

"No I do not want…. What flavor is it?"

Wes glanced at the packet. "It's berry."

"Okay," replied Talbot, taking a piece of gum and sticking it in his mouth he began to chew. "I've got a plan."

"What do you have in mind?" asked Wes, popping the last bit of gum into his own mouth.

Talbot outlined his plan and Wes nodded, blowing a huge bubble which popped right when Talbot finished his explanation.

"So what do we do after that?" asked Wes.

"What do you mean?"

"After we chop out his spine, what then?"

"I don't know," admitted Talbot, "but it's gotta be better than chopping off his legs a little bit at a time."

"Hey now, there was nothing wrong with that plan."

"What were *you* going to do once we chopped all his legs off?"

Wes rubbed his chin. "I dunno, but something would have come up."

"Well that's the same here!" replied Talbot, exasperated.

"Then why are we standing around talking about it?" asked Wes, drawing his sword. He marched toward the base of Prometheus's spine while Talbot spluttered and choked on a retort that just wouldn't come out. Wes turned back and waved him forward. "Let's go!"

Bastard.

Talbot jogged slightly to catch up with the Australian, drawing his Olympian sword as he did. Once he'd pulled alongside, Wes grinned cheekily and part of Talbot's fury died in an instant. Wes could be a real asshole – or *arsehole,* as he'd say – but he made no excuse for it, and in the end it was part of his charm and humor. It also helped cut through the tension during stressful situations.

Like this one.

They reached the slight lip between the spider's body and man's torso and climbed onto it, Talbot finding it gave him a nice platform a couple of feet wide upon which to work. Staring at the large humanoid vertebrae outlined beneath the taut red skin of Prometheus's lower back, the enormity of what they were about to do struck home. Wes seemed to realize this, putting his hand on Talbot's shoulder, supporting him.

"I can do this on my own, you know," he said comfortingly.

Talbot shook his head. "Let's take this bastard down together."

Wes nodded, grinned and patted him on the back. "Just don't freak out when he tries to swat us. Pay attention and get out of the way of his hands."

Talbot's heart leaped straight into his throat. He hadn't thought of Prometheus retaliating, though in retrospect he knew he should have. It was such an obvious concern, but Talbot had begun to forget the thing they were walking on was a breathing, highly intelligent creature. In fact, it was plausible that Prometheus was smarter than both Wes and Talbot; he'd certainly been manipulating them for ages in ways neither could have predicted.

Steeling himself, Talbot pointed his sword directly at the bulging vertebra, planning to carve through the spinal cord as swiftly as possible, hopefully crippling Prometheus and stopping him before he could harm anyone else. He tensed, noticing Wes was now in a similar position to his right, Laevateinn hissing and crackling, its strange, otherworldly power much more powerful than Talbot's regular Olympian sword.

But Talbot's 'regular' sword would be enough.

He bellowed his most fearsome war-cry – which wasn't very fearsome at all – and both of them struck at the same time. The weapons sliced through the red skin of Prometheus like it was pudding, and Talbot's nerves grated as he felt his blade scrape along the side of the bone, but he persevered, pushing it all the way in up to the hilt.

A horrifying howl, worse than any to emerge from Prometheus thus far, echoed against the rubble. As Wes had predicted, the right arm immediately swung around toward them. Talbot tried to pull his sword clear, but the suction of the wound prevented him from freeing it, clenching the blade like a fist, and he had to release his grip, throwing himself flat. From the corner of his eye, he saw Wes do the same thing, but he'd managed to get Laevateinn loose before dropping prostrate.

The massive hand slammed into the small of Prometheus's back a fraction of a second later, and Talbot felt the ensuing rush of wind pulling at his body as he lay face down. The primary result of Prometheus's action was to drive Talbot's sword even further into his back, like a large splinter.

Prometheus bellowed once more.

"When that hand moves, grab your sword and twist it to release it from the suction," hissed Wes. Talbot nodded, hoping Wes was actually looking at him to see the action.

Talbot felt more than saw the giant hand move away. He instantly pushed himself to his feet and rushed over to his sword, grasping its handle and twisting it savagely in the wound. A great sucking sound followed, and he easily dragged the blade from the gash.

"Don't just gawp at it, cut this bastard's spine!" shouted Wes.

Once again they simultaneously plunged their blades home, but instead of his sword being pushed aside by the bone of the vertebrae, this time it felt as though the blade slid between two sections. Talbot levered it side to side, sawing away at something deep within the new gash, something he hoped was the spinal cord.

Prometheus's bellowing became a shriek, high and piercing, and Talbot longed to cover his ears with his hands, but continued to saw away at the spinal cord like a lumberjack cutting down a great forest oak. Wes, seeming to sense he had everything under control, removed his sword and stood ready like a guard dog, controlled but expectant.

And he was right.

Prometheus swept around with his huge right arm once more, hoping to swat them. Talbot could feel the spinal cord beginning to part under the combined stress of his cutting and the general movement of the torso, and he was loathe to stop for fear that he would be unable to find the same place again. Indecision wracked him, and he froze, unsure of what to do….

But Wes knew.

The commando leaped directly in front of Talbot as the hand thundered toward them, bringing Laevateinn slashing down vertically at the same time. Without pause, the Olympian broadsword carved straight through Prometheus's sewer-pipe-thick wrist, slicing his hand straight off!

The unearthly screech filled the air once more, and Talbot risked a glance back to see the hand, as large as a small car, begin to shrink. First the huge, sickle-like claws retracted back into the skin and then the extra fingers crumbled into dust and disappeared. The skin turned from dark red to pink, becoming white as the limb shriveled to the size of a normal human – or Vanir – hand.

"Don't stop, you idiot!" yelled Wes, and Talbot realized he'd ceased moving while watching the incredible transformation of the dismembered limb.

Returning his attention to the task at hand, he began slicing the blade back and forth within the wound once more until he saw movement from the corner of his eye. Glancing to the left, Talbot saw Prometheus's other hand swinging around. Wes's attention was still directed the other way, anticipating another attack from the right. Rather than stopping, Talbot gave a tremendous wrench, and his blade finally slashed through the remaining threads of the inhuman spinal cord.

The hand froze mid swing.

A scream, horribly human this time, rang so loudly Talbot and Wes were both forced to cover their ears.

The spider-like body suddenly dropped like a puppet whose strings had been cut. Talbot felt himself momentarily suspended midair before plummeting down to crash atop the thorax as it hurtled to the ground. The gargantuan torso thrashed wildly atop the now motionless body of the spider, screaming and bellowing until it, too, collapsed forward.

Wes was instantly on his feet, sheathing Laevateinn and swiftly drawing Talbot's sword from the gruesome wound, thrusting it into his shaking hands.

"Let's go," ordered Wes hurriedly. "Now!"

Following the commando's lead, Talbot sprinted for the edge of the spider's body and speedily climbed down, jumping the last six feet and rolling upon the broken asphalt of a former road.

"What's wrong?" he gasped as Wes hauled him further away.

"That!" stated Wes simply, pointing back at Prometheus.

Talbot turned and saw the entire mutated creature begin to shake and tremble. Prometheus's skin started to vibrate intensely, like a naked man after an alpine dip. Talbot glanced at Wes, who was also keenly watching. Slowly, inexorably, the beast Prometheus had been began to shrink, its excess features – such as the spider's legs – either melding together or crumbling to ash like the extra fingers on the severed hand.

Prometheus was reverting to his original form.

Several moments later a man, naked and shivering, emerged from the transformation, lying on the ground in the midst of great piles of ash where the giant beast had stood only moments before. Shock suffused Talbot, but Wes grabbed him roughly by the arm, dragging him over to the figure.

It took Talbot a second to remember Prometheus wasn't originally a Titan; he had initially come from Vanaheim, and as such appeared a normal human being.

Apart from the fact his severed spine and wrist were healing while they watched.

Indeed, the gash in the small of Prometheus's back sealed itself as they stared at it, and the severed stump first budded with a tiny fist, which bloomed like an accelerated flower until a fully-formed hand remained. The naked body took a deep, shuddering breath. His regenerative powers had obviously returned upon reverting to his smaller shape.

Prometheus could heal himself again.

And they were just standing here watching.

"Shouldn't we hack him to bits or something?" Talbot asked Wes, panic causing a slight hitch in his voice. Ladon and the tank approached, rumbling in the distance, but Talbot's eyes never left their naked adversary.

"Let's just wait and see what happens," replied Wes calmly. "Control your hacking instinct."

Talbot risked a glance around the battlefield that had once been New York City and was amazed to see very few giants still standing. While he and Wes had battled to overcome Prometheus, it seemed the beasts from Tartarus had been incredibly effective in decimating the ranks of the giants, a fact which Talbot knew he shouldn't have been too surprised by, but found he was all the same. Two gryphons high above broke away from the rest of a group haranguing the few remaining valkyries and dragons and began flying directly toward where they stood.

Within moments both gryphons landed beside them and Kronos and Zoe leaped from their backs. The beating wings rose again behind them, and Talbot turned to see Zeus, Heracles, Apollo and Artemis swoop in on separate flying horses, looking bloodied and weary, but otherwise okay.

"Well, this is a wonderful reunion," commented Wes. "And perfect timing too."

"The battle is ours!" gasped Apollo.

"Yeah, that's awesome. But we have to figure out what to do with him." Wes pointed at the naked figure still writhing on the ground, his features obscured.

"Who is that?" asked Zeus.

"Prometheus," replied Wes, "or whatever Prometheus called himself before he became the Titan."

"He called himself Odin," said Zoe softly.

All eyes turned toward the beautiful young woman, and Talbot suddenly remembered that this was her father. To the rest of them, Prometheus had always simply been their enemy, throughout his many guises and machinations, but he was so much more to Zoe. He had killed her mother before her very eyes, kidnapped Zoe and used her blood to rejuvenate himself.

But he was also the man who gave her life.

Talbot wondered what torments Zoe suffered within her thoughts, but quickly decided he didn't really want to know, judging from the loathing on her face contradicted by the sorrow in her eyes.

Finally Prometheus roused and groggily looked around. Seeing his enemies gathered before him, he silently snarled and rose unsteadily to his feet, momentarily glancing at his naked form before a simple cotton shirt and pants appeared on his frame.

Prometheus in his original Vanir humanoid form, stripped of his disguises and monstrous visages, was decidedly plain, thought Talbot. He stood around five feet, ten inches tall and had messy brown hair which sat like a mop atop his pale, yet wild-looking visage. Dark-brown eyes stared haughtily at them all, and his beardless face sneered as he proudly faced them down. He might have been brought down, but Prometheus certainly wasn't finished.

"And what now?" snarled Prometheus. "Will you all take turns at trying to dispose of me?"

"Sounds good to me!" Wes leaped forward and in a single, smooth motion he drew Laevateinn and swiped it effortlessly through Prometheus's neck.

The surprised expression on Prometheus's decapitated head said what the others gathered felt. It slowly and ponderously fell to the ground with a dull thud, followed a fraction of a second later by the rest of his body, blood showering from the wound.

Stunned silence permeated the group, and Wes shrugged. "At least that shut him up," he said. The body twitched, and Wes rolled his eyes. "Of course he couldn't be dead. We should rename this bastard Jason Voorhees."

As the collective watched, the bleeding neck sealed, and within moments a tiny sprout appeared, swiftly filling out like a fast-motion video of a growing melon until Prometheus's head had regenerated completely, and he stood once more. The bloodstains on his white shirt swiftly disappeared. When Talbot glanced toward the decapitated head, only ash remained, blowing away in the light breeze.

"I really thought you would have learned better than that by now, Wesley," said Prometheus.

"I can chop you up all day, shithead. So just keep being a smartarse, and we'll start taking bets on how many body parts you can grow back before I get tired."

Prometheus sneered but said no more.

Zeus stepped forward. "What do you want? How can we end this enmity?"

Prometheus appeared thoughtful for a moment, his chin cupped in his hand, his brow furrowed. "Well, you could all die, that'd be a nice start. Starting with... *you*!"

Out of nowhere, a black blade suddenly materialized in Prometheus's hand, which he thrust like a lightning bolt straight toward Zeus's breast. Wes, his reactions like a cat, swept Laevateinn down in a sweeping arc, slicing cleanly through Prometheus's wrist – ironically the same wrist he had chopped through when Prometheus had been in his giant-form.

As Prometheus howled in agony and clutched his ruined arm, Wes chuckled cheerfully.

"I told you, dumb shit. I'm very good at this stuff."

Prometheus cursed them rapidly in more languages than even Talbot, with the skill of the Elder-tongue, could decipher. Even as he spoke, though, his hand began to reform.

"Hello... father," said a soft voice, cutting through his curses.

"You!" began Prometheus, pointing at Zoe, his hand now fully regenerated. "You are not my daughter."

"I miss mother too, father. But all of this won't bring her back."

"*THEY* KILLED HER!!!"

"No, they didn't," said Zoe calmly, her face sorrowful. "*You* killed her."

"*Bah*!" spat Prometheus, his expression once more scornful. "You're just like the rest of those Vanir fools; you think I'll fall for your tricks. Well they might have deceived you, but they won't fool me! I couldn't have killed Frigg. *I loved her*!"

"You killed her, father," persisted Zoe, her voice almost hypnotic. "You tore her to pieces when she argued with you about going to war with the Vanir Council."

"I... I could not...."

"And now I am here for the vengeance of a daughter wronged."

Zoe's voice had hardened, venom dripping from her every word.

Her hands suddenly shifted and reshaped into two ebony blades. Prometheus, focused intently on his twisted memories, hadn't seen Zoe's transformation. She plunged both black blades into his exposed belly eliciting an inhuman shriek. Talbot unintentionally took a step backward.

He had no idea what Zoe's hands were doing within Prometheus, but Talbot suspected they had turned into something other than blades. No matter how much Prometheus leaped and threw himself about, he found himself unable to get loose. Nor did it seem Prometheus was able to transform. Talbot wondered if, despite the recent casual altering of his appearance, their severing of his monstrous spine had somehow daunted his ability to change his shape. Or perhaps it was Zoe herself. Was she manipulating something within him which stopped Prometheus from shifting form?

Wes moved to assist Zoe.

"*Stay back!*" she snarled, battling furiously within Prometheus. Her hands – or whatever they were now – seemed to have expanded within the body of Prometheus. Talbot could see bulges and protuberances appearing all over Zoe's father as he writhed in agony.

Zoe wrenched her hands sideways, and Prometheus howled until his voice could produce no further sound. The lumps churning beneath the surface of his skin became more pronounced, and Zoe groaned slightly with the effort of whatever she was doing.

Talbot glanced sideways at Wes, seeing tension around the commando's eyes as he yearned to help, but had no idea how to. The battle being waged before them was between Zoe and her father. Any intervention from the rest of them might result in consequences none could predict, and Wes understood this.

But he clearly wasn't happy about it.

Prometheus's eyes snapped open, and he glared wrathfully at Zoe, grasping her wrists with his own hands and trying to draw her arms out of his body. But it was either too late or Zoe had invaded his body too far for him to stop her. He cried out once more as the entire surface of his skin swelled like a giant blister. Clawing at her desperately, his skin became increasingly translucent. Zoe's power, her manipulation, began to grow slightly more vicious as Prometheus's strength faded.

"No…. Please…." whispered Prometheus piteously.

Zoe's face softened slightly upon hearing the plea, but quickly hardened once more. "Isn't that what my mother begged before you tore her to pieces?" she hissed.

Prometheus threw his head from side to side, silently denying the accusation, but it no longer mattered. Judging from Zoe's expression it would make no difference what Prometheus now said, her decision had been made.

With a grunt and a prodigious show of strength, Zoe lifted Prometheus completely off the ground, and Talbot saw the probes she had within him suddenly flatten out like blades. A strange squelching noise came from inside Prometheus. A shriek rattled from his throat briefly, dying as he collapsed into shocked silence, his eyes bulging within their sockets, the lids then flicking closed – there was only so much a body could handle before shutting the mind off from the pain.

"You're not getting out of it that easily, you bastard," muttered Zoe, adjusting her arms to a slightly different angle.

A second later Prometheus's eyes shot open once more, and he screamed, long and loud, as his skin shredded and exploded outward. Thousands of thin, black, blade-like objects burst from his body, like ants from a sand hill, and Talbot suddenly knew what it had been Zoe had been doing inside him.

She'd been mincing him from within.

But there must have been more to it than that, because Talbot felt certain Prometheus would be able to survive even such horrendous injuries as she was committing upon him. Yet he continued screaming even after his skin had been flayed from within. His eyeballs burst as the tiny blades shredded them, his face now closely resembling the appearance he had adopted so recently as a mutated giant.

Talbot winced.

Zoe hammered the tattered husk to the ground, but still did not remove her hands.

"Talbot," she gasped, "repeat the words you used in Atlantis to weaken him. Do it swiftly. I don't know how much longer I can stop him from regenerating."

Talbot instantly understood what Zoe meant, and delved deep into his memory for the words she referred to. The incantation slipped to his tongue like he had used it only yesterday. He began to chant, recalling every word, every nuance of the mantra he had used so long ago, thinking back then that he was finishing Prometheus for good, not opening up the world to more of his machinations. But this time Prometheus was weakened unto death, with scant energy to regenerate his shredded body. Maybe this time it would work.

Talbot continued the repetitious chant. The gryphons which the Titans had flown in on took flight, fleeing before the chant could affect them. Ladon also instinctively fled beyond earshot.

The words on their own seemed meaningless; it was more the tone and rhythm of the phrasing which held the power. Talbot could physically see Prometheus's body recoiling from the influence of the chant. The shredded flesh, imbued with whatever genetic testing and manipulation Prometheus had performed upon it, began to shrivel and die as though it were being drenched with acid.

Zoe, her arms still embedded within the destroyed body of Prometheus, shrieked slightly, causing Talbot to pause.

"Don't you dare stop," she gasped. "No matter what happens, keep going. We won't get another chance."

Talbot nodded and resumed the chant, the words echoing hollowly across the ruins. He heard a sharp hiss from Wes and glanced up, seeing the commando biting his lip, staring across at Zoe. Talbot's gaze shifted to Zoe, and his chant momentarily faltered before he caught himself and continued.

Zoe skin was smoldering, her face contorted in agony as Talbot's words pierced her, rearranging whatever genetic mutations Prometheus had passed on by being her father. His taint went well beyond mere genetic meddling. He had passed this gift and curse onto his daughter.

She wept silently as Talbot continued his chant, but her arms never moved from within the body of Prometheus, even as the flesh sizzled and dissolved around her. Zoe's probing blades were now gone, but she still didn't remove her hands, determined to see an end to the man who had murdered her mother.

The flesh of Prometheus continued to dissolve as Talbot chanted, burning away like parchment put to a match. As he finished, and the last piece of their nemesis disappeared, Talbot looked to Zoe once more and saw that while her physical pain seemed to have ended, her tears remained.

CHAPTER 18

As the final ashes of Prometheus scattered across the broken land, and the terrifying Ladon returned to stand with the group, Talbot stared around him. Everywhere he looked revealed either giant corpses or enemies so beleaguered by allied attacks that they would surely fall at any moment.

The invasion was over. Earth was safe. They'd won.

But Talbot didn't feel victorious as he realized all that had been lost. His brother's death came bubbling back to the surface of his thoughts, along with everyone and everything that had been sacrificed along the way – including this beautiful city. He knew the buildings could be rebuilt, but would New York City ever regain the spirit it had once held?

He hoped so.

Wes moved forward to lift Zoe to her feet, wrapping her in a powerful embrace, tears cascading down her face unchecked. In that embrace Talbot saw their future would always be together, especially now that the threat of Prometheus had been removed. There was something kindred about the two of them, like two untamed animals who only found solace within each other's arms.

Zeus gave them a moment, and then cleared his throat politely.

Wes ignored him.

A second polite cough sounded.

Wes reached into his pocket, still holding Zoe with one arm, and produced a packet of something which he threw at Zeus. The packet dropped to the ground in front of Zeus, and Talbot saw what it was before choking on his laughter.

A package of lozenges rested at Zeus's feet.

"Wes," said Zeus softly, "we really need to talk."

"So talk, I'm not stopping you."

Zeus looked slightly uncomfortable. "It's about your true identity."

Talbot stared incredulously from Zeus to Wes, and then around at the other Olympians. Wes had finally looked up, a frown creasing his brow, but neither the Olympians, nor Ladon, appeared surprised by Zeus's revelation.

What the hell…?

Zoe's attention had also been grabbed, and she released Wes from her embrace. Her tears were gone now, replaced by curiosity. Wes glanced at her to make sure she was okay before turning to face Zeus fully.

"What are you talking about?"

Zeus took a deep breath. "You are not human," he said hurriedly.

Silence.

Finally, Wes spoke, his voice a rough whisper, almost a growl. "So, what am I?"

"You are an Olympian."

"I don't think so. I know my memory got scrambled when that thing attacked the base in Australia, but I'm pretty sure I'd remember being from a different dimension."

"It is true, brother," interjected Heracles. "You are an Olympian."

"Brother?" asked Wes. "You mean that figuratively, right?"

Heracles glanced at Zeus who said, "No, Wes, Heracles is indeed your brother. You are my son. Your name is Ares."

Talbot's jaw dropped.

"So how come I don't remember any of this?" demanded Wes, his hands on his hips.

Zeus sighed. "In the days after our original war against the Titans, we discovered whisperings of Prometheus's plans to once more invade our world. We had no exact details, but knew it would somehow involve the humans. And so you, as Supreme General of Olympia's armies, took it upon yourself to discover what this threat truly was. I met with the President of the land they call America, along with some of those he trusted closely, and opened their minds to the Olympian language – I must say that the secretary of his defense is a rather disagreeable individual. Only their President remembers any of this; he decided it was best the others remain ignorant and I wiped the meeting from their memories. After some discussion, I managed to convince them that our intentions were to benefit all our realms – Tartarus included. You had me... *implant*... memories into your mind which would serve as a cover while you infiltrated this world's government. You arrived under the guise of a human who had traveled through time instead of merely through dimensions."

"You mean Bessie, my ship, was Olympian?"

Zeus nodded. "Indeed. It was one of Hephaestus's greatest creations. I hope you took good care of it."

"Er... yeah, of course," replied Wes, his gaze dropping slightly. "But tell me more about what happened."

"In much the same way as I entered your mind when we met again atop Mount Olympus, I entered your mind, giving you false memories –"

"But what about my accent? I'm an Australian, and they weren't around when you guys interacted with this world... or were they?"

"From Olympia we have the ability to, shall we say, *glimpse*, this world from time to time without opening the rift gates. In this we had to be slightly less than honest with you in order to protect your cover and ensure the highest chance for the success of your mission. It was vital that you uncover Prometheus's plot."

"So I'm not real, is that what you're saying?"

"I'm not saying that at all! Your core character remains exactly the same; it's just your memories which are distorted."

Talbot glanced at Apollo and saw the Olympian readily nodding at Zeus's statement.

"So if you change me back, what happens then?" asked Wes.

"Your true memories return, replacing those I implanted in you prior to the commencement of your mission. Everything after this will remain the same; every action, every situation will be unaffected in your recollection."

"Is this why I lost my memory when the base was attacked back in Australia?"

"It's likely. The memories I embedded in your mind were only superficial, and any trauma would have certainly disrupted them. It's fortunate your true memories did not emerge instead of the fake ones when you recovered."

Wes looked at Zoe, and then at Talbot. "What do I do?"

Zoe moved over to him and silently lent her support, clasping his hand. Talbot shrugged.

"You just got told you're the Greek god of War, what do you want to do?"

"God of War?" said Wes, his eyes lighting up. "Now *that* is cool. I never thought about it like that. Let's do it, Zeus."

Kissing Zoe's hand, Wes released it and moved over to Zeus, who gripped his head with both hands.

"Hey Talbot," said Wes hurriedly. "If I turn into an arsehole, I'm gonna blame you." He closed his eyes.

A look of intense concentration came over Zeus's face as he silently rearranged the thoughts within Wes – or Ares – in such a way as to bring out the memories which had, up until this time, lain dormant. Within moments, Wes opened his eyes once more.

"Did it work?" he asked, his voice unchanged.

Zeus grimaced. "The injury you sustained in the southern land has prevented me from returning your voice to normal, but otherwise you are to as you once were."

"Fuck the voice. You guys all sound weird anyway. My memories feel... I dunno. It's strange, like my brain's been put through a blender."

"Your mind will return to normal within a few days."

"Hey, Wes," said Talbot before catching himself. "I mean, Ares."

"You can always call me Wes, cupcake. Just don't try to hump my leg."

Talbot smiled. "Well, are you going to go back to Olympia?"

Wes glanced at Zoe before nodding. "I think we'll go there for a while, just to feel things out. I mean, I am Supreme General and all that shit, so I guess I should really show my face there, don't you think?"

Talbot chuckled. "I guess," he said. "I can't believe you're Ares… but then again I can't think of anyone more suited to the job."

"Believe it. It's true, I know that much – I think I've always known. Just remember the reality of the situation. You've already met my father, Zeus, and my brother, Heracles. Is it any real surprise to find out I'm Ares? Put aside all the misconceptions you have about the Greek gods – we're a race of people from a different world who interacted with a more primitive race of people from your world. Of course they made us into gods; I mean, who wouldn't after seeing my arse? It truly is godlike."

"You make it sound so simple," said Talbot.

"It *is* simple, but you just can't get the concept of Olympians being gods out of your head. Maybe this will help: those Norse guys we were hanging around with way back when, you remember them?"

Talbot nodded.

"Well, chances are they made *you* out to be a god. I'm sure if you read deep enough through that crap you love so much you'll find reference to a nerdy scared god who does all sorts of cool stuff."

"Do you really think so?" asked Talbot.

"No, not really," replied Wes with a chuckle, "but the point is it *could* happen. And that's what's happened with us among your ancestors."

"But what about you?"

"What do you mean?" asked Wes.

"I mean… I don't know what I mean."

"Just spit it out! What's wrong now? I'm Ares, but I'm still Wes. Just think of it as a maiden name. I'm the same person you've been dealing with this entire time, just with more memories, so what's wrong?"

"How did you guys plan it? I mean… Wes arrived years before any of this happened."

Zeus spoke up. "As soon as word reached us from Tartarus that Prometheus was planning retaliation, we knew we had to get someone into your world. With his implanted personality, Ares – or rather Wes – crashed in a way as to arouse the most curiosity amongst your world leaders. With his cover story he was granted access deep into your government, a burning need implanted within him which ensured he would manipulate himself into a position to react when the time arose."

"You know how lucky you guys were, right?" asked Talbot. "I mean the odds were against a plan like that from the outset."

"Does this look lucky to you?" asked Wes, indicating the ruined city around them, the last of the giants from Valhalla finally succumbing in the distance, the skies finally clear of valkyrie and dragons. They had triumphed, but the city itself was still razed, millions of people around the world now dead as a result of Prometheus's war.

"I guess not," agreed Talbot.

"Mount Olympus remains destroyed," said Zeus.

"Not to mention the decimation of the Titans," observed Kronos quietly, speaking up for the first time.

"Exactly," said Wes. "All of these things are evidence of how shithouse this whole thing went."

"But you still got the girl," said Talbot.

Wes laughed and clapped Talbot on the shoulder. "I did indeed. And if I'm not mistaken, you are *just* a girl now, aren't you, Zoe? No more shape-shifting?"

Zoe smiled shyly. "Yes, I am just a girl. Talbot's chant seems to have drawn all remnants of my father out of me."

"Oh no!" said Talbot. "I'm so sorry, I –"

"Don't be silly," replied Zoe emphatically. "That was the last piece of his evil tainting my life. I am glad to be rid of it."

"Being able to change parts of your anatomy at will could have been a lot of fun, you know," murmured Wes. "I mean, if you were into that kind of stuff."

"Then it's lucky you're not, oh great God of War," said Zoe, laughing.

"Yeah, real lucky," grunted Wes.

Talbot gazed around at the devastated city for the umpteenth time, remembering the other cities across the globe left destroyed in the wake of the Valhallian Army. "How the hell are we going to fix all this?" he asked wistfully.

"We may be able to help," said Zeus.

"Really? How so?"

Zeus looked toward the shimmering black rift and grinned. "Perfect timing as usual," he murmured. In a louder voice he continued. "When I sent out the call into Tartarus for aid, I also bade Hermes search for one of our kind who was last seen going to the land of the Titans many of our years ago."

Talbot stared across the ground, spying a figure riding what appeared to be an old sway-backed donkey. "Who is that?" he asked hesitantly.

Wes looked toward the newcomer and chuckled, as did Heracles. "He always did manage to avoid the fighting," said Heracles.

The figure continued approaching, and Talbot squinted, making out the features of an intensely ugly man sitting on top of a dark-brown mule or donkey. The beast appeared similar in many ways to the Bronze Bulls of the Khalkotauroi which had drawn Wes and himself though Hades so long ago. He stared hard at the figure once more, an idea of who he was forming within Talbot's mind.

But it couldn't be.

"Talbot, let me introduce you to the elusive Olympian blacksmith and inventor known as Hephaestus," said Wes.

Talbot stared hard at the squat, hideous-looking figure sitting atop the artificial donkey. In his pack, a large blacksmith's hammer hummed with the same energy as the Olympian weapons, along with a set of tongs which hissed and spat power.

"What are you gawping at, you ridiculous pile of dung?" growled Hephaestus.

Talbot whirled around to Wes. "Can I come to Olympia with you guys?"

Wes's laughter rang out across the ruined landscape, echoing like the sound of hope for the future.

EPILOGUE

The President took a sip of coffee before sitting back in his high-backed chair and perusing his morning newspaper once more. The newly renovated Oval Office still smelled of fresh paint, and he leaned back, feeling the leather of his chair. He sighed softly.

They had survived.

New York City, while still far from being rebuilt to its former glory, was swiftly recovering. The tools and abilities the cranky Olympian named Hephaestus had provided were beyond astonishing, and the city was rapidly recovering mere months after the devastation which had taken place. He held up that morning's New York Times, reading that David Letterman had taken up residence once more in the newly rebuilt Ed Sullivan Theatre, and his first show had opened there last night. Such a small symbol was very telling in a city striving to recover.

The Government had covered up as much of what had really happened as it could – the general public was not yet ready to hear tales of Olympians and invaders from other dimensions. The conspiracy theorists were having a field day with the reports his cabinet had released, reports which had contended the giants had been a result of genetic experimentation by a terrorist group based in the Middle East. The rest of the populace seemed content with the lies. All that mattered to them was that the threat was gone, and America had prevailed where other countries had failed.

Hephaestus had returned to Olympia the previous night, confident they could finish the restoration without further aid. It was sure to be a difficult project, but an extremely satisfying one in its own way.

Having survived such a horrendous threat, many other world leaders – all of whom were apprised of what had really occurred with the Valhallian Army – had unanimously agreed to open more channels of negotiation between long-warring nations. Possessed with the knowledge of what potentially resided beyond the proverbial bubble of their own world, such petty disputes seemed much more trivial in comparison.

The other countries devastated by the invasion had also benefited from the techniques of Hephaestus, the irritable smith rebutting any arguments against the wisdom of such action for nations which could potentially become future enemies.

"Your nation could be a future enemy of Olympia," he'd snarled. "Does that mean I shouldn't help *you*?"

And so the collection of nations ravaged by Prometheus's invasion had received as much information about the techniques of Hephaestus as the United States. Some had almost reached the same stage of rebuilding as New York City.

The President sighed, leaning forward to take another sip of his morning coffee.

At least Hephaestus had left behind the device. The Olympian had almost taken it back, but he'd finally conceded to leaving it as Zeus had instructed him. However, he had lectured the President several times like a child on the seriousness of its use.

It was not a toy.

The small, rectangular box measured about the same size as a large cell phone. There were no numbers upon this device, however, merely a glyph-like design which Hephaestus had advised the President he'd need to trace his finger over in order to get the device to work. Unfortunately, he couldn't test it, and so had no idea if it would truly work. The Olympian smith advised him it was a single-use mechanism, and as such must be saved for only the direst of emergencies.

Only the President knew what the device did. It was designed as a distress signal straight to Olympia in the event an issue ever rose with the rift portals again. The hope was they'd never have to use it.

The President sighed again, pushing the problem from his mind and taking another sip of coffee. Once more his eyes were drawn to the Olympian device sitting on his desk, and he wondered why Zeus had thought they might need it.

What else could possibly be out there?

Printed in Great Britain
by Amazon